Murder on a Midsummer Night

Books by Kerry Greenwood

The Phryne Fisher Series
Cocaine Blues
Flying Too High
Murder on the Ballarat Train
Death at Victoria Dock
The Green Mill Murder
Blood and Circuses
Ruddy Gore
Urn Burial
Raisins and Almonds
Death Before Wicket
Away With the Fairies
Murder in Montparnasse
The Castlemaine Murders
Queen of the Flowers
Death by Water
Murder in the Dark
Murder on a Midsummer Night

The Corinna Chapman Series
Earthly Delights
Heavenly Pleasures
Devil's Food
Trick or Treat

Short Story Anthology
A Question of Death:
An Illustrated Phryne Fisher Anthology

Murder on a Midsummer Night

A Phryne Fisher Mystery

Kerry Greenwood

Poisoned Pen Press

Copyright © 2008 by Kerry Greenwood

First U.S. Edition 2009

10 9 8 7 6 5 4 3 2 1

Library of Congress Catalog Card Number: 2008937740

ISBN: 978-1-59058-632-7 Hardcover

Poisoned Pen Press
6962 E. First Ave., Ste. 103
Scottsdale, AZ 85251
www.poisonedpenpress.com
info@poisonedpenpress.com

Printed in the United States of America

This book is dedicated to Mark Pryor.
A verray parfit gentil knight—and a good judge of wine, as well.

Acknowledgments

Many thanks to Ann Poole for Mr Palisi, Tom Lane for his ancestor Mr Adami, and with gratitude to the usual suspects like David and Dennis and Alan and Samantha of Dragonfly. To my mother, Jeannie, whose memories and library I ransacked without pause. To Annette and Patrick, and to the amazing Beth Norling whose line would have made Erté scream with delight. And to my friends, for all those parties I never got to, all those birthdays I forgot, all those lunches we never had…thank you for forgiving me.

From the Greek of Tymnes

She came from afar, and her master said He had not such a dog in all his days. We called her Moll: she went into the dark. Upon those roads we cannot hear her bark.

And in devoted, loving memory of Monsieur, the elegant, gentlemanly, stripy cat, now residing in Bubastis.

Set me as a seal upon thine heart, as a seal upon thine arm: for love is as strong as death…Many waters cannot quench love, nor can the floods drown it.
The Song of Solomon 8:6–7 The Holy Bible

Chapter One

What if a little paine the passage have That
makes frail flesh to feare the bitter wave?

Edmund Spenser
The Faerie Queene

It had been such an agreeable day until then.

The year, aware that it was very new and ought not to put itself forward, was beginning its career as 1929 modestly. There were mild blue skies. There were sweet breezes (in St. Kilda they were scented with Turkish lolly and old beer, admittedly, but one could perceive that the year meant well) and cool water. Phryne Fisher had bathed early then plunged herself into a bracing shower. She had cleansed her admirable form with pine-scented soap and patted it dry with the fluffiest of towels. Her breakfast, prepared by that jewel of cooks, Mrs. Butler, and served by the gem of the butlering profession, Mr. Butler, had included homemade lemon butter for her toasted baguette and real coffee made from real coffee beans and not from a bottle with a man in a fez on the front.

Her household this sunny morning was disposed to be quietly industrious, from her two adopted daughters, Jane and Ruth, making a recipe file in the parlour to Dot mending stockings in the garden under the jasmine. Ember the black cat was hunting sparrows and Molly the black and white almost-sheepdog was guarding the kitchen door. It was not perhaps very likely that burglars would come in through the back door in broad daylight, but if they did, Molly was ready for them, and she was also within easy reach of a cook whose generosity with meat scraps was legendary in canine circles.

Mr. Butler was updating the cellar book, one of his favourite occupations. He had the drinks tray ready for when Miss Phryne might call for *citron presse*, a jug of which reposed in the American Refrigerating Machine with the shaved ice, lemon slices and mint sprigs.

Phryne was making a list of invitees for her birthday party. She would be twenty-nine on the thirteenth of January. A serious age. Most of her contemporaries were long married and rearing children, husbands and tennis coaches in utter suburban happiness. She caught a glimpse of herself in the drawing room mirror as she reached for a Turkish cigarette and her lighter. A small young woman with a boyish figure, dressed in a house gown of scarlet and gold. Her hair was as black as a crow's feather and cut in a cap, just long enough to swing forward in two divinely modish wings. Her skin was pale and her mouth red and her eyes a strong shade of green.

'You don't look twenty-nine,' she told her reflection. 'You're lovely!'

She blew the mirrored Phryne a kiss and rang for a lemon drink.

Just as Mr. Butler had borne in the tray with its icy jug, the front doorbell rang several times, sounding so abrupt in the silent house that in the garden Dot jumped and pricked her finger, Jane dropped the paste on the carpet, and Mrs. Butler lost control of an egg. It hit the tiled floor and smashed, where it was rapidly cleaned up by a grateful Molly. Ember swore as his sparrows flew off, chattering.

Mr. Butler shimmered away and returned with the news that Miss Eliza was at the door 'with a…person'.

'Right,' sighed Phryne. Her sister, Eliza, had taken to social work like a natural, and sometimes brought her most mysterious cases to Phryne with all the smugness of an Irish terrier producing a dead rat. But she did love Eliza, really, so she stood up to receive her visitors.

Eliza was a plump, bouncing daughter of the aristocracy, a fervent Fabian socialist and a woman whose claim to the title of worst hats in the world could only be challenged by her soul mate, Lady Alice Harborough. Today's production was of rigid yellow straw, plonked straight down onto the wearer's head like a candle snuffer. Someone devoid of any artistic sensibilities or shame had secured a dried hydrangea to it with a bakelite pin.

Eliza ushered her guest into a soft corner of the sofa and dragged off the offending headpiece.

'Oof! It's hot outside. Thank you for seeing us, Phryne,' she said, wiping strands of her fine brown hair off her rosy face.

'Lemon drink?' asked Phryne. 'Or shall we make some tea?'

'Lemon,' said Eliza. 'Gosh, thanks, Mr. Butler. Mrs. Manifold?'

'Nothing,' said the woman on the sofa.

Phryne looked at her and found herself examined by shrewd parrot eyes in a wrinkled face. Mrs. Manifold had long grey hair worn in a braid around her head, a loose brown dress made apparently of sacking, and sandals on her stockingless feet. Phryne searched for a fashion reference point and found the Pre-Raphaelites, which seemed unlikely. She sipped her drink and endured Mrs. Manifold's inspection.

'Phryne, Mrs. Manifold has a son,' began Eliza.

'Had a son,' said Mrs. Manifold in a flat, harsh voice.

'He was found drowned at St. Kilda beach,' continued Eliza. 'Wearing an old army overcoat with his pockets full of stones and the police think it's suicide.'

'Impossible,' grated Mrs. Manifold.

'So Mrs. Manifold told them and told them and made such a fuss that the police finally ordered a coroner's inquest, so there

was an autopsy,' Eliza went on, finishing her drink in a gulp and
holding it out for a refill. 'Here is the report.'

'Eliza, this is scarcely my business,' protested Phryne, taking
the document. 'The coroner will have to decide what happened
to…' She read the name on the file, 'Augustine.'

'The coroner has decided,' said Mrs. Manifold. 'He decided
that my Augustine fell in by accident while he was drunk.'

'Death by Misadventure?'

'Yes, the fool.'

'I see here that when they…sorry…opened his stomach they
found seven ounces of alcohol. Whisky, apparently.'

'And why should Augustine have whisky in his belly?' cried
Mrs. Manifold. 'He never drank but a glass of sherry at Christmas!
And if he wanted to die, he wouldn't have tried to drown. He
could swim like a fish! He's been murdered,' she declared in a
fierce, heartbroken undertone. 'My son was murdered.'

'Tell me more about him, and how you know Eliza here,
and you shall have a brandy and soda and maybe a few small
sandwiches,' instructed Phryne. Mrs. Manifold was haggard with
hunger, and Mrs. Butler's small sandwiches would slip easily past
the lump in a grieving mother's throat. Phryne was impressed by
the utter certainty of the bereaved woman. But utter certainty in
the matter of suicide was always suspect. Suicide, of all deaths,
was the most unchancy and dangerous. And one which could
render the survivors mad with guilt. 'If only he'd talked to me,'
people would say. 'If only I'd dropped in on him that night…'

But Phryne knew from her own experience that someone
bent on death cannot be deflected, and it is cruel to try. Because
she had tried, once.

Mr. Butler brought in a tray of crustless ribbon sandwiches
and distributed plates and napkins. Eating the first one taught
Mrs. Manifold how hungry she was, but she did not grab or
gulp. She was not disconcerted by being served by a butler. Mrs.
Manifold had evidently been raised in rather different circumstances than the ones in which she now found herself. Dot came
in and sat down, accepting a cool drink.

When Mrs. Manifold had eaten most of the tidbits and absorbed the strong brandy and soda which Phryne had prescribed, there was colour in her face and her eyes were less weary.

'Now, tell me all about Augustine,' prompted Phryne.

'He was my only son,' said Mrs. Manifold. 'My last baby. The girls have all grown up and married. But Augustine stayed with me. His father died ten years ago; poor man, he never did amount to much. He had a little junk shop, reclaimed copper, old wares. Dirty stuff. Augustine didn't object to getting his hands dirty, mind you! But when he took over the shop he said to me, "We have to move in better circles, Mother, than these rag picker's gleanings and bits of old metal. There's good stuff to buy and sell and we need to make a good profit, so you can live as you deserve."' She sobbed briefly, her hand to her mouth. 'So he started with a cart, going round looking for old furniture to mend and resell. He had a lot of that colonial homemade stuff which is now so popular.'

'Indeed,' murmured Phryne, who could not understand the fashion for stuff knocked up by an amateur hand in the legendary Old Bark Hut. 'Prices have been rocketing lately.'

'But he was educated, my Augustine,' said Mrs. Manifold. 'You only have to look at him. He wasn't strong,' she said with a sharp grieving sigh. 'His poor chest wasn't good. My mother said I'd never raise him. But I did.'

Phryne looked at the cabinet photograph which had been thrust into her hand. So this was Augustine. A weak, badly proportioned face, an absent chin, what might well have been watery blue eyes, a pouting mouth. A face only a mother could love, and this one evidently did. Phryne had lately been within a hair's-breadth of assassination by a very pretty young man and had almost gone off prettiness in young men. Augustine must have had virtues. And he could never have used his physical beauty to get what he wanted.

'I thought it was lucky when his chest kept him out of the war,' sobbed Mrs. Manifold.

Dot supplied her with more tea and a fresh handkerchief. Eliza took the photo.

'I've met him,' she told Phryne. 'Not a word to say to a goose but a perfectly nice man. Valued those sapphires for Alice, and when she came to sell them to the city jeweller, she got exactly what he estimated. That's when I met Mrs. Manifold. And I never saw Augustine drink, and he didn't go around with my ladies. They'd know,' she added.

Phryne nodded. Eliza had a flourishing friendship with all of the ladies of light repute in St. Kilda, and perforce had become acquainted with their clientele, if in a distant and disapproving way.

'Of course he didn't!' Mrs. Manifold had surfaced from her abyss of mourning at an inconvenient juncture. 'My Augustine wasn't interested in women. You're woman enough for me, Mother, he used to say. I never saw him ever look at a girl in that way. Mind you, he would have married, I expect. But not yet. Always working, my Augustine. He built that business from scratch, nearly. Got rid of the old metal. He was employing a man to do the carpentry and a girl to work in the shop, and he was always travelling. Buying, selling. It was a good business.'

'So he moved into paintings, then, and stamps, perhaps, small wares?' asked Phryne.

'Yes. I knew some artists once. In England. Before the War.'

'Ah,' said Phryne encouragingly.

'I was a model. No funny stuff,' she added hastily. 'I was a good girl. My sisters and I were all models. They called themselves a Brotherhood. Mr. Hunt was my artist. Mr. Morris was one of them. You've got some of his paper on your wall.'

'So I have,' said Phryne, enjoying again the mysterious complications of the William Morris design called Golden Lily, which gave her parlour its undersea greenish mystery. 'You were a model for one of the Pre-Raphaelites? How very interesting. I see now that your dress has a pattern, too—Daisy, is it?'

Mrs. Manifold almost smiled, smoothing the russet garment over her bony knees. 'Daisy it is,' she agreed. 'We used to help with the embroidery when they were doing a new design. Tapestry, too. We were good with our needles. Difficult, those Morris designs. All curves and waves. And precise to a stitch! It was worth our life to be one thirty-second of an inch out.'

'Very hard on the eyes,' sympathised Eliza.

'But so beautiful,' said Phryne.

Mrs. Manifold gave her a shrewd, appreciative look.

'Just so,' she answered. 'If you have to have the headache, better have it from making something ravishing. When Mr. Hunt didn't need us, we would all sit together and work on a big piece. We used to sing, sometimes. And Mr. Morris insisted on regular breaks, and the factory had a tea room, and lots of windows and very good light. It was a lovely place to work and a lovely time, before we all married and went away from each other and all this sorrow landed on us. Deborah dead in France and her husband and baby with her; a stray shell landed on her house. Me, a widow in Melbourne. Might as well be at the ends of the earth. And Lizzie, well, Lizzie went down the wrong path and we never spoke of her. And I thought I was the lucky one. Until now.'

'Quite,' said Phryne.

'Sometimes when the artists couldn't pay us they gave us a painting. I brought a lot of them with me. Augustine was going to sell some of them.'

'Ah,' said Phryne. The Pre-Raphaelites were good solid artists. Definitely worth collecting. Outmoded now, but might easily come back into fashion. Phryne herself loved them, and might be putting in an offer for some of Mrs. Manifold's store, though now was not the time to mention this. The widow was speaking of her son once more.

'But he was educated, Augustine was. His father wouldn't let him go to the university, said it was above our station—he was a fool—so Augustine read books. In Greek. And Latin. And he was selling coins and antiquities. And someone killed him,' she insisted, returning to her original point.

'How old was Augustine?' asked Phryne.

'Twenty-nine,' said Mrs. Manifold.

Something decided Phryne.

'Very well,' she said. 'I will look into it. First, I wish I could tell you that I will find out what you want me to find. But I might not. I might not be able to solve this, or I might find that Augustine killed himself. I can't skew the results. Do you agree?'

Mrs. Manifold fixed Phryne with her savage eye.

'I know he didn't kill himself, so it doesn't matter. You look into it, and I'll pay you whatever you ask. I've got the shop and Augustine left me well off.'

'We shall see if I deserve any payment,' said Phryne, unaccountably depressed. 'I'll come around to the shop this afternoon. About three? Good. Eliza, can you look after Mrs. Manifold? I'll see you later.'

Mr. Butler escorted the visitors to the door and returned, looking grave and ushering Jane and Ruth before him.

'Yes, Mr. Butler?' asked Phryne, expecting some important announcement or serious confession.

'Miss Jane wishes to apologise for spilling paste on the parlour carpet, Miss Fisher,' he said.

'It's only a carpet,' said Phryne, and laughed with relief. She hugged the culprit, admired the recipe file, and recommended that Mr. Butler call the excellent Mrs. Johnson, cleaning lady supreme, to come and remove the stain.

Phryne ascended the stairs to put on junk shop visiting clothes: a light summer suit in a mixed pattern which would be easily cleaned. She had never met a junk shop which didn't specialise in various forms of dust, from greasy oil-soaked dust to floating varnish dust to the fine oatmeal coloured powder of vellum, which stuck to all fabric and clung like a suitor.

Dot had chosen the suit and was now replacing Phryne's mended stockings in her drawer. She had also allotted the most mended for this afternoon's excursion. The other thing which junk shops had were a plethora of hosiery-destroying snags.

'Well, Dot dear, we have a suicide to investigate and a junk shop to visit. Would you come with me? You know how I value your domestic knowledge.'

'Yes, Miss, if you like,' said Dot. 'But I don't know anything about paintings and things.'

'No, but you know the difference between an old piece of cloth and a new one,' said Phryne. 'And you know a flat iron from a potato masher, which I don't. Here's the young man,' she said, handing over the photograph.

'Never make the cinema his career,' considered Dot. 'But it's not a bad face.'

'No,' agreed Phryne. 'And he loved his mother and swore he would never leave her.'

'Oh,' said Dot. Her education in the stranger byways of love had been startlingly augmented by employment in Miss Fisher's household. 'You think he was…'

'Maybe. But perhaps he never found a girl to equal his mother,' Phryne commented. 'Now there's a strong-minded woman. She says he wouldn't have killed himself.'

'People always say that,' said Dot, picking up strewn garments. Phryne always marvelled at the way they just fell limp into her hands and then threw themselves into perfect folds.

'Yes, but she made a good point. He was found drowned, in an overcoat with pockets full of stones. But he could swim like a fish, she said. If you can swim you wouldn't choose drowning.'

'Why not?' asked Dot, who considered water an alien element to be entered only at the very edge and then only up to the knees.

'Because when you learn to swim, sooner or later you get in above your head and swim for the surface and take one breath of water before you get out, and it hurts, Dot, like you wouldn't believe. Plus you spend the next hour choking and throwing up and feeling as though someone has beaten you across the ribs with a rubber hose. Those who say drowning is a nice peaceful death are lying.'

'And no one has come back to tell us that it is true,' declared Dot.

Phryne chuckled. 'Exactly. Mrs. Manifold is right in saying that anyone who can swim would not try drowning as a suicide method. There are so many others—hanging, shooting, throat cutting, poisoning…'

'Miss!' objected Dot, hugging her armful of scarlet and gold cloth.

'Well, well, not to offend your sensibilities, Dot dear, I will just say that there are a thousand exits for those determined on self-slaughter.'

'It's a mortal sin,' said Dot, shivering.

'To Catholics, yes. I didn't ask about Augustine's religion. Even so, Dot, some Catholics have killed themselves. And some coroners have brought in Death by Misadventure or Suicide While the Balance of the Mind is Disturbed so that they can be buried in sacred ground.'

'But they have to be mad,' said Dot. 'Don't they? To want to die?'

Phryne looked at her companion fondly. Dot had been starved and badly treated and at her wits' end, and her response had been to consider homicide, not suicide. Of all suicidal subjects, Dot was the most unlikely. And a stalwart fellow traveller for this journey, which might prove harrowing.

Why had she agreed to accept the task? Perhaps because of Mrs. Manifold's unrelenting belief. Or perhaps—was it that Augustine was the same age as Phryne? Or was she remembering a suicide she had tried to prevent, a long time ago?

Dot called her attention to the state of her shoes, and Phryne shelved the matter for later consideration.

'Lunch,' she said. 'Then a little research on some artists, and then ho for the relics.'

Two soldiers surveyed the landscape. There was not a lot to survey. It was limestone, picked out in a sickly yellow, with sandstone outcrops.

'When we first came here, Vern,' growled Curly, reaching for his tobacco pouch, 'I thought it was the driest desert, worse than back o' Bourke, worse than the great Artesian, dry as a lizard's gullet.'

'And now?' asked his companion, pushing an enquiring horse's nose gently aside. 'Give over, Ginge. We'll find some water soon.'

'Now I reckon it's worse,' said the first, lighting his cigarette with a sulphurous fume. 'It's a flat, stony, waterless vision of hell, that's what it is.'

'Too right,' said Vern.

Chapter Two

Lay up not for yourselves treasures upon earth, where moth and rust doth corrupt and thieves break through and steal...For where your treasure is, there shall your heart be also.

Matthew 6:19–21 The Holy Bible

The shopfront was modest. Phryne knocked at the bright green door with the firm hand of one who is expected and was admitted by Eliza.

'Mrs. Manifold is lying down,' she explained. 'It took a lot out of her, talking to you. I said I'd show you around and she said you could see anything you wanted, she has no secrets. I say, Phryne, isn't this strange? I've never helped investigate a murder before. It's quite exciting.'

'I suppose so,' answered her sister. 'Let's have a look around. Dot, can you help me here? Poke about and tell me what his stock is worth.'

The shop had a very clean plate glass window with an internal shutter. Dot moved this back against the wall and fastened it. The bright day poured in, hard-edged, making all the goods seem old and shabby, the beams dancing with dust motes. It was the kind of light never seen in Europe, harsh and strong. Whenever Phryne saw it she thought of spring cleaning. It was this summer radiance which had always triggered off the scouring reflex in her mother. Then it was down with the curtains and soapsuds everywhere. Her nostrils remembered the sour smell of newly washed wooden floors. Eliza was struck with the same memory.

'Washtubs,' she murmured. 'Why am I thinking of washtubs and soap bubbles?'

'Spring cleaning,' replied Phryne. 'Come along. To work.'

'Of course,' said Eliza. 'You used to tell me stories when we were banished to the front step, out of the way of all that scrubbing.'

'That was uncharacteristically nice of me,' replied Phryne, unwilling to reminisce. Eliza took the hint and pottered away to examine the household goods laid out on tables. Dot ruffled through a pile of folded cloths and observed, 'Lots of tapestries. Aren't they beautiful? Laid up in camphor, not napthalene. No moth has laid a tooth on any of them.'

'These dishes are the same,' said Eliza. 'Though not a set amongst the lot. All whole and not chipped or cracked, but a harlequin collection. Most of them are good,' she said, turning up a cup to show the Royal Doulton mark on the base.

'Just the place to find a replacement for that cup the temporary kitchenhand smashed after our big dinner party,' said Phryne. 'People love truffling through mixed goods.'

'Yes,' said Dot. 'My sisters do the junk shops and secondhand dealers every fortnight. On a Saturday. Can't see it myself. I'd like all new things, if I was buying, not something which someone else has used.'

'When you get your own house, Dorothy, will you furnish it all new?' asked Eliza, carefully checking for silver marks on a series of partly polished dishes.

'Oh, yes, Miss Eliza. Woolworths if I have to, until I can afford something better. Anyway, cheap china's the best. Things get broken, and if you can replace it by paying sixpence, no one gets upset when something smashes.'

'A good philosophy,' said Eliza. 'These silver dishes are all silver, Phryne. No Britannia metal or E.P.N.S.'

'What's E.P.N.S?' asked Dot.

'Electro-plated nickel silver,' explained Eliza. 'A lot cheaper than real silver but eventually the silver coating wears off. What have you got over there, Phryne?'

'Cutlery,' said Phryne. 'Knives and forks and soup spoons. All, as you say, silver. This is a very expensive junk shop. Looks like the others but the goods are definitely above average.'

'And no prices,' said Dot. 'Usually there's a sign saying something like "Anything on this table threepence" and I can't see any price tags, either.'

'No, this shop was run on personality,' said Phryne, feeling a rising respect for the commercial acumen of the deceased. 'Ladies would come here and bargain for their Spode saucer or their Morris dishtowel. It would be the high point of their week and I just bet Mr. Manifold left his mother well off. It's set out like an ordinary second-hand shop, but it isn't. More like a *brocante* in Paris, where you have to summon all your eloquence to persuade the *patronne* to sell you anything. Very clever, Mr. Manifold. So, Dot, how would you sum up this room?'

'Full of pretty things,' said Dot. 'Lots of things to look at. But no useful stuff. No pots and pans, no wooden spoons, no kettles. Only decoration.'

'Eliza?'

'The same,' said Eliza. 'A lovely place to potter around in.'

'And with enough left for the client to do so they can feel that they have discovered a hidden treasure. An artful film of dust over the china, the silver half-polished. Careful selection of stock so that the lady customer feels that thrill of adventure and discovery. For instance, I noticed the mate to that Royal Doulton cup on the other end of that bench, and two matching saucers in that stack. Impressive. Let's go on.'

Eliza led the way into an inner room, which had a locked door at the far end.

'This is the fine arts room,' she said. 'And they are fine, Phryne. I think that's a Burne-Jones chalk, and the lady with the polar bears is Edmund Dulac. It has his blue, the *bleu du lac*.' Eliza heard the note of pleasure in her own voice, remembered her socialist principles, and added, 'Disgusting that capital should be tied up like this, when it could be used for housing and feeding the poor.'

Phryne chuckled, but quietly.

The fine arts room was hung with a hundred pictures. Every inch of wall space was covered. Phryne walked slowly around the room, examining every one. It was an interesting collection, with something to please everyone, from European oils almost indistinguishable under a century's varnish, meticulous seascapes with distressed ships; farmers, trees, horses, cows; and a lot of small children: offering each other flowers or nursing lambs or staring innocently out of the picture. There were also a goodly array of kittens, in baskets, puppies, in hay, and several studies of clothed mice.

But as Eliza had said, amongst the oil-cloth prints were genuine treasures: the Burne-Jones angel, the Dulac lady with polar bears and the Greek icon of the Virgin, who stared with her wide open eyes at the strange company in which she found herself. Phryne examined a little landscape which might have been a Sisley and a muddy oil of a clumsy nude which had to be a Sickert. Two gorgeous enamelled tiles, twining with jungle vines, were definitely Morris, and Phryne coveted them. But knowing Mr. Manifold as she was beginning to, she was sure that she could not have afforded them. She noted that he had not confined his buying to the previous century. There was a Picasso horse in Indian ink, a Cezanne sketch of a table with glasses, and some flower-studded grass by a Fauve of some sort. No major works, of course, and none of the really outré artists. But a lovely collection to sell, for it contained plenty of simple paintings for the 'I don't know about art but I know what I like' school, and a secret cache of treasures for the cognoscenti. The room smelt sweetly of frankincense from a charcoal burner on the table.

This also held an ashtray in blue and white china, a vase of gum tips and a large folio of sketches in cardboard sleeves.

'Do me a favour, Eliza—go through all the sketches and note anything interesting. Is there another room?'

'Yes, here's the key,' said Eliza, sitting down on a Charles Rennie Mackintosh chair and opening the folder. 'What am I looking for?'

'Anything odd,' said Phryne. 'And an inventory,' she added, unlocking the inner door.

The room was lined with glass cases and the light, when she switched it on, was bright. This room had no windows. Rightly so, because the cases all contained jewellery, small sculptures and coins, glinting in the glare. Phryne took a breath and Dot gasped aloud.

'Look at all those diamonds!' she said.

'No, they are rhinestones, paste, but this is a very expensive collection, Dot dear. Here are works of the Art Nouveau masters, including what I would swear was a necklace by Fabergé. Gosh. I wonder what he inherited from his dad's junk shop and what he bought himself? This stuff is very tasty indeed.'

'It looks like the sort of thing you wear,' Dot observed, stooping over the Fabergé necklace. 'It's mistletoe, isn't it? The little moonstones are the berries and the diamonds are the flowers. And those greenish stones the leaves.'

'Yes. Jade, moonstone and rhinestone, with a little enamel to fill in the gaps. Fabergé's trademark. A lovely thing in itself, leaving aside the value of the gems. Now this stuff is more what I would have expected,' she said, indicating a tray of heavy discoloured 'diamond' rings and gold watches from which the faintest tick had long ago departed, despairing of further life.

'What they used to call estate jewellery,' said Dot.

'Wrenched off Grandma's fingers before she was cold,' said Phryne in distaste.

'Better us than the undertaker,' said Dot stolidly, veteran of several deathbeds. 'But I know what you mean, Miss, this isn't classy jewellery, like the other things. This must be bought from people in St. Kilda.'

'Yes, he must have bought locally.' Phryne inspected another glass case, filled with 'curiosa', including a very convoluted netsuke of several people in interesting conjunction. There was also an intricately carved jade ball with a lot of other orbs inside it, and a few fans of startling beauty. 'But the bulk of his stock came from elsewhere. Those paintings are from England, presumably some of the ones owned by his mother from her artist's model days. I expect he traded down at the docks for sailors' toys and went travelling himself. And what have we here? A scroll, a real scroll written in…' She peered through the glass, 'an unknown script, and another in Greek.'

'Can you read Greek, Miss?' asked Dot, impressed.

'Just enough to sound out the letters. It says "Josephus". Could be the Josephus of *A History of the Jewish Wars*. That would make it very old. A few little icons, a terracotta tile figured with a Medusa's head, something which might be a horse's bit…'

'And a relic of Saint Cecilia.' Dot crossed herself. 'Look, Miss! It says *St. Cecilia* on the front of that little gold case.'

'So it does. Patron saint of music, as I recall. Probably contains a fingernail or a harp string.' Phryne was about to say something scornful about relics when she saw Dot's face and didn't. 'Mr. Manifold got around. A very ingenious young man.'

'Who wouldn't be likely to kill himself, with his business going so well,' commented Dot.

'Indeed,' Phryne agreed, prospecting further. 'His business was flourishing, though we need to inspect the books; he may have had huge debts. Then we shall have to find out about his heart.'

'His heart?' asked Dot, confused.

'Men have died, and worms have eaten them,' said Phryne. 'But not for love. As it happens, there the bard was inaccurate. Didn't Mrs. Manifold say that there was a girl who worked in the shop?'

'I don't recall,' said Dot.

'You know, Dot, an old policeman told me you could always tell who had drowned themselves for love and those who had died because of debt. The lovers' fingers were always torn, scrabbling on the jetty to get out, to escape. But the ruined ones just went straight down.'

'I wish you wouldn't tell me things like that, Miss Phryne,' shuddered Dot.

'Sorry. Let's see what Eliza has found, eh?'

What Eliza had found was a fight. While she was firmly on the side of the working man, this did not extend to his self-perceived right to belt the working woman over the ear with a spade, and when Phryne and Dot entered the yard at the back of the shop, from whence the yelling was emanating, they found Eliza grimly clutching the spade by the haft and addressing the wielder in flow of language which he was not accustomed to hear from a lady. The young female victim was kicking him in the shins, which did not assist his control of his temper.

'All right, everybody drop your weapons,' said Phryne sternly. 'Miss, stop kicking right away. Eliza, take that shovel and give it to Dot. You, sir, stand up straight, tuck in your shirt, and wipe your face.'

'Blimey,' said the spade wielder.

'Well you might say "blimey". You might go so far as "gosh" or even "golly", not to mention any of the epithets which my sister was using in her free socialist manner. Who are you and what is this all about?'

'Just sack me,' said the man sullenly.

'No,' said Phryne. 'Answer my question.'

He took a look at her. She was small and adamant and he fancied that even Ma Manifold might have met her match in those emerald eyes. The girl had burst into tears and flung herself on Eliza's bosom, quite the most comfortable bosom available at that time. This showed good judgment.

'Got any beer?' asked Eliza, astounding the man.

'Some in the Coolgardie in the kitchen,' he said. 'But the old chook saves it for her guests.'

'We are guests,' said Phryne. 'Go get a few bottles, will you, Dot? And the gin which will be somewhere in that kitchen, and a few other things which will occur to you.'

'Yes, Miss,' said Dot, thoughtfully taking her spade with her.

'And you, stop crying now, you aren't hurt,' Phryne ordered the girl. 'What's your name?'

'Sophie Westwood,' sobbed the girl.

'And you?'

'Cedric Yates,' said the man, standing to his full height and shoving back his lint-pale hair. He had light blue eyes in a ruined complexion and skin pale as paper under his blue singlet. Phryne grinned.

'Relative of Cecil Yates, taxi driver and wharfie?'

'Cousin. His dad and mine are brothers,' said Cedric. 'Oh, jeez, you ain't Cec's Miss Fisher, are yer?'

'Guilty,' said Phryne.

'Oh, jeez,' said Cedric again. 'And I nearly beaned yer with a spade!'

'No, you didn't,' said Phryne briskly. 'I had no intention of allowing you to bean me with anything. Now, let us sit down in the shade, and you can tell me what this is all about. I am investigating the death of Mr. Augustine Manifold,' she added, drawing the tall man down to a suitable log under a skillion roof. Eliza placed her charge on the other end of the log and sat herself firmly between them. Just in case hostilities broke out again. There was a strong agreeable scent of wood shavings.

'Sorry I went crook, Soph,' said Cedric. 'It was what you said.'

'And I'd say it again,' said Sophie, a thick-waisted, unattractive girl with pimples. 'All soldiers are—'

'Don't say it again,' advised Phryne. 'You can tell me later, if you wish. In private. Ah. Beer.'

Dot had found a tray, some glasses, and the requisite alcohol. She busied herself with pouring and serving. Cedric Yates downed his bottle of beer in one long, practised gulp and reached for the second.

'Not so fast,' said Phryne, possessing herself of the bottle. 'Answers first. You worked for Mr. Manifold?'

'Yair. Matter of seven years. Lost one of me props in the war and trained as a carpenter. Fine woodwork. Not a lot of call for it and I can't go the roads like other blokes. I was doing a perish until I met Aug. He needed a woodworker and I needed a job. I used to fix the old furniture he bought. Most of it was bonzer. Beaut wood. Just needed a few reglued joints, maybe a bit of missing carving redone, bit of a sand and polish. Sometimes I had to make, say, a new leg or a drawer or something. He was pleased, said he was lucky to get a craftsman like me.'

'What was he like?' Phryne was still cradling the beer bottle so Cedric kept talking.

'Mum's little angel,' grinned Cedric. 'Nothing good enough for my boy. Took himself very serious, flannel next to the skin if he had a cold. But a good enough boss. Now she's a terror, old Ma Manifold. Wants to drive down the wage and up the hours, she'd pinch a penny until it squeaked.'

'You're a—' Sophie began. Eliza hushed her.

'Much as I support free speech, young lady, I do not approve of bad manners,' she said severely. Phryne waited for Sophie to protest but she just gave Eliza an adoring smile. Eliza is better at women than me, Phryne thought. I might leave Sophie to her and concentrate on Cedric. Who was getting restive and very, very thirsty.

'Tell me about Mr. Manifold. Was he depressed? Sad? In some sort of trouble?'

'Before he offed himself? Nah. Could have knocked me down with a feather when he came back "found drowned". Never thought he'd do that. Coroner asked me that too. He was cock-a-hoop, said he had some big deal coming up, would make his fortune so his old mum could retire. He said he'd build her a house in Toorak and she'd never have to lift a finger again.'

'He said that,' affirmed Sophie.

'Anyway, he was doing good-o,' said Cedric, reaching an imploring hand towards the bottle. 'Can I have me beer now, lady?'

'Here.' Phryne supplied the amber fluid. 'Did he have any friends?'

'Dunno,' said Cedric.

'Sophie?'

'Yes,' said Sophie, who had drunk half a glass of gin and lemonade and was feeling a little giddy. 'Lots of friends. Lovely clothes. They came into the shop almost every day.'

'Lady friends?'

Sophie shook her head and then seemed to regret it. 'I don't know,' she said. 'His mum told him he ought to marry to keep the business in the family and he just laughed and said he was happy as he was and far too busy to take a wife. I never saw him with any girl, not particular. I s'pose Gerald would know.'

'Gerald who?'

'Atkinson. Mr. Manifold's best friend. He came in almost every day and took Mr. M to lunch. In a beautiful big car.'

'Rolls-Royce Silver Ghost,' observed Cedric. 'Toffy type in big fur-collared coat. La-di-da voice. Knows a lot about furniture, but,' he added, trying to be fair. 'Drew out designs for the new stuff. Arty type of bloke. Takes all sorts, I reckon,' he added, allowing Phryne to pass him the last bottle of beer.

Sophie flushed purple, which made her pimples glow like lanterns.

'You, you…you're a peasant,' she said to Cedric.

'That's me,' he said complacently. Sophie's fingers twitched as if seeking a weapon and Eliza interposed her person.

'That's enough! How long have you worked for Mr. Manifold, Sophie?'

'Three years, since I left school.'

'And what were your duties?'

'I opened the shop in the morning, posted the letters, answered the phone, I dusted and mended and did a little light cleaning, I showed the things when Mr. M asked me.'

'So you know the stock?'

'Yes, Miss.'

'Good. I have the inventory. Later we will go through it to make sure that nothing is missing. For now, I need to know how you saw Mr. Manifold.'

Sophie folded her hands in her lap and prepared to confide.

'He was such a nice man. Never tried…tried anything, you know, Miss.'

Cedric made an uncomplimentary sound and Phryne clipped his ear. He subsided in case she took his bottle away. Sophie executed a sitting-down flounce, which Phryne assessed at a high degree of skill. Sophie had an annoying voice, shrill as a mosquito.

'Well, he never did. And he paid me well, more every year as I learned about the business. What sort of things to show what sort of people. When to help and when to leave the customers alone to find things on the tables. Lots of important people came to the shop. I was getting good at it! I don't know what will happen to us now he is gone!'

She began to cry again. Eliza patted her shoulder.

'We shall make some provision for you,' she soothed. 'Cedric too. Mrs. Manifold may be keeping the shop going, you know.'

'But it was Mr. M who attracted all the people,' sobbed Sophie. 'He had such a lovely voice, deep and…and he knew where all the valuable things were in Melbourne. When there was an auction he was always there. Especially deceased estates. He used to say he knew more about the riches of the city than any burglar. And he bought things that you wouldn't think would sell, like that awful colonial furniture, wood with the bark still on, like that three-legged table,' said Sophie, pointing out a roughly circular table made of a slice of tree for the top and three not very similar branches for the legs. It had clearly been recently repaired and was clamped until the glue set.

'It's rubbish all right,' commented Cedric, who was sipping his final beer to make it last. 'Like you said, Soph. Old bushies made stuff out of unseasoned timber tied together with spit and baling wire because they didn't have nails or planes or any of them other things. Then rich people actually wanted to have this stuff in their houses, when they could have a Sheraton chair—I dunno. But I remember the first lot of colonial rubbish, came out of a farmhouse in Horsham, I laughed when I saw it, but Aug said, "You mark my words, this will be worth our while, Cedric," and blow me down if he wasn't right.'

'He had very good judgment,' said Sophie. 'They call it a nose. He had a lot of friends amongst the dealers and the junk shop men, old friends of his father's, and he went round to all the shops, even the really dreadful old wares ones, just in case.'

'Old wares?' asked Phryne.

'The ones which stock old tins and rusty screws and bunches of keys without locks and chain link fencing without any links,' put in Dot.

'That's right, Dot dear, you're a rubbish pile veteran, aren't you? Have you ever seen anything worth buying in an old wares shop?'

'No,' said Dot. 'But I wasn't looking too closely.'

'But the boss, he would look,' said Cedric. 'He used to come home filthy—and didn't his mum create!—because he'd been burrowing into a pile of old iron. And like as not he came up with something we could clean up and sell.'

'Yes, remember when he found that big silver platter? It was tarnished black and the old wares man sold it for tenpence,' put in Sophie, showing her first signs of animation. 'Took me eight goes of bath brick and then three of Silvo to clean it up. Had to do the curlicues with a matchstick. But it sold for fifteen pounds and Mr. M gave me a commission for the extra work.'

'He was good like that,' said Cedric, putting down the empty bottle. 'Well, this is nice but it ain't buying socks for the baby. You want me to keep on with the work?' he asked Phryne.

'Yes,' she said. 'Whatever you have in hand. Mrs. Manifold shall pay you until she decides what she is doing with the shop or I'll know the reason why.'

'Reckon you will,' said Cedric, nodding, and went back to his bench. Now that she knew, Phryne could see the drag and swing of his artificial leg. He was conscious of her gaze. 'Nice bit of mahogany here,' was all he said, but Phryne looked away quickly.

'And you,' Eliza told Sophie. 'You can help with the investigation.'

'Well, why don't you both stay here and go through the inventory with Sophie,' Phryne suggested. 'And if she can give me the address, I'll be off to see Mr. Manifold's best friend, Gerald Atkinson.'

Phryne collected the address and left. She could leave Eliza to cope with Mrs. Manifold's wrath when she found her beer gone and the level in her very own private gin bottle sensibly reduced.

◇◇◇

'What do they call this place, sir?' asked Vern.

'The desert of Sinai,' replied the officer. 'No, sorry, the bloody desert of bloody Sinai.'

'In bloody Palestine,' Vern completed the ritual.

'Never mind, we'll be going back after remounts soon,' said the officer. 'After Roumani.'

There was a silence. The stars blazed as close as lanterns.

'After we copped it at Roumani. You remember Bill the Bastard?' asked Vern.

'The horse that never galloped without bucking? Of course.'

'He did after Roumani. He came out of the bloodbath carrying five men: two behind the rider and one on each stirrup. Never even tried to buck. 'Course, he must have been carrying half a ton in soldiers alone.'

'Is that why he's now my packhorse?' asked the officer.

'Yair. Poor bugger deserved a rest. But the yeomanry copped it worse than us.'

'Yes, they copped it...'

'It'd be beaut if our CIC was closer to the enemy than the front bar at Shepheard's Hotel in Cairo,' said Vern, without moving his lips. The hand-rolled cigarette stayed in the corner of his mouth as if glued.

'I'm sure Sir Archibald Murray knows about being a commander-in-chief,' said the officer with a toneless lack of conviction.

'Yair, my flamin' oath,' agreed Vern.

Chapter Three

Happy is the child whose father goes to the devil.

Proverb

Phryne took a taxi to the mansion of Mr. Gerald Atkinson. She could have called home and had Mr. Butler collect her but she was feeling, for some reason, pressed for time. This proved to be an error, because as she left the taxi and began walking up the garden path, one of those impromptu cloudbursts which made Melbourne weather the proverb it was fell upon her unprotected head. Within moments she was soaked to her French undergarments and partially deafened by thunder booming apparently some three or four feet above her and slightly to the right.

'Thunder on the right is supposed to be a good omen,' she said to herself as she completed her trek through a rather nice formal garden to the front door and rang the bell with some force. 'This may prove to be an interesting interlude.'

The door opened and a magisterial butlerine figure enquired as to the lady's business. His tone indicated that Phryne had only merited the term 'lady' out of charity and she had better have a good story if she wanted to get over the threshold in that condition.

Phryne was in no mood to be buttled at. Her shoes were full of water, her dress was behaving like a dishcloth, and her stylish cloche had wilted around her head and was acting like a cold compress. She walked in, straight past the black and white man, and beamed a sunny smile up into his face.

'The Hon. Phryne Fisher to see Mr. Atkinson. Before which I need a towel, a warm garment, and a telephone.'

'Yes,' said the butler, hypnotised. Only the really rich or really aristocratic had this kind of certainty. They knew that the world would unhesitatingly bend itself to their will, and it always did. 'If your ladyship would follow me…'

Squelching, Phryne followed him upstairs into a small bedroom, where the butler was supplanted by a fascinated housemaid, introduced as Gertrude. She supplied a towel and helped Phryne to remove her soaked dress, which was clinging like a corn plaster to her rapidly chilling limbs. When Phryne was dry, the maid helped her into a truly sumptuous gentleman's lounging robe, of scarlet padded silk with damask collar and cuffs in a sprightly spring green. Phryne resolved not to look at herself in strong sunlight in case of self-combustion.

The silk was luxurious and Phryne sat to allow the maid to dry her hair.

'That's Mr. Gerald's favourite robe,' Gertrude told her. 'Mr. Nunn must really like you! Oops, sorry, Miss, I mean, m'lady. I'm not used to being a lady's maid. Usually I do the parlour and the door but Mrs. Patterson's down with her leg again and the boy's gone to the dentist and I've been helping Cook. Sorry.'

'That's all right,' said Phryne, reflecting that the gossiping ladies at various tea parties were right, for once. Australians did not make good servants, thank God. There was something indefatigably democratic about them. But Gertrude was a nice girl who was trying hard and should be encouraged. 'That'll do for the hair,' she said. 'There's a comb in my bag. How about my shoes?'

'Soaked,' said the maid. 'I reckon they'll dry out bonzer if I stuff them with newspapers and leave them near the stove.'

'I'll ring and get someone to bring me some more clothes,' said Phryne. 'Amazing how wet you can get in such a short time!'

'Yes,' said Gertrude. 'And it's stopping now, look—the sun's coming out.'

'So it is,' said Phryne. 'How long have you worked for Mr. Atkinson?'

'Six months,' said Gertrude. 'Six months more and I'll marry my young man. He's a baker. We're saving up for a house. He's got his own business.'

'Congratulations. I hope you'll be very happy. What's Mr. Atkinson like?'

'All right,' said the girl slowly, applying the comb to Phryne's straight black hair. 'Bit high-handed and Old Country and he has noisy friends and noisy parties. And the fits he throws if someone moves one of his precious bowls or statues! They're a task to dust, I can tell you, not to mention his dirty bronzes and horrible carved lumps of rock. But I'm not here for fun, and he pays well enough. I go home every night. Mrs. Patterson's the housekeeper, I don't see much of Mr. Atkinson.'

And that, clearly, was fine with Gertrude. Phryne smiled and shook her head.

'Can you lend me a pair of slippers?' she asked, holding out a folded note.

Gertrude grinned. 'For that, m'lady, you can have them,' she replied.

So it was that Phryne Fisher, trailing the skirts of her lounging robe like a ball dress, came down the stairs to meet Mr. Gerald Atkinson. The first thing he noticed about her was a pair of very new bright pink slippers, with pompoms. The next thing was the upraised head on the slim neck rising from the green damask calyx like a lily. And the third was her jade green eyes.

'Miss Fisher?' he asked, holding out a hand.

'Mr. Atkinson,' she replied, allowing him to take her hand and either shake it or kiss it as he felt inclined. He paused for a moment, then kissed. Phryne allowed him to conduct her to a parlour into which the riches of Europe appeared to have been sent, possibly for storage. Phryne noted a near-Bernini salt cellar, a miniature statue of Michelangelo's David, a copy of a Tiepolo

banquet, several faux Canalettos and shelves full of assorted bric-
a-brac as she was led to a deep chair and allowed to sit.

'As my cousin Sir Eldred always said, "bit of a wetting never
hurt no one,"' he told her.

Gerald Atkinson was tall and skinny, with a haughty arch to
the brows which might easily have been accentuated by skilled
plucking and a rosebud mouth with just a trace of lip rouge. He
was dressed in a very nice tweed suit which was just a bit too
new and a cravat which was just a smidgen too bright, with a
stickpin in which the diamond was just a soupçon too large. If
he was not a baptised bachelor, Phryne considered, he was certainly a confirmed one. This was no bar to Miss Fisher's regard.
She had many friends whose interest in young men was just as
fervent as her own.

'And as my father the baronet says, "What a man needs after
a good soaking is a good whisky,"' replied Phryne.

'That can be managed,' said Gerald Atkinson, brightening at
the mention of Miss Fisher's titled relatives. 'Irish or Scotch?'

'Mind you, he'd say the same after a good sunning,' said
Phryne. 'Scotch, please, with water.'

Mr. Atkinson obliged, pouring a small glass for Phryne and a
tumbler for himself. Miss Fisher sipped at her very good whisky
and looked around the room, wriggling her toes into Gertrude's
pink slippers.

'I know all about you, Miss Fisher!' he exclaimed.

Phryne privately considered this very unlikely, but was still
trying to place Mr. Atkinson, so she merely inclined her head
and smiled.

'And I know nothing about you,' she said. 'So you can
start.'

This disconcerted the young man, who had clearly prepared
an elaborate compliment. He took a gulp of his drink and
began.

'Born: Cairo. My father was a diplomat. School: privately
educated. Came to Melbourne in '13, family fearing war. In

which they were right, of course. Family settled in Camberwell. I inherited this house, so came to live here.'

'Alone?'

'Sometimes,' said Mr. Atkinson ambiguously. Phryne let that one lie for the present.

'Occupation?'

'Gentleman,' he informed her stiffly. Aha. One of those. Phryne was familiar with the insistence of the upper middle class on idleness as a measure of social status. They had, of course, not met people like Lady Alice Harborough, Eliza's friend, who worked harder than any skivvy at her chosen avocation, which was rescuing the women of St. Kilda from penury and crime.

'Yes, but even gentlemen have occupations. My father, for instance, is a baronet and also a Justice of the Peace and a Master of Fox Hounds. My sister Eliza is a social worker, and I am a private detective.'

'Oh, I see what you mean. I'm a collector of antiquities,' said Mr. Atkinson, mollified. Phryne waved a hand at the shelves which Gertrude found such a trial to dust.

'Yes, I can see that. Care to show me some of your collection?'

'Certainly!' Mr. Atkinson's eyes lit up and he looked almost attractive. 'If you would come this way?'

'First, I need to call my house and get someone to bring me some clothes,' she said. 'I can scarcely travel in your very delightful gown.'

He almost blushed. 'This way, Miss Fisher.'

The telephone was in a library which Phryne longed to explore. Mr. Atkinson did not appear to be bookish. There were no volumes open on the desk or the library table, no bookmarks, no signs that anyone had ever read any of the opulent sets of classics and half-calf bindings. Only the collectors' texts were well-used: Gibbons on stamps, the standard authorities on coins and on porcelain. And, for some reason, Roman plays.

Phryne made telephonic contact with Mr. Butler and gave him orders in relation to the clothes and the address at which he was to call with all convenient speed. He was reminded to bring an umbrella and Phryne hung up.

'What a lovely library,' she said, meaning it.

'I inherited it all from my grandfather,' said Mr. Atkinson, carefully not mentioning the name or profession of the said ancestor. Which meant, Phryne knew, that he had been In Trade.

She considered this philosophy extremely silly. If there were no trade, nothing would ever get done or made. And if her own grandfather had not married a Trade heiress, the Fisher family would be as poor as church mice and eking out a living by taking in washing. No point, however, in imparting her own views to this deluded person. He would only be shocked and she didn't want to shock him yet.

'Your grandfather had excellent taste,' she observed, swishing her gown as she moved. The drag of the heavy silk was most pleasing.

'Indeed. Now, if you will come this way,' he said, and Phryne was plunged into the world of the collector.

She had been there before, of course. Sometimes it was fun— like the man who collected Fabergé eggs, or the charming woman who collected children's toys. Sometimes the wit and charm of the collector could overcome the tedium of the collection, such as the delightful Jane Wright, who had a collection of hair ribbons which covered walls, but was very funny about them, as far as anyone can be funny about hair ribbons. In the case of Mr. Atkinson, it was going to be a long day. He collected broken bits of old rock, about which he knew far too much, and Phryne dropped instantly into the trance she employed when stuck in an all-too-familiar church service or a parliamentary debate. She surfaced briefly to nod at 'Mesopotamian' and 'Old Petrie' and 'cuneiform' then slid effortlessly back into her meditative state. More bits passed under her gaze.

'Of course, if you remember your Aramaic,' he was saying when she dropped in again. She nodded solemnly and he continued. 'And this was sent to me from a dig in Gaza. You see the curve?'

It was a shard of terracotta, broken from a bigger pot. Mr. Atkinson's hands described a cylindrical shape.

'It would have held a scroll,' he said. 'The Bedouin bring such things into Cairo occasionally, or Alex. They will never say where they have found them. A few complete ones have been sold, far beyond my touch, alas!'

'I find such things fascinating,' lied Phryne. 'But this is too much to absorb at one time. Let's go back to the parlour and I'll tell you why I came to see you.'

'But the rest…' cried Mr. Atkinson, as distressed as a doting mother with a reserve of fifty-seven cabinet photographs of her infants still to exhibit.

'I will come back and see them,' promised Phryne, laying a hand on his arm. 'Now we need to talk about the sad death of your friend, Augustine Manifold.'

'Oh, poor Augustine,' said Mr. Atkinson, allowing himself to be led back into the parlour and sinking down onto the couch. 'I'll never know why he did it.'

'Tell me about Augustine,' prompted Phryne.

'He was my best friend,' said Mr. Atkinson, groping for a handkerchief.

'How did you meet?'

'I went to his shop,' said Mr. Atkinson. 'He had some bits and pieces that I found quite irresistible. Rarities, you know. And we got talking and I found that he knew a lot about antiquities, especially considering that he had never been to university.'

'Self-taught is often best,' agreed Phryne.

'He knew all the archaeologists,' continued Mr. Atkinson, finding the handkerchief in his trouser pocket and wiping his eyes. 'They sold him duplicates and broken stuff, things you couldn't put in a museum. I remember we spent a whole night putting together a Greek pot, using his special glue. The best sort of jigsaw puzzle, and it was a kylix with a dancing maenad in the middle, a real find. I've got it in that glass case over there, you can hardly see the cracks.'

Phryne got up and looked. It was a lovely thing. The maenad tossed her hair and brandished a lyre, which was polite of her, considering what else, being what she was, she could be brandishing.

'That glue must be amazing stuff, to join such friable material together,' Phryne commented.

'His own invention. He made another one for furniture. The carpenter chappie said it was better than any he'd ever used. You didn't have to keep it hot, see. But now I expect that it will vanish, unless Augustine wrote down the recipe. That old mother of his hasn't a particle of Augustine's initiative or sense—she'll just sit on the inventions and the collection like a foul old broody hen.'

'Indeed,' murmured Phryne.

'He was such a good fellow!' Mr. Atkinson burst into sobs. 'We used to talk all day and all night, sometimes. I took him to lunch on the day...on the day he...'

'How did he seem?'

'Just as ever, but excited. He said he had some great enterprise on foot. Something which would make him rich. He was going to buy a lovely house for his mother so he could live alone at last. But he wouldn't tell me what it was, this deal. And now he never will!' he said sadly.

Phryne looked away, in charity, from his tear-blubbered face.

She was still in two minds about Mr. Atkinson. A snob, certainly, one who had never bothered to learn the name of the carpenter who did such lovely work on the dead man's furniture. He didn't like Mrs. Manifold, but he would be in good company there. And he seemed genuinely affected by the loss of his friend. But there was some character trait in him that she had yet to elicit, and she did not know what it was. Some buried emotion which she could sense lurking under his civilised surface.

'I am investigating Mr. Manifold's death,' she told him.

'Good,' he said through his handkerchief. 'Then when you find out, you can tell me why. Because I don't know,' he wept. 'I don't know!'

He fled from the room, leaving Phryne still puzzled.

She pottered around the collection until the bell rang, her car arrived, and the maid Gertrude escorted her to her previous bedroom, where she assumed her clothes and shoes and returned, with some regret, the sprightly gown.

'Here's my card,' she said to the maid. 'If you can think of anything strange about Mr. Manifold's death or life, call me. There's a reward,' she added. Gertrude's eyes gleamed and she stowed the card in her apron pocket.

'Right you are, Miss. M'lady.'

Phryne took her bundle of rough-dried clothes and her newspaper-stuffed shoes and entered the big car. All the way home she was silent. Mr. Butler did not know if this was deep consideration or pique and took care around corners, so as not to joggle his employer out of a train of thought.

But all she said, as he closed the front door of her own house on her and hefted the bundle, was, 'Odd.'

Mr. Butler did not know what to make of this, but considered that lunch was in order. And perhaps a strong black coffee.

'Has Dot returned, Mr. B?' she asked.

'No, Miss, she is still with Miss Eliza at the shop. She left a telephonic communication that she expected to be engaged for the rest of the day.'

'And the girls?'

'Have gone to visit their school friend, Miss. They were collected by the Laurens' chauffeur half an hour ago, also expected home for dinner.'

'Then it's just me for lunch?'

'Yes, Miss.'

'Ask Mrs. Butler to do me some fish,' said Phryne. 'I need brain food. Or steak, of course.'

'Yes, Miss Fisher. A few of the flathead tails, crumbed, Miss, some French potatoes, a little green salad? And an apple pie to follow.'

'Scrumptious. I will be in the parlour,' she told him, and took herself firmly into the sea-green room. Notes. She needed to write all of this down and then it might make more sense. She was annoyed at Mr. Atkinson's flight, just when she was getting a handle on him. Of course, that might have been the reason that he had fled.

She took a new sea-green silk-covered notebook from the stack in the bookcase, uncapped her fountain pen, and began to write.

Mr. Butler saw her suitably occupied, brought her a cup of strong black coffee, and left her undisturbed until he called her to lunch.

Lunch was excellent. Phryne appreciated the crispness of the fresh fish, the crunchiness of the fried potatoes, and the spiced heartiness of Mrs. Butler's famous apple pie. With the meal she sipped away two glasses of an athletic hock from the Barossa; a little young and foolish but perfectly agreeable company. She had made all the notes she usefully could, and was about to propose lying down for a brief nap when the doorbell rang and Mr. Butler returned with his silver salver. On it reposed a card. In good style, Phryne observed; neat lettering, engraved, very much a gentleman's card. Mr. Valentine Adami, Barrister at Law, apparently wished the favour of speech with Miss Fisher.

'Show Mr. Adami into the parlour, Mr. B,' she said. 'Break out the port.'

Mr. Adami presented no difficulty in classification. He was well, but not too well, dressed. His hair was stylishly cut and his eyes were bright and he was a charming specimen. A successful immigrant, Phryne diagnosed, comfortable and attractive. Nice suit, too. She waited until he was properly seated and had sipped his port before she asked, 'Well, Mr. Adami, I see that you are a lawyer. What can I do for you? I have to tell you in advance, I don't do divorce.'

'Neither do I,' he said in his pleasant, hardly accented voice. 'I have been advised to see you by…' he lowered his voice, 'a very exalted personage indeed. In the Church, you know.'

Phryne was puzzled. Had she obliged any Princes of the Church lately? Of course—the exceptionally reverend Daniel Mannix, in that strange affair of Jock McHale's hat. Mr. Adami was well connected. Phryne made a little bow.

'I am honoured by his confidence,' she said.

'Indeed. He holds your skills in high regard,' said Mr. Adami carefully. Phryne appreciated the nuance. 'He said that if anyone could help me, it would be you.'

'Indeed. What is the problem?'

'It's an estate,' he said, putting down the port glass with appropriate care. 'The estate of a very old lady who died last week. Her name was Mrs. Mario Bonnetti.'

'She was Italian?' Phryne sipped at her own port. It really was superb.

'No, not at all. That being the problem, as I hope I shall explain. Let's see…' He unfolded a bundle of papers and scanned them. 'She was born Kathleen Julia O'Brien on the twenty-fifth of May, 1848. In Melbourne. Her father was a lawyer, a propertied man who bought and sold land and built houses.'

'Fairly oofy, then,' observed Phryne.

Mr. Adami registered the slang, clearly did not approve of such levity on the serious matter of money, but went on without comment. 'Yes, a wealthy man was Daniel O'Brien, and so was his wife, the former Miss Bridget Ryan. The family's wealth was in land and manufacturing so it was not destroyed by the crash in 1880. However, Miss Kathleen Julia was a clever girl and her father sent her to school; not to a convent school, as was usual, but to a school run by some rather advanced ladies, where she showed a great talent for languages, mathematics and music.'

Mr. Butler shimmered into the parlour, refilled the port glasses, laid down a plate of cheese straws, green olives and black olives, and dematerialised in his own remarkable fashion. Mr. Adami took an olive, tasted it, and said with more than common politeness, 'The Archbishop said that you were a truly sophisticated lady, Miss Fisher, and I see that he was understating the matter. Real Sicilian olives! What a treat!'

'Have several,' urged Phryne. So far the story had not engaged her interest but she could not help liking this dapper Italian. Mr. Adami obliged her by eating three olives then returned to his discourse, refreshed.

'So, we have Miss Kathleen Julia at sixteen, accomplished and intelligent, in post gold rush Melbourne. She goes to suitable concerts with her sisters, properly escorted, of course. She visits the conservatorium. She attends suitable parties for young persons. Then there is a sudden break in her life. Abruptly and without explanation she is withdrawn from school and sent to stay with her Aunt Susan in the country. And there she stays until she is seventeen, a whole year. When she comes back she attends no parties and goes to no concerts, is not seen in public and her piano is given to her younger sister. Then, when she is twenty, in 1870, she marries Mr. Mario Bonnetti, a gentleman forty years of age.'

'Curious,' said Phryne, who had an easy explanation for that rustication.

'Significant,' said Mr. Adami. 'But she made him a good wife, according to all accounts. He was an indulgent husband who allowed her to resume her music. He liked her playing, it is said. And she bore him many children, four of whom are still living. I have their names here, and a family tree.'

Phryne looked. Giuseppe, known as Joseph, born 1872. Maria, born 1874. Patrick, born 1875—he died young— Sheila, born 1878, and Bernadette, born 1880. In between, the solicitor had recorded, were three babies dead before they were a year old and five stillbirths. Phryne sent up a brief but fervent prayer of thanksgiving to Marie Stopes.

'And these four are still alive,' she prompted.

'Yes. Maria is now Sister Immaculata, and belongs to a teaching order. She inherited her mother's talent for music. The others are all married with children of their own. I am instructed that it was a happy family.'

Phryne noted the use of 'I am instructed'. It conveyed what the lawyer had been told without any indication of his opinion as to its veracity.

'Fruitful, certainly,' she commented.

'And Mr. Bonnetti died at the age of seventy-two in 1903. He was a man who did not like lawyers and he wrote his own will and testament.'

'They say that all the lawyers in Gray's Inn raise their glasses once a year to the man who makes his own will,' said Phryne.

'As well they might,' said Mr. Adami with feeling. 'This one was unusually inept. Mr. Bonnetti left all his worldly goods to his wife. Not just for her lifetime. Outright.'

'I begin to see where this is heading, Mr. Adami,' said Phryne, taking another olive and holding out the plate. Mr. Adami took two to soothe his feelings.

'Mrs. Bonnetti did employ a solicitor. My firm, in fact. She was adamant about the terms of her will. She left everything, except for some trifling legacies to servants and so on, to be divided equally between her children. The issue of her body, that is.'

'Oh,' said Phryne.

'Not just her legitimate children,' elaborated Mr. Adami.

'And you suspect that there may have been a child back in 1864 when she was sent to…where?'

'Ballarat, I believe.'

'She didn't leave you a letter or a document about this possible child?'

'No.'

'And have we any more clues?'

'Just this,' he said, and gave her a miniature. Phryne switched on the table lamp, with its Tiffany jewels, to examine it.

The setting was skimpy, a gold border barely a sixteenth of an inch wide, and the backing was of base metal. Not a very well painted miniature. It showed a young man with dark curly hair and blue eyes. He was wearing a tight high collar with a severe necktie and a penitential pin. Under the painting was his name in small even letters.

'Patrick,' read Phryne. 'I see. Anything further known?'

'I can't even give you the names of the old lady's friends,' he said worriedly. 'Because they have predeceased her. You see my problem, Miss Fisher. I must assume that the child is alive—though he or she would be sixty-four years old—or, if not, might have left children who will inherit the share which their parent might have had if they had survived. I cannot distribute the whole estate without knowing about the putative child. And Mr. Bonnetti once received a note which said "the child is among you". Someone knows something! And I cannot put an ordinary private enquiry agent on this case. The good name of a lady…'

'Yes, I see,' said Phryne. 'Leave it with me for a few days, Mr. Adami. I have another case on foot as well. But I will look into it,' she said.

'Discreetly?' he begged, taking her hand. 'Discreetly,' promised Phryne.

◇◇◇

'Where did you get the black eye?' asked Vern. 'Bit of a difference of opinion with the MPs in Cairo,' said Curly, lighting a cigarette. His knuckles were skinned raw. 'Ah,' said Vern. 'Marquess of Gooseberry rules?' 'What's them?' asked Curly. 'If you see a head, kick it,' instructed Vern. Curly grinned around his split lip. 'Too right,' he said.

Chapter Four

Errors, like straws, upon the surface flow;
He who would search for pearls, must dive below.

John Dryden
All For Love

The girls and the old wares contingent returned at five, Eliza and
Dot filthy and thirsty and Jane and Ruth agog for information
on this new case.

Phryne banished them all to bathe, dress, and come down
to dinner in a sober and industrious frame of mind at which,
she said, she would lay out for them the whole extent of both
problems. Then she went to do the same herself, giving Eliza
the bath and contenting herself with a brisk splash in cold water
and a clean dress.

'I say, Phryne, this is lovely soap,' commented Eliza as Phryne
was brushing her hair before the bathroom mirror.

'Castile, double milled, scented with freesia,' said Phryne.
'For the invention of baths one could forgive the Romans the
imperfect subjunctive. Take a cake with you. Very good for the
complexion. By the way, you have to watch the sun in Australia,
Eliza, it will burn your milk and roses into blackcurrant jelly
and beetroot.'

'Yes, that's why Ally always makes me wear a broad-brimmed hat. I've had such an interesting day, Phryne. That little man had a remarkable stock. And I've convinced the shop-girl Sophie to come to our Girls' Social Club. We wanted to call it Working Girls' Club, you know, but that would not do. She lives alone in a nasty little room in a boarding house and I believe that she would improve with some company.'

'Yes,' said Phryne affectionately. Eliza loved the whole world. If Jack the Ripper dropped in with his case of scalpels she would try to convince him to doff his cloak and join a woodworking class. And she might succeed, too.

'Lady Alice is coming round with a change of clothes for you, Eliza dear, I'll send her up as soon as she arrives. Want a little pre-dinner drink and a few cocktail biscuits?'

'Rather!' said a voice from the steam. Eliza usually lived an austere life and liked to wallow in luxuries if she could manage it without offending her socialist conscience. In this case, she was filthy and therefore must bathe before dining with civilised persons, and if she happened to be bathing in Phryne's porcelain tub big enough to lie down in, using Phryne's endless hot water and her superb soap, towels, powder and scent, then that was a bonus. Even Fabian socialists were allowed to like freesias.

'Good, I'll arrange it,' said Phryne. 'Enjoy yourself!'

'Oh, I will,' promised the voice from the mist. Phryne closed the door on the sound of happy splashing.

Descending the stairs, Phryne found Jane and Ruth, polite and scrubbed in their dinner gowns. They were very good looking, she thought, her orphans; Jane with her blonde hair in pigtails in her decorous blue silk and plumper brown-haired Ruth in apricot. Lin Chung had provided the fabric and Madame had made the dresses, with just a little beading around the neckline and hem—'*Très jeune fille, mais un peu soigné*'. Their childhood had not allowed them any luxuries at all and they got as much of a thrill out of new clothes as Phryne did herself. Except that Jane had to be prodded to notice the new garment, of course, as she was thinking about the physics of meteorites. Or that is what she had said on the occasion of trying on this dress.

When Lady Alice arrived, Phryne sent her with two attendant girls, one carrying a tray with the decanter and glasses and one carrying the selection of tasty biscuits, up the stairs in grand array. Dot joined Phryne in the parlour. She was conspicuously clean and had re-plaited her hair into a sedate French pleat. In honour of guests for dinner, she had put on her favourite terracotta, beige and fawn house gown and a bandeau with an orange geranium in it.

'Well, Dot dear?'

'It was a bit of a hard yakka day, as my dad would say, Miss. More stuff in the shop, and in his rooms and in store, than you could stuff into a rubbish truck.'

'A bit unkind,' observed Phryne.

'I wouldn't give any of it house room,' declared Dot stoutly, taking a glass of sherry from Mr. Butler's tray. 'Thank you, Mr. B.'

'Well, well, it is all a matter of taste,' said Phryne. 'Didn't you like anything you found?'

'Oh, yes, some of the glass was first rate,' said Dot, sipping the sherry. She had only lately become habituated to a pre-dinner potation and she was still not sure if it came under the heading of the Demon Drink. Miss Phryne's Grog Blossom definitely did. 'Some lovely jewellery. But a lot of it was just old stones and coins where you couldn't see who issued them. Miss Eliza said they were thousands of years old. Before Christ, she said. Such things shouldn't be. There wasn't anything left after the flood.'

'True,' said Phryne, a little shocked by the depth of Dot's ignorance. 'But after the flood they did rebuild the world, you know. It says so. In Genesis, as I recall. Never mind, Dot dear, don't concern yourself. Ah, here come our guests. Nice and clean, Eliza?'

'You could eat your dinner off me,' beamed Eliza, rosy with hot water and scented with flower essences. 'If you should want to, which I trust that you don't. I've allowed the girls a half glass of sherry each, is that all right?'

'Of course,' said Phryne. 'It's a good idea to get used to the idea of drinking at home.'

'It might have made a difference to some of our girls,' agreed Lady Alice. In honour of Phryne's dinner, she had put on her much mended black satin dress and such of her sapphires as she had not sold to relieve the poor. She was sipping whisky, her favourite extravagance. Phryne decided that she and Eliza made a lovely couple. They had certainly thrown everything away to be together: social position, hunt balls, membership of some exclusive charities, and incidentally as foul a concatenation of relatives as Phryne could imagine. And England, of course. And winter.

Mr. Butler intimated that dinner was served, and the company filed into the dining room.

'So, Eliza, how was your day?' asked Phryne.

'Fascinating,' said Eliza. 'We went through the entire inventory, such a lovely collection! Inscriptions from Mesopotamia, enamels from Egypt, even a few cuneiform tablets. And so on through the ages, one could say. Right up to a Picasso sketch and some Fauves. And only one thing missing,' she said, accepting Mr. Butler's assistance in sitting down at the dinner table.

'What?' asked Phryne.

'A scroll,' said Miss Eliza. 'A copper scroll.'

'Odd,' said Phryne.

The dinner progressed through a delicate vegetable soup, some baked lemon-festooned fish with a tomato salad, a roast chicken with sage and onion stuffing with accompanying *légumes maison*, a dessert of fruit salad and ice cream and, finally, a savoury of anchovy toast and some thin chocolates for those with a sweet tooth. Phryne delighted to see her guests eat with pleasure. The menu, with its emphasis on delicate savours and fresh ingredients, was one of Mrs. Butler's triumphs. Mr. Butler's choice of the Rhine riesling for the soup and fish and then a Portuguese rosé for the chicken was extremely acute. Phryne allowed him to fill a minuscule glass with her liqueur of choice, green chartreuse, and expressed proper congratulations.

'Do tell Mrs. B that the dinner was superb,' she said, to a murmur of agreement from the guests. 'And your choice of wines most ingenious.'

'Thank you, Miss Fisher, I shall convey your good opinion to Mrs. Butler,' he said and bowed, a feat considering that he was holding a silver tray with a full set of tiny Waterford glasses. At no point did they even tinkle together. Phryne was impressed. So was Jane, who began to calculate the years of practice it must have taken to keep the hand and arm steady while moving the body from the waist. She was having trouble working out where his waist might theoretically be, since years of buttling and port had expanded Mr. Butler's corporation to the size of an American oil combine. But she assumed that if she drew a line through the watch chain it might approximate to a median…

'A copper scroll, Eliza?' Phryne was asking, and Jane stored the calculation for later consideration. She often kept abstruse puzzles for when she couldn't sleep due to Ember deciding to repose on her chest, inducing dreams of mines collapsing, or Ruth snoring.

'Copper, yes. It was supposed to be in his manuscript collection in that inner room, Phryne, and we could see where it had been. A little dust around it. Sophie was ordered always to leave a little dust on the antiquities. So they looked, well, old.'

'You know, I'm really sorry I never met Mr. Manifold,' said Phryne, enchanted.

'He does seem to have been a heaven-born salesman,' agreed Eliza. 'We don't know anything more about this copper scroll except that it wasn't copper. Sophie handled it and said it was a common vellum scroll, rolled around two spindles, written in Greek.'

'Perhaps it was in a copper housing,' suggested Jane.

'Possibly,' said Phryne. 'Mr. Atkinson said that scrolls were commonly found in terracotta sort of pot things, sealed at both ends. He has the shards of one in his collection. Might have had decorated ends, of course. Good thought, Jane, keep thinking. You are going to help me read the autopsy report later, if you please.'

Jane wriggled with pleasure. Ruth made a grimace of disgust.

'The inventory doesn't tell us where he got the scroll. The acquisitions book just says 'Simon'. He got a lot of archaeological stuff from this Simon, but Sophie says she doesn't know him. I asked Mr. Yates, and he says all he knows about Simon was he used to call after dark, had a motorbike, and carried his goods in an army knapsack. Mrs. Manifold was still too upset to talk to me.'

'Odd,' said Phryne. 'I would have said she was a woman of iron grey purpose. Not prone to have hysterics.'

'Er...I believe that they might have been...so to speak... induced...' hedged Eliza.

'She was drunk?' demanded Jane, cutting through Eliza's attempt at politeness.

'Yes,' said Dot. Jane and Dot exchanged a glance of solidarity; the only two straight speakers in the house. Neither of them had any difficulty in calling a spade a spade, or indeed a shovel, and found the rest of the world annoyingly prone to euphemism, which they felt was perilously close to untruth.

'Yes,' said Eliza. 'I think it was the relief she felt that you had taken on the case that made her hit the bottle. Before she came to see you, Phryne, no one would believe her.'

'I don't know if I do, either, yet. Right, tomorrow I am taking Dot off this case, provided you can carry on for a few days, Beth.'

'I can spare the time,' said Eliza, getting an affirming nod from her partner.

'I can manage the mothers' group and the girls' friendlies,' said Lady Alice. 'If you come back at night and help with the hostel.'

'I'll be there,' promised Eliza.

They smiled fondly at each other.

'What do you want me to do, Miss?' asked Dot. She had felt a little left out what with Miss Eliza's presence in the case, and her knowing so much more about art and things than Dot.

'Something much more suited to your natural talents,' said Phryne. 'I am now about to impart the problem of Mrs. Mario Bonnetti's will, so everyone get a drink and find a comfortable position, because I don't want to be interrupted or I might lose my place.'

Jane got another cup of tea, Ruth a glass of milk. Phryne was supplied with a pot of coffee and a jug of iced lemonade. Her sister accepted another kirsch and Lady Alice's whisky was replenished.

Phryne told the story of Mrs. Mario Bonnetti, nee Kathleen Julia O'Brien, her strange interlude in Ballarat and her marriage to a forty-year-old Italian. Phryne recited the names of the children, including Sister Immaculata, and the problem of the division of the estate. Then there was a silence.

'And we need to find out not only if there was a child, but if it lived?' asked Lady Alice. 'Such children usually do not live, especially then.'

'What do you mean?' asked Phryne, who never thought about children if she could help it.

'Well, dear, consider. The mortality rate even amongst healthy legitimate children at the time was one in five before their fifth birthday. People didn't know about feeding pregnant women then, and mothers usually got the keelings of the pot or the leavings of the plates, whatever was left over after the Master of the House had been fed. Men were the breadwinners and had to get the most; women were at the bottom of what biologists call the food hierarchy.'

'Still are,' said Dot. 'In my house, my dad got the pick of the food, then my brothers, then my sisters, then me, then Mum and the baby.'

'Which means a lot of weak mothers who can't survive the labour and exhaustion of childbirth,' explained Lady Alice. 'And a lot of babies malnourished in the womb, so they cannot undertake the effort of living.'

'Miss, should the girls be hearing this?' asked Dot, worried.

'Yes,' said Phryne. 'There is nothing immoral about biology. Or sociology. By itself, I mean. Knowledge is power, Dot dear.'

'But it's always been like that,' Dot protested, shelving her concerns for the girls' immortal souls. 'Men work hard, they need the food.'

'And women don't work hard?' asked Lady Alice gently.

Dot subsided. She had never thought of this before. It was revolutionary. And probably against the law of God. Or maybe not.

'So a child borne by an unmarried mother probably went to an orphanage,' continued Lady Alice, who knew when to leave a socialist concept to soak in. 'There must have been some good ones, somewhere, but most were baby farms, where babies lay all day in soaked napkins, if they had napkins, fed occasionally on watered cow's milk, and died in droves. The poor mites. Children of sin. Such cruelty. Now in a rational state—'

'This was an important family,' said Phryne. 'Would they give the child to an orphanage? Wouldn't they arrange an adoption?'

'Might have,' said Eliza. 'But they were Irish. The Irish were very hard on unmarried pregnant girls. Harder than the Italians, even though they are both Catholics. If so, it would be a poor family with no children. And they would have paid for its keep. That might be a way of tracing them.'

'And the girl wouldn't be living in Ballarat,' said Dot, who was still thinking about who got the most food and why. 'You couldn't keep her hidden all that time without someone knowing. She would have been on a farm or something, out of the town. Probably working for her living,' said Dot.

'Cruel,' said Phryne. 'So, she is stripped of her rank and all her pleasures, sent off to Ballarat, then further degraded into a farm servant. Why didn't they just kill the baby at birth and bury it under the pigsty?'

'Oh, no, Miss!' Dot was aghast. 'That'd be murder! It'd have to be baptised, too. Before they did whatever they did with it.'

'Aha,' said Phryne. 'Baptismal registers. We are going to have fun, Dot dear. Tomorrow I want you to come with me to talk to a nun.'

'Why are you choosing the Sister to begin with?' asked Eliza.

'Because she owns no property and therefore isn't actuated by greed,' Phryne replied. 'And because I have been recommended to Mr. Adami by the Archbishop. That ought to be convincing.'

'What did you do for the Archbishop?' asked Eliza suspiciously.

'I found a hat.' Phryne took a gulp of coffee. 'I'll tell you about it another day.'

'Very well,' muttered Eliza, disappointed that one of her own family should be assisting a minion of the Bishop of Rome, purveyor of opiates to the people.

'We shall be quiet and respectful and wear attar of roses,' Phryne told Dot. 'Now, if everyone would like to mull over our problems, Mr. Butler will put on some quiet music and I will go and read that autopsy report with Jane.'

'Better you than me,' murmured Ruth to Jane.

'Yes, isn't it lucky?' replied Jane with a blissful smile.

Phryne had always suspected Mr. Butler of a carefully concealed spark of irony, and this was confirmed as she and Jane sat down at the table to the strains of *Danse Macabre*.

The report was brief. '"The body of a well-nourished man now known to me as Augustine Manifold. Height five feet six inches. Weight nine stone eleven pounds. Hair, brown. Eyes, brown. No tattoos, scars or other distinguishing marks. Bruises and abrasions on arms, hands, knees and head, most likely post-mortem and a result of the body tumbling against objects in the water by the action of the tide."'

'Hang on,' said Jane. 'What objects? He was found on the sands.'

'Nice point, keep reading,' said Phryne. The sketch of the male body showed that the abrasions had been mostly on the knuckles and the shoulders. Had Augustine Manifold been forced into the water and hit his attacker? Still, there was no telling about water damage and at least he had beached before the crabs and crayfish had nibbled at him and thereby put Phryne off seafood for weeks.

'"Opened, the abdomen smelt strongly of alcohol. Six ounces of whisky were recovered from the stomach, along with starch, fruit pulp and a sugary liquid. Liver, spleen, heart, kidneys and intestines: normal. Brain showed signs of asphyxiation. Eyes had petechial haemorrhages. Lungs contained froth and water. Froth in mouth. Cause of death: drowning."'

'I don't call that a proper examination,' said Jane indignantly. She felt that poor Augustine Manifold had been short-changed.

'No,' said Phryne. 'One thing leaps out, doesn't it?'

'No,' said Jane.

'They didn't test the water in his lungs,' said Phryne. 'So...'

'So they don't know if he drowned in salt water or in fresh!' Jane exclaimed. 'You mean, someone might have drowned him in a bucket, or the bath, and then dressed the body and thrown it into the sea?'

'It's a possibility, isn't it? His liver was normal but he had a killing load of whisky inside him. The murderer would just have to wait until he passed out.'

'Yes,' said Jane. 'But how can we test it now?'

'Ah,' said Phryne. 'If the body is still in the undertaker's fridge, then we can do a little light burglary. We shall see. The examiner may have kept his samples. We shall consider this further. Now, can you open that box for me and lay the contents out on the table?'

'What are these things?' asked Jane, doing as she was bidden. She wrinkled her nose at the odour of fermenting seawater which billowed out as she prised off the cardboard lid.

'What was in Augustine's pockets,' said Phryne. 'What do we have here? One handkerchief, mouldy. One wallet. Opened, it contains—here, Jane, you tease out that paper and lay it flat on a napkin. Then we might be able to read it. One pocket watch, soaked. Would probably go again if cleaned and dried. One pencil, propelling, and a little case of replacement leads for same. One notebook, also mouldy. Sevenpence in change. One gold coin—very old. One pocket-knife, rusted shut. Nothing unusual. I'll just go and get some blotting paper for the notebook.'

When Phryne returned Jane had managed to roll the papers out of the wallet around a pencil and was laying them out on her handkerchief.

'This is a banknote, one pound,' she told Phryne. 'This is another—ten shillings. This is a page out of a sewn book. Maybe that one, it's the same size.'

'Anything written on it?'

'Yes, Miss Phryne, but it doesn't mean anything.'

Phryne looked. In the middle of the sheet a firm hand had drawn an equilateral triangle and next to it a vertical line.

'I know what it could be,' she told Jane. 'But you need a classical education—which, of course, Augustine had.'

'What?'

'A Greek letter,' Phryne told her. 'Delta. Or it might just be a triangle. A design for some piece of furniture? The start of a map?'

'It looks finished,' objected Jane. 'It was in his wallet. I think you're right, Miss Phryne. I think it's a delta. We use them in astronomy, you know. For stars. Alpha is the brightest star in a constellation, beta the next brightest, gamma the next after that and so on through delta and epsilon.'

'Somehow,' said Phryne, 'I don't think this is about stars.'

The man with the keys jingled them. It was half dark and no one was about in the hot, windy street. He opened the postbox and groped inside. He detected an envelope and drew it out. There was nothing else in the box.

He tore the letter open. His ten pounds had gone from the envelope. In its place was another of the dreaded letters.

The Child Is Among You it said. *Twenty pounds, next week. Or else.*

There was no signature. He closed and locked the box.

Where was he going to get twenty pounds?

Chapter Five

Nuns fret not at their convent's narrow room; And hermits are contented with their cells.

William Wordsworth
'Nuns Fret Not at Their Convent's Narrow Room'

Phryne found it hard to sleep. This was probably because of the weight of Ember, who had decided to grace the Mistress' bed with his dark (hot, heavy, furry) presence. And the rising whine of the north wind, which promised scorching temperatures on the morrow. Phryne had always hated being cold; in her first summer in Australia, she was beginning to wonder what was so bad about putting on a lot of clothes and walking in snow. It had been fresh, certainly, and the fingers and toes had tingled…

Phryne sat up and put on her bedside light. There was never any point being cross about weather, it was like politicians: to be borne patiently, because it was compulsory. The wind began to howl, causing the vine outside her attic window to rake agonised fingers across the glass. Unsettling. Phryne decided on a trip downstairs for that jug of lemonade and her detective story, which she had left in the parlour.

She did not put on any lights but drifted down the stair in her dark green silk nightgown like the ghost of a cinema star.

She had gained the parlour and was feeling for the light switch when she heard a scratching noise which wasn't caused by the wind.

Mice? Phryne cast a reproving glance at Ember, who had followed her on the off-chance that there might be milk. He was listening intently to the same sound, but he had not sunk into a stalking crouch. Therefore, not mice. Or rats. In fact few rats swore softly when they dropped something, which was what this rat had just done. He was outside the parlour window, fiddling with the catch. Phryne was not in the mood for burglars. This one was booked for an uncomfortable half an hour before the constabulary came to his rescue.

But it would be nice to know what he was looking for. If he was a local bad boy rummaging for jewellery, she could just bean him with the poker and call the police. No burglar could complain of such treatment; after all, like foxes, as Phryne was always being informed, they probably enjoyed the chase. Or not, as it happened; she did not care, at least in the matter of burglars. Trespassers Will Be Hit Over The Head With Something Conclusive was her watchword.

Phryne drew back into the shadow of the door as the swearing man finally managed to get the window open and climbed in.

He had a shaded torch. He had a paper in his hand. A shopping list, perhaps. Phryne sank into her cat's resting trance, which kittens learned at their mother's paw but Phryne had had to acquire by hours of Lin Chung's mind exercises. In this state one could not be bored, one did not notice a mosquito bite or a cramp. One just existed in the night, part of it. In this case, Phryne allowed herself to melt into the shadows of the parlour wall and watched as the burglar swore again, dropped his jemmy, froze and listened for movement, moved again, tripped and almost fell over a chair…Then he began rummaging through the books, dropping one in three.

At this rate he would make an unwise noise and rouse the household and the wrath of an outraged Mr. Butler if he didn't get a wriggle on. Ember, slightly interested and wondering if this nocturnal visitor might be persuaded to open that obdurate Refrigerating Machine which guarded the milk can from its proper warden, strolled across and uttered a cordial meow of greeting.

The burglar gave a screech, dropped his jemmy again (missing Ember by inches) and dived for the window, which was still open. By the time Phryne had followed him he was a running shape, fleeing wildly down the Esplanade. All she had seen of him were his hands, manipulating the torch. They were handlike, with five fingers each. Neither huge and calloused nor small and delicate; just hands. He was of medium stature, though he was wearing a jacket so it was hard to tell. And from the turn of speed he exhibited in his retreat he was probably quite young. And really not cut out for a life of crime, to judge from his evident nervousness and his tendency to drop things. Somewhere a motorbike hammered nails into the night.

Phryne swore softly in her turn, climbed back through the window and closed it carefully, noting that the lock had not been broken but the bars had been taken down neatly and disposed against the fence. That would have to be remedied. In the morning. She built a nice pile of expendable objects on a small table and placed them where they would be knocked over if the burglar came back, put on the light, and surveyed the room.

He had been looking at the books. Several thick tomes had been taken down and shaken, if the litter of chocolate wrappers, tram tickets, bits of ribbon and other impromptu bookmarks were evidence. Phryne looked at the titles. All in Latin: Plautus, Terence, Julius Caesar, Epictetus, and the maunderings of Marcus Aurelius. No common factor there. The burglar had left his jemmy, which Phryne carefully picked up with the tongs and placed on the big table. Marks were visible on its slightly greasy surface. Tomorrow she would ask her old friend Jack Robinson to have someone comb through the fingerprint archives for her intruder. Phryne gathered up all the bits of paper and found one which did not seem to belong. It was a torn-off piece of cream-laid notepaper, as sold to ladies for their social correspondence. It smelt faintly of lilies. But it was not informative. On it was drawn that tiresome triangle or delta, the word *one* and *Brothers*.

'Hmm,' said Phryne. She found her novel, put a 'do not touch' note on the jemmy, and wafted into the kitchen for her lemonade, preceded by Ember, who radiated the smug satisfaction of a cat who deserved the milk which was about to be dispensed to him, considering that he had nearly lost another life to falling implements in order to obtain it.

'Though actually, it would have been nice if you had waited just a little bit longer before scaring him away,' Phryne told him, pouring milk into his special dish, a chipped piece of famille rose which he considered his due as an aristocrat. Common cats drank out of Woolworths china. He drank out of porcelain. As long as it contained the creamy milk which Mrs. Butler bought from her favourite hygienic dairy, which was staffed by Jersey cows who were shampooed daily by attentive milkmaids. It did, and he lapped delicately.

Phryne watched him as she gulped down her first glass of lemonade and listened to the wind howl and claw at the house. A few days of this, she thought, and I shall be storing myself in the American Refrigerating Machine along with the milk.

Now that the excitement was over for the night, Phryne yawned, took another glass of lemonade and ice and wandered back to bed. Ember bestowed a parting lick on the bowl on which the design was now clearly visible and followed her up the stairs. *Finis*. Curtain.

Morning announced itself with Dot and coffee. Dot had now known Phryne long enough not to bother her with questions like 'By all the saints what has been happening in the parlour God protect us did we have a burglar?' before the lady had absorbed her coffee and a small biscuit, drunk her glass of cold water with lemon juice, and taken a brisk cool shower. Dot occupied the time with putting out clothes, finding matching stockings and removing Ember from the disordered bed so that it could be made. This was always a touchy manoeuvre. But on this morning he rose unbidden, stretched all of his elegant black limbs and sauntered to the door, intent on breakfast.

Dot made the bed with five skilled flicks and opened the window. Then she shut it again on a gust like a furnace exhaling.

'Going to be hot,' she ventured. 'I'll pull the curtains as soon as you're dressed, Miss Phryne.'

'Wouldn't opening the window be better?' asked Phryne, towelling her hair.

'No, Miss, if it's going to be really hot you need all the shade you can get, to keep the cool in,' Dot instructed.

Phryne accepted this, donned a loose cotton shift and went down to breakfast. There she ate poached eggs and crispy bacon with grilled tomatoes and advised her household of the nocturnal caller. She ordered a visit from an ironmonger to replace the bars, and watched Mr. Butler wrap the jemmy for dispatch. The girls had already breakfasted and were agog. Their reactions were distinctly different. Ruth, who had not much imagination, was a little excited. Jane, who did, was a little afraid. But both of them were restrained from interrogating Miss Phryne at table by Dot, who agreed with Jane. Burglars should not be tolerated in a lady's house.

This might also have been Mr. Butler's opinion, but this could only be guessed at by the keen observer, who might have noticed an intensifying of his customary imperturbability from that of a stunned mullet on ice to that of a stuffed, as it might be, moose. He supplied Miss Fisher with more coffee and said nothing.

'Today, Dot, we are going to visit Sister Immaculata,' said Phryne. 'She's teaching at an infants' school in Port Melbourne. I'm hoping that she might be able to impart some family secrets and save us from having to dig deeper. Eliza is going back to Mr. Manifold's shop to assist Sophie and poke around a bit.'

'School's out,' observed Ruth, with some satisfaction. 'The teachers are on holiday, like us.'

'Sisters,' said Dot severely, 'are never on holiday.'

There, it appeared, she was wrong. On arrival at the bluestone reformatory, it appeared that the school was indeed closed for the summer. It was deserted except for the sound of scrubbing and shrill conversation, which indicated that a few of the congregation had been strongarmed under threats of eternal damnation into scouring the place with sand soap and carbolic, to judge by the scent. The convent next door had a dread portal doorway with a wicket gate inside it. Phryne knocked, clutching at her straw hat which the wind was trying to steal, and made her request.

'Sister Immaculata?' repeated a plump, sweating young nun, clearly perishing beneath her wimple. 'She's on holiday in a boarding house in Williamstown. I can give you the address. She's been a bit unwell and the doctor ordered sea bathing,' said the portress, scribbling on a spare service card and handing it through the bars. 'Gosh! I wish it was me! Going to be another scorcher, isn't it?'

'I'm afraid so,' agreed Phryne.

She took her leave and ordered Mr. Butler to drive to Williamstown. It was still early and the day promised, at least, a pleasant lunch at some seaside cafe. Or cool hostelry. The hostelry, perhaps, might be better. In Phryne's experience, the hostelry was always better, due to the patrons voting with their feet if the lunch wasn't up to scratch…

Dot was outraged when she mentioned this.

'Miss, we can't take a nun to a pub!' she objected. Phryne had tried her very high. Her employer really was a Godless heathen.

'Of course not, how very silly of me.' Phryne patted Dot's hand. 'That's why you're here, you see? To stop me making terrible errors.'

'All right, then,' muttered Dot, still quivering. Her own early education had given her a great respect for nuns. Some of this respect had been instilled with a slipper. Some of it had been engendered by her deep love for the young and beautiful Sister Scholastica, who had taught her to read and write her beautiful cursive hand. She had once, on a never-to-beforgotten day, broken up a fight and taken the bruised and winded little Dorothy into the very convent itself. There Dot had been hugged in a flurry of starch and robes, given lemonade, had her torn dress mended with fine stitches and had her skinned knee patched with sticking plaster. After which Dot adored Sister Scholastica with her whole heart. Miss Phryne, she reflected, just didn't understand about nuns. But Sister Scholastica would have wanted Dot to forgive her, so she did.

The weather was not going to perturb Williamstown. Built mostly of bluestone, it laughed at gales and was mildly contemptuous of hot winds and high seas. Blow thy belly full, it might have been heard saying. The Esplanade was chattering with school children, flushed and sticky with ice cream. The back beach was thronged with lunatic holidaymakers, emerging from the wooden bathing pavilion in fewer garments than they usually wore, except for a few fathers who were sticking to their work trousers, though they had removed their coats and were freely displaying their braces to an indifferent world. Sandcastles were being constructed in the face of the destroying blast. Solemn babies sat in puddles, patting the water with wooden spades. Harassed mothers distributed sandwiches in which the sand had suddenly become a prominent ingredient. Brown boys as beautiful as any Greek bronzes dived headlong into the sea, daring each other to go deeper.

The ice-cream man was coining money. Over the howling of the wind Phryne could hear some hardy soul's wind-up portable gramophone declaring that yes, they had no bananas.

'Here, I believe, Miss Fisher,' said Mr. Butler, drawing up at a bluestone building with a cheerful green door. The green door was a bit of a shock. Phryne got out. The door was ornamented with a fat porpoise in brass, very well polished. She grasped the cetacean and knocked.

It was answered by a doleful elderly woman in a drab wrapper and carpet slippers on heavily bunioned feet which clearly gave her hell.

'Miss Fisher to see Sister Immaculata,' said Phryne.

'Come in,' said the drab.

'I was rather hoping that she might come out,' said Phryne, oddly unwilling to enter the dark hall, but entering anyway.

'I'll ask,' said the unhappy lady, and limped away.

She had left Phryne standing in the hall. This was rude, even if practised on a heathen—and how did she know Phryne was a heathen, anyway? Phryne looked at Dot, who shrugged. Minutes passed. Then a small nun came bouncing down some invisible stairs and rushed to take Phryne's hand.

'I'm so sorry. Mrs. W is a good woman, of course, but she hasn't any manners. I think they keep her on to remind us to be charitable even to the irritating. I'm Sister Immaculata. My brother says you are going to help us. Mother says I can go out without a chaperone, which will be very nice. Where shall we go? The Ozone, perhaps?'

Since this was going to be Sister Immaculata's day, Phryne nodded and watched her secure her wimple over her cap, flip on her veil and flick her hood over her head with the skill of long practice.

The Ozone tearoom was a long, light, very clean establishment, fairly cool and not very crowded. Sister Immaculata sat down on a chair which faced the sea and folded her hands.

'It's so big,' she said. 'Endless. Nothing between us and Antarctica bar a few islands and Tasmania. Teachers can easily forget that there is a world outside the classroom. Now, I understand that I am to answer your questions as fully as I can.'

'But first,' said Phryne firmly, 'you are to have tea. And scones and cakes and sandwiches without the sand and whatever your heart desires.'

'The Lord must have sent you to turn me away from sin,' said Sister Immaculata with a twinkle in her eye. 'I have been craving chocolate eclairs for weeks.'

Phryne waved over the waitress.

'Chocolate eclairs, cakes, scones and cream,' she ordered. 'And tea for three, please.'

Phryne beguiled her tea with wondering about Sister Immaculata. She was stocky and brisk, perhaps a little pale, and none of her hair could be seen under the ecclesiastical headgear. But she had been born in 1874, which meant that she was fifty-four, an age at which most women without upper-class privileges were crones, either toothless and stringy or epicene, moustached and fat. Her skin was soft and almost unwrinkled and her movements were sure. And her appetite, as she reached for the plate of cakes, was excellent. She and Dot accounted for most of the food, while Phryne drank sugarless tea with lemon and tried not to melt.

She envied Mr. Butler, who had probably slipped into that neat-looking little pub and was doubtless sinking a well-earned beer by now.

The fourth eclair defeated Sister Immaculata. She looked at it longingly, reached out for it, then sighed. She drank off the lees of her tea and set the cup down with a decisive little click.

'Thank you,' she said. 'That was a wonderful tea. I only have a light dinner, you see, because I have to go into the water after dark, and you mustn't bathe with a full stomach. Shall we walk? I should like to breathe some fresh air.'

'Into the gardens,' suggested Phryne, who had seen a high fence with a rank of thick pine trees inside it just down the road. Those barriers might deflect this tearing north wind a little.

'Tell me the subject of this enquiry, Miss Fisher, so I can order my thoughts as we walk,' suggested the nun.

'We want you to remember your mother,' said Phryne. 'It is possible that she bore a child, long before she met your father, and we need to find out if that is so. And there aren't a lot of people we can ask.'

'I see,' said Sister Immaculata. She folded her hands across her well-filled middle and preceded Phryne down the road to the garden gate. The wind tore at her veil, but she did not unclasp her fingers to subdue it. She glided ahead like a plump, self-contained ghost and Phryne followed her.

The gate clicked open, and then shut. At once the wind was defeated and the sound of it died down to a gentle murmur. Inside the garden, it was still. A few of the sandy holidaymakers had penetrated its silence, but they too seemed to have been hypnotised by the aromatic quiet and were lying on the grass, dozing, their sunburn slicked with milk of roses, their children and goods piled around them. Phryne thought they looked like refugees from some war against the weather.

Sister Immaculata led the way to the lily pond, which had real lotus blossoms rising from its muddy depths, and across a little rustic bridge to the aviary. There she sat down on a bench and motioned Phryne and Dot to sit beside her. In the huge enclosure, a peacock thought about displaying his magnificent tail, lifting it with a froufrou as from a silk petticoat, then decided it was too hot even to impress the brown undistinguished peahens and put his head back under his wing. A scurry of quail ran across the floor of the cage, like little clockwork birds. They were so charming that Phryne was just crossing them off her list of edible poultry—with regret—when the nun began to speak.

'My mother was not a happy woman,' she said, looking down at her hands, now holding her rosary. 'I don't think she had ever been happy. My father was a good man and did all he could to please her, but…she wasn't happy. She was lovely,' said Sister Immaculata. 'So beautiful. When I was little she used to let down her hair over me, like a waterfall of black silk. Scented with lilac. I always think of her when I smell lilac.'

'She married an older man,' hinted Phryne. 'And not an Irish Catholic.'

'Yes,' said Sister Immaculata. 'I always wondered about that. Not at the time, of course, a child does not wonder about her parents, but later. Why we never saw our other grandparents except at christenings. They gave us each a christening mug and a Bible. But that's all. I believe that my brother tried to visit them once, but they would not receive him. He was very cross, poor Joe! I believe that she liked my father well enough, and she almost loved us, but…there were bad days. On bad days she would lie in bed all day and say that she wanted to die.'

'Is that why you decided to become a nun?' asked Phryne.

'Oh, no, dear, God decided that,' said Sister Immaculata with perfect conviction. 'I have a vocation. I knew all my life and I went into the convent when I was sixteen. My father was not altogether pleased, you know, but Mother was. Ah, well, they are all with God now,' she mused. 'God be good to them!'

A parrot interjected 'pretty boy!' with some satisfaction. This set off several others, who all had their favourite line.

'Polly wants a cracker!'

'Pretty boy!'

'Drop dead!'

This appeared to subdue the others. Sister Immaculata smiled.

'Now, tell me, why did you want to know about my mother?'

'Because it appears there is a problem with the distribution of her estate,' said Phryne, and explained poor Mr. Adami's problem. 'It seems that there may have been another child, and I thought I would start my enquiries with you, because…'

'I don't own anything? A good notion,' said the nun, looking as though she was on the point of rewarding Phryne with a gold star or a boiled lolly. 'Not owning anything set me free,' she told them. 'I had drawers full of clothes and dozens of toys and I left them all behind without a thought. Except the books,' she said, as an afterthought. 'But I work with books. If you have a couple of pennies, Miss Fisher, shall we buy some peanuts for those parrots?'

As Phryne could see that the nun had something more to say, she complied. A couple of pennies in a machine caused a bag of peanuts to come shooting down a green-painted chute. A macaw, a green parrot, a cockatoo and a couple of galahs came down the bars, helping themselves along with their meat-shears beaks, to partake of the bounty and comment 'Polly wants a drink of water' and 'you beaut!' Sister Immaculata fed them. Phryne looked at her, a strange survival in her medieval robes, the gaudy new world birds screaming and fluttering at her fingertips.

'My mother left me a package,' said the nun, when the final peanut had been crunched. 'It's with Mr. Adami. I have been struggling in prayer about what to do. Tell him that you have my permission to open it. Then tell me what it contains. I have always known that there was something wrong. It would be a relief to know that my mother was suffering from loss and terrible grief, not from...'

She had no need to go on. Terrible grief was not inherited. Madness and melancholia were.

'Well, we had better be getting you back,' said Dot to Sister Immaculata. 'You've been ill and you're supposed to be resting.'

'Yes. I am a little tired,' said the nun politely, getting up and patting Dot's hand.

'Goodbye, Polly,' said Phryne to the birds.

'Ribuck,' said the cocky.

'I wonder who teaches them all those words?' asked Dot, making conversation.

'Someone with a lot of time on their hands,' said Phryne.

They walked the now-silent Sister Immaculata back to her convent and watched the green door shut behind her. Mr. Butler had returned to the car and was reading the *Hawklet*.

'Where now, ladies?' he asked.

'Home, if you please,' said Phryne. 'The day gets hotter from noon, doesn't it? I'm sure there's some meteorological reason why it shouldn't.'

'Always does, but,' said Dot. 'Cool change tonight, Miss Phryne. You'll need your blanket.'

'Oh, indeed,' said Phryne in a tone which indicated deep scepticism. 'I need to telephone Mr. Adami to bring that parcel around, and then we might get somewhere.'

'But wasn't she nice, Miss?' asked Dot.

'I wish she'd been my teacher,' Phryne replied.

◇◇◇

Simon hauled the heavy Harley-Davidson onto its centre stand. Now that old Augustine was gone it seemed pointless to continue his trading amongst the sailors and thieves. But he had another reason for visiting the shop. He settled his hair, smoothed his leather coat, and sidled towards the back gate of the yard. The guard dog Binji knew him, and did not bark.

Chapter Six

Memento mori. (Remember you must die.)
Proverb

Phryne made her phone call and Mr. Adami agreed to have the parcel brought to her house within the hour. Meanwhile, the afternoon post brought her a sad black-bordered card—with a gloomy quotation from Ezekiel, advertising his opinion that all flesh was grass, on the top—which invited her to mourn the death of Augustine Manifold on the morrow.

'The coroner's released the body, of course,' she commented. 'Jane? Would you like to come and help me rob a funeral parlour?'

'Yes, please,' said Jane with ice-cold aplomb.

'Right, then we need some anatomy lessons,' said Phryne. 'No, sorry, Jane, I should have said, some extra anatomy lessons. I know you have that Christmas copy of *Gray's Anatomy* by heart by now. Wait until I get Dr. MacMillan on the phone, and you shall be instructed. Meanwhile, I will go and have a cold shower and change this dress.'

'Into burglary clothes?' asked Ruth, who felt the heat and was refreshing herself with cold lemonade.

'Something like that,' replied Phryne.

Dot had already taken herself off to her own room to lie down in the cool dark. It had not been scorching long enough to really heat up Phryne's stone-built house, though once it got hot Dot suspected that it would stay hot. Miss Phryne wouldn't need her to rob a funeral parlour—the things she said—and she had a headache. She took two aspirin with her lemonade. It had been that hot and bright outside!

She allowed her eyes to close, remembering Sister Scholastica and the scent of roses. 'St. Elizabeth of Hungary,' Dot murmured, and fell asleep.

A refreshed Phryne came down to the parlour to find that everyone had gone. Ruth had taken her lemonade into the kitchen, to watch Mrs. Butler making sorbets. Jane was on the phone to Dr. MacMillan. Phryne could hear her precise Scots voice saying, 'You must push the needle directly through the chest...' and didn't listen to any more. She examined the card. The mortal remains of Augustine Manifold were to be viewed at the establishment of Mr. Leonard Palisi, coffin maker and undertaker, of Smith Street. She had a feeling that she might have seen him before at some Church jollification. Tall, thin, always dressed in a black suit, Parade Gloss on his shoes, always wore a hat, even inside, except in the church. Beautifully bald, not a hair to his name. Yes, that was him. Kept birds, Phryne thought, I believe it was birds.

Mr. Palisi? Ah, yes, the amiable and efficient undertaker who had not blenched at being asked to arrange a funeral for the mummified remains of one Thomas Beaconsfield, scion of the aristocracy. It had been a small but tasteful service. The only mourners had been Phryne's own family, a dwarf and two nuns, Sister Mary Magdalen and Sister Elizabeth from the Convent of the Good Shepherd. Phryne smiled at the memory. The Fishers were a dissolute family, but they always kept their promises.

She sipped her lemonade, called Mr. Butler to augment it with a suitable amount of gin, and waited for her minion to be ready.

Jane came back, flushed with excitement.

'I know how to do it,' she informed Phryne. 'I just need to stop at a pharmacy to buy a syringe with a long needle. People use them for killing woodworm, the doctor says, so there shouldn't be any trouble getting it. And the doctor says she'll test for seawater in the hospital laboratory. Isn't this exciting?' she asked.

'Indeed,' said Phryne, sipping.

'Miss Phryne, why don't we just ask Mrs. Manifold if we may?'

Phryne sipped again while wondering if she was going to shock her adopted daughter. Still, even shocks can be salutary.

'Because Mrs. Manifold might have killed him. I know, it's unlikely. But we can't rule anyone out, Jane. And if he wasn't drowned in the sea, then where was he drowned? Come along,' said Phryne, getting up and leading the way to the door. 'And put on your hat,' she added.

'Yes, Miss Phryne,' said Jane obediently. She crammed the straw on her head and fell in at Miss Fisher's elegant heel. Jane wouldn't have missed the chance to practise her anatomy for quids. Life with Miss Phryne was all that Jane could have desired.

The syringe was obtained without difficulty, though Phryne had to fight off a pressing offer of the proprietor's patent woodworm-exterminating liquid. Under Phryne's expert control, the big red car cut through traffic. Jane closed her eyes and thought about Gray's display of the dissected chest and lung cavity. It was better than estimating how close the car was to that hysterical fruit truck, whose peaches were even, at this moment, beginning to spoil.

The funeral parlour was a small elegant building with black glass windows in the bottom storey. The door was mahogany and beautifully carved with angels by someone who had seen a Tiepolo. Phryne pushed it open and the dust and noise was instantly shut off. Just like the gardens, she thought, though this is the peace of death, not life. The cool air smelt, oddly, of flowers, polished floor tiles, cold stone and fresh sawdust. Jane vibrated at her side.

'Mr. Palisi?' Phryne asked as the tall man in the black suit advanced almost noiselessly. 'I believe you might remember me?'

'No one could forget you, Miss Fisher,' he replied. His voice was even and modulated, but his eyes were warm with admiration. He might be a well-preserved fifty, Phryne thought, or a prematurely aged thirty; it was hard to tell beneath his undertaker's manner. 'Have you come to see one of my people?'

'Augustine Manifold,' said Phryne.

'I am so sorry.' Mr. Palisi took Phryne's hand in his own cool fingers. 'Mr. Manifold was returned from the coroner's office in…in some disarray. We do the best we can, of course, but he… is not in a suitable condition for viewing.'

'They butchered him?' asked Phryne coarsely. Mr. Palisi winced.

'In a word, Miss Fisher, yes. Samples of course were taken for various reasons, and we have done our best with stitching and wax, and naturally the embalming smoothes out the skin, but…sorry, young lady?'

Jane had uttered a modified yelp of disappointment.

'He's been embalmed?' she asked.

'Well, yes,' said Mr. Palisi, taken aback. 'Rather necessary in this heat.'

'Of course,' said Phryne, suppressing Jane with one hand on her shoulder. There was no hope for it now but the truth. 'We were rather hoping to get a sample from the body, you see. I am attempting to find out what happened to him, and the medical examiner didn't test for certain things.'

'And he didn't know his left hand from his right,' said Mr. Palisi. 'I like to do my best for the deceased, you know. For the relatives, really. There is no one else here at present so I might allow myself to express the opinion that it doesn't matter to the dead how we treat them but it matters a great deal to those who loved them. Perhaps I might suggest that some of the samples might still be retained by the coroner? I can make a call,' he suggested delicately. 'Perhaps you might like to sit in my private rooms. Just up the stairs, Miss Fisher.'

Phryne accepted. It was very cool in the funeral parlour and if the body of Augustine Manifold wouldn't tell her where he had been, perhaps the coroner might. She propelled Jane up the stairs in front of her.

The parlour was a surprise. Clearly Mr. Palisi owned the whole building and lived, so to speak, above his work. It was a conventional room, sparkling clean, with several comfortable chairs, fresh roses on the table, and a whole window filled with an aviary. Jane flew to the library of interesting anatomical treatises. Phryne looked at the birds.

They were a mixed flock of canaries and budgerigars, a bird for which she had an affection. They were so unlikely, like a lot of Australian birds. Phryne did not approve of caged birds, but these ones seemed happy, and were not at risk of having their song abruptly terminated by a prowling cat. There were fresh branches of gum leaves in the cage and the scent lent a medicinal quality to the air.

Two canaries were perched by the window, each trying to outdo the other. Their songs were tuneful and charming and very, very loud.

'You wouldn't think that two ounces of feathers and beak could make such a noise,' she commented to Jane, who was enthralled by some back issues of a trade publication called the *Undertaker's Gazette*.

Phryne left her to it. Mr. Palisi appeared at the door. He seemed to have the same ability to move without being seen to move attributed to some saints, the devil, and Mr. Butler.

'Beautiful birds,' said Phryne.

'They're my little singers,' he said, his face transformed. He opened the cage and one budgie flew out and landed on his shoulder. It examined Phryne with some care and then turned its back on her. Whatever the test was, Phryne had failed it.

'Now, Geoffrey, be civil,' said Mr. Palisi. 'I have ascertained that some samples have been kept by the coroner's office, but I cannot imagine how you can get to them, Miss Fisher.' He stopped, removed the budgie to his finger, and cleared his throat. 'I am about to have an afternoon pick-me-up. Could I…perhaps…could I ask you ladies to join me? I seldom have any company.'

Phryne was about to refuse when she decided that she really couldn't. This was a very pleasant, very lonely man. Even his budgie didn't seem to like him much.

'Thank you, Mr. Palisi, that would be lovely. Your house is beautifully cool in this weather,' she said, sitting down in one of the armchairs.

Mr. Palisi blushed with pleasure all over his head. He opened a cabinet and revealed a collection of bottles.

'I usually have a gin and tonic at this time,' he said.

'Excellent choice,' said Phryne. Jane opted for barley water, never taking her eyes off the gazette.

'Your young colleague seems fascinated by my trade,' he commented.

'She will be a very good doctor,' responded Phryne, 'when she learns some more about people. Tell me, Mr. Palisi, isn't yours a very sad profession?'

'Not at all,' he demurred, sitting forward on the chair. 'Someone must care for the dead, make them presentable so their relatives won't be stricken.'

'It is one of the corporeal works of mercy,' said Phryne.

'Yes, you visit the prisoners and captives, and other people feed and clothe the poor, and I prepare the dead for their longest sleep. My father was a carpenter and coffin maker, and I inherited the business. I fear that no one will follow in my footsteps, however, as there is no Mrs. Palisi.'

'Never despair,' said Phryne bracingly. She liked Mr. Palisi and if he splurged on shaving he didn't break the bank on shampoo. 'There is always hope. You do meet a lot of eligible widows, don't you?'

Mr. Palisi did something which undertakers rarely do. He laughed. Geoffrey the budgie squawked and fluttered on his finger. He raised the bird to his face and made a kissing noise, which the budgie reciprocated. Perhaps Geoffrey was better company than Phryne had thought. Perhaps Geoffrey didn't like visiting ladies who might have designs on his master. And

Geoffrey ought to improve his manners or he might become cushion stuffing, given the wrong kind of lady.

'Well, agreeable as this has been, we must away. Jane, put down the magazine and say goodbye to Mr. Palisi.'

'Goodbye,' said Jane. 'You have a fascinating profession. Might I perhaps come in some day and watch you at work?'

'You are an amazing young lady,' he replied, comprehensively taken aback but recognising real enthusiasm when he saw it. 'Perhaps when you are a little older, and if Miss Fisher gives her permission.'

'And perhaps we would like to invite Mr. Palisi to dinner, Jane?' asked Phryne.

'Oh, yes, please.' Jane was delighted.

'I will send you a card, Mr. Palisi.'

Mr. Palisi blushed again. It was as though the sun was setting over his hairless pate.

'I am overwhelmed, Miss Fisher. Thank you, I shall certainly come. Now, as you say, you must go. I'll see you downstairs. Say goodbye, Geoffrey.'

Phryne left, a little stunned. She had never been sneered at by a budgerigar before.

'To the morgue, Miss Phryne?' asked Jane, skipping as though she had just been offered a trip to the zoo.

'Yes, that's in Batman Avenue and it's getting late, so hold onto that hat.'

Jane held onto her hat, shut her eyes, and tried not to hear what the other drivers were saying about Miss Phryne's skill, morals, antecedents and the marital status of her parents. Not to mention the screeching of brakes and an outraged shout from a traffic policeman who had nearly lost several toes which he valued.

'That was a red light, Miss Phryne,' she ventured.

'Yes, it was,' returned Phryne, unmoved.

Jane tried to think about anatomy. Anatomy was dead. And safe.

Like the funeral parlour, the morgue was cool, but it smelt of decomposing flesh and phenol, neither being attractive scents.

Fortunately, the office was just closing as Phryne arrived. A conspiratorial boy grabbed Phryne's sleeve as she mounted the worn stone steps. He was clad in a white overall with splashes of unnameable fluids on the front. He was red-faced and his mother should have done something about his wiry, curly hair, though shaving his head might have been the only answer.

'I'm Mike. Mr. Pally says you want the Manifold samples,' he whispered. 'I can show you where they are but someone'll have to distract the doorman.'

'I'll distract,' Phryne told Jane, still moving. 'You get the sample. There'll be a reward in this for you,' she told the boy. He spat on the step.

'Don't care if they sack me. No life for a man, this. Cutting up dead bodies. I'm just waiting till I'm old enough to get into the engine drivers' union.'

'Go on,' said Phryne. Jane accompanied Mike through a lower entrance and Phryne found herself talking to one of those cross-grained old soldiers who made entry into Melbourne's public buildings so colourful and demotic an experience.

''Scuse me, Miss,' he said, touching a finger to his cap. 'Offices closing in a minute. Have to wait till tomorrow.'

'Oh, what a pity,' said Phryne, patting her bosom with one delicate hand. 'My editor said I had to get the opinion of the people in the business about the state of the morgue. You'll have to do,' she added, and brought out a notebook and pencil. 'What's your name, sir?'

'What d'ya want ter know me name for?' he growled.

'So I can attribute your quote. How long have you been working here, Mr...?' She paused invitingly.

'Burwood,' he snarled. 'Kev Burwood. You want to know what it's like working here? It's crook. Out on the steps in all weathers, rain or shine. I asked 'em for an umbrella or even a chair and they turned me down flat. Suffer chronic with me chest in the cold.'

'And with the heat?' asked Phryne, having successfully tapped into a rich vein of complaint.

'Yair. I sweat buckets in this serge uniform in the summer, and can I get a lightweight one? Not in the budget, they say. And then there's the smell. You smell it?'

'I can smell it,' agreed Phryne, making fraudulent pot hooks in her notebook.

'Turn a man's stomach. Mind you, the Lord High Mucky-mucks don't smell it, not them, they've got those gauze masks. Whole place is swilled down every night with phenol as if it was a piggery. Can't smell a thing but phenol for hours and it makes me tea taste crook. Missus says it don't matter what she cooks 'cos I can't taste it anyway. I told 'em, what about carbolic, it's a nice clean smell, they even put it in them soaps that ladies use, but they says, too expensive and phenol does the job. You gettin' all this down?' he demanded.

'Every word,' lied Phryne.

'Then there's the people. There's a mob up and down these steps all the day long—cops, doctors, relatives, and most of them ain't good company. Blubberin' widows, sons whose old man has just kicked the bucket, girls whose young feller has just thrown a seven. All that stone motherless misery gets me goat.'

'Why do you stay?' asked Phryne, who had seen Jane returning with the curly-headed boy, Mike. She slipped Jane a coin to hand on and saw it trousered by the future driver of the Indian Pacific.

'You mad?' asked Mr. Burwood belligerently. 'It's a job, lady. Long as I stay on these steps I've got a job. And they ain't too easy to come by, these days.'

'That's true. Well, thank you, Mr. Burwood, it's been nice talking to you.' She really was going to go to hell for fibbing, she thought.

'Lady!' the gnarled hand came out to grab at her arm. 'I need this job. Don't put me name in the paper, eh?'

Phryne, feeling a little ashamed of herself, agreed that it was highly unlikely that it would appear in any newspaper, and, gathering Jane, went back to the car.

'You've got it?'

'I've got it,' said Jane, alight with purpose.

'Then off with us to Dr. MacMillan at the Queen Victoria Hospital. Want me to wait?'

'Oh, no, Miss Phryne,' said Jane, shutting her eyes again as the big car slid into traffic. 'I can catch the tram.'

'You're sure?' asked Phryne, avoiding immolation by police van by two inches.

'Absolutely sure,' promised Jane, conscious of a sixpence in her knicker leg. Petty theft in the name of medicine was one level of risk. Driving with Miss Phryne was another thing altogether.

Phryne arrived home feeling as though she had been simmered on a stove, probably with vegetables. The heat was making her sluggish. She had a slight headache after absorbing gin during the day. Also, the air felt impatient and portentous, as though a storm was brewing. From the hall table she took Mr. Adami's parcel. It was a well-wrapped box, starred all over with sealing wax into which someone had repeatedly impressed a signet ring.

This will never do, she said to herself. A mystery of my very own and I'm so tired and grimy and hot that I'm not excited by it. Well, this box has waited a long time to be opened. It can wait until I have had a little nap and am feeling more the thing.

The admirable Mr. Butler had noticed how his employer felt about the weather and had decided to compensate for the temperature. As Phryne opened her boudoir door after a brief wash in lukewarm water, a rush of cold air caressed her undraped form. For a moment she stood naked in the cold blast and smiled seraphically, though seraphs generally wore more clothes. How had this miracle come about?

Mr. Butler had placed a large lump of commercial ice in a washtub on a chair, and directed over it the breeze from the tall electric fan. Phryne sank down supine on her bed and let the cool air flow over her. The Roman emperors, she recalled, had caused slaves to run ice convoys from Mount Hymettus to cool their rooms in the same way. Utterly content and mildly imagining the matched Circassian twins she might have bought for her own delectation in the old days, she fell into a light doze.

She woke to a growl of thunder outside and went down under paw as Ember crossed her body on his way to her wardrobe. Ember had been found by Jane as a mere slip of a soaking wet kitten, lost in a tempest, and this had evidently caused the feline equivalent of shell shock. As far as Ember was concerned, the only place from which to watch a good thunderstorm was inside a closed mahogany wardrobe within a stone-built waterproof house, preferably with a few crushed silk blouses to repose upon. If they weren't crushed silk to begin with, he was happy to provide that service. Phryne heard the *ping* as the shirt parted company with its hanger and the click as the door closed behind the fleeing black tail. Ember was earthed for the duration.

Phryne rose and dressed and pulled back her curtains. She opened the window. A louder growl muttered across the horizon. The hot air outside was as heavy as wet velvet and full of expectation. There was a flutter of sheet lightning across the sea. Phryne turned off the lights and the electric fan.

With a high explosive thud and a crash the storm arrived. Water impacted the window as though thrown from a bucket. The skies lit, once, twice, with fierce actinic light. Trees thrashed under contrary winds. The vine raked the window as though desperate to get in out of the wind. The temperature dropped twenty degrees, flooding the house with the scent of hot asphalt doused in rainwater, one of the premium scents in the world. The flies that had been tormenting Phryne all day whisked away and vanished. Rain poured down in a constant stream.

Phryne laughed, wrestled the window closed, bade Ember to stay where he was, and went downstairs. Now that someone mentioned it, she was hungry, and that was the dinner gong sounding in the hall even now.

Mrs. Butler opened the kitchen door and ordered Mr. Butler to put out all the house plants so that they could get some refreshing rain. She herself added a tub to catch rainwater for washing her own hair. Then she modified her menu. The cold salad dinner was transformed into a thunderstorm change-of-temperature dinner by the simple expedient of heating up the cold potato and leek soup and the vegetable hash to go with the rewarmed corned beef. Phryne's family sat down to an ideal dinner for the change, with both cold and hot components, and sweet, sour, salty and bitter elements. Mrs. Butler had never heard of the theory of the four humours, but she knew what made a good table.

And when in the middle of the soup course the lights went out, Mr. Butler lit branches of candles and continued serenely on his butlerine way.

'Isn't it romantic?' breathed Ruth.

'It's a lovely light,' agreed Phryne. 'My great-grandmother was a beauty in her day, and she always refused to have the electric lights on when she came down to dinner. She said that women over a certain age should never allow themselves to be seen in electric light. Far too harsh, like the Australian sun.'

'Bit difficult to manage now,' commented Jane.

'And an awful lot of work,' said Dot. 'Someone has to clean and polish all the candlesticks and pare, snuff and replace all the candles.'

'Yes, I imagine there was a candle boy,' said Phryne airily. The soup was superb, the corned beef in its blanket of mustard sauce was just the ticket, and she was feeling refreshed. 'Before my time, of course. No, thank you, Mr. Butler, just some more lemonade. Well, we have advanced in our case, with the help of Jane doing the Sexton Blake and me doing the distracting. Did Dr. MacMillan allow you to watch the tests, Jane?'

'Oh, yes, in the hospital laboratory, it was so interesting! She let me do the testing. She's wonderful,' said Jane dreamily.

'And after dinner you shall tell us all about it. Dot, dear, are you well?'

'Just a bit off-colour, Miss. I got a headache and then I fell asleep. I'll drink some coffee and I'll be fine.'

'Good. I have Mr. Adami's package, which we shall open later.'

'Tell us about your great-grandmother,' said Ruth. 'Was she very beautiful?'

'Oh, indeed, Arcadia was a tall, strong, robust woman, big bosomed like the last century preferred, with china blue eyes and golden hair which almost reached her knees. She was an American, a rich heiress, but they say that after a few years she was an English aristocrat to a T. She fell in love with my scapegrace ancestor when he was rusticated to Chicago for some mad gamble on a cross-country horse race. She just bundled up her hair and kilted her skirt and followed him, despite what her papa said about penniless noblemen. And eventually her papa forgave her and handed over the dowry.'

'And did they live happily ever after?'

'Tolerably so,' said Phryne, not wanting to bruise Ruth's romantic heart. 'They had eight children, and she transformed the big house: heating, lighting, plumbing. When she was old she used to have her chair pushed to the top of Dewberry Hill to watch all the lights put on at once, so that she could see the house lit up like a birthday cake. I've got some of her jewellery: the diamond tiara, parure, clips, earrings and bracelets. And the big ruby.'

'Eton mess!' exclaimed Dot as dessert and coffee were brought in. 'Wonderful.'

Phryne stuck a pleased spoon into the mixture of raspberries, cream and broken meringues. Despite the feral weather, she felt that she was very lucky to be living at 221B the Esplanade, St. Kilda, Victoria, Australia.

Jane stood herself on the hearth rug in the standard gentleman's position, back to an imaginary fire, and began to expound.

'With Mike's help I managed to get two ounces of…the fluid.' She was about to mention the absorption ratio of water into lungs in drowning and decided that her audience was far too squeamish. 'Dr. MacMillan said that there are two tests for saltiness. One is the silver nitrate test and one is the electrolysis test. We did the electrolysis test first because it doesn't diminish the specimen. It's easy. You just put the fluid in a chamber and pass a current through it and measure the amount of electricity which passes through it on an ammeter. Salty water conducts electricity while fresh water doesn't. We had a standard sea-water sample and ran a current through it with a set voltage. The ammeter showed point four of an amp. The same current passed through the sample would not necessarily mean it might be seawater, but it would be salty. In this case, we only got two thousandths of an amp.'

The flickering light was making even Jane's round childish face hollowed and strange. No doubt, thought Phryne, the sibyls of the oracle of Apollo at Delphi had looked so, in their laurel-scented cavern over the abyss. And this was a modern sibyl, proclaiming the manner of a man's death.

'Then we took a small part of the sample and added silver nitrate, which, if there is salt, will precipitate a thick white paste like office glue. It didn't. So from the tests, we knew that it didn't conduct electricity and it didn't precipitate silver,' ended Jane, triumphantly.

She noticed that she had failed to carry her audience. Phryne, Ruth and Dot were looking at her in mute incomprehension.

'So, what does that mean?' asked Phryne, after a pause.

'Oh,' said Jane, making a mental note not to underestimate the scientific ignorance of the layperson. 'He was drowned in fresh water, not salt. Dr. MacMillan did a few more tests, which I would be happy to tell you about—'

'Perhaps later,' said Phryne. 'What conclusion did you two alchemists come to?'

'Oh, it was clear,' said Jane. 'Beyond doubt. He was drowned in fresh water with soap in it.'

The thunderstorm, feeling itself about to die, gave one last shattering crash which seemed to shake the house. The candles flickered.

Dot crossed herself. 'He was drowned in the bath,' she said.

'God have mercy on his soul.'

◇◇◇

The priest at St. Mary's was about to knock off for a cup of tea with maybe a whisker of the cratur, for it had been a long night confessing the lost and strayed, when he heard someone come into the confessional and pulled the stole back over his shoulders.

'Bless me, Father, for I have sinned,' came the whisper through the grating.

An elderly man, he diagnosed. Ragged-voiced with strain. Educated accent. Well, the middle class were as sinful as anyone else, God forgive them.

'God bless you, my son. How long has it been since your last confession?'

'Ten years, Father. I have just found out...found out something...'

'Yes?' asked the priest testily, longing for his tea and whisky, as he heard nothing for some time. He got up slowly and pulled the curtain aside.

The confessional was empty.

Chapter Seven

Good night, good night! Parting is such sweet sorrow,
That I shall say good night till it be morrow.

William Shakespeare
Romeo and Juliet

'Miss Phryne?' Jane was looking concerned, her pale face white in the candle light.

'Yes, Jane?'

'Why does Dot think it's better that Mr. Augustine was murdered rather than it being a suicide?'

'Ah, there you have me,' Phryne temporised. What to say about this touchiest of all touchy topics? 'Dot's religion tells her that killing yourself is a mortal sin.'

That was not going to be enough, Phryne could tell.

'What do you think?'

'Well, if you would have my plain answer, however brutal, Jane dear, I think that someone who has decided to die should be allowed to make their own choice. I stopped a suicide once, in Paris. Etienne. His father was making him leave his life in Montparnasse. He was going to have to work in a bank, marry a suitable lady, and be a *bon bourgeois*. He said he would rather die, and he took a lot of chloral, and I found him and called an ambulance and they pumped his stomach. The next day he went home to his father and married as required. I met him a few years later, walking his children in the park, and he gave me a look of such hatred that I can still feel the sting of it. So my advice is, try not to get involved.'

'And if you can't help getting involved?' asked Jane keenly.

'Then just do the best you can,' said Phryne.

Jane thought about this. She nodded. She collected Ruth, and they went to play an engrossing game of snap. Mr. and Mrs. Butler cleared and cleaned and retired for the evening. Phryne and Dot took a branch of candles into the small parlour and sat down at Phryne's little table. Outside the storm had gone, and a cool wet wind swept in through all the windows, which Phryne had personally opened and would, in due course, personally close and lock. Dot had put on a cardigan and Phryne was enjoying the cool.

'Whoever sealed this wanted it to stay sealed,' said Phryne, slicing through another wad of wax with her sharp letter knife. 'If the lady has left her daughter a letter which mentions the child and his or her fate this will make our job a lot easier, Dot.'

'Things are never that easy,' said Dot practically.

'True. But I feel fine! The rain is over and done and I am expecting the voice of the turtle to make itself heard any moment now.'

'I think I've got this corner undone,' said Dot.

She slipped the stout paper aside and turned the box around in her hands.

'Pretty thing,' she said admiringly.

'It is a very pretty thing,' agreed Phryne. 'A jewellery box, I suspect. Rosewood, eighteenth century, inlaid with maple, oak and mother of pearl. Chinoiserie at its best. The Prince Regent would have swooned over it. Let's get it open.'

'Don't wrench it, Miss Phryne, here's the key.' Dot applied a delicate little golden key to the golden lock. 'There. What's this?'

'Draw it out carefully, it's been there a long time,' instructed Phryne.

Dot pulled out and unfolded over her hands a bundle of some soft thread. She slung it deftly over a chair and it fell in a spiderweb tracery, the colour of milk or ivory, unstained by its long confinement.

'A cashmere shawl,' said Dot soberly. 'For the baby, perhaps. Lovely work! You can't hardly see the lace-maker's knots. It must have taken ages to make.'

'Nine months, possibly? What else is in this box? We have letters.' She laid out the artifacts as they came to hand. 'One bundle, tied with pink ribbon. We have a little painting. We have some jewellery. We have some coins. And some cuttings, they look like newspaper. A little bound book. Drat this candlelight! I've got used to electric light, Dot.'

'Might have to wait till morning,' said Dot. 'This writing is a real scribble and it's crossed. No, we're going to need sunlight to read it. What about the jewellery, Miss?'

Phryne sorted rapidly through the glittering pile, holding each piece up to the candle. Little reflections of coloured lights blinked on and off in the lacquer of the Chinese box.

'It looks good, but not excellent. A garnet set, they used to be very popular, especially for young women and those who could not afford rubies. Like the box, the setting is eighteenth century, as is this bracelet, and these rings, one of which is a gentleman's signet.' Phryne peered at the bezel, squinting in the candlelight, then shook her head. 'Might be an armorial bearing. Eliza would know. Some kind of beast, I think. And this necklace made of sunstone daisies would be a lovely present for a little girl. Quite nice things, might have been an eldest daughter's share of the family boodle. But this is entirely trumpery.'

She gave Dot a pot metal ring in the form of two hands holding a crowned heart between them.

'I've seen something like that before,' said Dot. 'But I can't remember where.'

'It's not the sacred heart, is it?' asked Phryne, who relied on Dot's knowledge of all things religious.

'No, and that's what's missing, Miss Phryne. There's no crucifix, no rosary, nothing religious, like she might have left to a daughter who's a nun. She might have left her the jewellery because they have to go to the eldest daughter, like you said, and I can see her sitting there making that shawl for her baby, poor girl. And maybe the letters will tell us more. But where is her rosary, Miss Phryne?'

'Nothing else in the box,' said Phryne, taking it up carefully, inverting it, and shaking it over the table. 'Nothing but a little dust. Drat. I was hoping to get some clue to be going on with tonight.'

As though her petition had been heard by some electrical goddess, the lights winked on. Dot laughed and began to blow out candles.

'Leave us one,' said Phryne. 'I don't entirely trust the weather. Or the supply. Come now, Dot dear, you can have first go with the magnifying glass. Let's have a look before the lights go out again.'

They worked silently for half an hour. Then Dot put down the letters and rubbed her eyes.

'Love letters?' asked Phryne, hoping that Dot's delicacy was not going to be outraged by long ago evidences of Irish passion.

'No, they're from her friend, a female friend. She lived in St. Kilda, I think, from what she says about going down Acland Street for cakes. Or perhaps she was on holiday here. People used to come to St. Kilda as a watering place, you know. So far it's just gossip, schoolgirl's gossip.'

'Well, if you don't mind, can you spend tomorrow morning making a fair copy for those without your pinpoint vision?'

'Yes, Miss, of course. What's in the little book?'

'It's in code,' said Phryne. 'Alphabet substitution, I think. I'll break it. In all probability,' she added, in case the goblins of obscurity could hear her. 'The cuttings are from the *St. Kilda Times*, and either she wanted a knitting pattern or a review of *Romeo and Juliet* as put on by the St. Kilda Players, an amateur group who look absolutely dire. What was her girlfriend's name?'

'Margaret,' said Dot, pouring herself a glass of lemonade.

'Might be the Miss Margaret O'Rourke who played the nurse in this production. The little painting is good. A watercolour of a young man in costume. No title or signature that I can see. Still, Dot, I suspect that this is the father of the child.'

Dot turned the little unframed sketch to the light. It had faded and foxed over the years but it was still a fine-spirited piece. The young man was wearing tights and a doublet. In his hand was a skull. His face was alive: wide mouth, bright blue eyes, prominent nose and jaw. Not beautiful, but very attractive. And very young.

'An actor. Looks like a wild boy,' she commented.

Phryne, something of an expert on wildness in both genders, agreed. 'A wild boy, indeed.'

Dot yawned and took herself off to bed. Phryne hastily scribbled the alphabet on two strips of paper and began to attempt the breaking of the cipher. She surveyed the page, which seemed to have a lot of *b*s in it, assumed *b* would be *e* and slipped the alternative alphabet along. This yielded, at the first try, from QEFP YLLH YBILKDP to THIS BOOK BELONGS and constituted the fastest time in which Phryne had ever broken a code. Admittedly, it was a code only used by children under the age of sixteen, but she was proud of herself anyway.

The girls came to say goodnight and went off to their own room. Molly assumed her usual place on Phryne's feet. She gently altered this by slipping off her shoes and putting her feet on Molly. The dog was warm, like a breathing, affectionate hot-water bottle. Phryne read on, writing out the decoded pages as she went in the sea-green notebook which she assigned to each new case. From notebook to notebook her pen went flying. She fell into the cipherine's trance whereby she was merely the bridge between the code and the clear, not truly aware of what she was writing, only of the words unfolding under her fingers. By the time the storm returned and the lights went out again, she had finished the diary and was unstiffening her maltreated wrist.

'Phew,' said Phryne, and loaded all the goods, except for the shawl, back into the rosewood coffer. She took the box to the foot of the stairs and left it there as she lit a few more candles and carried them with her as she carefully closed and locked every window. Then she bore Kathleen O'Brien's legacy up to her own boudoir. If there were any more burglars, thought Phryne, they would have to fight her for the treasure. Tomorrow she would attend Augustine Manifold's funeral. Tonight she would read the diary of that sixteen-year-old who had left her children such a puzzle to solve.

Phryne washed briefly, donned a nightgown and took the Fisher silver candelabra which she had salvaged from her family's trove when she left old England forever. She sat down by the window. With a little help from lightning, she ought to be able to read her own writing, starkly black against the bone-white page. ABXO AFXOV it began. Dear Diary. Phryne settled down, took a soothing mouthful of gin and lemonade, and started reading with attention.

Dear Diary. It is the 25th of May in the year of our Lord 1863. Today is my fifteenth birthday and I was given this diary by Miss Beale and told that I ought to write an account of my thoughts every day, and also copy down any poetry or observations I make. She said this would allow me to examine the state of my soul and my affections. So I am doing as she said because Miss Beale is a very wise lady. My name is Kathleen Julia O'Brien and I live in Saint Kilda in the house of my father Daniel. My father is a lawyer who argues in court. Soon he is to be a member of the Governor's Council. He is a very important man. I live with my mother Brigid and my sister also called Brigid and my brothers James and John who are all older than me. My favourite occupations are reading and playing music on my piano which my father bought for me. I am reading Shakespeare and Carlyle and working on a nightcap for my father. It is of Italian trapunto work and I am finding it quite difficult. Miss Beale says I will be a good housekeeper once I learn to add up properly. My household accounts always come out wrongly and besides I have rubbed them out so often they cannot be easily read. Otherwise I learn geography with the globes, mathematics, geometry and algebra, literature, cookery, tatting, lace-making, music, Proper Supervision of Servants and dancing. I love music more than anything. I am learning a Chopin polonaise for our school's afternoon tea for the parents and I love it so much. Even though it is so difficult that I could not get my stupid fingers to do as I asked and I felt like slamming the piano lid down on them. Miss Brougham, my teacher, found me in tears and told me that I was too ambitious in my choice of piece. But I will learn it.

Phryne stopped reading and gazed out the window. A strong-minded young woman, this Kathleen. Not daunted by advice to try something easier. Not a survival trait, necessarily. The little book was not so much a diary as a commonplace book. And Kathleen had an irritating habit of not dating her entries.

Sunday. After we came back from mass we settled down to Sunday occupations, which means no noisy games or running about. Papa found my brothers playing cards and thrashed both of them, so they are in disgrace for gambling on a Sunday. Or gambling at all, Papa is very set against gambling. We girls were lucky to avoid his wrath because we were trimming a hat, which would be frivolous and worldly, but when we heard him coming we put it aside and took up the altar cloth which we are mending. He grumbled a bit about sewing being work but agreed that mending an altar cloth was a suitable occupation for a Sunday. In fact he was pleased with us and sat down to read to us from O'Reilly's Consolations while we sewed so we had to mend the whole cloth and it was so scratchy and dusty! It just served us right for our improper intentions!

But I really cannot like Father O'Reilly's book. He is so dreary. And he does not console me at all. But when we finished the cloth Mama came in and told us to put on our jackets and we all went out for a walk in the garden. Except for the boys who were confined to the house. Papa is rather severe with them. I'm sure they never meant to be impious.

Phryne shook her head. Papa was severe, but thrashing bad boys was not uncommon. And it was pure defiance to play cards on a Sunday. Phryne's own grandmother had considered even jigsaw puzzles to be unacceptably frivolous. Oh, those long Sundays, with nothing to do but stare out the window or read sermons. Phryne was willing to bet that O'Reilly's *Consolations* were just as dire as *Christian Thoughts For Little Ones*, her own Sunday reading. She had beguiled the tedium by filling in all the *o*s and writing *I hate Sunday* in very small writing over all blank spaces. For which, come to think of it, she had been spanked.

'Dear Diary,' resumed Miss Kathleen, some days later, 'Today is washing day so we are all at liberty provided we do not give trouble. We are sitting in the garden. I have my favourite seat under the willow tree. It hangs down like a fairy curtain, so green and lacy. Margaret is visiting because it is washing day at her house too. We are working at embroidered slippers. We are making two pairs, one for her papa and one for mine, but it is easier if we do a slipper each so her papa's will be finished first. Gerald was meant to read to us but he went to play football with some other boys, so Margaret's brother Patrick is supplying his place. He is reading a Shakespeare play called *The Tempest*. We are supposed to use a special Shakespeare which omits the parts unsuitable for young ladies but we cannot find it so he is reading the whole play. It is very exciting and has spirits in it. Patrick wants to be an actor. He is a very good reader and dancer but his papa will never permit him to take up such an occupation which is not for gentlemen's sons. His father is a lawyer like mine and wants Patrick to be a lawyer too. He tells me that he will never be a lawyer, but an actor as soon as he is eighteen and can join the actors' theatre. Then he will marry me as we have always intended. We have been in love since we met at Margaret's sixth birthday party.

Phryne stretched. The candlelight was flickering. She trimmed her candle and moved the book a little closer. Patrick was the man for Kathleen, then. What had happened to these two tender lovers?

The journal then gave the reader a recipe for kangaroo tail soup, one for seed buns and one for potato scones. Phryne blinked at a recipe for Marlborough cakes which took eight eggs and required whisking for an hour to make it light. Miss Kathleen enclosed a sketch for a pair of detachable sleeves called engageantes and an embroidery pattern for a summer petticoat.

Mama says that now I am sixteen and out and have put up my hair I may have a crinoline, and today one was fitted. I am to practise four hours a day walking and sitting in it. It is strange at first because there is no weight of undergarments and skirt. The skirt of the gown seems almost to float. But it swings easily and I knocked a lot of china off the little table in the nursery with it before I began to become accustomed to the movement. I am sure that I will be much more comfortable in summer with this admirable contrivance. But I can't run anymore, and I cannot sit in the willow tree in a crinoline. I suppose I am becoming a young lady. I am working very hard at my music and watercolours and reading that beastly Carlyle on the French Revolution which was awful, the poor Queen and King and the poor little Dauphin. I am now responsible for the flower arranging for the parlour and the public rooms and Mama is teaching me to make potpourri today. The last of the roses are blooming even now. There is a very good song about the last rose which Margaret sings very pathetically and makes us all cry.

Which was all very well, thought Phryne, who agreed with Kathleen about Carlyle. And she remembered leaving childhood behind, but she never remembered missing it at all. Phryne's childhood had been endured but rarely enjoyed. And in the clothes she was presently wearing—which Miss Kathleen would not have thought decent as undergarments—she could climb as many trees as she pleased. Things have got better, thought Phryne.

'Now we are plunged into a great jam-making,' said Miss Kathleen.

> All the trees seem to come ripe at once and everyone helps Mrs. Clitheroe and the maids. There is just a cold dinner on jam-making days. I had a terrible time making my apricot jam jell. It just wouldn't wrinkle on the little plate until Patrick and Margaret came to help and Patrick put lemon juice in it. He said his mother always did so. My darling Patrick! I can hardy wait until he is eighteen— and it is tomorrow!

Phryne rubbed her eyes. There was something attractive about the fresh enthusiasm of Miss Kathleen. When was doom going to land on the poor girl?

There followed comment on Motherhood and Noble Women and several hints on the care of the skin (wash with milk, rub in until dry), removal of freckles (lemon juice and glycerine) and care of the hair (wash once a month, massage with coconut oil if dry). Then the ciphering became unreliable and Phryne had to guess at the meanings.

> Patrick went to speak to my father and Papa laughed at him! Then he came up the stairs to me and said very gruffly 'Do you mean this nonsense?' and I told him indeed, indeed I meant it and it was not nonsense, and he grew very angry. He forbade me to leave the house and

has told Miss Beale that I will not be returning to school. I am to stay with my sister and my mama and not go out alone. And he says he will take away my books and my music and that I am no longer to come down to dinner at seven, when the grown-ups dine, but stay in the nursery with the children. This is hard. I begged him to have mercy but he laughed. Today I shall tell him again that I and my Patrick are in dead earnest.

Phryne shook her head. This struck her as unwise. So it had, in fact, proved.

I spoke to Papa again and he struck me a great blow across the face and said that I would never marry if he had any choice in the matter. I fell over and was too horrified and grieved to get up. He just stared at me and then he went out of the room, and Mama came crying and took me back to the second floor and washed my bruise in arnica. All she said was 'Poor child! Poor child!' and would not say why Papa was so angry. Mama bade me stay in bed today and I have been weeping. But I will stop soon. I will eat the chicken fricassee and the junket which Cook has prepared for me. Then I will see Patrick again, if I have to climb down the ivy...

I did it! I climbed down and into the back garden and out the back gate and there he was, waiting, like the note which Minnie smuggled upstairs said he would be. We fell into each other's arms and I wept and he wept too. He said my father and his were on opposite sides of some financial thing and each thought the other had cheated him and we were all forbidden to have anything to do with each other. He gave me a letter which Margaret had sent to me, saying goodbye. But any number of Papas cannot come between me and my only love. Patrick is to make the arrangements and I will contrive to see him again in three weeks' time. Then no Papa can keep us apart.

It sounded like Miss Kathleen was going to fling her bonnet over the windmill, all right. A risky move. Especially in 1864, when Papas were Papas and domestic tyranny was a virtue. Phryne felt the need for a drink, went downstairs and got a consoling gin, and was followed up to her room by Ember, who liked people to be awake when he was awake. He sat down, purring, in the window niche. Phryne stroked him absentmindedly as she read.

'It's done!' announced the diary.

I got leave of Papa to go to the doctor, and bribed Minnie with my pearl earrings. The whole thing was over in half an hour. Then we went to the doorkeeper's house at Patrick's place, which is empty, and we stayed there all day. Then I had to go home with Minnie, but I shall come again. And he is my golden man, my beautiful boy, my only love, my Patrick.

There were a few more recipes after this, for family dinners. Sea Pie, Boiled Potatoes, Vegetable Marrow with Gooseberry Fool for dessert. Or even simpler: French Onion Soup, Bread, and Apple Compote.

I am paying strict attention to everything Mama says about running a household as I shall have one of my own before long. If the soup is too salty, cook a raw potato in it and it will take up the salt, or add a spoonful of sugar. A greasy pot full of boiling water and soda is already washing itself. Remove the smell of onions from knives by thrusting them into earth. Use Jones' Patent Flour. Never buy green pickles, make our own in season. How long will I have to wait? Oh, Patrick, come and take me away!

Ember purred. Phryne stroked. Something awful was coming, she could tell. The sky gave an obliging growl and lightning flicked across the page.

Patrick has a position as an actor! This is wonderful, but he is going on tour, to Castlemaine, Bendigo, Ballarat and other places, with the troupe, and I must stay in my father's house though I am so loath to be here. Father looks on me very darkly when he sees me and never speaks. I am glad of this because I might faint if he did. I have been keeping to my room. I am not very well at present. Although I only ever used to see Patrick during the day, tonight I imagine him lying here beside me, his dear head on my breast, his sweet eyes devouring me. I think there is going to be a storm. LATER. Mama has the headache she always has before a tempest, and there are important people to dinner, so she has taken some laudanum and steel pills and laid herself down on my bed. She will have a cup of black coffee when she gets up after half an hour. She is asking me what I am writing and I have told her, my diary. Then she said a strange thing. If I could help you to your Patrick, my dear, she said, I would, but your papa has other plans for you. When I asked her what other plans she said suitable marriage and would not say to whom. But now she is gone and I am worried. I cannot marry anyone but my Patrick!

Oh, poor girl, said Phryne to herself, drinking the gin and stroking the nightblack fur. There was not really going to be a storm, of course, because the best lightning conductor in the world could not fool Ember. If it was going to thunder in earnest, he would not be lying on the window sill, purring.

Phryne forced herself to read the last page of the cipher. 'Patrick will come for me,' said Miss Kathleen.

Now that I am in disgrace and have nothing to lose I am sure that he will come whatever his papa says. I know that the troupe are coming to Ballarat where I now am. I cannot even remember the scandal and the scenes. I collapsed during them and was taken away and put to bed and had brain fever for three weeks. Even in this hostile place the Sisters do not dare to actually mistreat me or set me to unfamiliar work. The other girl here does the washing, a horrible, hot, exhausting task. But I am not asked to work. I am allowed to read the Bible and I have been reading it. May God's vengeance fall upon my father and Patrick's father. I have started a cashmere lace shawl for the baby. And I wait. Patrick will come for me.

And there the story ended. Poor girl! No Patrick ever came for her. She had returned without the infant, been imprisoned again by the stern Papa, then been sold to Mr. Bonnetti, who seemed to have been kind to her. By then her heart must have been so very broken that nothing much would bother her again.

Phryne drank the rest of her drink, blew out the candle, smoked a silent cigarette in the dark and put herself to bed with the black cat for company. She did not want to read. She had heard enough stories for one day, and didn't even want to dream.

'It's very plain, sir. I was beetling along over Turkish lines when the old Sop suddenly cut out on me and down we went, fearful smash, my leg was caught in the wreck of the fuselage and I daresay I was shouting a bit, the fire was already at my toes. Then these soldiers appeared out of the night. One of them told me, "Stop squealing, you bloody idiot, you'll bring the bloody Turks down on us and we'll be buggered!" I think they were Aussies, sir.'

'The language sounds familiar,' said the officer. 'What happened then?'

'I don't know,' confessed the pilot. 'There was a whooshing noise and when I woke up next I was secured in a stretcher on a camel and my bus—or the bits of it, at least—was secured on another camel and we were on our way to hospital. They think I shall keep my leg, sir. Can we get them a medal, sir?'

'Either a medal,' said the officer, 'or a reprimand for leaving their posts. With this command, you never know.'

Chapter Eight

My shroud of white, stuck all with yew, O prepare it!
My part of death no one so true Did share it.

William Shakespeare
Twelfth Night

Phryne rose in just the right mood for a funeral: sombre. Her mood was sombre, her charcoal suit, grey stockings and black shoes were sombre, even her flat grey felt hat was sombre. So was the day. Everything matched. Dot, who was staying home, struck an uncharacteristically bright note in her terracotta house dress and brown cardigan figured with autumn leaves. Phryne gathered up her bag and gloves and her light outer coat and proceeded to the door, where Mr. Butler was awaiting her. He was wearing his livery cap and coat. The Hispano-Suiza was already purring.

'To the church, if you please, Mr. Butler,' she said.

'Nice day for a funeral,' he replied, and let the great car glide into the street.

Phryne realised, as she walked into the church, that she was in for a full requiem mass. That being so, she settled down to enjoy it, sniffing appreciatively as a cloud of incense billowed around her. A little acolyte with a large heavy censer had found that if he swung the censer hard enough the reciprocating motion had the same effect on him and there was something of a blur of frilly robe and feet as he and the censer went orbiting around the church and around each other. The attendance was not large. Presumably all those people who had been flattered into buying Royal Doulton cups and saucers didn't feel any need to come see Augustine off to the Higher Regions. Gerald Atkinson was there, holding a handkerchief to his lips. He was accompanied by several young men and a couple of ladies. Cedric Yates was there in his demob suit. The girl Sophie was there, in drab black borrowed from the wardrobe of Mrs. Manifold, who was a pillar of stygian grief, draped in black down to her stockings and her veil. Eliza and Lady Alice attended her.

'Stabat Mater,' murmured Phryne.

The young woman next to her stifled a giggle.

'Yes, but she really is stricken,' she reproved. 'Poor woman.'

'I know,' said Phryne. 'Funerals bring out the worst in me. Phryne Fisher,' she said, extending a hand.

'Rachel Phillips,' replied the young woman. She obviously didn't own any mourning clothes, but had managed with grey and beige. She had black hair and dark eyes and a profusion of gold jewellery. Phryne thought her stylish and comfortable in what she had always thought of as a very Jewish way.

'Augustine used to buy a lot of stuff from my dad,' Rachel explained. 'Rosenbergs, in Little Collins Street. Stamps, coins and small treasures. Dad says he couldn't really bear to come to the funeral—in a Christian church, yet—but I can cope; I married out, and poor Augustine was a good customer.'

'I'm looking into his death,' murmured Phryne, watching the rapidly revolving acolyte collide with a burly priest, who caught the child in one hand and the censer in the other. That was a relief. Some of that really superb lace might have got singed. And the child, of course.

The congregation found seats and settled, opening the order of service and focusing on the small print.

The significant dates of Augustine's life were there, and a very stern verse from Ezekiel, again. With a few added jolly comments from the preacher on vanity. Phryne tried not to allow the gloom of the service to ruin her day. She said as much to her seat mate.

'You should go to a Jewish funeral,' observed Rachel. 'Well, you shouldn't, *kine hora*, of course, but that is even more realistic. They're dead, they're gone, and we owe them nothing but memory and truth. Plain pine coffin and no decorations.'

'A rational people, I have always said,' agreed Phryne. 'But possibly too realistic. I have no patience with people who insist on calling a spade a bloody shovel.'

'That is an opinion,' said Rachel carefully.

'Do you know all these mourners?' asked Phryne, changing the subject. One should not debate comparative religion with comparative strangers, she told herself. One of them might be an evangelist. Or an axe murderer.

'Yes, most of them. You already know Sophie and Mr. Yates from the shop? That man is a magician of a carpenter; he made some cabinets for us once and they were works of art. The old man with the gorgeous head of white hair is Professor Rowlands, from the university. A perfectly civilised being with a tendency to lecture on languages, which are his field. Ancient languages. The tall young exquisite is James Barton, famous family, and the pretty girl in the dreadful clothes is his sister, Priscilla. Next to her is her constant companion, Blanche White.'

Phryne giggled into her prayer book.

'Yes, I know, has to be an assumed name. I mean, look at her. From Cairo, she says. I'd think she was a closet Jew if it weren't for the fact that I don't like her and I don't want her in my family.'

Miss White was svelte, dressed entirely in black, and smooth as a cat. Her hair was slicked down and folded into a bun at the nape of her neck. Her eyes were artfully outlined with kohl and her shoes and hat were the last word in elegance. What was she doing with Priscilla Barton, who looked like she had dressed from the ragbag and was wearing a hat which would have been spurned by a not-very-picky dustman's horse?'

'I do see what you mean,' agreed Phryne.

'Then there are the followers. Luke Adler has brown hair, Valentine Turner is the blond, Stephanie Reynolds is the one in the red sari and Veronica Collins is the plump girl next to the gentleman in the black suit.'

'I know him,' said Phryne, not disclosing the presence of her favourite policeman, Detective Inspector Robinson. 'So these were Augustine's friends?'

'Yes,' said Rachel Phillips. 'I suppose so. They feted him rather, took him out to lunch and so on, but I never could work out if they liked him at all. Or if he liked them, indeed. He was not a man to wear his heart on his sleeve. I'd better hush, the ritual is starting.'

'*Requiem aeternam dona eis, Domine,*' said the priest in a no-nonsense tone, '*et lux perpetua luceat eis.*'

Rest eternal give to them, Lord, and let perpetual light shine upon them, translated Phryne to herself. She wondered how Rachel would feel about the next lines, assuming she understood Latin.

'*Te decet hymnus, Deus, in Sion, et tibi reddetur votum in Jerusalem.*'

You are praised, Lord, in Zion, and homage will be paid to you in Jerusalem. Phryne stopped translating and allowed the service to flow over her, sonorous, plaintive, strong. *Kyrie eleison*, murmured Phryne. *Christe eleison.* Lord have mercy on us. Christ have mercy on us. *Kyrie eleison. Dies Irae. Tuba mirum. Rex tremendae.*

She surfaced from her trance somewhere near the middle of the Recordare, when a titter could be heard from the pew in which Augustine's friends were sitting. Priscilla Barton was giggling, a high hysterical noise, which increased when Mrs. Manifold turned to glare at her. Irritated, her brother James jumped to his feet, dragged her roughly up by one arm and hauled her out of the church, his face red with shame. What had brought that on? Phryne wondered. What was in the Recordare? Remember kind Jesus, requests not to be forsaken, I moan as one who is guilty…Perhaps Miss Barton had been tickled by the request at the end, which had always struck Phryne as funny.

Inter oves locum praesta, et ab haedis me sequestra. Place me amongst the sheep and separate me from the goats. Well, yes, it was a comical image, but not enough to make you laugh in the middle of a requiem mass. Miss Barton seemed a little unstable. But her brother was clearly used to her hysterics, as well as annoyed and embarrassed by her. He had got her out of public view smartly, if not gently.

The door swung shut on the high-pitched noise as the priest, offended, put his shoulder into the denunciation of *confutatis maledictis*, when the accused are confounded, adding an extra growl to the *flammis acribus addictis*. Doomed to the flames of woe. Sounded bad. Phryne shifted a little and found that Rachel Phillips was also anxious.

'Never mind. The Lacrimosa, the weeping and mourning, is next, then we get into the more comfortable stuff and into the final straight,' she whispered. Rachel gave her a weak smile. Mrs. Manifold was weeping along with the prayer.

Phryne pulled herself together and watched what she could see of that pew which contained the bright young things. It was there, she felt almost sure, that the mystery of Augustine Manifold would be solved.

An organ, played rather well, accompanied communion. Half of the congregation knelt at the altar rail, including, Phryne noticed, Gerald Atkinson, which was a bit of a surprise.

Domine Jesu passed without incident, though Phryne caught Miss Collins mouthing a peppermint. Benedictus. Sanctus.

And in the middle of the Agnus Dei the whole group murmured. Something to do with sheep, definitely. Phryne hoped that someone would tell her the joke.

Finally the request to shed eternal light on the deceased was repeated and the mass was over. '*Ite, missa est*,' said the priest, and gathered his acolytes to lead the coffin out of the church and into Mr. Palisi's commodious, rubber-tyred motor hearse, which must have been a considerable investment. However, one could rely on people dying.

While it was not common for ladies to accompany the body to the cemetery, Mrs. Manifold was being helped into an undertaker's car, so Phryne invited Rachel Phillips to accompany her. Mrs. Phillips shook her curly head.

'But I'll see you at Augustine's house later,' she promised. 'I've had enough religion for one day, that's all.'

Phryne felt the same as she got into the big red car and leaned back against the leather upholstery. Mr. Butler diagnosed exhaustion and said over the noise of engines starting, 'Basket next to you, Miss Phryne. Mrs. B's compliments.'

Phryne opened the basket and found a flask of cognac, a thermos of strong coffee, a paper bag containing coconut macaroons and a big white napkin. In a wash bag reposed a clean handkerchief, a little crystal bottle of smelling salts, a small spray bottle of eau de cologne and a comb and mirror. Phryne combed her hair, sprayed herself with eau de cologne, poured and drank two cups of coffee and ate a macaroon during the journey across town. For Augustine was going to rest with his fathers in the Melbourne General Cemetery in Carlton. Funeral processions were interesting, she found, not having ridden in an Australian one before. Traffic allowed them to pass. People stopped in the street. Men took off respectful hats as the cortège passed, and Phryne fought down a strong impulse to wave regally. She screwed the cup back onto the thermos and stowed all the belongings away. She felt much better.

'Your wife,' said Phryne, as the big car turned into the gates, past the Gothic keeper's cottage, 'is a jewel among women.'

'I have always thought so, Miss Phryne,' Mr. Butler said complacently, aware that the said wife had also packed him a basket, containing a thermos of sweet milky tea and a packet of cold lamb sandwiches with homemade chutney. He knew a place where he could park in McIlwraith Street in order to enjoy his picnic in peace. Mr. Butler did not like the idea of all those dead people lying there and envying him his lunch. He bought an armload of blue daisies from the flower stall, gave them to his employer, and took the big car away.

It was a rather nice cemetery, Phryne thought, hoisting her bouquet and walking slowly in procession behind the coffin carriers. The monuments tended to the large and sad—broken columns, spilt urns, weeping women—without the element of macabre which affected places where people had been buried for longer. Phryne recalled Kirkwall in Orkney, where all graves, even those of children, were ornamented sternly with skulls and bones. She noticed the huge monument to Burke and Wills and the grave of King, the only survivor. She sang 'I know that my redeemer liveth', the phrase on the grave of a singer. She veered aside from the procession to lay some flowers on the grave of the miner Thomas Beaconsfield and, further along, the last resting place of that Queen of the Gilbert and Sullivan stage, Dorothea Curtis. Though properly she should have had violets, the diva's favourite flower. Pity that so many of her clients were dead, but that was the way of the detective trade.

And life had improved, she considered, as she read *Erected by William Witheridge in remembrance of his beloved wife Johanna who departed this life aged 31 years. Also to the memory of his five infant children requiescant in pace.* No longer did a woman have to lose five infant children before she gave up the ghost herself, probably with a sigh of relief. Phryne read the next stone. *Sacred to the memory of James…for he was a promising and engaging boy whom it has pleased Divine Providence to take from his fond and beloved parents after two days' illness. Sweet innocence fond lies here—lamented by a mother dear Who hopes by faith in endless joy To meet again her lovely boy.*

A red rose had climbed over little James' stone and almost obliterated his dates. It was blooming in hot, scented, vibrant life, and Phryne was suddenly moved almost to tears. She hurried on, embracing her flowers.

The weather was getting into its stride. The sombre morning was clearing, the mist lifting, the sun emerging and striking sharp and hot. Phryne was glad of her hat. She noticed that the group of Augustine's friends were clinging close together. Priscilla Barton had rejoined them and was walking along beside her brother James, clutching a vial of smelling salts in her hand.

Phryne wondered about the state of mind of a woman who would wear a red sari—decorated with golden sequins, indeed— to a funeral. It might be a defiant gesture. Looking at Miss Reynolds' pretty, vacuous face ornamented with the red caste mark, Phryne did not think she exhibited enough character to make such a gesture. The young men Adler and Turner were beginning to perspire in their suits, though Gerald Atkinson remained as cool as several cucumbers in a cold frame. Miss Blanche White stalked beside Miss Barton in a long-legged ballet dancer's glide which she was maintaining even over grass and cobbles. A notable feat. And Miss Veronica Collins brought up the rear, complaining about the heat and fanning herself with the funeral card.

Implacably mournful, flanked by two equally elderly ladies and followed by Eliza and Lady Alice, Mrs. Manifold, scorning assistance, stumped along behind the coffin of her only son. Somewhere Phryne had seen depictions of three old women like these. As she came in sight of a statue of Michael the Archangel with his flaming sword, she remembered where. In a book about Icelandic legends. The three sisters who controlled the fate of men, living in a cave with only one eye and one tooth between them. Edmund Dulac's depiction of the Norns.

Sobered, Phryne reached the end of the journey, especially for Augustine Manifold. The coffin was lowered, extra prayers said and Phryne cast some of her flowers into the grave. This custom did not seem to have travelled across the seas and she attracted some puzzled glances from the friends. Mr. Palisi, however, approved.

'A pretty notion,' he said to her as the priest and the mourners left and a couple of muscular men began to fill in the grave.

'I thought so,' she replied. 'A very good funeral, Mr. Palisi, conducted just so.'

'Thank you, Miss Fisher.' He accepted the praise as his due. Then he removed his tall hat, wiped his bald head with an irreproachable black-bordered handkerchief, bowed and took his leave.

Phryne headed for the McIlwraith Street exit, bestowing flowers as she went. No sense in wasting them.

In affectionate remembrance of Robert Bettargh who departed this life at 28 years of age. He was an affectionate husband and a kind father—the rest of the stone was weathered illegible. Just above the moss, Phryne could read *See all things else decay.*

She gave him some flowers.

Just as she was leaving the Catholic section, she noticed an unassuming stone on which the name was almost rained away. She knelt on one knee to read it and recoiled as if the stone had harboured a hidden tiger snake.

Patrick O'Rourke, the stone declared. *A fellow full of the most excellent jest. Born 15th June 1846 Co Limerick died 25th May 1914 Melbourne.*

If this was *the* Patrick O'Rourke—the birth date was right and the inscription could only be for an actor—he had lived a long time with his guilt at abandoning poor Kathleen. If he had any guilt, of course. He might have just been an ordinary young man, pollinating his way through the flowerbed of maidens like any drone with no regard for consequences. Twenty-fifth of May? It rang a bell. And might be significant, Phryne thought…Yes, she had recalled it. He had died on Kathleen's birthday.

Phryne sat back on her heels and contemplated the stone. Then she scraped away the moss at the root and read: *This stone erected by the Actors' Benevolent Society and a few sorrowing friends.* Was the Actors' Benevolent Society still extant? Would they know anything about this Patrick O'Rourke? In any case, since it seemed that he had abandoned the girl and the child, would that help at all? He had never married and had a family, it seemed plain, if the Benevolent Society had to bury him. Had he mourned for his lost love all his life, never finding another, as she had mourned for him and the baby?

Patrick will come for me, the girl had written in her small, clear handwriting, perfectly sure. Perfectly betrayed. Perfectly abandoned. Patrick had never come to rescue her.

Phryne did not give Patrick any flowers.

Just as she reached the gate, however, she turned back and threw the rest of the spicy stems in front of the worn stone.

'It might not have been your fault,' she told him. 'And you were very young.'

She found Mr. Butler waiting for her as she came out into tree-lined McIlwraith Street and blinked at the sudden green.

'Home?' he asked, replete with tea and sandwiches.

'Mrs. Manifold's house, if you please,' Phryne replied. 'I'll just finish up the coffee, but not the cognac. Though I've had a bit of a shock in connection with my other case, so maybe just a sip or two. From the look of that gaggle of Augustine's intimates, I'm going to need my wits about me.'

'You'll get to the heart of it, Miss Phryne,' he assured her. 'You always do.'

Phryne found this factitious but comforting.

'So far,' she said, pouring out the last of the coffee and adding a few fluid ounces of brandy. 'So far, Mr. Butler, I have been lucky.'

'Lucky's as good as right, my grandpa used to say,' he returned equably.

Phryne did not wish to debate this, and cast her mind back to the coroner's scanty inquest and the shamefully small amount of evidence requested from Augustine's friends as to his last night on earth.

They had all been at dinner together, they had said, Augustine and all seven of them; both Bartons, White, Adler, Turner, Reynolds and Collins. At Gerald Atkinson's house. Augustine had seemed more cheerful than usual. He was talking about a deal he had made which would make him rich. He had repeated what Gerald had told Phryne; he was going to buy his mother a house and give her an annuity and live by himself. He wouldn't tell any of them what this deal was, or even whether it involved a painting or an artifact. None of them had any idea what it was. They said that he was customarily secretive and loved to surprise them with some new thing.

Their evidence, Phryne remembered, had been as close fitting as a jigsaw puzzle. No one had joined the party, no one had left. They had farewelled Augustine together and watched him walk away to his death. And they had stayed together for the rest of the evening, only parting at four in the morning when cars and taxis had been summoned. Neat. But perhaps a little gaudy.

She leaned back and closed her eyes.

When she opened them again she felt better. Cemeteries were lowering to the spirits. Her spirits had now recovered. The big car had stopped outside Mrs. Manifold's house, where it was going to be a squeeze stuffing all those people into the parlour. Phryne gave her hair a last flick and got out and Mr. Butler settled down with his pipe and the *Hawklet* to wait. Miss Fisher, to add to all her other virtues as an employer, did not object to the smell of pipe smoke.

Rather sensibly, Mrs. Manifold had not tried to hold Augustine's wake in her house, which looked small. She had spread a buffet in the shop itself. There was a funeral wreath on the door and the knocker had been tied up in a black glove; all the proprieties were, it appeared, to be observed. Phryne went in and was immediately collared by the woman in the red sari. Stephanie, Phryne remembered from her briefing, Stephanie Reynolds. One hand was clutching her arm and the other hand was forcing a glass of port into her grasp. Phryne grasped it, as spilled port would not improve her grey suit. Phryne only drank very good port and her first sniff of this one told her that it did not fall into that category, being the noxious grape-derived fluid supplied to the drunks of St. Kilda at threepence a pint and otherwise known as 'dog's nose', for some reason lost in the mists of lexicology. However, there was probably a pot plant around tough enough to survive a libation or two.

'Miss Reynolds,' she said politely to her assailant. Pale eyes met hers and straggling brown hair was shaken away from an undistinguished face.

'Oh, you're Phryne Fisher, aren't you, the Hon. Miss Fisher, I ought to say. I met you at the opening of that play, now what was it called? I can't remember,' said the woman in the sari blankly, scratching at her caste mark. This meant that she released Phryne, which was a relief. 'But it was very clever and you were there with a beautiful Chinese man in the most gorgeous suit and James said…I don't recall what James said but it was very funny.'

'It doesn't matter in the slightest,' Phryne assured her truthfully. She didn't care what anyone said about the association of Phryne and Lin Chung, especially James, who was leaning against the white-painted wall, looking exquisite and drinking his third glass of the revolting port. That appeared to be the sum total of his social skills but Phryne supposed that he might have hidden depths.

Gerald Atkinson was sitting by himself in the inner room, weeping discreetly into a pale blue handkerchief. It was probably pure coincidence that it was Dulac blue.

'Priscilla and Blanche are so upset,' Stephanie informed Phryne, looking rather wildly around the room. 'They liked Augustine. And Gerald, of course. I've told them and told them that he has just been translated unto another and higher sphere and we should be able to get him by planchette in a few weeks but they didn't take it at all well. The master says…'

At this juncture Phryne, while preserving the perfect appearance of a lady who is listening closely to the wisdom of the master, tuned out like a Marconi apparatus and considered the room. She had heard a large number of the more theosophical of her acquaintance talk about their masters and she didn't need to hear it again. For one thing, they all sounded the same and they all demanded the same: total subservience. Phryne thought that she must have missed the vital subservience enzyme or vitamin or whatever it was that made people rush forward to surrender their will to someone else. Miss Reynolds was a natural slave and presumably relished her slavery.

Mrs. Manifold and her two sisters were drinking a colourless fluid which might be water or might be straight gin, as they had every right to do, and looking at a huge album of photographs, probably of Augustine as a baby on a sheepskin rug. Priscilla Barton and Blanche White were a picture in contrasts, one looking like a female tramp and the other like the veiled woman in Sapper, who at any moment might start diffusing exotic perfumes and stealing the Naval Treaty. But they were both weeping, Priscilla noisily and Miss White quietly. Rachel Phillips was sitting with Sophie and Cedric Yates, trying not to sip the disgusting port and talking, by the gestures, about furniture. The plump girl, Veronica Collins, was patting Priscilla on the shoulder, and Luke Adler and Valentine Turner, brunette boy and blond boy, were propping up either end of a display case like bookends. From their mutual expression, which was almost identical, they were embarrassed and nervous and had decided that immobility would best preserve them from social errors. Rabbits in headlights laboured under the same misapprehension.

Phryne thought that the person she most wanted to meet was the rubicund, white-haired professor, and she detached herself gently from Stephanie Reynolds and drifted in his direction. He was looking in a glass case. His lips were moving. Translating, perhaps. Phryne joined him and leaned over the case at his side. He was reading a scroll.

'I don't know the language,' she observed. 'What is it?'

'Aramaic,' he said. 'Hello! I saw you at the funeral. Don't drink that ghastly stuff,' he warned her. 'It would bleach a black dog.'

'I'm just looking for a pot plant,' she assured him.

'Try that vase of lilies, they couldn't be more dead. I've a notion that if we wander over to the bereaved mother we might get a snifter of something better.'

'With a double dose of bitter aloes,' said Phryne, tipping her glass as instructed. The deceased lilies rustled sadly. Professor Rowlands looked regretful.

'True. Poor Augustine, it does seem unfair. You're Miss Fisher, aren't you? You know that he was on the verge of a wonderful discovery?'

'Yes, but no one knows what it was.'

'You're looking into his death, aren't you? Well, I can tell you what Augustine was expecting to find.'

'Yes, but will you?' asked Phryne.

He smiled down at her, looking like a younger, slimmer version of Father Christmas. 'I will,' he told her. 'It was treasure.'

'So how'd you manage on your little holiday in the prison camp?' asked Curly.

Vern grinned. 'Did a bit of a perish for terbacca until Bill came up with a lurk.'

'How? You can't get anything into the camp, it's guarded and them guards ain't got no sense of humour.'

'Nah, well, you know how Bill's always looking at insects and worms and snakes and vermin? He found out that scarab beetles always like cooler sand and they can follow a path. So he lay down all casual-like at the fence, drew a line in the sand under the wire, and set his little beetle mates trundling under it, each one with a cig attached by a thread. All I had to do was take off the cig and send the beetle back. When one went on strike he'd get another one.'

'He's a clever bloke,' commented Jim.

Chapter Nine

I hate ingratitude more in a man Than lying, vain-
ness, babbling drunkenness, Or any taint of vice whose
strong corruption Inhabits our frail blood.

William Shakespeare
Twelfth Night

Phryne had no time to ask any more questions. She gave the
professor her card and asked him to call on her at his earliest
convenience and stood respectfully to listen to Mrs. Manifold
speaking her valediction of her lost child.

'He was a good baby,' she said, her rough voice creaking as
though she had torn her throat with screaming. 'He was a clever
boy, always loving. He worked hard and when his father died he
worked harder. He made me happy every day that he lived.'

'He was a good fellow,' said Gerald. 'We all loved him. We'll
all miss him.'

Priscilla and Blanche wept afresh.

Miss Collins said in an unexpectedly beautiful, operasinger's
voice, 'He was such a nice man.'

'He was a shrewd and honourable trader,' added Rachel
Phillips.

'He was a good boss,' said Cedric Yates firmly, and Sophie
burst into tears. 'And a good bloke,' he added.

He raised his glass.

'To Augustine,' said Cedric, and they all drank.

Then it was time to condole with the bereaved and go home. Phryne distributed her cards to Rachel and the others and took her leave of the old woman. Even as she watched, Mrs. Manifold filled with renewed power. She had buried her son fitly and mourned him as she would for the rest of her life. But she had something still to do. It was revenge. She straightened a little, put back her hair, and took Phryne's warm hand in her two cold claws. She had a grip like an eagle, and it is never wise, Phryne thought, to rob eagles of their chicks.

'Do you know anything more?' she grated.

'I will come and see you soon,' Phryne said. 'When I know more.'

The talons relaxed their grip. Phryne bent to kiss the icy cheek and went out into the sunshine, where Rachel Phillips was drawing a deep breath of smoky St. Kilda air as though it was straight from bracing Skegness.

'Phew!' she said.

Phryne had to agree. 'Can I give you a ride?' she asked.

Rachel shook her curls. 'I'm going to walk,' she said. 'By the sea. And muse on mortality and other things. I'll call you,' she promised.

Phryne was about to enter her car when the bright young things came out in a group and lit cigarettes to soothe their feelings. Phryne did the same and accepted a light from Valentine.

'We're going back to Gerald's house,' said Stephanie. 'Would you like to come too, Miss Fisher? Augustine deserves a real wake.'

Phryne did not relish their company, but accepted in the interests of detection. Professor Rowlands emerged from the house of woe, bowed, replaced his hat, and strode away. She hoped that he would call her as soon as he could. Treasure, eh? What kind of treasure?

Cedric Yates and Sophie came and shut the door and locked it with a curiously final click. Manifold's was closed, possibly forever.

'Very well, but I need to go home first,' Phryne said to Stephanie. 'I shall join you later. At Gerald's house, is it? Then I shall see you there.'

She smiled on the others, got into the car and said to her chauffeur, 'Get me out of here, Mr. B, and with all convenient speed.'

The big car drew away from the pavement.

Phryne arrived home to find that she had a visitor. She didn't want one but it was the point-device Mr. Adami and she could not refuse him an interview. He was as beautifully dressed as ever and looked concerned. A solicitor who looks concerned is always a bad omen. Dot accompanied her into the room, trying to field her coat and hat, which Phryne had flung to the winds. Dot succeeded, due to wicket-keeping for her little brothers as a girl, and stood clutching the garments to her demure bosom. Her employer was, evidently, in a mood.

'Hello, Mr. Adami, do sit down,' Phryne said crossly, flinging herself into a chair in the small parlour. 'Dot dear, can you get me a cup of tea? And perhaps ask Mrs. B if there is any leftover lunch? Tea, Mr. Adami?'

'No, Miss Fisher, very kind of you but no, I am in haste,' he said in his precise English. 'I came here to deliver an invitation from the head of the Bonnetti family—that is, the eldest son, Joseph. He has called a family council about the will of his mother and he would very much appreciate your presence, Miss Fisher.'

'Oh, very well,' said Phryne ungraciously. She was in possession of a magnificent fit of temper which she would have to dissipate soon or self-combust. She wondered where it had come from. 'When?'

'On Friday afternoon, Miss Fisher. Here is the address. At three, if you please,' said Mr. Adami, and made his escape, feeling, not for the first time, that his profession was a lot more dangerous than the general public would credit. As the front door shut safely behind him Phryne swore loudly.

'I am quite out of sorts, Dot, and I am going for a swim. When I come back I would like some strong tea to take the taste of funeral liquor out of my mouth and perhaps a toasted sandwich or an omelette. I am going to have to keep up with what I judge is a hard-drinking crowd and my stomach will need lining. Back soon,' she said, ran upstairs for her bathing costume, ran downstairs and out of the house all in a moment, slamming the door on the way out.

'Funerals,' said Dot to Mr. Butler. 'Do funny things to people.'

'She's had a tiring day,' said the butler solemnly. 'And borne it pretty well up to now.'

'She'll be better after a swim,' said Dot, smoothing the coat as though its feelings might have been ruffled.

Phryne ran across the prickly grass and the hot sand, tore off her loose shift and walked into the water and out as far as she could wade, then dived and swam for the horizon. In her present incandescent state, she thought, it was amazing that the tide was not seething around her. She duck dived over and under the waves as though she was swimming for her life from some sort of shipwreck.

After half an hour she was beginning to recover. Her hair was soaked, as she had been unable to find her bathing cap and had not the patience to search for it. It clung to her sleek head like a seal's fur, deliciously cold. Her arms and shoulders were agreeably tired and her temper tantrum appeared to have been washed away in the cool salty water. Moreover, she was getting weary and the sun was killingly hot.

She walked home and climbed the stairs to a cool shower and a change of garments, washing away the salt with the fury and soothing her skin with milk of roses lotion (as used by royalty). By the time she had donned a silky violet afternoon dress and sandals she was ready to descend and be affable to her staff, who drew surreptitious breaths of relief and tended her cautiously, as though she might bite.

Phryne ate her omelette, drank a glass of milk and toyed with a meditative banana, sliced, with ice cream, chocolate syrup and nuts. It sweetened her afternoon in a very satisfactory manner. She looked at her companions and saw their wary expressions.

Oh, dear. She must have been really uncivil. Again. Time to start mollifying everyone's feelings.

'I'm so sorry, Dot, I really loathe funerals. I beg your pardon for being so rude. Poor Mr. Adami went out of here like a rocket.'

'He'll be all right,' said Dot. 'He's a lawyer. They got thick skins, my mum always said. You sure you want to go to this bunfight, Miss?'

'I don't,' said Phryne, stretching as she stood up. 'But I'm going. Don't delay dinner for me, God knows how long I'll be away with the fairies. If a gentleman called Professor Rowlands calls, ask him to lunch tomorrow. If I'm not home in the morning, call Jack Robinson. He was at the Manifold funeral, so he must think there's something wrong with that death. How do I look?'

'Chic,' said Dot. 'That violet is a lovely colour with your skin, Miss Phryne. Aren't you going to wear stockings?'

'Not with sandals. I need a hat, though—come and help me choose one? And why not ask Mrs. B to slice up that roast beef for salad tonight? You know how you like cold roast beef.'

'Thank you,' said Dot, who recognised an apology when she heard one. 'That would be nice.'

Later, wearing a perfectly darling black straw hat with a pale heliotrope ribbon, Phryne was driven to Gerald Atkinson's house, whence there was a sound of revelry by day. As Valentine opened the door, she was regaled with a little song, a little song entitled 'No Matter How Young a Prune May Be, It's Always Full of Wrinkles'.

It seemed scarcely decent, but she walked inside anyway.

The party was in the parlour, a large room in plush and gilt, filled presently with dancers. Valentine said over the roar of the gramophone, 'Do help yourself to a drink, Miss Fisher, I've got to mind the door.'

Phryne stood still. The room was half lit by hundreds of candles. The air was thick with a sweetish heavy smoke. Incense, but not Church incense, unless it was another kind of church altogether. Under the cloud of sandalwood she could smell a sour reek she associated with Morocco—what was it? That scent of burning rotten leaves was familiar. Of course. Kif. Phryne sneezed discreetly and moved through whirling figures until she reached the far wall, where the door into the next room stood half open and a comprehensive bar had been established.

Phryne looked at the profusion of glittering bottles. Lavish and very expensive. Everything that any drinker had ever wanted to imbibe: chartreuse in both colours, strange Greek and Slavic brandies, schnapps, cognac, whisky and whiskey, bourbon and rye, vermouth and Pernod, even including absinthe. She resisted *la Fée Verte* firmly and poured herself a very modest gin and tonic, with just enough gin to flavour her breath. This was no company for teetotallers and she wanted this group to confide in her.

If they ever stopped dancing. Valentine was minding the door, Luke was playing the gramophone. Rachel Phillips must have been and gone, also the professor. Gerald was dancing with Veronica, Priscilla was dancing with Blanche, James was dancing with Stephanie in a whirl of red sari. At least they were tired, which would limit this shameless exhibition. Phryne saw that two of the three couples were now performing the Nightclub Glide, where the female of the pair wreathes her arms around the male partner's neck and the two lean inwards, providing mutual support to the terminally intoxicated. Fairly soon, they would have to sit down, or fall down.

The gramophone began to play a charleston and that sprightly dance proved to be an impossible task. Gerald sank down onto the sofa and Luke allowed the music machine to wind down. 'The Varsity Rag' wailed into silence, which spread and pooled like milk. The dancers were too breathless to speak and Phryne was not going to start. She was hoping that she would not become too affected by the kif if she sat in a draught of fresh air. She had smoked it overseas and it always made her very sleepy and indiscreet, though the indiscretion (which took the form of stroking the nearest available male flesh) might have been inherent, rather than drug-induced.

'Divine Phryne!' exclaimed Gerald Atkinson, stretching out a languid hand. 'So good of you to come and help us mourn poor, poor Augustine!'

'Poor Augustine,' repeated Phryne insinuatingly.

'He was such a nice man,' sobbed Priscilla. She had collapsed into an armchair and was ransacking her bag, looking for a handkerchief.

'A good fellow,' sobbed Blanche, wiping her kohled eyes with a wisp of silk which showed not a trace of black when she let it fall.

'No, he wasn't,' said Veronica Collins, leaning both plump elbows on the table and supporting her dimpled chin in her hands. She spoke with the authority of the very drunk, a state which had degraded her private girls' school accent a class or two. 'He wasn't a nice man at all.'

'Ronnie, please,' said Gerald.

'In what way?' Phryne's voice, just audible, floated on the smoky air.

'He wouldn't tell,' pouted Veronica.

'I said we could get him on the planchette when he's had a chance to settle down in the afterlife,' objected Stephanie. 'He'll tell us then, just have patience.'

'Steph, you really are such a fool,' said James Barton, who had clearly reached the limit of his patience with female sensibilities.

'How dare you?' shrilled Miss Reynolds, shocked. 'You've seen what the Hidden Masters can do! You...you...unbeliever!' She threw this epithet at him like a curse.

James grinned. It was rather too close to a baring of teeth for comfort.

'I am an unbeliever,' he said flatly. 'I don't believe in any of your spiritualist nonsense. I don't believe that Augustine knew where it was, and I don't believe he was going to tell us anything, and I don't believe that he'll be any more amenable because he's dead. He cheated Gerald. He cheated us. He was a twister.'

'Oh, James, how unkind,' wept Priscilla. 'You always were unkind. Mother always said—'

'Don't talk to me about Mother!' James snarled. 'You always throw Mother at me when I show signs of sickening of all this… mawkishness, all this join-hands-and-sing-a-hymn, "Is there-anybody-there?" foolery. I'm sick of it. I'll have no more of it, Pris, do you hear? No more!'

'I will not desert my masters,' said Priscilla with unexpected firmness.

'Then you can play with your ouija board without me!' James flung around and was at the door when Valentine laid a hand on his shoulder.

'I say, old man…' he began.

James shrugged off the hand and Valentine was joined by Luke, who applied another hand to the other shoulder.

'You're upset,' soothed Luke. 'Come and have another drink.'

James pushed Luke aside and shoved his way into the hall. Valentine stood in front of him and Luke flanked him. Both of them were sounding very sober, all of a sudden.

'No, really, old chap, we can't let you drive a car in this state,' said Luke.

Phryne found their cooperation slightly menacing. They were like two hunting dogs, reacting to each other without having to look. However, James really should not be allowed out in this state, in the interests of the national death rate. It was a kind action to restrain him.

Without violence the two young men shouldered James into the room again, and Gerald gave him a large glass of brandy.

'Drink it down, old boy, and you'll feel more the thing,' Luke encouraged.

James complied. He shuddered and sat down rather quickly.

'There,' said Valentine.

'Where?' asked Priscilla. 'Did you hear what he said about my masters?'

'Yes, I heard it,' said Blanche calmly. 'It is strange how different two siblings can be! One open to all sorts of possibilities, another closed up tight as a drum, and so angry!' She wavered closer to James, trailing her graceful fingers across his face, and cooed, 'Is the great big man angry?'

'You should see your aura,' Priscilla informed him.

James batted ineffectually at the caressing hand.

Gerald took another deep breath of the drugged air and said, 'But we are forgetting our guest! Come and look at the pretty things which Augustine found for me.'

Phryne, who had thought the quarrel strangely compelling, rose and accompanied her host as he wobbled from glass case to glass case. 'Here is a Ming Dynasty lady,' he said, peering through the glass at a tiny maiden carved in blackwood.

'The Taoist flower maiden,' said Phryne, who had been given a much larger, more intact and more valuable jade version by her lover, Lin Chung.

'Quite right!' slurred Gerald. 'What a clever girl you are! Can you tell me what this is?'

'A ceremonial cup,' said Phryne. 'Bronze, Chinese, fifth century, perhaps?'

'And the incense burner that goes with it,' agreed Gerald. 'How about this?'

'Egyptian.' Phryne was beginning to enjoy herself but was watching her host closely. A collector should not be outfaced amongst his own collection. He would be nettled and he could have weapons. It would be interestingly historic to be battered with a ninth-century Chinese warrior's club, but it would also hurt. 'It's a faience scarab, perhaps one that the Pharaoh had issued to mark particular triumphs. This one has soldiers and captured enemies on it, so is it Ramses the Third?'

'Egypt's Napoleon, yes,' agreed Gerald, who seemed rather pleased than nettled by Phryne's erudition. Veronica Collins, who had trailed along, observed, 'I always loved this one.'

'It's a putto,' said Phryne, who had a limited tolerance for small, fat, nude children, even if they did have wings. This one appeared to be simpering. 'Not classical. From a grave, possibly, or maybe a mantelpiece? One can see the little tongue of stone where it was attached to something upright. Eighteenth century. Italian. Is this some sort of test, Mr. Atkinson?'

'Everything's a test,' mumbled Gerald. 'This is Pris' favourite.'

Phryne could see why. It was a small iconostasis, about the size of a paperback book for railway reading. It was hinged in the middle. The outside was wood, carved and gilded. The inside revealed a glorious gilded Madonna surrounded by angels with lapis wings on one side and a morose man, attired in an airy sheepskin, staring cross-eyed out of a bush of thorns at a woman in a ruby-red dress. St. Anthony being tempted and the Madonna being praised by angels. The blues were astounding, so fresh, so bright. Periwinkle, thought Phryne, hyacinth, Greek midday over Hydra.

'Where would we be without Charging Elk, I ask you?' Stephanie was demanding of the company, having joined the guided tour. 'Where would we be in our quest without Selima and Zacarias? Nowhere. Augustine wasn't going to tell us anything else, but my spirit guide knows…'

'Yes, yes,' soothed Blanche White, slinking along after Pris like a cat after a bird. 'That is a lovely thing, Gerald.'

'It's Greek, isn't it?' asked Phryne. 'Precious.'

'Very precious,' agreed Gerald. His colour was heightened, perhaps with a touch of rouge, his eyes dilated almost black by the kif, and his bee-stung mouth was smiling. He looked like a Saint Sebastian drawn by Félicien Rops. Reynolds was joined in conversation by Priscilla and Phryne was listening to both her and Gerald, a skill learned at school and sharpened by many dreary cocktail parties.

'This?' asked Gerald, indicating a handful of broken coins.

'No idea,' confessed Phryne promptly.

'It's pieces of eight,' said Veronica.

'Really? As in Long John Silver and "Sixteen Men on a Dead Man's Chest"? Pirate treasure? Fascinating,' said Phryne, rather disappointed.

'They had better plunder. Moidores, Louis d'or, gold cups and chains. They say that Blackbeard had fifteen caches of treasure, and only eight have ever been found.'

'Charging Elk said, "How! Seekers must look to the West!"
You remember, don't you, Pris?'

'Of course,' said Pris. 'And when we looked to the west we
found Zacarias.'

'What about this?' asked Gerald. Phryne detected something
creeping up behind her and felt Blanche White's hand stealing in
between her arm and her side. She crooked an elbow to defend
her breast.

'It's a Colombian statue, Maya or Inca or something like that,
a beast eating a man.'

'A jaguar, and here is the companion piece,' said Gerald.

'I compliment you on your sense of the macabre,' said
Phryne. The companion piece was a crude wooden statuette
of a tiger eating a white man, legs first, so that his screaming
face and his top hat were still visible—and indeed might easily
prove inedible if the tiger had any delicacy of taste, which Gerald
apparently didn't.

'You could call it the art of rebellion,' he told her. 'This was
made in India before the Mutiny.'

'And Charging Elk said that we wouldn't get any help from
Augustine—he said, "Curio man speak with forked tongue,"
you remember?' insisted Stephanie.

'Yes, so he did,' said Pris. 'And he was right.'

Phryne, with Blanche White glued to her side, moved to the
next case. The air was clearer. It was cool in the rooms, evidently
a ventilation system was in operation to preserve the antiquities.
She knew the little woman in the next case.

'Ishtar. Lady of stars and goddess of Ur,' she told Gerald.
He nodded briskly and led the way to a glass dome over a small
thing. It looked like a little terracotta pillow on which a drunken
sparrow had been roosting.

'A cuneiform letter, Gerald,' she said. Blanche White was
so close to Phryne that she was reminded of Alice and the Red
Queen. She looked around. All of the group were in attendance. Luke and Valentine were inspecting a case full of coins.
James Barton was standing with them, holding his forehead

as though his head was insecurely gummed on, and Stephanie and Priscilla were next to the anthropophagus tiger, still talking about seances.

Blanche and Phryne moved to the next case, in which was displayed a red figure vase—a rude one. Phryne loved these little round two-eared cups, the Ancient Greek equivalent of Woolworths china. They were made quickly and thrown away in huge numbers and often had a cartoon on them, whatever the cup maker had on his mind when he had fired a few hundred of them in a day. In this case, it was satyrs and their indecent ways. This satyr was demonstrating a method of becoming one with one's flock. The goat looked relaxed about it. It was grinning.

'Red figure is my favourite,' observed Phryne, without turning a hair. This wasn't in the first hundred of indecent things she had seen, not to mention taken part in. 'Where did Augustine get it, I wonder?'

'Sicily, he said.' Gerald was amused. Phryne felt that she had passed some sort of test. 'That's what set us off laughing in church—disgraceful of us! Huge deposits of Greek leftovers in Sicily. Syracuse, you know. More intact temples there than in Greece, and Lord knows how the temples are going to fare if Greece turns to war now, what with all these bombs and so on. I look on collectors as salvaging what they can from a violent world which does not care about beauty.'

'Or even wit,' agreed Phryne, shifting a hip out of Blanche's reach. What was the woman after? By now she must know that Phryne was not carrying a gun. She must know what sort of undergarments she was wearing.

A white figure vase reposed in the next case. It was a tiny thing, decorated with a sad maiden casting a wreath onto a tomb.

'To hold tears,' Veronica Collins informed Phryne. Phryne shrugged off some of Blanche's embrace and bent forward. The vase was intact, except for a chip on one side which alone disqualified it as a museum piece. The range of Augustine's stock was astonishing. Phryne wished more than ever that she had met him when alive. The man who could assemble this remarkable collection must have had agents all over the world.

'Did Augustine speak any other languages?' she asked.

'Oh, yes, lots,' said Stephanie, unexpectedly coming out of her diatribe about spirits. 'Italian and Greek and Spanish and Italian, and some others, I believe. He was a wonderful man,' she said, and she and Priscilla burst into tears again.

Blanche released Phryne, to her great relief, to go to her friend, and Gerald moved on.

'A flint arrowhead,' she said. 'French?'

'From Abbeville,' he agreed. 'Marvellous how they made them. It's as sharp today as it was ten thousand years ago.' He opened the case and drew the point across his wrist. A red line sprang up behind it. Phryne stared. Gerald tied his handkerchief around his wrist, to defend his faultless cuff, and put the arrowhead in her palm. It was a lovely, deadly thing. Phryne imagined the maker striking hundreds of shards off a flint until he had the exact shape, then flaking it so accurately that the head formed the shape of a leaf.

'Lethal,' she said, giving it back.

A flat lead disc figured with an eagle was the next exhibit. It was not a coin. There was a hole in the top. It was meant to be worn. And it was thicker than a coin.

'It's a bulla, the Roman seal of freedom,' said Gerald. Letting his blood had apparently had a sobering effect on him. 'There's a space inside for one's manumission.'

'I am a citizen of no mean city,' quoted Veronica.

'I always thought that showed the saint in a very poor light,' said Phryne. 'The soldier says to him, "I'm a Roman citizen too, cost me a fortune," and Paul says, "I was born a Roman." Pure arrogance. No wonder the centurion sent him on.'

'To Caesar hast thou appealed, to Caesar shalt thou go,' said Gerald.

'And this?' asked Phryne. 'I don't recognise the style. It's a flower, around the cup, isn't it?'

'An almond flower,' said Gerald. He paused, but apart from the fact that almonds were very tasty, Phryne knew of no special significance in almond flowers. 'Persian,' he added.

'Oh,' said Phryne. 'Very…old.' It was lumpy as cups went and seemed to have no grace in its making. Though it was pure gold, which made it valuable.

'And these are some coins,' said Gerald. 'Shekels. And now, Miss Fisher, perhaps you would care for some Turkish coffee? My man makes it very well.'

'Thank you,' said Phryne, smiling sunnily into his face. 'I adore Turkish coffee.'

She was glad that Blanche had released her, or she might have felt a reaction. Why had Augustine been drowned with one of those golden shekels in his pocket?

'I fear,' said the officer, 'that Judea has lost its bloom.'

'Yer mean because it's freezing cold and raining and snowing and there's no cover and the tents are all leaking, sir?'

'Could be that,' said the officer. 'Anyway, some of the Christmas parcels got through. There's one for your mate Jim.'

'Whacko,' said Bill.

They crammed into one tent to open the parcel. It was a heavy, solid parcel laden with possibilities. Each item was taken out and admired as the 1917 winter sleeted down outside.

'Cake, Jeannie makes good cake,' said Jim hungrily. 'Baked in the tin and sewn into sailcloth. Socks and underwear, you beaut, mine are in rags. Lice powder, Fuller's for the Feet, soap, boiled sweets, papers, matches, pound of tobacco, dried fruit, and—this.'

They all looked at it.

'She's a good woman, all right, your Jeannie,' said Curly solemnly.

Wrapped in drying eucalyptus leaves was a bottle of overproof rum.

'Merry Christmas,' said Bill.

Chapter Ten

For wisdom is better than rubies.

Proverbs 8:11 The Holy Bible

The coffee was thick, black and dangerous, as the best Turkish coffee always is. It was served in gem-like Lalique tea glasses in holders woven of golden vines. Phryne drank only one cup, in deference to her chances of sleeping any time soon, but the company gulped as if coffee was about to be banned under the *Drugs and Poisons Control Act 1926*. This must be their standard mode of behaviour, Phryne thought; to stoke themselves up on kif and alcohol, then caffeinise themselves into sobriety again, in time to go home to their respective respectable homes. She tapped into the general chit-chat and obtained some information right away.

'You live with your mother, Miss White? And you live with your brother, Miss Barton? My sister is in Australia but we thought it best for her to have her own establishment.'

'Siblings,' said Veronica. 'Rivalry.'

'Indeed,' lied Phryne, who now got on swimmingly with her sister Eliza.

'That's what Augustine wanted, to give his mother a wonderful house so he could live alone. A natural solitary, Augustine.

Like one of those old hermit johnnies. Loved to be alone. Hated company, most of the time,' said James Barton.

'Didn't appreciate your cocktails?' insinuated Phryne over the rim of her coffee cup.

'Oh, no, he didn't go that far,' asserted Gerald. 'Liked a drink as much as the rest of us.'

'Indeed,' murmured Phryne. 'Your tea glasses are Lalique, I think? Beautiful things. I must say that your range of liqueurs would not disgrace the Ritz, Mr. Atkinson. Do you collect them as well?'

'Ah? Yes, well, yes, I suppose so.' Mr. Atkinson seemed distracted. 'I always pick up a bottle if it looks interesting. And I buy a lot from the agent. Hard to get real absinthe these days, for instance; they dilute it with anisette.'

To Phryne, all aniseed liqueurs tasted the same, from Pernod to raki to ouzo to absinthe. Though only absinthe had the extra mind-wrecking, brain-rotting wormwood which had sent so many of the intelligentsia of Paris out of their collective heads. She didn't like aniseed. She had even given her black jellybeans to the Fisher dog. Terpenes had never been her tipple.

She sipped her coffee and nodded in assent. It was definitely time she got out of this appalling atmosphere while she could still remember her own name. But she had one thing to do first. She put down the cup, approached Miss Collins and murmured into her silky soft ear a certain request.

Veronica led her out of the rooms to—drat!—a downstairs WC with nothing else in it but a small basin and a mirror. Not the bathroom which she was convinced must exist in such a well-appointed house. Phryne made use of the facilities then announced that she really must tear herself away.

Veronica protested a little too much and Phryne repeated her desire to depart. Veronica flushed an unbecoming red which went all the way up to her blonde curls and called out to Gerald Atkinson, 'Miss Fisher says she has to go home!'

There was a note almost of panic in her voice which set all the hair on Phryne's neck to bristling.

Gerald got up. 'Oh, no, Miss Fisher, beautiful Miss Fisher, do honour us with your presence. We're going to dance some more and then we will be dining early. Do stay,' he said, his hand closing around her wrist.

'No, really,' said Phryne, moving towards the door. The others had all risen and gathered around.

'Do stay,' cooed Priscilla Barton.

'Do stay,' said Blanche White, advancing.

'Do stay,' groaned James Barton.

Phryne scanned the room. The situation was not good. Valentine and Luke stood between Phryne and the door. She had a strong desire, suddenly, to shriek and claw for eyes. She was greatly outnumbered; too many people to fight.

Instead, she dropped her purse, said, 'Oh, how clumsy of me!', bent to pick it up, kicked it through the doorway between the two young men, stooped to retrieve it, nudged it again and was at the front door before the company could mobilise to arrest her escape.

She took her hat from the hallstand, smiled ravishingly, and was gone. She slammed the door and ran down the steps and into the car.

'Home?' asked Mr. Butler.

'And that right speedily!' she replied.

The car was already in the stream of traffic before Luke and Valentine arrived on the pavement. Phryne waved at them. They did not wave back. Phryne fanned herself and blinked away a few terror-induced tears.

'I think, Mr. Butler, that I have just escaped a fate worse than death. Not for the first time, however. It's still daylight. I expect it's still January, too. What time is it?'

'Barely six, Miss Phryne,' he said comfortably.

'Wonderful,' said Phryne, and sank down against the car's upholstery, breathing hard. 'I shall be in time for dinner, and I am starving.'

Dinner was everything her kif-maddened hunger could desire. The vichyssoise was properly iced. The salad was fresh, the potatoes waxy, the carrot and celery curls crisp, the roast beef sliced as thin as paper and the green tomato chutney Mrs. Butler's sister's finest. Phryne ate like a wharfie and drank three glasses of a light moselle which the Barossa Valley was making so well before she looked up at her family. They were so normal, the girls and Dot: well fed, a little shiny with perspiration, and discussing Jane's newly found interest in coral.

'I know that people make it into teething-rings and neck-laces,' said Phryne. 'But nothing else. Do tell!'

Jane, delighted, began to inform her adoptive parent about corals, their reefs and their strange, eerie method of releasing all their eggs when the moon was full and the tide at its high-est. The others ate more beef, Phryne drank more wine, and contentment settled over the house. While she could not have passed any reasonable exam on corals thereafter, Phryne loved the sound of Jane's enthusiastic voice. She was suddenly so glad to be home that she had to take another glass of wine with des-sert, which was a matchless pineapple sorbet. And then a glass of the good cognac with her coffee.

The girls went to the small parlour after dinner to play the gramophone and Dot sat down with Phryne. Dot had some mending and Phryne was writing up her notes. When her eccen-tric employer finally capped her fountain pen, Dot ventured, 'Was it bad as all that, Miss?'

'Yes, it was thoroughly vile,' said Phryne. 'The only one who might crack, however, is James Barton. I may have to dine with him. What a bore!'

'Professor Rowlands called and I gave him your message, Miss. Lunch tomorrow, he said he'd be there. He sounded like a nice man.'

'That will be an improvement,' said Phryne. 'Dot, do you know of any special significance of almond flowers?'

'No,' replied Dot, after deep thought. 'They're very pretty, almond flowers. Large white blossoms. Smell sweet. Nothing I can think of, Miss Phryne.'

'No religious connection?'

'Not that I know of,' said Dot, picking up an errant thread and securing it firmly. 'There's flowers in the Bible, you know, the rose of Sharon and the lily of the valley. And there's the lilies of the fields.'

'Anemones,' said Phryne.

'Not the tall white arums, then?' asked Dot, who had always wondered what Our Saviour was talking about when he said that Solomon in all his glory was not arrayed as one of those boring white lilies.

'No, not them. Anemones. Windflowers. You know, the spring flowers, purple, blue and red with a black centre. Of course, purple was the imperial colour, only kings and emperors wore it.'

'Oh,' said Dot, possessed of an image of a stern bearded Old Testament person shining in silks of red and blue and purple. 'So that's what he meant.'

'Who?'

'Jesus, Miss Phryne. Our Lord,' said Dot, in case Phryne had altogether missed out on Christianity, crossing herself unobtrusively.

'Oh, him.'

'Why do you ask?' Dot was curious about this sudden religiosity.

'The degenerate Gerald showed me a rather clumsy, badly made golden cup and said it was shaped like an almond blossom. He then paused, as if waiting for some comment. His collection is noticeably of beautiful objects—rare and beautiful. Well, except for the satyr and the goat, perhaps. And that at least is rare. So why have a gold cup which looked like it had been made by an apprentice? Ah well, I am going to bed, and perhaps tomorrow might be more amusing. And with any luck, less threatening. Mr. B will do the locking up. And I hope for sweet dreams.'

'Sleep tight, Miss Phryne,' said Dot. 'God and His angels protect us all.'

Phryne, exhausted, settled for no dreams at all, or none that she could remember when she woke to find it was morning and the world was up and doing.

She turned over and went back to sleep. The world could get on with it without her for a few hours. The sunlight, through her dark green curtains, was a pleasant glow. She imagined that she was a koala, sleeping in a gum tree, and closed her eyes, snuggling into her soft grey fur and wriggling her flat black nose…

She was roused by Dot reminding her that she had a luncheon appointment with a professor and what did she want to wear? Phryne abandoned her marsupial persona and got up to shower and don undergarments, and then to ponder what costume would convey the right impression to a university man.

'I think I'll wear the azure cotton with the Greek masks in black,' she decided. 'It's got arms and a higher neckline than he is used to. I don't want to be confused with any of the female persons at that appalling wake.'

'Really?' Dot was always interested in wicked people. 'What were they wearing?'

'Very little,' Phryne replied, as her head cleared the conservative neckline. 'I'll just have my coffee and a croissant, Dot, it's scandalously near to luncheon. Oh, I see you have anticipated me.' The tray with Hellenic coffee, a glass of water and a croissant was already on her little table. Phryne sat down to sip. As Dot was evidently still agog for descriptions of the demimonde, she went on kindly, 'Well, Miss Blanche was wearing a red dress secured only by the thinnest of straps, which left her back and most of her front bare. And she was relatively respectable. Miss Collins was half naked, and she is far too plump to expose all that flesh—draped in quite the wrong shade of electric blue. Priscilla Barton was costumed in an orangey confection straight from the ragbag, and Stephanie Reynolds was positively swathed in her sari. They really were the nastiest collection I have met in many a party, Dot dear.'

'And this professor is one of them?' Dot clasped her hands.

'No, I believe that he was only at the funeral because he knew and liked the deceased. He seemed quite civilised, as did Rachel Phillips. However, handsome is as handsome does, as you keep telling me. We shall see.'

'Indeed,' murmured Dot. 'I went and searched for that certificate, Miss Phryne. For the young man in the cemetery?'

'Oh, good, yes, our other problem. What did the Actors'
Benevolent Society say?'

'No one there, Miss, I'll call again today. It's just a little cubby
hole of an office near the Princess Theatre. But Births Deaths and
Marriages had his death certificate. His name was Patrick James
O'Rourke, born in County Limerick, Ireland, in 1846. That
makes him eighteen at the time of the...er...incident, Miss. I
mean, if he was the father of the baby. And Miss Kathleen would
be sixteen in 1864, she was born in 1848. Otherwise it's not a
lot of help. Next of kin is marked unknown and the death was
registered by Mr. Albert Wright of the Princess Theatre. That
must be the Actors' Benevolent people, I think. They ought to
still remember him, he only died in 1914.'

'How?' asked Phryne, her hand on the doorknob.

'Miss?' asked Dot.

'How did he die?'

'Accidental gassing, Miss,' said Dot, reluctant to think of that
mortal sin, suicide.

'On the anniversary of his sweetheart's birth,' said Phryne.
'He never married?'

'No, Miss, never married, no children, no next of kin.'

'Just actors,' said Phryne. 'Well, he could have done worse.'

'How?' asked Dot, but her eccentric employer had already
gone.

Professor Edwin Dafydd Rowlands had done the unthink-
able: he had arrived early for luncheon. Mr. Butler had coped
with this social solecism by showing him into the smaller parlour and supplying him with a strong whisky and water, a plate
of Mrs. Butler's excellent cheese straws, and a newspaper. He
was, however, prowling Phryne's bookshelves when his hostess
entered, looking cool in a dress the colour of a Greek summer
sky, patterned with the masks of comedy and tragedy. He turned
to her with a copy of Plautus' plays in his hands.

'I am so sorry,' he apologised. 'I just can't resist other people's books. What a nice collection of classics you have.'

'Thank you. Translations, of course, my Latin is minimal. But there are people I really appreciate.'

'Ovid, perhaps?' asked the professor, with a twinkle.

Phryne returned the twinkle with added interest. 'Him, and Herodotus—my favourite gossip—and some others.'

'Plautus?' he asked, putting down the volume of plays.

'Much funnier than Terence,' she said. 'Come and have some lunch?'

'Delighted.'

He offered his arm and escorted her into the dining room. It was pleasantly cool, the heavy curtains excluding a raking north wind which had decided to see how much of St. Kilda's sand it could transfer into St. Kilda's gardens, birdbaths and sandwiches. Phryne surveyed her professor. Well dressed in a light grey suit. Smells pleasantly of soap and pipe smoke. Pale rather than tanned. Robust rather than sprightly. Greek rather than Roman.

Ember floated in as Mr. Butler brought the soup. Professor Rowlands bent to offer a hand to the black cat, who sniffed it and then allowed the royal ears to be briefly caressed. Ember then wound a couple of times around Phryne's ankles as a courtesy then followed Mr. Butler out.

And the professor is a cat person rather than dog person, thought Phryne. Still that was no guarantee of virtue. Dr. Nikola, the arch villain of Guy Boothby's shockers, had a cat of which he was presumably fond—and it liked him, for it sat on his shoulder, sneering, as screaming victims were pushed into the scorpion pit. Where did he get so many scorpions? From a scorpion breeder? In London?

Phryne shook herself, allowed Mr. Butler to seat her, and reached for her large white serviette. The soup was a delicate, very hot, beef consommé, served with sippets of toast. The professor ate neatly. Another good point. Most men slurped.

'Apicius would not approve,' he commented.

'Indeed, why not?' asked Phryne.

'Roman cooking was always heavily seasoned with fish sauce, a dreadful condiment made by putting a lot of innocent fish into pickle and burying the whole concoction until it was—excuse me mentioning such a thing at this excellent table—rotten. After which it was, regrettably, dug up again. And slathered over everything. At one point in his book, he says, "Don't worry if you haven't got the right meat for the occasion. With enough fish sauce, no one will be able to tell." Must have been ghastly. Unless, of course—'

'You liked fish sauce. Australians drench everything in tomato sauce, probably on the same principle,' she said.

'And the English consider HP or Worcestershire the epitome of taste.'

'Sad, isn't it? When there is such excellent food in the world.'

'You know, when I came here from Wales, I was astounded at the richness of the Australian diet. Such milk, such eggs, such ice cream! I thought it a land of milk and honey.'

'Ah, a green salad, *salade russe*, and Mrs. Butler's special poached chicken,' exclaimed Phryne greedily. Her hashish hunger had not quite left her. She allowed Mr. Butler to carve the chicken, which he did with stately grace, and then piled her plate with goodies. The professor gave her an amused smile.

'This is a feast! I wonder, Miss Fisher, at your slenderness! If I ate like this every day I would not fit through a door, unless liberally greased. Beautiful chicken,' he added, tasting a slice of the moist delicate flesh. 'Lovely salads. Now tell me, Miss Fisher, if you would be so kind, what caused you to ask me to this Lucullan banquet?'

'I am investigating the death of Augustine Manifold, and hoped you might be able to tell me about him. I haven't got any clear picture, you know. And although I did attend his wake at two separate parties, I still haven't got him clear in my mind.'

'Oh, I see,' replied the professor, possibly a little cast down. Still, the food was wonderful and Miss Fisher kept the best in wine, as well. He sipped a little of the moselle and began, 'He was a good fellow, Augustine...'

'That's what everyone says,' exclaimed Phryne crossly. 'It doesn't mean anything, you know.'

'No, it doesn't,' he agreed.

'In any case, the port and coffee stage of lunch would be a good time for an interrogation,' she told him. 'Now is a good time for discussing neutral topics, like how do you like Australia? And are you staying? And how is the university treating you? And things of that order.'

He smiled again and ate a forkful of creamy *salade russe*, with its beetroot and potatoes and mayonnaise which had not come out of a jar. 'I like it here,' he said. 'I never want to be cold anymore, and I never am, not cold like Wales, where you look out in meagre daylight in January and know that there are three more months of misery and gloom before you see a glint of the sun. I can manage the hot days by staying inside and reading Xenophon. I have a nice house in Parkville and a housekeeper who can cook. Everything is so new here, so fresh, so unlike Europe, laden down with its horrible history of war and death. I had quite enough of war in the Middle East. The university appreciates my scholarship—such as it is—and I have enough time to get on with my book.'

'Indeed? Thank you, Mr. Butler, perhaps half a glass. What is your topic?'

'Xenophon,' he said, accepting another glass of wine. '*Anabasis*.'

'What I Did On My Holidays,' said Phryne.

'Now, now,' he chided. 'Xenophon is relevant. Modern, even. Consider our recent history. A Polish legion fought its way across Russia and Siberia during the revolution, and when they finally saw the sea, bless them, they didn't call out in Polish but in Greek—'

'*Thalassa, thalassa!*' echoed Phryne. 'Yes. True. Same went for Mawson, who had crawled the last few miles, when he realised he was at the end of a terrible journey. "*Thalassa, thalassa!*" It means "Home, home!"'

'Or, "Rescue, rescue" or, perhaps, "We are, in all probability and against all odds, actually going to live through this." Yes, indeed. How I recall—'

He broke off and Phryne's thumbs pricked.

'You recall something about the war?' she asked. 'I never went near the Middle East, I was in France, driving an ambulance.' Professor Rowlands looked at Phryne and decided, visibly, to trust her with his reminiscences.

'Yes, well, I was in Palestine with Allenby, a consultant about things classic, incomprehensible or archaeological. He was an amazing man. Looked just like an Empire hero, you know: tall, bluff, built like an ox, temper like Zeus Pater, chin you could strike matches on. The troops called him The Bull. When he was on one of his lightning inspections they'd radio ahead, "BL" which stood for "Bull Loose". But he was remarkably learned and interested in everything.'

'Archaeology?'

'Certainly. And birds. No, thank you, I really couldn't eat another crumb.' Mr. Butler cleared the table as the professor went on. 'Storks, for instance. He had all the lookouts reporting when they saw storks flying and in what direction. Big puzzle in the ornithology world, apparently, where did the storks go when they migrated into Africa. Allenby solved it. Admittedly most ornithologists don't have an army to do their observations. And whenever the troops found anything buried when they were digging—lot of digging in army life, you know—he'd send me to find out what it was. They found at least two beautiful pavements, one Roman and one Hellenic, probably Herodian. And bones, lots of bones.'

'Fascinating,' said Phryne, as Mr. Butler brought in the sorbet of tropical fruits and the ice cream.

'It really was,' said the professor. 'I didn't want to be there, but then, neither did Allenby. He'd been sent to Palestine to fail. They said he called Haig a blithering idiot.'

'No argument here,' said Phryne, who had her own opinions on that general.

'No, nor here—and his only child, a son, had just been killed in France. He was sick of soldiering and just wanted to go home to his birds. So he wanted to finish the war, and the only way he could do that was to win, and he rather efficiently did that, in a very short time. He took Damascus, cleared the Turks and Germans out of the whole of Palestine, and became Governor of Jerusalem, much against his will. He did it so well that the Jews thought he was pro-Arab and the Arabs that he was pro-Jew.'

'Nice,' approved Phryne. 'I remember seeing the newsreel film of him walking into Jerusalem.'

'Yes, well, he was far too modest a chap to ride into the Holy City. Considering the precedent, you know.'

'Quite,' agreed Phryne.

'I was working with Richard Meinertzhagen, the spy. Clever Dick, the soldiers called him. He was a very cunning chap. Been with Allenby since the Boer War. We worked out a series of codes based on Plautus. That's why I've never been able to read the plays without remembering the war, you see.'

'*Thalassa?*' prompted Phryne.

'Oh, yes, we were lost in a dust storm in Judea, in the wilderness. Terrible storm. Dust in everything, mouth, ears, eyes, bitter dust. Hot as the depths of the inferno. We knew we would die if we didn't find shelter soon. But no use sitting down and crying, so we staggered on. Up, always up, hoping to get out of the dust. Then it cleared and we saw the River Jordan, and we cried "*Thalassa, thalassa!*" as we rolled down the hill and into the water. Oh, it was lovely, so wet and cold. And fresh. If we had gone on in the way we were supposed to go on, it would have been the Dead Sea, and that would not have been refreshing. Dear me, I am prosing on. What did you want to ask me, Miss Fisher? Ah, yes. Augustine Manifold. He was rather all things to all men, you know, which is perhaps why you can't get a clear picture of him. The single most important thing about Augustine Manifold was his ambition. He was going to get on, make his big transaction, settle his mother, and lead his own life, if it killed him.'

'As it did,' Phryne put in.

'Yes, apparently.' The professor sighed. 'Well, let's see. He was one of the finest self-taught minds I have ever encountered. Learned languages like a child, by listening, though he got his Hebrew from the elder Mr. Rosenberg and his Greek and Latin from a cramming class. Of all people he reminded me of George Borrow, who got drunk on words. And his discernment was remarkable. He could look at an object from a civilisation he knew nothing about—Mesopotamia, for instance—and say ancient or modern, fake or real. It was uncanny, almost supernatural. You know there are people who claim to be able to tell things about the previous owners from touching something they owned?'

'Psychometry,' said Phryne.

'Yes, well, Augustine was like that. But he kept that skill well under his hat; he didn't want anyone to think he was a lunatic. He did it for me, once, as a favour, with a Greek pot. He described the girl who had broken it, a Circassian slave, as if she had been standing in front of him. He kept saying, "But she's got blonde hair," because he thought all Greeks were dark. Bless him. But he was a chameleon, you know. A salesman. The ladies who bought his porcelain thought him deferential. His workers liked him. He is a great loss,' sighed the professor, drinking his coffee.

'What did that strange crowd of Gerald Atkinson's want with him, then?' asked Phryne.

'Oh, they are hunting treasure,' said the professor with a wicked grin. 'And now they will never find it.'

'Oh,' said Phryne.

Dark, again, and hot, with a tearing wind, and the tall man unlocked the postbox. His hand trembled so much that he could hardly manipulate the keys. He found the envelope. His hoarded notes were gone. Inside was a folded note. Same handwriting, same paper.

Fifty in two weeks, or I tell.

He stood with the paper in his hand for so long that a passing policeman diverted from his beat to ask if the gentleman was ill. His face, in the streetlight, was as white as the paper he held in his hand.

The man gave a muttered excuse about the heat and hurried away.

The policeman watched after him. He would go down in his notebook, along with everything else that happened on this hot night, when the dogs were cranky.

Chapter Eleven

The best actors in the world, either for tragedy, comedy, history, pastoral, pastoral-comical, historical-pastoral, tragical-historical, tragicalcomical-historical-pastoral, scene indivisible, or poem unlimited.

William Shakespeare
Hamlet

Phryne put down her coffee cup with a click. 'Treasure?'

'Yes, you see, it fascinates everyone, the idea of treasure. Gold, jewels, buried in the ground, free to all finders. Except it isn't, of course.'

'What sort of treasure?' demanded Phryne, not to be deflected.

He chuckled. 'The usual sort, see previous reference, gold, jewels, coins etc.'

'You, sir, are trifling with me,' she told him.

He smoothed back his white hair and smiled at her. 'Sorry. It's just so ridiculous. Well, Miss Fisher, to break a confidence, they told me that Blackbeard the pirate—that is, Edward Teach—had buried many hoards, and they wanted one of them. And it was no use me saying that the treasure might have been buried by the said pirate, but who was to say that it was still there? I was reminded of Maes Howe in Orkney. There is a Viking inscription on the wall. "Treasure lies to the South East. Happy the man who finds it."'

'And I was the man, and I'm very happy?' guessed Phryne.

'How acute you are! *The Orkneyinga Saga* says that they did indeed find it, and had a great deal of trouble—even for Vikings, who were used to trouble, mostly causing it. They said that two of their number went mad, and it was very inconvenient carrying them and the treasure with the dead kings throwing gold cups at them all the time.'

'Haul comrade ten yards, drop comrade, go back for gold, haul gold ten yards, pick up comrade. Yes, I can see that it might have been inconvenient. I have been into Maes Howe and it is a haunted dark place. Gave me a case of the willies which I have not had since Mycenae, which it strangely resembles.'

'Yes, it's one of the puzzles,' he agreed, picking up a biscuit. 'It's a perfect Mycenaen chambered beehive tomb, and it's in the middle of nowhere—as far as the Greek world was concerned, of course.'

'Mysteries,' said Phryne.

'There are lots of them,' he agreed, and crunched his biscuit. 'Fortunately.'

'About this treasure,' she pressed. 'What had Augustine to do with it?'

'He sold them various artifacts which he said came from the hoard,' he replied. 'Pieces of eight. Gold chains. Things which might indeed have been of the right century. But nothing that pinned it down. So the next step was…'

'A treasure map? Of, as it might be, an island? With an X marks the spot on it?' demanded Phryne sarcastically.

'And palm trees and directions like "fifty paces north from the place of skulls". Yes. I fear so.'

'It must have been a hoax.'

'And yet, I never thought Augustine a humorous man, and I knew him as rigidly honest. Even as an antique dealer. He never said something was original if it wasn't. He made rather a point of showing that, for example, a painting had been retouched or a furniture leg repaired. His patrons loved him for it and bought even more from him. Would he so lightly throw that reputation away?'

'Hmm,' said Phryne. 'So they are now relying on the spirits?'

'Are they? Mediums, I suppose I ought to say media, no, that doesn't sound right either. Good Lord.' The professor drank some more coffee. 'Well, I hope it leads them to wealth, but I, for one, will not be holding my breath.'

'Indeed. Are there lots of hoards lying around?'

'No—well, it depends on to whom you are talking. There's always been a lot of interest in the Temple treasure.'

'Which temple would that be?'

'The Temple of Jerusalem, the Great Temple. Built by Herod. Destroyed by the Romans. Picture the scene. You're a priest. The Romans have captured Jerusalem. They have started out being civilised, but they are already borrowing a few talents from the treasury and you can see that if anything goes wrong, they will sack it. So what do you do?'

'You sneak the treasure out in man-loads, every night, and bury it,' said Phryne.

'Exactly. That Temple mound is honeycombed with paths and tunnels. By the time we get to the Jewish rebellion in AD 67 there would still be enough left for the Romans to pillage and, outside, enough concealed to begin life anew outside the Holy City. I suspect—I hope—that the Temple library was concealed somewhere safe, as well. Libraries are far too inflammable for my taste. The Romans made new coins with some of the Temple treasure. Judea Captiva, in chains and in mourning. They were not a subtle people, the Romans. Previous coins had plants on them. But even if the Temple treasure was distributed like that, who is to say that it is still there? There is a scroll which seems to set out where it was hidden. And, of course, spots marked X, or rather, spots marked epsilon or alpha. But it says things like "by the base of the hill shaped like a bull's horn, ten talents of silver" and the chances are that the hill shaped like a bull's horn…'

'Isn't there anymore. I see. Any more missing gold?'

'For that you will have to go to South America, and there find blood-stained gold in plenty on the sacrificial altars of their frightful gods.'

'Let's change the subject.' Phryne did not need sacrificial altars at luncheon.

Mr. Butler brought in the salted nuts and dried fruit which Miss Fisher liked with her after-dinner cognac. She picked up a nut. 'Do you know of anything significant about almonds in the classical world?'

He choked a little on the coffee, wiped his mouth, and objected, 'Really, Miss Fisher, that was an inquiry out of the blue! And I hardly know how to answer a lady at her own respectable table.'

'Assume it is not respectable,' she ordered.

'Very well. Zeus, the king of the gods, spilled his seed upon the ground, and from it grew a double-sexed monster, called Cybele/Agdistis. A hermaphrodite, you understand. The gods conferred and thought that they really couldn't have that sort of thing, so they decided the creature should be female and…er…'

'Castrated it,' said Phryne.

'Quite so. The castrated hermaphrodite, now female, was called Cybele, mother of all. From her excised portions an almond tree grew. Nana, a nymph, put one of the almonds in her bosom and conceived and bore Attis, a beautiful youth with whom Cybele fell madly in love. One version of the story says that she drove him mad, and he performed the same operation on himself, under a pine tree, and bled to death. From his blood, violets grew. Another version says he was killed by a boar, but I think that's a borrowing from Adonis, another dead boy. Like Tammuz. You know, in the Bible, the prophet heard at the temple steps the voices of "the women weeping for Tammuz"? In any case, there was a cult, much disapproved of in Rome, of Attis and Cybele, in which the priests, the Galli, castrated themselves and threw their…er…parts at a pine tree which was cut down, brought inside, wound around with woollen ribbons and decked with flowers.'

'An interesting early form of the Christmas tree,' commented Phryne, unmoved by this barbaric recital. Professor Edwin Rowlands was taken aback. He had never met anyone like Phryne before. And she looked so demure in her azure dress.

'A fascinating theory which needs thought,' he assured her. 'If you remember your Catullus you might recall poem sixty-four. No, it's sixty-three. "*Ego mulier, ego adulescens, ego ephebus, ego puer, ego gumnasi fui flos*: I to be a woman, who was once a child, once a youth, once a boy, I was the flower of the playground…" Then he says "*iam iam dolet quod egi, iam paenitet*: Now, now, I rue my act, now, now I would it were undone." And Catallus concludes with an invocation to the goddess who causes men to do such things. "*Dea, magna dea, Cybebe, dea domina Dindymi, procul a mea tuos sit furor omnis, era, domo: alios age incaitatos, alios age rabidos*. Goddess, Great Goddess Cybele, Lady of Dindymus, far from my house be all your fury Lady and Queen: drive others to a frenzy, drive others to madness."'

'A good poet,' said Phryne. 'Frenzy and madness. The same might be said of treasure hunters.'

'Indeed,' agreed Professor Rowlands, selecting an almond from the bowl of fruits and nuts, and biting it.

Dot reached the door of the Actors' Benevolent Society and settled her hat, which the wind was trying to tear from her head. She had coiled her long plait into a bun and pinned it firmly, or the wind would have had the hair off her head as well. She had cotton gloves in deference to the heat, and she knew her hands were sweating. And she hated seeing new people. But Miss Phryne had sent her, so she must think that Dot could manage this interview, and rather than disappoint Miss Phryne, Dot would prefer to be publicly whipped through St. Kilda at the tail of a cart.

The door opened to her knock and she was blown inside. When the door shut again, an aged but beautifully groomed gentleman was offering her a chair.

'And perhaps a glass of cold water, or a cup of tea?' he added.

'Thank you!' gasped Dot. The wind had taken all the breath out of her.

'Shocking weather, this,' commented the aged gentleman, allowing his guest time to settle her garments and regain her composure. He poured cold water from a thermos, and lit the flame under a spirit stove. His movements were very slow and painful.

Dot drank the cool water and smiled at her preserver. He was dapper to a degree. His shirt front was blinding, his suit old but meticulously pressed, his white hair glossy with care and even his shoes were shining. He sat down at the desk. Dot was struck, suddenly, by a pang to the heart. She knew this was Albert Wright. She had seen him before, when Dot's mother used to save up to go to the theatre every six months. She had last seen him young and now he was old…

'I saw you on stage,' she told him. 'You played the gentleman in all those comedies. You sang and danced. When I was a girl—' she broke off and blushed. 'I had ever such a crush on you, Mr. Wright.'

'My dear girl,' he said, smiling and taking her hand. 'That's the nicest thing anyone has said to me for a week. Ah, yes, I could dance then! And sing! They were such fun, those comedies. Silly, innocent things. I would prance on and say, "Anyone for tennis?" and the audience used to applaud. Great days, great days.'

'You don't act anymore?' asked Dot, forgetting her reserve and her anxiety about talking to new people.

He grimaced. Then he rose, silenced the kettle and made the tea. He sugared his liberally and explained.

'The pins, dear. I got arthritis and that was the end of my dancing days. But I toiled on, you know, never say die. Had singing jobs, some straight parts, second extra gentleman in Shakespeare. But Shakespeare's terrible, because unless you're King you never get to sit down. Didn't really suit me and I wasn't very good at it, to tell you the truth. Then my uncle died and left me a modest competence and I secured this position. No one needs benevolence like actors do. I was one of the lucky ones. Usually if we get sick they might as well shoot us, like broken-down horses.'

'That's a terrible thing to say,' said Dot.

'True, O King,' he said. 'But never mind. *Toujours l'audace*, as the dear Emperor said. Now, what can I do for you? You're not in the profession, dear. How can I help you?'

'Oh!' Dot had remembered her orders. She took an envelope from her purse and gave it to Mr. Wright. He slit it open and his eyebrows rose. It was a rather large cheque signed *Phryne Fisher*.

'Munificent!' he said. 'We can get old Charles out of the doss house and into a clean apartment with a paid companion. He was wonderful in his time, you know. His Othello sent shivers up my spine. Now he's doing Lear, of course, in real life. You're not Miss Fisher, dear,' he said curiously. 'I mean, I beg your pardon, but I've seen her at the theatre quite often. Small woman, carriage like an empress, magnificent clothes, attended mostly by a Chinese chap dressed by Savile Row.'

'No, I'm Dorothy Williams, her confidential companion.'

'That,' said Mr. Wright, 'must be an interesting profession.'

'Oh, it is,' Dot assured him. 'She wants to know about a man you buried in Melbourne General Cemetery in 1914.'

'Then we will finish our tea and consult the books,' he told her. 'My dear Miss Williams! What a wonderful day,' he added, tucking the cheque into his wallet and patting it close to his heart. 'And it seemed so unpromising when I got up and realised that it was going to be fearfully hot again. I sometimes feel it would be soothing to be a savage,' he added. 'And then all one would have to wear would be a lap-lap and a few pieces of shell. Still, it wouldn't do,' he said, sipping his tea. 'It wouldn't do for Melbourne at all.'

Dot peeled off her wet gloves and agreed.

An hour later Mr. Wright found the entry he was seeking.

'Really, the books are in a shocking mess. We've only had someone in charge all the time since '23. Before that it was whoever was resting and had the time, and the treasurer used to write his bank statement in eyebrow pencil on the back of a playbill. True!' he said in reply to Dot's shocked exclamation. 'See, here's one of them—and it's the one we want.'

Dot scanned the playbill. In suspiciously dark and greasy pencil—perhaps it really was eyebrow pencil—someone had written *service and interment of poor Pat O'Rourke, wake and headstone poor fellow no harm in him shame to treat a sweet swan so...* There followed a series of calculations, much crossed out, and a final *twelve pounds, eight shillings and tenpence halfpenny, which leaves eighty-three pounds ninepence in the fund.* Mr. Wright raised an eyebrow. Now that she was close to him, Dot was aware of his scent of eau de cologne and powder. Did this delightful man use theatrical makeup even though he had retired from the stage?

'Sorry about the accounts, they kept a running record, but half the time the treasurer was doing his work in the wings and they did get a little confused. I remember him. Patrick O'Rourke. Never really succeeded, poor chap, though everyone said he was a sweet boy. Old man, when I met him, of course. Living in a wretched room in Fitzroy. No one could quite understand how he came to be gassed. Didn't have any family here. Irish, you know. Though perhaps he had some distant relatives, several people came to the funeral which we didn't know. Otherwise it was just the theatre chums. We were the only family he had ever known.'

Dot sensed a clue, jumping up and down and yelling 'here I am!' into her ear.

'Mr. Wright, this could be very important. I would like you to cast your mind back and tell me everything you can recall about the other people at the funeral.'

'Oh, my dear, that'll be a stretch of the old memory! Not as young as I was.'

Dot knew that she was expected to say something flirtatious but she really didn't know how, so she said, 'Nonsense! You're as young as you ever were. When I saw you dancing on stage, doing "Top Hat and Tails" with Margaret Arnold.'

'Oh, yes, that was our star number,' he said dreamily, beginning to hum the tune. 'Come to think of it, Maggie was at that funeral. It was a freezing day and she was wearing her furs—the price of virtue, I hasten to add; she had married that newspaper magnate by then. I found a new partner, Jessie, darling girl she was, died young. Like too many of us. Cold day, I had my astrakhan coat. Maggie had her furs. Johnnie was there, yes, and old Freddie, weeping into his hankie. Gorgeous Gwen Powell with that reprobate, Hayward Rendell. Most of them were old—I thought them old. Then. Oh, such a long time ago.'

'Let me go and get us a nice cool drink,' Dot offered, having seen the restorative effects of alcohol on Phryne's clients.

'I'll send the boy down to the theatre bar,' he told her, 'if you've got the wherewithal.'

'Oh, certainly,' said Dot, who had an emergency fund of Miss Phryne's money for contingencies like sudden thirst, immediate taxis, witness expenses or bribes. She turned her back to extract the little folder from her undergarment. Mr. Wright smiled at her. He really was a charming old man.

He took the note, called 'James!' down the stairs, and after a short interval a pale, panting boy appeared. Too much greasepaint and not enough sleep, Dot diagnosed.

James booked an order from Mr. Wright and took off again. He clattered down and, in due course, plodded up. On one hand, like a waiter, he held a tray with several glasses, an ice bucket, a bottle of tonic and a bottle of gin. James offered Dot the change and she nodded at him to keep it. He blushed with pleasure and for a moment looked quite healthy. James bowed elaborately, putting back the skirts of his imaginary brocaded coat, flourishing an imaginary feathered hat. Then he was gone, in case Dot changed her mind.

'Going to be good, that boy,' commented Mr. Wright, loading ice into both glasses and pouring a solid dose of gin into each one, topping it up with tonic.

'Mud in your eye!' he said cordially, then leaned back, sipping, closing his eyes. Dot got out her notebook and began to make a list of names as he spoke them.

'Maggie, of course, and me, then old Charlie and Freddie, that was Charlie Latham, fine dancer in his time. The Russian—Serge was his name? Came out here with the Ballets Russe and never went home to the steppes. He was a dear friend of the deceased, but Paddy had crept away from all of his old friends. Serge never even knew where he was living, come the last act. None of them did. Thought he'd gone back to Ireland, perhaps. Serge always said that Paddy had a secret sorrow. Only one who knew where he was was Archie, now Archie ought to be able to tell you who was at that funeral, good memory, old Archie, and he used to take our little donation over to Paddy every Thursday. Archibald Lawrence. You might have seen him on stage, Miss Williams. There was a woman in a dark suit, very antique, long skirt, big hat. Hard to see her face. And two men; both much of a muchness, can't recall anything about them, sorry, except they were wearing ordinary clothes and they slipped away from the church, didn't even follow the coffin to the grave, though some people are just too sensitive to do that—poor Serge had to be carried away by Freddie when he wanted to fling himself in, you know how emotional those Russians are...Tell you what,' he said, sitting up and opening his eyes suddenly. 'I believe that Archie is at home, he hates the heat. Let's call him on the telephone and invite him to have a drink with us.'

'Yes, let's,' said Dot, who had been hoping for a chance of disposing of her drink. She never drank gin and especially not in the morning. There was no suitable receptacle to pour it into and anyway she hated wasting things, and this was expensive gin.

Fortunately Mr. Wright excused himself to go and use the box office phone and Dot noticed that the silent boy James had reappeared. He was looking hungrily at the tray. She beckoned and offered him her glass. He smiled, drained the glass, refilled it with tonic and returned it, all without a word. Then he gave her his court bow again, and vanished. He would do well on the stage, Dot thought, as long as he didn't have a speaking part.

'That boy been here?' asked Mr. Wright as he struggled up the stairs again. 'He's a mumchance brat.'

'Can't he talk?' asked Dot.

'Oh, yes, nice little voice, but he's on tonight and he's saving it. Have to conduct all my conversations with him in dumb show. Old Archie's delighted with the invitation and should be here soon. I think that calls for another round, don't you?'

'I'm still drinking this one,' said Dot truthfully.

'Now, how can I amuse you in the interim, Miss Williams?' asked Mr. Wright. 'We have some scripts, and a rare collection of playbills and scrapbooks.'

'Tell me about when you were on stage,' invited Dot. Nothing could have pleased Mr. Wright more. He sipped his gin and began to reminisce.

Dot soon got lost in the Freddies and Charlies and Jimmies and Roses and Julias, but she was fascinated. The theatre flowed over her like a highly flavoured river of pink champagne, fizzing with gossip and spiked with refreshing malice like the Angostura bitters in a cocktail. When she heard footsteps on the stairs, Mr. Wright was describing a phenomenon called 'corpsing'.

'You see, after a while, in a long run, you start to sleepwalk through the part. I remember when we were doing one of those Cheltenham tragedies, all sound and fury, you know, I started making a shopping list, and when I got to the end of it, reminding myself that we were out of soda water, I found that I had denounced my wife, disinherited my son, and turned my daughter out of the house with her child of shame. I came to myself in front of seven hundred people in the full glare of the footlights without the faintest idea of what I was going to do next. A terrible feeling.'

'What did you do?' gasped Dot. He waved an elegant hand.

'Oh, I coughed myself over to prompt and got the line. No one took those melodramas seriously, you know.'

'Luckily for you,' commented a spare man from the doorway. 'Has young James been struck dumb? He wouldn't announce me.'

'Saving his voice,' explained Mr. Wright. 'He's Ariel tonight.'

'Oh, ah,' said the spare man. He held out a hand to Dot. 'I'm Archibald Lawrence, as this oaf does not seem to be willing to introduce me.'

'Dorothy Williams,' said Dot, flustered by being so abruptly dragged out of her theatrical river. The hand was smooth and cool.

'Pleased to meet you,' said Mr. Lawrence, dropping into a chair and reaching for the gin. 'Filthy weather, isn't it? Your employer has handed over a cheque of special generosity, bless her, so we are at your service. About time someone took notice of poor old Paddy. I always felt he had a hidden sorrow.' His drink vanished almost instantly, as though he had a secret siphon.

'Hidden bottle, more like,' said Mr. Wright. 'Another half, Archie?'

'Don't mind if I do,' said Archibald Lawrence.

Dot looked at the two gentlemen. One thin, one comfortably stout. Mr. Lawrence was shabby but clean, Mr. Wright more prosperous. Mr. Wright had abundant silver hair and Mr. Lawrence almost none. But they were similar. Both had the sonorous diction of those who had to be heard at the back of the stalls. And both had the excellent skin, hardly lined at all, of those who never saw the sun and who wore greasepaint every night of their lives, plus matinees on Wednesdays and Saturdays.

'We're trying to remember who were the strangers at old Paddy's funeral,' prompted Mr. Wright.

'Ah, yes, well I recall the day, it was so cold I had two coats on. And, yes, Albie, you are correct, for a change. Two men, coat collars turned up, hats pulled down. And a woman in a black cloth coat with a draggled rabbit fur around her shoulders. It had been rained on, you know that look. Shabby. Didn't speak to any of us.'

'Do you think they were all together?' asked Dot.

'Interesting. I can see them clearly, you know. Good memory and it hasn't departed like other things. I would have thought the men were together and the woman alone. What do you think, Albie?'

'Yes,' said Mr. Wright slowly. 'I suppose so. I didn't pay much attention to them.'

'Well, I did,' said Mr. Lawrence with some asperity. 'Actors' Benevolent couldn't find any relatives and we had to lash out for the whole funeral. I thought I might sting them for a contribution if he was their connection, but they slipped away so quickly that I never got to put the arm on them. But I had a brief rummage through my papers and I found the book for that funeral. We ought to be able to eliminate all the theatre names, and the ones that are left will be the strangers.'

'Assuming that they signed in,' said Mr. Wright. 'Well, furnish it forth, dear fellow, and let's have a squiz.'

Mr. Lawrence produced a folder, nicely edged in black, with the details of the funeral on the first page and a scribble of signatures on the second, facing page. Mr. Wright took a pencil, sharpened it with a slow deliberation which made Mr. Lawrence quiver with impatience, and they began to tick off the known attendees.

'That's Serge, he was so Russian, poor fellow. And there's me, and you, little cramped letters.'

'Better than that scrawl of yours,' snorted Mr. Lawrence.

'Made signing autographs a lengthy business,' preened Mr. Wright. 'But you didn't have that trouble, of course. Here's Althea, and here's Thomasina, and McKenna Jordan—God, she was gorgeous; those long, long legs, dark eyes and that famous *poitrine*—excuse me, Miss Williams.'

Dot nodded, unoffended. She knew what a *poitrine* was. Bosom would have done as a translation, and why shouldn't an actress have a famous bosom? Mr. Lawrence was hastening into speech.

'Even so, she was a fine actress when she was older. I saw her do a Gertrude that would blow your hat off. Absolutely exuded "it". To Johnson's Hamlet—of course, they were close, you know.'

'Really?' asked Mr. Wright. 'I mean, I heard rumours…'

'Gentlemen,' reproved Dot.

'Ah, yes, of course. Well, there's McKenna and right next to her—you see?—old Tommy himself. Then there's…'

They went on. It had been a well-attended funeral. Dot's attention wandered to the walls, plastered with posters for benefit nights. So much work, just to amuse the world! A world that ate toffee and drank ginger pop and probably dropped paper bags in the stalls…

'Aha!' said Mr. Wright. 'Here they are. Everyone else accounted for, you agree, Archie?'

'I agree,' said Archie, and poured himself another drink, adding lumps of ice.

'They are rather hard to read, so we'll give you this document to show your Miss Fisher, if we can have it back for the archives, please?'

'Of course,' Dot agreed.

'The names seem to be T. Johnson, S. Barton, and this might be Gaston, or Geston, maybe? Blasted pen has spluttered.'

'Thank you,' said Dot. 'That's wonderful. Miss Fisher will be very grateful.'

'She has already expressed her gratitude very handsomely,' said Mr. Wright. 'Anything else we can do for you and her?' His gesture offered her the whole theatre and everything in it.

'What do you recall about Mr. O'Rourke? What was he like?'

'They say he was a fey creature when he was young,' said Mr. Lawrence. 'I never knew him then. By the time I saw him he was old and doing bit parts in Shakespeare. Beautiful voice. Remnants of a career, of course. They say he did a very good Hamlet in his time. But the drink got him. Occupational hazard in our line of work, eh, Albie?'

Mr. Wright looked solemnly over the rim of his glass. 'Certainly. It's only when we've safely retired that we can tope a bit. Or a lot, of course. Bottoms up, dear boy! I've still got the figures to do.'

'Leave them until tomorrow,' suggested Mr. Lawrence.

'I've got a couple of fine cigars here to go with the drinkies. Haven't chatted with you for an age, Albie.'

'Oh, very well,' agreed Mr. Wright readily. 'Wretched weather destroys my arithmetic, anyway.'

'Talk about fading memory,' said Mr. Lawrence. 'No one to claim them, see, so we kept them. If your Miss Fisher is investigating, these might be helpful.'

Dot took charge of a small box. Then she took her leave of the two actors, and heard, as she went down the stairs, the rollers of theatrical gossip surging afresh above her.

She had to speak to herself sternly. She really, really wanted to go back and listen.

◇◇◇

Simon parked the motorbike and scratched his head. Would she be waiting? Had she got his message? He had been refused at the shop by that dreadful old woman. She had turned into steel since Augustine died. Despite the heat, he shivered. He didn't want to ask the terrible woman who kept the Atkinson house. Last time she had showed him the ulcer on her leg.

He saw her coming down the street. She ran forward into his arms.

Chapter Twelve

I am all the daughters of my father's house,
And all the brothers too.

William Shakespeare
Twelfth Night

Miss Fisher was still toying with the remains of her mixed fruit and nuts and musing on her recently departed luncheon guest when Dot came back from the city, flushed with triumph, bearing spoils of war, and more than a trifle dishevelled.

'It's blowing a gale out there!' she exclaimed. 'I'll just run upstairs and take off my hat, Miss Phryne. How did you manage with the professor?'

'I fear that I have been managed rather expertly,' Phryne replied, eating another muscat. 'Don't run, Dot. Walk slowly. How about lunch?'

'Oh, I forgot,' said Dot. 'I'll ask Mrs. B for a sandwich or something. I've had such a morning. Back soon.'

She deposited the folder and the little box on the table. Phryne did not touch them. They were Dot's revelation.

Instead she walked into the smaller parlour, found her encyclopaedia and looked up Edward Teach, known as Black-beard. Why that mark of significance? she wondered. Black beards must have been fairly common at the time. Which was circa 1680.

Born in Bristol. His ship was called *Queen Anne's Revenge* and he ruined lives and stole fortunes around the Caribbean. Privateer during the War of the Spanish Succession, which Phryne had never understood. He didn't seem to have actually killed anyone, Phryne noticed as she read on. Just held up their ships and looted them down to the smallest coin, earring and gold tooth. Blackbeard because he filled his beard with pistol wadding and lit it when aroused. He lived on Nassau, where the Governor was in his pay. When offended, he had once blockaded Charleston. Finally he retired full of bad works to Ocracoke Inlet to put his sea boots up and there he was attacked by men of the Royal Navy under Lieutenant Maynard, who sneaked in and ambushed him. '*He drank damnation to me and my men, calling them cowardly puppies, saying he would neither give nor take quarter.*' He was thereafter shot four times, stabbed more than twenty times and died in a sword fight with Lieutenant Maynard, who eventually managed to cut off his head. End of career of notorious pirate. Supposed, on not very good evidence, to have left buried hoards all over the Caribbean.

There was a sentence from a book which she could not quite find, itching at her memory. She relaxed and allowed her mind to drift. Then she had it. '*Don't know Captain Flint? You've heard of Blackbeard? Blackbeard was a child to Flint.*' *Treasure Island*, of course. Robert Louis Stevenson.

Phryne didn't like pirates. She had never considered them romantic. One of them had removed Lin Chung's ear, and had come damn close to killing him. And Phryne, of course. Were ancient pirates more romantic than modern ones? Probably not. Parading Teach's head—complete with beard—around to prove that he was dead was just a touch barbaric, though it was instantly convincing.

Could anyone really believe in pirate treasure in this year of grace 1929? Of course, with enough kif and absinthe, one could believe anything; fairies, pelmanism, politicians. Now what had those wasters and bounders said about their spirit guides? 'Zacarias', yes, well, one of Blackbeard's crew was called Israel

Hands. And 'look to the West', which didn't mean anything. From the right point of view, everything was to the west. And what did one make of the otherwise honest Augustine Manifold carrying out such a thumping great hoax? As soon as it was exploded there would go his commercial reputation, even if the police didn't have enough evidence to charge him with fraud.

Phryne shook her head. She could, regrettably, easily see Gerald Atkinson fitting out a boat of some kind—probably a lugger—and heading off to the Caribbean to search for pirate treasure. Probably dragging his protesting clique with him. As long as someone else did the sailing, the provisioning, the navigating and the cooking. What she couldn't see was Gerald Atkinson actually finding any treasure.

She shelved the problem as Dot came back, freshly rinsed and wearing a loose beige cotton shift and sandals. Outside, the north wind clawed at the shutters.

'I had such a lovely talk with Mr. Wright and Mr. Lawrence,' said Dot, accepting a glass of iced orange crush. 'Ooh, how nice! It's so hot outside. I spent a pound out of special expenses on gin and tonic for them,' she told Phryne.

'A pound well spent,' Phryne replied. Mrs. Butler refilled her own glass of orange drink, made by juicing a lot of oranges and diluting the juice with sugar syrup and soda water. The lemon version was also very good. 'Make sure I top it up. One must always have an emergency fund. Pass me my purse and I will do so now, before I forget and you are too polite to remind me. Well, what did they say, these superannuated actors?'

'Lots of things, but these are the important points. Patrick O'Rourke was never very successful, though he played Hamlet when young.'

'As did our Patrick,' said Phryne.

'He died in poverty and misery and no one could quite understand how he gassed himself,' said Dot, still skirting the suicide taboo. 'But he was buried properly and there were three strangers at his funeral. Here are their names,' she said, producing the document with all the pride of Ember producing a dead rat.

'The gentlemen sorted through all the names and these are the only three that they did not know. The others were all actors.'

'Good, Dot, good!'

'I can't read them very well but you might do better in a good light. Looks like T. Johnson, S. Barton and Geston or Gaston. Two men, they had the impression that they might have been together, and a woman in a shabby black cloth coat—on a freezing cold day.'

'I'll examine it with the magnifying glass later. And what is in this box?'

'Patrick O'Rourke's possessions, Miss. They didn't have anyone to give them to, so they kept them. They're very honest, in a way. Very innocent, too, in their way,' observed Dot.

Phryne gave her an approving smile. 'You are very wise, Miss Williams. Shall we open the box?'

'Oh, yes,' said Dot, and fetched the scissors.

The box had been sealed with a couple of sealing-wax wafers and a piece of sticking plaster. As she opened it Dot could smell alcohol and scent; eau de cologne and greasepaint, of which Mr. Wright had been redolent. In it was a wodge of papers, a small package, and a gold watch. Phryne examined the watch, pulling over a light.

'Cheap, gold foil, not working,' she said, giving it a delicate wind and hearing the works ratchet and fall silent. 'Could possibly be fixed, I suppose. Give me that butter knife, Dot, and I'll open the back.'

Dot, who had been unfolding very delicate old paper, obliged and Phryne gave the secret cleft in the pocket watch a light twist. The back popped open.

'Ah,' said Phryne. 'What do you have there, Dot?'

'Letters,' said Dot. 'From a girl called Kathleen who is expecting a baby. From Ballarat.'

'I see,' said Phryne. 'And here I have a miniature of the very same Kathleen.'

'It's her, isn't it?' asked Dot, looking at the colours, still fresh after all this time, protected by the closed watch case.

'It's her,' said Phryne. She levered the picture out and on the back was written *Mo Cridhe*.

'My heart,' said Dot. 'It means "my heart" in Scotch, which I suppose is also Irish.'

'We've got the right Patrick O'Rourke, then. What's the playbill?'

'He was playing Hamlet in Ballarat. At the Theatre Royal. Lord, what were the dates?'

Phryne fetched her notebook.

'He was playing Hamlet on the dates that she was writing to him from that place,' said Dot. 'And he never came for her.'

'There might have been a lot of reasons for that,' said Phryne. 'He might have felt that she was better off with her family than following an impoverished actor around the traps, hungry, unsettled, sleeping in lodgings.'

'He might have been wrong,' said Dot fiercely. 'He broke her heart.'

'So he did,' said Phryne. 'And his own as well. Why else should he kill himself on the anniversary of her birth? No use being cross with the dead, Dot. What's in the other little packet?'

Dot opened it with difficulty. It had been sealed and sealed again, as though it was very precious.

'It's a guinea,' she said, holding it up to the light. 'A golden guinea. And he was so poor, and never spent it!'

'There's writing on the paper,' Phryne pointed out.

'Can't read it,' said Dot. 'It's in Irish, as well. "*Tá sí milse ná seo rud eile.*" Whatever that means.'

'Tomorrow,' said Phryne, 'you shall go and find me an Irish priest who can read it for us.'

'All right,' said Dot. 'Father Kelly at St. Mary's will know. And I'll light a candle for his betrayed girl when I'm there.' She thought a moment. 'And for him, as well,' she added reluctantly.

'Stout fellow,' approved Phryne.

Mr. Butler shimmered into sight, advising Miss Dot that her lunch was laid out in the breakfast room and that Detective

Inspector Robinson had called and asked for an interview with Miss Fisher.

'Good,' said Phryne. 'Have some lunch and then some rest, Dot dear, this weather would fell an elephant. You've done very well,' she added, as Dot went out to nibble her chicken sandwiches with banana ice cream to follow and Phryne welcomed her old friend into the parlour, where he fell into a chair with a groan. His unremarkable face was flushed red and he appeared to be steaming.

'Mr. Butler will help you off with your jacket,' she said sympathetically. 'Shirt sleeves are good enough for me, Jack dear. Then you will drink a pint of cool soda water and then a large amount of beer. You have to replace the water first or you get drunk intolerably fast, and now that I am here in summer I have begun to understand this Australian insistence on cold beer. Only ice cold beer could enable anyone to survive in this intolerable climate.'

Mr. Butler had discorporated in his inimitable way and now reappeared to supply the soda water, which Jack Robinson engulfed without blinking, then a cold beer from a bottle reposing in a large metal ice bucket on which clouds of condensation were forming. Jack Robinson drank the beer in one long, satisfying draught, excused himself to the downstairs washroom, and came back much paler and wetter, having apparently put his head under the tap.

'She's a killer outside,' he said, taking his second glass more slowly.

'So Dot says.' Phryne was on her third glass of orange crush. The heat was leaching fluid out of her body, she felt, as though hungry for her fleshly moisture to alleviate the extreme dryness of the air.

'That really hit the spot,' said Jack Robinson. 'Didn't know about drinking soda water first, though. That's a bonzer notion. Seen plenty of blokes down a couple of cold beers when they were hot and suddenly they're roaring. They say it'll be cooler tomorrow, though. This north wind comes straight off the desert. When it changes it'll take the edge off the heat.'

'That will be nice,' said Phryne. 'How about some bread and cheese and pickles? Bet you haven't eaten lunch.'

'That'd be good,' said Jack Robinson. 'Anything that's kicking round the kitchen, Mr. Butler,' he said to that stalwart figure. 'Don't want to give any trouble.'

After a pause for a shudder in reaction to the idea that any guest in Miss Fisher's house would be served something which happened to be lying around even so well conducted a kitchen as Mrs. Butler's, he vanished again. He was back in moments with a tray on which reposed freshly baked bread, the cheddar cheese which Mr. Robinson liked and the pickled onions which he favoured.

Phryne walked away to the window to allow him to dine in peace, and listened to the wind claw dust across the glass, a very unsettling sound. The trees were being lashed and whining under punishment like schoolboys under the birch. The house was creaking plaintively. Phryne suddenly wanted to be out of Australia altogether, on a boat going somewhere Aegean, with fresh fish for breakfast and azure skies above.

But then, every country had its mistral, its meltemi, its own terrible wind. And in England she would be frozen to the bone, wearing three layers of clothing plus a coat, there would be only five hours' daylight and that murky and grey, and the entire Fisher family would be trying to get close to the ancestral log fires, which baked the shins and left the back exposed to the chill of the ancestral draughts.

Could be worse, thought Phryne. She considered Jack Robinson, her favourite policeman. He was very hard to recall when he wasn't there. His hair was mid brown, as were his eyes, and his complexion was—ordinary. As were his clothes and his figure, which would be described as 'medium build'. His anonymity had stood him in good stead when arresting criminals and had not been so extreme as to deny him promotion. While he did not approve of Miss Fisher's investigations, he approved of Miss Fisher, and had frequently assisted her in various unofficial ways. And she doted on the wholehearted way he ate pickled onions.

When the tray was devoid of any crumb, Mr. Butler bore it away. Mrs. Butler would be pleased. She loved enthusiastic eaters, and since the advent of the American Refrigerating Machine, she had been able to do a lot of the cooking in the cool morning and reheat it for dinners, which made her less hot and cross. She had even made a supply of sandwiches and put them into the machine, which meant that late lunchers got cold food, which pleased them. And all Mrs. Butler had to do was put them on plates, which pleased her.

'Well,' commented Jack Robinson, relaxing and relishing his third glass of cold beer. 'Augustine Manifold.'

'Yes,' said Phryne.

'I gave those samples the old Scotch doctor supplied to the Government Analyst and he agrees with her. Not a word of apology, mind, for missing it in the first autopsy. Not testing the water in the lungs, I mean. Not a word about that. Just agrees that the water has no salt in it and has got soap in it, so tends to suggest that the deceased might have been drowned in a bathtub.'

'Tends to suggest, eh?'

'I know. But that's the best we're going to get out of that old grampus. They shoulda sacked him years ago and replaced him with his boy—he's a sharp one.'

Phryne refrained from mentioning that she had met the young man in question and that his burning desire was to be an engineer.

'So, what have you been doing, Jack dear?'

'Reported to the Powers That Be that we had a homicide, had it registered and a file opened. It's now a homicide case. That was the hard part. Took me the best part of a day.' Jack sipped a little more beer. 'Then got a list of suspects and I'll be working my way through them. First, the mother. Not likely.'

'I agree. She was devastated by his loss. And she asked me to look into his death, you know; you had it written up as a suicide.'

'Could be a double bluff. Some murderers are real deep.'

They both thought about Mrs. Manifold. Harsh, yes, strong-minded, savagely reserved. But murderous, no.

'She adored Augustine,' Phryne told Jack. 'Scrub her off your list.'

'For the time being, all right. Girl who works in the shop. Sophie Westwood. Not strong enough. Takes a lot of heft to force someone's head underwater. Even a mostly unconscious person will struggle if they can't breathe. Besides, she was doing good in the shop, the boss was pleased with her, and now she might be out of a job, and things are pretty crook for finding another. She's not pretty or taking. Not likely to get anything but factory work, and that ain't no fun. Vague sign of a boyfriend, don't know anything more. I think we scrub her, as well.'

'Agreed,' said Phryne.

'Reach me my notebook? It's in my inside pocket.' Phryne fetched it from the policeman's suit coat, which Mr. Butler had hung neatly over a chair. He riffled through the pages. 'Yair. Then there's the odd job carpenter, now he's a possibility. Cedric Yates. Strong enough, even though he's only got one leg. He could hold the deceased down until he drowned. I got his history. Discharged honourably from the army with a missing limb. Was sent to Alexandria and then home. Soldiers' rehab got him onto carpentry and in the end gave him a carpenter's ticket. His teacher said he was a natural with wood. Didn't talk much but got on all right with the other blokes. Nothing on his military record. Got a decoration for rescuing a pilot in Palestine. But he's cousin to your Cecil Yates, and they're all red-raggers, wobblies. Workers of the world unite. You know the sort of thing.'

'Really, Jack, you don't think that poor Augustine was the victim of a revolutionary outrage?'

Jack Robinson drank deeply of a refreshed glass and had the grace to hiccup. 'Nah, not really. Main reason why I don't think it was, say, Yates and Westwood working together, is that there's no bathroom in Manifold's house. A wash-place and a WC in the garden, but that's all. There's a tin bath but it has to be filled from the copper, which is only lighted on Mondays for the household washing. Augustine most likely died on a Saturday or a Sunday, he hadn't been that long in the sea. If anyone lit the copper on a day when they weren't washing, then Mrs. Manifold would know the reason why. She keeps a very tight hand on the expenses. Pinch a penny till it squeaked. And if anyone had lit the copper and drawn a bath, despite the old chook, the whole household would have known about it, and someone would have told me.'

'Indeed,' murmured Phryne.

'So then we come to his friends. That's why I was at the funeral, to get a squiz at them.'

'And you got more than you bargained for,' guessed Phryne.

'That woman in heathen dress—red—at a funeral! That slinky woman in black straight out of Sapper! What a collection! Young blokes in clothes which must have cost the earth and all completely—'

'Outrageous?' hazarded Phryne.

'Yair. You could say that. The sane ones were Rachel Phillips, married, two children, nothing known. Her dad, Mr. Rosenberg, runs a stamp and coin shop in the city, respectable old coot, pillar of the local synagogue, very devout. Wears one of them skullcaps. Mrs. Phillips works for him, believed to be real good at stamps. The old Mr. Rosenberg thinks the world of her. Disinherited his son, who was a waster, and is leaving the shop to Rachel.'

'His son is a waster?'

'He's a drunk. You don't see that much amongst the Jews. Named Zachary, calls himself Simon. Spends his time sponging off his younger sister. Does a little dealing of this and that, we've had him on the list for years. Sooner or later he'll sell something he really has no title to and we'll get him. So far he's on the edge.'

'Greyish, but not black.'

'Yair. Greyish. But getting darker. Mrs. Phillips had no motive to murder Augustine. She didn't even know him real well, as far as we've been able to find out.'

'She told me she went to the funeral because her father didn't feel comfortable entering a Christian church.'

'Yair, well, that'd be right. Professor Rowlands works up at the university. Lives in a nice house with a housekeeper to look after him. Bit of an eye for the ladies but nothing permanent so far. Gossip says he's much run after but so far won't let himself be caught.'

'That would be right. A twinkle in the eye and a flirtatious manner which never goes too far. A charming man. I had him to lunch today.'

The beer was beginning to catch up with Robinson. His next glass was filled with ice cold soda water by the observant Mr. Butler. Robinson didn't seem to notice the substitution.

'Did yer?' he asked Phryne. 'And?'

'I was much amused but I am not sure that he told me the whole story about Augustine. I suspect he knows more. But he told me what the frightful Atkinson clique wanted with Augustine.'

Phryne explained the treasure of Edward Teach and the fact that Augustine seemed to have found part, at least, of the hoard. And was about to sell them a treasure map.

Detective Inspector Robinson sprayed soda water all over his chair. 'Treasure map? I never heard such stuff.'

'Yes, me too, but those Atkinsons are strange. I went on to their version of a wake after the funeral and I must say, Jack, I have been in some awful company before—I have dined with torturers and Apaches and strict Plymouth Brethren and politicians—but I never met such vile company as those people. Each in his or her own way, they were frightful.'

'Do tell!' urged Robinson.

Phryne ordered her thoughts, opting for a glass of the soda water in which lumps of ice were floating. The heat was affecting her mind, taking the edge off her recall. She concentrated on that disgusting afternoon, recalling the scent of incense and hashish.

'When I came in, they were all dancing,' she began. 'Luke Adler and Valentine Turner were minding the door and the gramophone, respectively.'

'Turner has a police record for assault,' said Robinson. 'As does Adler. Street fights.'

'Near certain public toilets, perhaps?' asked Phryne, wrinkling her nose.

'As it happens…' Robinson spread his hands. 'No street offences, though.'

'I see. Then there was that unbalanced pair, James Barton and his sister Priscilla. She's an hysteric who clings to the slinky lady, Blanche White, in whose name I, frankly, do not believe.'

'Still trying to find out about her,' Robinson admitted. 'The Bartons are clean. Both of them get an income from a trust fund set up by their uncle, who was in wholesale chilled lamb.

'Export, you know. James Barton went to university but failed his first set of law exams and has drifted ever since. She's been hospitalised for an attempted suicide by drug overdose.'

'Then there was Stephanie Reynolds in her red sari. She is a fan of the hidden masters and has a spirit guide called Charging Elk. I suspect she is sincere in an entirely bird-witted way. She seems to have been conducting seances for them, seeking treasure. Now don't choke, Jack dear, the opinions of the Atkinsons are not those of the management. She has called up two spirits from the vasty deep, one called Selima and one called Zacarias. They have told her that Augustine was not to be trusted.'

'Hmm,' said Robinson.

'Veronica Collins didn't make a lot of impression on me, except that I might have told her that one with so Restoration a figure should not wear clothes designed for the thin.'

'Nothing known,' said Robinson. 'Lives with her mum in a small house. The Widow Collins takes in lodgers.'

'She's sinning above her station, then. And then there is Gerald himself, a poisonous little numero with, I suspect, a line in drug dealing.'

'Is on the watch list,' agreed Robinson. 'He received a parcel from South America with a lot of cocaine in it, but those morons in customs grabbed him before he could open it. The cocaine was hidden in some real ugly terracotta figures, so he could say—possibly even with truth—that he didn't know the drug was there. And wasn't charged. He buys a lot of stramonthium and marijuana cigarettes for—he says— asthma. Got his money from Daddy, who died last year, just when son Gerald was on his arse bones.'

'Suspicious death?'

'Car accident. Brakes failed. Ran straight into a snow gum. We looked at the car, but no real evidence of tampering. Driver was drunk, anyway, as apparently he had been every day except Sundays for his whole adult life. Gerald was all right at school and started an antique shop, but it failed because he kept taking things home and not selling them. Now he lives on a whopping lot of rents. His dad owned most of Emerald Hill. Never married, no police record.'

'And a nasty piece of work. I bet he's got a bathroom.'

'Several, I should think.'

Mr. Butler refilled glasses in the silence. Then Phryne protested, 'The only thing, Jack, is that they all said—even the spirits—that Augustine wouldn't tell them what they wanted to know. If he was planning a massive fraud, wouldn't he have told them? Showed them the map? Let them test it to find that the parchment was the right age and the ink wasn't modern?'

'Could Augustine have made a thing like that?'

'Oh, I expect so. There are always leaves of old parchment knocking around, in the mountings of pictures, for example. And I could make you a good medieval ink if you could find me some oak galls in Australia, and some vinegar and soot. I had a friend in London, Ambrose, who used to make what were known as facsimiles. For museums, he said. So their real documents wouldn't get exposed to the sun and air. Ambrose would have been able to construct a convincing pirate map in an afternoon.'

'And yet everyone says that Augustine was straight as a die,' observed Robinson.

'Yes, it's a puzzle, isn't it?' said Phryne, and they both fell silent, listening to the mad wind trying to tear the roof off the house.

Simon kicked the big motorbike over and the engine roared.
Not much longer. Very soon the right amount of money would
be in his pocket, and then the longed-for revenge could begin.
He savoured it, licking his lips.

Chapter Thirteen

For you there's rosemary and rue; these keep
Seeming and savour all winter long.

William Shakespeare
The Winter's Tale

Miss Fisher retired for a rest after Mr. Butler had shown a much refreshed policeman to the door. Her room was cooled with ice and the electric fan and she lay down in the breath of winter with great delight. The cool air fanned her forehead, blowing delicate wisps of silky black hair across her eyes. She closed them. Just for a moment.

When she awoke the wind had changed. The dreadful sense of assault by weather had gone. Apart from the humming of the fan, the room was silent. She stretched and found that she had been joined by, on one hand, a finely framed, perfectly black cat, extended to his full length asleep with his head on her pillow. On the other hand, a half-naked, beautifully smooth Chinese man; also sprawled, also elegant, also asleep.

The situation was novel and delightful and Phryne did not want to disturb the lovely picture which they made. She settled down again between them, but the siren call of the carnal woke both of her male bed-companions before long. Ember flowed up into a meticulous stretch, yawning and showing his pointed teeth, on the arrival of the fishmonger at the kitchen door.

Phryne rose to open the door for him and he passed her with a regal nod. Lin Chung had other ideas, but they did not involve food.

'Come back to bed,' he suggested.

'We'll get hot,' she said, putting one hand on her hip.

'But there is plenty of ice left,' he pointed out. 'So we can get cool again.'

This argument convinced Miss Fisher. She watched hungrily as Lin stood up to remove the rest of his clothes. She shucked the single garment she was wearing.

And then she sprang on him like a small, impassioned tiger.

Lin went down under this avalanche of kisses that were almost bites and surrendered to his fate. Strong arms held him down, strong thighs rode his flanks. The world dissolved into a white chrysanthemum behind his eyes.

Some time later he realised that he was being covered with a discreet gown and Phryne was talking to someone at the door.

'Just a light, simple dinner, cold salmon and salad, and can you open a bottle of Veuve? Thank you so much, Mr. Butler.'

She came back and bathed in the cold air as he had seen her bathe in a hot shower, turning each part of her admirable form to the stream. Her beauty always amazed him. Her passion had surprised him. He felt gingerly over his body, ascertained that it all appeared to be present, and wrapped himself in a green satin sheet. Lin Chung felt almost cold, a great luxury in such a climate.

'Ah, Phryne. Jade Lady,' he sighed.

'Beautiful man,' she responded, and rubbed her naked body the length of his, a cat-like movement, finishing with her nose in the hollow of his throat. 'I've ordered us a simple little repast. We don't have to get up until the weather changes.'

'This ice-and-fan arrangement is wonderful,' he said. 'I will institute it at once. Grandmamma feels the heat terribly and never gets a lot of sleep during the summer, and consequently neither does her household. Her view is if she is awake, everyone else should be awake. Her maids were overheard conspiring to put chloral hydrate in her late-night tea. And I happen to have a rather nice collection of ceramic pots, fully big enough, just off the ship from Hong Kong. I shall have one sent around tomorrow: the green porcelain with the blue lotuses, I think. It would suit the room better than the tin bath. Very clever, Jade Lady.'

'Not me—Mr. Butler. He might, of course, have been thinking of putting a mickey finn in my late-night cocktail. I have been wandering around at night because I couldn't sleep. And there was a burglar, of course.'

'Poor man,' sympathised Lin Chung. 'What did you do with the body?'

Phryne slapped his wrist. 'I let him go,' she said. 'He was not a very skilled burglar and he didn't take anything. Might have just been a wandering thief. I've been having such a puzzling time, Lin dear.'

'Tell me about it?'

'Wait for the champagne,' she told him, and kissed him again.

By the time the champagne arrived an hour later, delivered by Mr. Butler, along with the 'simple repast' on a covered trolley, Lin felt in need of something strengthening. Phryne drank a glass of the Veuve rather more quickly than its antiquity warranted and it shocked her into speech.

She told Lin about the Atkinsons, then all about the case of the missing child. Lin sipped gently. The savour was of spring, strawberries and hyacinths, with the uniquely French yeasty sparkle which caressed the palate. He shook his head over the tragedy of the drunken actor's suicide and the forsaken maiden's respectable fate.

'Could have been much worse,' he said lazily. 'She could have been thrown out into the street with her baby, and then what would have happened to her?'

'I don't know.' Phryne sat up abruptly and reached for the bottle. 'But she could have determined it on her own. Dot said the same thing, come to think of it. She might have decided that she couldn't care for the baby on her own and that adoption was an answer—though there were a lot of spare babies then, and baby farmers, and not a lot of the poor little creatures survived. She might have starved and begged with her actor husband. She might have gone on the streets and taken to gin—or become a famous whore with a pink feather boa. Or even a rich courtesan with one parliamentary lover and a little house in South Yarra.'

'Or killed herself and her baby one night with a cry of, "Oh, the river, the river!"' replied Lin Chung. The sight of a drop of champagne running down Phryne's rounded chin and thence down her pearly breast to her admirable navel was ruining his concentration.

'Dickens himself knew that most prostitutes didn't kill themselves,' she retorted. 'It's just that he wasn't allowed to put it in a book. Public taste required poor Little Em'ly to die— or go to Australia, which was much the same thing. Ironic, really. But it was all decided for Kathleen O'Brien, poor girl. Her parents knew better.'

'At that time,' said Lin carefully, 'that was the general belief. They thought they were handling the matter with tact and care. They didn't send her away after the baby was born, and they did find a suitable husband, this Bonnetti, for her, who was kind to her, as you say. She had her music and her children and lived a long, comfortable life.'

'Oh, well, damn it, I suppose so,' admitted Phryne grumpily. 'How have things been with you? I haven't even asked, I'm sorry.'

'Well enough. Grandmamma has not been healthy or happy in this weather, though I now have a remedy for that which will increase our harmoniousness.'

'Did you sack the maids who wanted to drug her?'

'No, just warned them not to try it. Unless instructed by me. Many more nights of scolding and shrieking would not be good for the old lady. But if anyone is going to drug her, it is going to be me. Better drugged than poisoned.'

'That could happen?'

He shrugged. 'I hope not, of course. But she is very exigent and lack of sleep is a well-known torture. What has Mr. Butler given us? I can't keep drinking champagne on an empty stomach...'

'Let's see.' Phryne collected the trolley and wheeled it inside, within easy reach of the bed. She began lifting lids. 'Simple little repast,' she said admiringly. 'A little caviar, perhaps, Lin dear?'

Lin loved caviar. He accepted a plate and loaded caviar, sieved boiled egg and chopped onion onto a sippet of rye toast. The next course was perfectly cooked salmon, with mayonnaise and a bitter-leaved salad. And for dessert, Phryne found, they had Mrs. Butler's famous tropical fruit sorbet, luscious with slivers of pawpaw and mango in a pineapple and passionfruit base. Phryne settled back into the envelope of cool air and sighed with pleasure.

'Are you staying for breakfast?' she asked Lin.

'Since I cannot get any ice at this late hour, and therefore cannot alleviate Grandmamma's discomfort until tomorrow, I would be delighted. And so would Ember,' he added, as the black cat strolled into the room, tail as erect as a taper, scenting caviar and salmon, his favourite fruits.

Because he did not demand, but sat collectedly at her feet, tail curled round paws, radiating 'I am a good and deserving cat' so effectively that she could almost see the halo around his ears, Phryne awarded him a portion of salmon and a teaspoonful of caviar. He ate them with great neatness, polishing the plate and then positioning himself in the ambiance of the fan to wash and brush his already immaculate fur. He knew Phryne very well.

She could not be forced, but she could always be seduced.

Phryne reposed that night in the cool damp air, between the purring black cat and the luxuriating Lin Chung, and slept like a baby.

When she woke Lin had already washed and dressed and was leaning down to kiss her. Ember had vanished, presumably seeking bacon rind. It was eight o'clock.

'I must go and arrange about the ice and the fan,' Lin said. 'I will send the porcelain bath over as soon as I can. Thank you for last night,' he added, kissed her again, and left.

This suited Phryne, who was never keen on company for breakfast. If ever there was a woman born to be a concubine, she told herself as she turned on the shower, it is I. A night of passion, and then the loved man wafts away. No domestic dramas, no domesticity at all, in fact, and if I need a man as an escort I can always find one. Perfect, she said to herself as the hot water cascaded over her shoulders. Phryne liked the twentieth century. It had had its unfortunate events—like the Great War—but with any luck, that would be the last one for the duration. And no parent could now stop Phryne from living exactly as she wished.

She dressed in a light shift and went down to breakfast. Dot and the girls had already eaten. Phryne and her newspaper were alone with the croissant, the cherry jam and the pot of coffee.

Dot came in as she sipped the last sip and nibbled the last crumb.

'Cooler today,' she observed, 'now that rotten wind has dropped. You've got the meeting with the Bonnettis, Miss Phryne?'

'Yes, and it is not likely to be amusing. I haven't got any information about the child, only about the father, and that's a sad story in itself. Would you like to come with me?'

'Me?' asked Dot, taken aback.

'Yes, you. You did most of the research. You talked to Sister Immaculata. And there is almost guaranteed to be a priest present and you know that priests make me nervous. I never know if I'm supposed to kneel or bow or whether a simple handshake will suffice.'

'You just have to shake his hand,' Dot instructed. 'You're not part of his congregation.'

'Right. Well, up to you,' said Phryne.

'All right, Miss Phryne, if you like. I'll put on some good clothes.'

'And so will I,' said Phryne. 'At least we are not going to melt. Oh, Mr. Butler, Lin Chung is having a porcelain bath delivered today to take the place of the tin one in your admirable air cooling system. Make sure that you get the carriers to move everything for you. That's what they are for. Should we hire a house man, do you think, for the heavy work?'

The butler bowed from the waist. 'If you would be so good, Miss Fisher, there is a large young fellow, a connection of my wife's, who would do admirably and could be paid by the hour. He's out of place, due to no fault of his own.'

'Good, hire him immediately. I don't want you to throw your back out hauling heavy loads, Mr. Butler.'

'No, Miss Fisher.'

'I'm taking the car to attend this Bonnetti meeting, is she fuelled and ready to go?'

'Yes, Miss Fisher, filled her up yesterday.'

'Wonderful. Carry on, Mr. Butler.'

Dot was having second thoughts about accompanying Phryne anywhere, if she was the chauffeur.

'Are you driving, Miss? Can't Mr. Butler drive?'

'He has to wait for the porcelain. Don't worry, old thing! I'll drive like I'm carrying a cargo of little lambkins, Dot, I promise.'

'Very well,' said Dot reluctantly. She knew how Phryne drove. It put the 'neck' into 'neck or nothing', and the neck was Dot's.

Her fears were, unhappily, realised. By the time they arrived in Kew, with the heartfelt curses of half of Melbourne's motorists (and that poor cyclist) following, Dot was worn out. If Miss Phryne had been driving lambkins, she thought crossly, they would have the world's curliest wool before they arrived at their destination. With their nerves, also, in rags and hardly a bleat between them.

'Here we are!' exclaimed Phryne, allowing the big car to roll to a halt. 'You can open your eyes now. Nice house, Dot.'

Dot opened her eyes as ordered. 'Expensive,' she said, looking at a vast black marble pile with a long line of stairs up to the front door, flanked by black marble walls with flowerpots flowing over with white and scarlet ivy-leafed geraniums, mostly dying of drought.

'Old money,' Phryne said. 'Well, old for Australia. Come along. Let me just put your hat straight, and you shall do the same for me.'

Dot imitated a lambkin. The big house overawed her. But nothing overawed Miss Phryne. She marched up the steps as though she was a duchess condescending to view a peasant's hut. Dot followed the violet silk flicker of Phryne's skirt up the steps, of which there seemed to be thousands. They arrived, panting a little, at the top, a glassy black marble pavement as big as a tennis court and as welcoming as a tombstone.

'Vulgar,' observed Phryne to her shrinking handmaid. Then, as the massive door opened, she turned the full measure of her personality on a butler so terribly well dressed and so freezing in manner that Dot almost squeaked and fled.

'The Honourable Miss Fisher and her companion Dorothy Williams,' she announced, in a tone so icily flat that Dot began to shiver and even the butler flinched a little. He stepped back and they walked in.

'I believe that Mr. Bonnetti is expecting you,' he intoned.

'I believe that he is,' said Phryne flatly.

'I will announce you,' said the butler, giving up the effort to impress this obdurately unimpressionable guest. He knew sheer unadulterated aristocratic arrogance when he saw it. 'If you would come this way, ladies…'

They followed him through a hall hung with oil paintings, presumably of ancestors. The house was dark and close and smelt faintly musty, as though the carpets could do with a good going over with vinegar and tea leaves. This must be the family home, Phryne thought. She had seen bigger, and better furnished.

Resolutely unconcerned, Phryne allowed the butler to announce her and Dot, then entered after a studied pause. And there were the Bonnettis, in council.

The children of Mario Bonnetti and his wife, Kathleen, nee O'Brien, had been as follows, Phryne recalled: Giuseppe, or

Joseph, born in 1872, now fifty-six; Maria, born in 1874, now a nun called Sister Immaculata, who was not present; Sheila, born 1878, now fifty; and the youngest and last living child, Bernadette, born 1880 and now forty-eight. All of whom had married and presumably had children of their own. The room seemed crowded, though it was very large. Mr. Adami, looking dapper but worried, conducted Phryne to the head of a solid walnut dinner table, where a large man was standing. There was a priest, as Phryne had expected, next to him. An old priest, which might be an advantage.

'Mr. Bonnetti, this is the Honourable Phryne Fisher,' said Mr. Adami. Phryne put her hand into the hard, strong hand of the head of the family. Mr. Bonnetti had dark eyes and white hair and a commanding presence. This was someone used to being in charge. After all, his father had died more than twenty years ago, and he was the only male heir.

'I am pleased to meet you,' said Phryne. 'This is my assistant, Miss Williams.'

Dot's hand was also taken and pressed.

'Very kind of you to help us with our little problem,' Mr. Bonnetti told Phryne. There was not a trace of an Italian accent in his voice. 'Let me introduce the council. This is Mr. Adami, whom you already know.' Phryne smiled at the harassed lawyer. 'This is Bishop Quinlan, who has agreed to assist us.' Phryne shook the old man's hand, cool even in the summer heat.

He had a benign, closed, close-shaved countenance. Dot dipped gracefully and kissed his ring. 'This is my sister Sheila and her husband Thomas Johnson.' Phryne shook the hand of a thin, faded woman with a nervous twitch to the eyelids. All her nails were bitten to the quick. Her husband was large and florid, with blue eyes and thinning hair. 'And this is my sister Bernadette, she is a widow, and her doctor, Dr. James.'

Bernadette did not extend her hand but stared blankly down at her handkerchief, which she was folding and unfolding. She had the almost unlined countenance of the mentally bereft and a mass of beautiful hair, still reddish. Dr. James gave Phryne's hand a fast medical examination squeeze. Behind Bernadette's chair stood a woman wearing the black dress and white apron of a household servant in the old days. Phryne smiled at her and she blinked timidly at this brightly dressed lady.

'And this lady?' asked Phryne.

'Oh, that's just Tata Guilia, she cares for Bernadette. Cared for all the children, and still here, eh, Tata?' said Mr. Bonnetti heartily, as though to a small child. Tata Guilia smiled a small, shy smile. 'My sister Bernadette never really recovered from the birth of her last child,' Mr. Bonnetti told Phryne. 'But sometimes she comes back to us so I thought she should be here.' He shot a challenging glance at his brother-in-law, Thomas Johnson, who huffed. 'Well, now, let us all sit down and let Miss Fisher inform us as to the results of her investigation.'

Phryne sat at the bottom of the table and surveyed the room. The chairs were heavy walnut, the walls were hung with dusty velvet curtains in faded red, and there were far too many ornaments, most of them precious, all of them needing a good wash. Phryne particularly liked a Staffordshire pair, maiden and swain, who had been grape picking, and were now returning with baskets on head and hip, depending on gender.

The maiden was wearing a shawl of grey dust and there were cobwebs on the young man's flowery hat. There were various gaps in the dust where things had been removed. How Augustine Manifold would have loved this house, she thought. Poor Augustine. Mr. Bonnetti saw her glance.

'We haven't used this room for a long time. Not since mother became ill. I thought that I ordered it to be cleaned,' he said meaningfully to a man standing by the door.

'*Patrone*,' said the factotum indignantly, in a heavy Italian accent. 'Mr. Johns, 'e no let us in. Troppo val'able things in 'ere, 'e said. 'E call us *ladri*—thieves!'

'I shall speak to Mr. Johns later,' said Mr. Bonnetti. There was an undercurrent of menace in the statement which made all present glad that they weren't Mr. Johns. Phryne hoped that he was the butler, who deserved a little putting-down. 'But for the moment, forgive us our squalor and inform us, Miss Fisher.'

Phryne looked at Dot, who was far too overwhelmed to speak. So she began, 'The first thing you asked me to find out was, was there a child? And due to the researches of both myself and my assistant, I can confirm this. There was a child. He or she was born in Ballarat at a home for fallen women run by the Sisters of Mercy on or about the fifteenth of January 1865. He or she was sent out to be adopted—'

'Wait a moment.' Thomas Johnson raised a plump red hand, glinting with rings. 'You say he or she. You don't know which, girl or boy?'

'No,' said Phryne. 'Not yet. It has been quite difficult to get even this far, you know. If I might continue?'

'How do you know the child didn't die?' persisted Thomas Johnson. He was sneering at Phryne, and she had never been very tolerant of being sneered at.

'I don't,' she responded. 'Yet.'

Mr. Johnson stood up. 'Seems to me you haven't got a lot of information for our money,' he insinuated.

'Happy to resign the case any time you like,' said Phryne, putting her hands on the unpolished table, preparing to rise.

'No, no, no!' scolded Mrs. Johnson, Sheila Bonnetti as was. 'Thomas, you said you'd be good and patient. You promised!'

'This is a waste of time,' he growled at her. 'It's just dragging the process out, so that you get less of your mother's money than you should. We need that money. My business is—' He had said too much. He sat down again, leaving his heavy hand on his spouse's fragile shoulder. She winced and bit her lip.

'Your business is in trouble?' asked Mr. Bonnetti, quietly. 'Again?'

'Just needs an injection of capital to turn the corner,' bluffed Mr. Johnson.

'It seems to me that it has already turned a number of corners,' said Mr. Bonnetti. 'And it seems to me that all of Sheila's dowry has been expended in driving it around the corners, eh?'

'Ridiculous!' said Mr. Johnson violently. 'I lavish every luxury on her. Don't I, dear?' he said to Mrs. Johnson, squeezing her shoulder.

'Oh, yes, dear,' she responded in a faint voice.

Phryne was disgusted. Dot was interested. She had not known that rich people behaved just the same as poor people. Only the surroundings were different. This was just like her uncle claiming that Dot's grandmother had left the money to him, not his wife her daughter, and he could spend it as he liked. Which had been down at the pub buying beer for his mates. Uncle Jim had had that exact tone of voice, and that exact shade of brick red in his complexion, while he was telling Dot's father that his wife was a happy woman.

She hadn't believed Uncle Jim, either.

'It was always about money,' announced Bernadette, suddenly. Dr. James took her wrist in his and began counting her pulse. 'First Father's money, and weren't you angry with Mother for getting it, and didn't you come almost every Sunday, Thomas, begging her for more money for the house, for Sheila, for the business? And didn't you take a lot of her money for the dowries for your children, Joseph?'

'Your children aren't precisely begging in rags,' sneered Mr. Johnson.

'She was pleased to set up a trust for the girls,' protested Mr. Bonnetti, sounding for a moment less sure of himself. 'Bernadette?'

But Bernadette had gone again. Dr. James shrugged. Tata Guilia produced some drops and beckoned to the man at the door to fetch something. He came forward with a glass of water. Everyone watched as the doctor measured out twenty drops, mixed it with a little spoon, and gave the glass to Tata Guilia. Gently, slowly, the old woman coaxed Bernadette to sip the mixture, though she made a face as if it was bitter.

'Perhaps we might return to the object of this meeting?' asked the Bishop in a creamy Irish voice. 'Miss Fisher, could you forgive this interruption and proceed with your report?'

Phryne obliged. She was getting very tired of family scenes, of which she had experienced enough in her own family.

'The father of the child was an actor called Patrick O'Rourke, who died in poverty and misery and is buried in the Melbourne General Cemetery. He left his child a message, but I have yet to puzzle it out.' For some reason she did not want to expose that sad scribbled piece of paper to this well-fed prelate. 'I can make further enquiries,' she said, looking straight at Thomas Johnson. 'If you wish me to do so.'

'Of course,' said Mr. Bonnetti, standing up and folding his arms. He looked like he was posing for an heroic picture. The Patriarch, perhaps. 'If you would be so good as to continue, and report your results in—say—a week's time? Then we will all be in better humour,' he said. 'And this room will be fit to sit down in.'

'Very well,' said Phryne, and Mr. Adami escorted her and Dot out. Warfare broke out behind her as she left.

'Are they always like that?' she asked, as the iron butler unbarred the portal and they were out in the sunshine again.

Professional confidence warred with what seemed to be real distaste. Mr. Adami, Phryne realised, was a very honourable man.

'Always,' he said.

'I reckon it's a pavement,' opined Bill.

'Nice bit of work,' said Jim. 'Considering that the prof says it's two thousand years old.'

'What about the bones, then?' asked Vern.

'Chaplain sent the message to HQ. "Have found the bones of saint," he said. HQ sent back, "No record of trooper Saint. Please supply full name, number and identity disc."'

'Them blokes,' said Vern. 'Wouldn't know a tram was up 'em till the conductor rang the bell.'

'Too right,' said Curly.

Chapter Fourteen

Out of my lean and low ability I'll lend you something.
William Shakespeare
Twelfth Night

'Phew,' commented Phryne, starting the big car and allowing it to slide into the street, inches away from the elevated nose of a highly affronted Rolls-Royce.

'Phew,' agreed Dot, closing her eyes. It really was better if you closed your eyes while driving with Miss Phryne. You couldn't see the near misses, just hear the horns and roars of fury. Due, doubtless, to the special intervention of her guardian angel, she never seemed to hit anything. Dot wondered what Phryne's angel might look like. Overworked, she decided. Ragged, exhausted, lacking a lot of feathers and greatly in need of a heavenly tonic and a rest on a nice soft cloud, she thought, and giggled to herself.

'Another frightful gathering,' said Phryne, giving the steering wheel a deft twiddle to avoid a tram. 'What did you make of all of them, Dot?'

'Something cruel,' Dot replied. 'Not that I haven't seen that sort of kerfuffle before. It's just you don't expect it in rich people. I thought if you were rich, had a bed and a roof and three meals a day, nothing to worry about, you'd have to be happy.'

'You'd think so, wouldn't you? Never mind, Dot dear, we're happy, despite having all those things. Now, put your detective hat on and tell me about the people in that room.'

'Well, Miss—' Dot inadvisedly opened her eyes, gave a faint shriek and closed them again. It did help to think about something else, apart from how close that radiator had been. 'I didn't take to Mr. Thomas Johnson. I reckon he beats his wife. She was shrinking away from his hand, you saw.'

'I did,' agreed Phryne. 'That might have been a marriage for love to begin with, but now he just wants her for her money. And she is probably desperate to keep him, so she gives him whatever she has.'

'And it isn't enough. You heard him say his business needed more capital.'

'There isn't enough capital in the world to prop up an idiot like that,' sniffed Phryne. 'The perpetually unsuccessful could fail to make a profit at a knocking shop on navy night—sorry, Dot, at a drinking school in a brewery, I should have said. And perpetually angry, too; sure that the world is cheating them of their deserved success. Tiresome, very. Sheila's heart didn't seem to be in this family conclave, though.'

'Don't imagine the poor woman has any spirit left,' said Dot, hanging onto her hat.

'How old do you think he is?'

'I don't know, Miss. He certainly isn't young but it's hard to tell with gentlemen.'

'Well-groomed, well-fed gentlemen, yes.'

'Why do you ask?' Dot opened her eyes and saw that they were on the Esplanade and close to home.

'This child of shame, Dot, would now be sixty-five. It would be piquant if he happened to have married into the family.'

'Lord help us!' gasped Dot. 'But that would mean…'

'That he had married his half-sister. Indeed. Let us hope that it is not so. There, it wasn't so bad as all that, was it?'

Dot got out of the car on wobbly legs, privately swearing she would never enter it again.

'No, it was worse,' she told her employer. 'But it was fast!'

Phryne laughed and tore off her respectable hat. 'Come in, then, and Mr. Butler shall make you a sherry cobbler. We might even drink it in the garden. Now the wind has gone, it's a very pleasant day.'

'So it is,' agreed Dot.

When they were settled at the white wrought-iron table with their drinks before them, Phryne asked Dot to continue her impressions of the Bonnetti family.

'Well, Miss, there was Mrs…I never heard her married name. The sick lady, Bernadette.'

'With the very attentive doctor.'

'Yes. I saw why Mr. Bonnetti wanted her there. When she's herself she's very acute. She knew all about the money.'

'So she did. I wonder about her illness, you know. Did you notice those drops? They were valerian, very strong—I could smell it across the table.'

'Yes, Miss, it's used to calm people down. My mum swears by it for nervy people who can't sleep.'

'But too much of it for too long unbalances the mind. I remember one aunt of mine who used it so much that she did nothing but cry all day. The doctor sent her to Switzerland to recover. Which she did, after about six months of mountain air and huge meals and healthy walks along the snow line. Also, she fell in love with an alpinist and caused a scandal, but that does not concern us here.'

'What was wrong with the alpinist? What's an alpinist?' asked Dot, drinking deeply of her sherry cobbler.

'A mountain climber, and he was very lower class and— gasp—he was an Italian Catholic. But she married him anyway. The Fishers have always been strong-willed.'

'So they have,' said Dot, smiling at Phryne. The ground had stopped whizzing away under her feet and the sherry cobbler was very refreshing.

The hot sun was shining in an agreeably muted fashion through a canopy of strongly green leaves, jasmine and honeysuckle and clematis. The salty, plant-killing wind was repelled by high bamboo fences. Although the sweet spring flowers had gone, there were still bright pink, bright red and scented geraniums, and Mrs. Butler's herb garden, fertilised by the three chickens who clucked amicably in their run behind a bamboo screen. Mint grew at Dot's feet, sheltering under the table. She recalled her task and resumed.

'Mr. Bonnetti's wife wasn't there,' she observed. 'You'd think she would be, at a family council. I gather he's got a wife?'

'Oh, yes, she does a lot of good works in the Italian community, runs boarding houses for immigrants and so on. I believe I have actually met her. At the Lord Mayor's Show, I think. Robust woman in an overloaded hat. Possibly she had another engagement. Or possibly she isn't interested.'

'Still,' said Dot. 'It was strange. I thought it was strange.'

'Anything else?'

'Yes, Miss, that butler. Mr. Johns. I never saw such a terrifying person! And the houseman told Mr. Bonnetti he had given orders not to go into the room. Mr. Bonnetti was not pleased by that.'

'It's all bluff, butlers—they're servants,' Phryne told her, sipping her cocktail. 'Just look them straight in the eye and state your business. It would be funny if it was Mr. Johns,' she said idly. 'But either of the two could have been the people at the funeral. T. Johnson, that was the signature. Either Mr. Johnson or Mr. Johns.'

'Yes, but that would mean they knew that Patrick O'Rourke was the father of this missing child,' protested Dot.

'Yes, it would mean that, and the matter now becomes impossibly complex. We are going to leave it to percolate, and we are going to have a nice talk about new curtains. Your room, Dot. Those flimsy ones were only a stopgap when I was furnishing the house in a bit of a hurry. What do you say to some heavier ones?'

'The sun wakes me up very early,' conceded Dot. 'But it seems a shame to waste the cloth, and they're such a nice pattern, those pretty birds in all my favourite colours. Maybe we could get a blind? Or a shutter?'

'That's an idea. But have a look at the catalogue, Dot, and see if we should get you some new ones. Use the flimsy ones in winter, perhaps, or have them lined?'

Phryne opened the huge Myer catalogue, and soon they were both absorbed.

Presently, they heard voices in the house. Lin Chung's porcelain bath had arrived. It was being hauled up the stairs by two Chinese carriers and a giant. That was the initial impression. Phryne assumed that this broad expanse of muscle, lightly covered by a stretched blue singlet, shorts and boots, was the 'large young fellow' who was a connection of Mrs. Butler's and who was now to be hired to do the heavy lifting. He looked perfectly capable of lifting anything, up to and including a heavy goods motor vehicle.

Phryne and Dot watched as the large package was manhandled up the stairs and into her boudoir.

'I'll just get the broom and clean up the packing,' worried Dot.

At that moment the doorbell rang and Mr. Butler paced magisterially off to answer it. There was a flurry of footsteps and a young man scrambled inside, found Phryne in the parlour, and flung himself at her feet, panting, 'You have to help me! They're all mad! They're going to kill me!'

It was James Barton.

'Shut the door, Mr. Butler, if you please,' said Phryne calmly. 'We shall conduct Mr. Barton into the small parlour, and perhaps you can supply some very strong coffee? Never mind the packing, Dot, go to the spyhole and tell me what you can see.'

Dot obeyed. There were little telescopes built into several places in Phryne's house. She examined the front gate, then moved to the girls' part of the house and examined the side way.

'Nothing there,' she reported. 'No people. No car, either.'

'All right. Come along now, old thing,' she encouraged, hauling James Barton up by the shoulder. 'Come along with me and you shall have coffee and I will protect you, in all probability.'

'They're all mad…' he shuddered, but cooperated enough to allow himself to be lowered into a soft chair and supplied with a handkerchief, a glass of cold water and, in due course, a cup of coffee so strong that Mrs. Butler sent it into the parlour in a kitchen cup, not being too sure of the strength of Miss Phryne's Clarice Cliff or the good bone china. It was heavily sugared, for shock. His hands were shaking too much to hold the cup.

Phryne watched as Dot helped the young man absorb the dangerous fluid. There was enough 'awake' in that coffee to keep him alert for the term of his natural life. Though he seemed convinced that that would not be long. He was genuinely terrified, Phryne thought; sweating, shaking, eyes dilated black.

Jane and Ruth came in, attracted by the noise, were warned by Dot and went out again, though Phryne was sure that they would be loitering just outside the door. James Barton did not seem to see them. He was still sobbing. And Phryne had thought him the most sane of the Atkinson clique! Of course, that wasn't saying much…

The doorbell rang again. Mr. Butler went to answer it and James Barton curled into a ball and screamed, 'Don't let them in!'

But the visitor was Lin Chung, looking concerned.

Phryne left James in Dot's care and watched as Lin dismissed the Chinese carriers, blinked respectfully at the large young fellow, and conducted Phryne upstairs to view her latest acquisition. She was delighted. It was a large porcelain tub, spring green in colour, with blue lotuses depicted as if floating on the water. It would hold a large block of ice and was altogether an improvement on the tin bath. She kissed Lin's smooth-shaven cheek.

'Thank you! How is your Grandmamma?'

'Not sure if a Chinese doctor would support such a new-fangled apparatus. I sent Dr. Shang to talk to her. He says that the only way to balance a Yang wind—hot and dry—is to use Ying methods—cold and wet. Besides, he is a good influence on her, he is almost as old as she is and remembers the old days. He will prescribe a soothing tea for all of us and I suspect that I am better out of the way. I am glad you like the tub. Now, Phryne, I never interfere in your affairs, but I couldn't help noticing…'

'The screaming young man? Yes. One of the Atkinson lot, and I would have said the most sane, though I could be wrong. He says they are going to kill him. I haven't been able to get a sensible word out of him, he's beside himself with terror. Would you like to stay? You might pick up something extra, it's always useful to have a second auditor. And I've got an idea about the Atkinsons, which will require you to remember what you learned as a stage magician.'

Lin bowed, both hands together, and said in stage Chinese. 'As you prease, little Missee.'

Phryne clipped his ear. Lightly.

Downstairs, the situation had settled. The carriers and Mr. Butler's large young fellow had gone. Phryne assumed that someone would eventually tell her his name.

Dot was trying to calm James Barton, Mr. Butler was putting the chain on the front door and Mrs. Butler was asking how many people would be in to lunch. This being the most important issue at stake, Phryne informed her that there would be six, if James Barton had recovered enough to eat. If not, then the table would not be too put out.

'Always better to cater for more than less,' approved Mrs. Butler, and went back to her kitchen to pulverise chicken livers for what Miss Phryne called 'pâté' but she called 'potted meat'. Lin accepted a cool drink and sat down on the sofa. Dot was still kneeling beside the terrified young man, encouraging him to sip more coffee. She had never seen a grown-up man so absolutely distrait.

Phryne, who had, thought of shell shock and drugs.

'Tell me, James, what have you taken?' she asked in a clear, business-like voice. 'I need to know now.'

'Just smoking,' he said. 'I didn't drink…I didn't drink the…'

He broke down again. Dot, Lin and Phryne looked at him.

'I am reluctant to suggest more drugs,' said Lin Chung. 'But perhaps Dr. Shang could help?'

'Of course,' said Phryne, who was considering 1) valerian and 2) a clinically measured belt over the bonce as a cure for the young man's neurasthenia. Any potion from Dr. Shang would probably be more efficacious.

'I will telephone,' said Lin Chung, and went into the hall to do so.

Dot managed to get the rest of the coffee down the young man's throat and let him lean back. She fetched a cool cloth, wrung out in water and eau de cologne, put it over his eyes and then lowered the blinds, as he seemed sensitive to light. His sobbing died away, but he retained his clutch on Dot's hand. Dot gave Phryne a questioning glance.

'Just sit with him for a while, Dot, if you would,' Phryne told her. 'This is a crisis and, with any luck, we might find out what is going on in the Atkinson menage. There's no harm in him,' she added.

'No, Miss, he's like a babe with a nightmare. I'll be all right for a bit if you can pass me that cushion to kneel on.'

Phryne passed her the cushion and went out to explain the situation, as far as she knew it, to her family and staff.

'Girls,' she said, knowing that they were hiding just behind the larger parlour door, 'come out and listen to me. There is a break in the Atkinson case, but it means that we must keep a sharp lookout and not take any risks. What were you going to do this afternoon?'

'Nothing, Miss Phryne, we were just going to read in the garden and maybe go swimming a bit later, when the sun's off the water. Jane got a bit sunburned yesterday,' said Ruth. 'And I've got a cooking lesson with Mrs. Butler at three. Ice cream,' she added. 'You make a chocolate custard and then—'

'Good. Don't go out unless you have my permission, all right?'

'Right,' said Jane solemnly. Then, eagerly, 'Is the young man ill? Is the doctor coming?'

'Yes, he's having hysterics, and no, the ordinary doctor isn't coming, my medical student. Instead, you can see a real Chinese doctor in practice if you promise to sit quiet and not ask any questions until he has gone. Agreed?'

'Agreed,' said Jane, eyes shining. This was better than swimming, which she did not particularly enjoy. One got sand in uncomfortable places and her shoulders were red and sore from yesterday's sun. Her burned epidermis had already begun to desquamate.

Mr. Butler accepted Miss Phryne's orders that she was not At Home to anyone except Dr. Shang, the police or the fire brigade, and conveyed her request for Chinese tea to Mrs. Butler. She was used to this and sent in the tiny cups, spirit stove, kettle, teapot and the canister of Buddha's Tears tea of which Lin Chung was particularly fond. Dr. Shang arrived, was admitted, and was conducted into the smaller parlour by a deferential Lin Chung.

He was a short, robust doctor, with such a beautiful lined oval face that Phryne longed for him to have been rendered in ivory. His Western clothes hung on him like a sack and Phryne considered that a robe would have suited him much better. In front of an enthralled Jane, he took James Barton's wrist in his strong fingers and sat as if listening. Then he took the other wrist out of its desperate grasp on Dot's hand and listened to the pulse tick along inside it. Then he opened the patient's mouth by squeezing his cheeks, grunted and said something to Lin Chung.

The doctor opened his bag and Jane saw, as she crept closer, a fascinating collection of herbs, spices, weeds, and—could they really be dried cicada shells? Dr. Shang made a selection, placing the harvest in a square piece of white paper, which he folded neatly and handed to Jane.

'Take it into the kitchen and boil it in a pint of water for five minutes,' instructed Lin Chung. 'Then strain it into a china jug and bring it back. And bring a tablespoon, if you please, Jane.'

Jane flew, immensely flattered that he had entrusted her with this crucial mission. Dr. Shang sat down and accepted some tea. He drank a cup, smoothed his moustache, and made a comment.

'The doctor says that you have excellent servants,' said Lin, annoyed. 'I shall correct his mistake.'

'Don't bother, just don't tell Jane,' said Phryne.

'Very well.' Lin supplied the second cup.

'Do I pay a fee to the doctor himself?' asked Phryne.

'No, he will send an account when we see how the patient does. He only gets paid if his treatment works, you know.' Lin poured the ritual third cup for the elderly man. He smiled and made an admiring comment about the tea.

Jane came back with the medicine. It had a peculiar and rather penetrating scent, like old leather shoelaces cooked with grass clippings in vinegar.

'One tablespoon every hour,' instructed Lin Chung. 'I will see the doctor out, Phryne. Good luck getting the boy to drink that stuff,' he added, as Dr. Shang bowed a little, patted Jane on the head and gave her a coin, and went into the hall.

'Well, Dot, he trusts you, see if you can get him to drink it,' Phryne urged.

'Rather him than me,' muttered Dot. She took the spoon and touched James' lower lip with it. 'Swallow this, there's a good boy,' she coaxed. 'Then you shall have a peppermint.' James, who was receptive to a firm female voice, swallowed as ordered. His eyes shot open and he sat up, retching. 'What was that stuff?' he choked. 'Medicine,' said Dot. 'Here's your peppermint.'

'You're drugged,' said Lin Chung, coming back. 'Our people indulge in opium. We know a lot about treating opium poisoning. You need to cleanse your system. Then you might be able to tell us what this is all about and why you need Miss Fisher's protection.'

'Am I safe here?' asked James, staring around wildly. 'As houses,' said Phryne. 'Come now, who is trying to kill you?' 'My sister,' said James. 'Blanche White. Val and Luke.

Stephanie. Veronica. And that bastard Gerald Atkinson.' 'Oh,' said Phryne blankly. 'Why?' 'Because they think that I'll tell about the treasure.' 'And about the murder of Augustine Manifold?' 'Poor Augustine,' said James, suddenly and inconveniently sleepy. 'He was a good fellow.' And he fell deeply asleep, leaving Phryne exasperated. 'Lunch!' announced Mr. Butler.

He opened the postbox in fear and trembling, because he had not been able to raise fifty pounds. All he could squeeze out of the pawnbroker had been twenty-five. And that was going to cause trouble when she searched for her garnet set. Still, she hardly ever wore it.

The envelope was there. The enclosure said *Fifty next time*.

He drew a shuddering breath, almost of relief.

Chapter Fifteen

We know one thing about the spirits. We know that they lie.

Harry Price
The Detection of Fraudulent Mediums

James Barton slept the rest of the afternoon, which was full of incident. The first caller was Eliza, who came to report on the state of Augustine's shop.

'Mrs. M is going to keep it going,' she confided. 'As a monument to Augustine. Put a spoonful more sugar in my tea, will you, Phryne? Mrs. Manifold keeps a very bare table. And she likes that herbal stuff that tastes like grass. Perhaps it is grass, that would be cheap. But she accepts that she has to pay Sophie and Mr. Yates a fair wage for their skill and expertise. Cedric Yates has agreed to stay, the man really is an artist in wood.'

'But he doesn't talk much,' put in Phryne, passing the ginger biscuits.

'No,' responded Eliza, gobbling two of them. 'And I think it would be better to get a young chap, or even another young woman, for the shop. It isn't good for a young woman to be alone all the time, there are nasty people about, and I am concerned about Sophie.'

'Are you, Eliza? What's wrong with her?' asked Phryne.

'I am not sure, but I'd say it was the usual problem.'

'A pregnancy?' asked Phryne with her sister's bluntness.

'No, no, my dear, at least not so far as I am aware. I mean a man,' said Eliza.

'Really?' said Phryne without noticeable tact. 'But she's… not prepossessing.'

'No, but there's someone for everyone, they say. That certainly worked for me,' said Eliza, smoothing down her shabby dress. 'Sophie giggles at nothing, blushes unexpectedly, and watches the door like a hawk, especially towards closing time. I've asked Mr. Yates, but he just said—'

'Dunno,' quoted Phryne. Eliza nodded. 'Well, they sound like all the symptoms of love, I have to say. Worse, I expect, if you know you aren't pretty and this man might be the only one you're going to get. Jack Robinson said there was a sniff of a boyfriend, but he didn't know anything more. This could be important, Eliza, can you do some spying for me? I need to know who that boyfriend is.'

'All I know about him is that he rides a motorbike,' said Eliza.

This struck a spark somewhere in Phryne's memory but she could not drag it to the forefront. She abandoned the attempt for the present.

'Lurk,' she told her sister. 'Hire a taxi and sit in it all night if you have to, here's some funds. Take a picnic and Lady Alice and you can do your accounts in the car. But I need that boyfriend, and I need him soon. I've got James Barton here in a state of collapse, saying that the Atkinson clique were trying to kill him. Things have come to a pretty pass and I need to solve this before anyone else gets killed.'

'Do you think that they killed Augustine?' asked Eliza, accepting the money and levering herself to her feet.

'Hard to think of anyone else, isn't it?' Phryne replied.

Eliza kissed her and took her leave. She'd never been a spy before. It was all very exciting.

Hardly had Mr. Butler cleared away the tea things than the bell pealed again. He went out, and returned despite her orders, escorting an incandescent gentleman. Phryne recognised the apoplectic complexion and the sneer.

'Mr. Johnson?' Phryne stood up. 'What can I do for you?'

'You have to stop!' he shouted.

'Stop what?'

'Stop investigating,' he jerked out the sentence. 'Meddling, busy women, always poking their noses into other people's lives!'

'Mr. Butler, see Mr. Johnson out,' said Phryne, stepping back out of the way of the grasping hands. 'He's leaving now, and he won't be back.'

'You've got to listen to me!' he cried. 'Stop this now, you silly bitch!'

'Sorry,' said Phryne, 'Mr. Butler, would your large young man still be in the kitchen?'

'I believe so, Miss Fisher,' said Mr. Butler calmly.

'You might fetch him, if you please,' said Phryne, without taking her eyes off the madman.

Mr. Johnson dragged a wad of cash out of his pocket. He flourished it at Phryne. His face was purple and he was sweating like a pig.

'I'll give you all of this if you'll mind your own business!' he grunted. 'Take it!'

Mr. Butler had returned with the giant. Phryne examined him. Several axehandles across the shoulders and gentle brown eyes like a Jersey cow.

'Hello,' said Phryne. 'I'm Phryne Fisher.'

'Ted Rowntree,' mumbled the large young man, taking her hand with wincing delicacy and then giving it back uncrushed.

'Could you do me a service? Put that wad of bills back into Mr. Johnson's pocket and escort him to the door. Then shove him through it, and I would not object too strenuously if I saw him bouncing down the steps.'

'My pleasure, Miss,' said Ted. He dispossessed Mr. Johnson of his money, stuffed it into his inside pocket, then picked the man up by one shoulder and his waist and carried him into the hall. Phryne heard the door open and close rather conclusively. Ted and Mr. Butler came back.

'We should have hired a chucker-out before,' Phryne told Mr. Butler. 'It's so easy if you weigh half a ton and have a grip like a gantry. Thank you, Ted. Expect a little extra in the pay packet for this additional labour. And you too, Mr. Butler. Mrs. B must be feeling like she's running a hotel.'

'Luckily, both the girls are helping her, and Miss Dot as well,' he said, suppressing the fact that Mrs. Butler had indeed delivered herself of such sentiments not ten minutes ago. 'But Mrs. Butler always appreciates a new hat, Miss Fisher.'

'She shall have one with feathers on,' Phryne assured him. 'And an extra half day in which to go shopping, when we get to the end of this case. Cases. I promise. And I will hold my birthday party at the Windsor. I shall owe far too many people an invitation. And I hope that this flood of visitors will dry up fairly soon! I am astonished. Now, should I wander into the kitchen in, say, ten minutes, to congratulate our valiant skivvies?'

'Ten minutes, Miss Fisher, that would be appreciated, I expect.'

Even Mr. Butler was not going to second-guess a cook in her own domain. Phryne lit a cigarette and considered Mr. Johnson. Then she considered the Bonnetti case. Then she stopped considering it and read a copy of *Australasian Home Beautiful* because she felt that what her mind needed was less concentration and more distraction. An article on the latest developments of art moderne glass kept her interested for the required time. Musing on her cases, she suddenly said, 'Simon!'—the motorcyclist and the supplier…and Sophie? Time to talk to the staff.

The kitchen was full of steam. Jane was washing up. This was a good division of labour, because although she was blindingly intelligent, Jane wasn't very coordinated, so Ruth was drying. Dot was peeling potatoes. Mrs. Butler was piping cream onto a gorgeous but wobbly pink jelly, seemingly composed of strawberries. She completed the cream and stored the shape in the American Refrigerating Machine, then wiped her hands on her apron.

'I'm so sorry about the visitors,' apologised Phryne. 'I had no way of knowing that they would come. There's a new hat in it for you, Mrs. Butler, and my sincere admiration.'

'That's all right, Miss,' said Mrs. Butler. 'I've got lots of help.'

'So I see. Think of a treat, Dot, girls. After today you will deserve one. Drat, there it goes again, that doorbell!' exclaimed Phryne, leaving the kitchen in a hurry. 'Who is it this time?'

'What would you like to do?' asked Dot of the girls. 'She means it about a treat.'

Jane was about to propose a visit to the Medical Museum at the University of Melbourne but caught herself in time. She had finished all the dishes and cutlery and was now emptying the sink in order to refill it with fresh hot water to rinse glasses.

'What about the theatre?' said Ruth diffidently. She hadn't got used to treats.

'Oh, yes, please,' said Jane.

'That would be nice,' said Dot, who would not have suggested it. 'We can go to the new musical, *Variety!* Shall we?'

'Oh, yes,' said Ruth and Jane.

'Then keep drying,' instructed Mrs. Butler, imagining her new hat. Something light in pale straw for summer, she thought. With white feathers and maybe a pink flower or two. She knew just the milliner. Her old summer hat had been caught in the rain and was uncertain as to brim and discoloured by water. For this, Miss Phryne could have as many visitors as she chose.

The next one was a depressed Jack Robinson, who came to drink beer and report nothing much happening in the Manifold case.

'I've got a new murder down at the docks. Fifteen men in the offing and they were all in the toilet when it happened. A two-man toilet. They must have been sitting on each other's laps. Thanks, Mr. Butler. That's bonzer.' He drank deeply, downing first the mandatory soda water and then the amber liquid. 'So what I have to tell you, Miss Fisher, is that unless you can give me a good lead in the Manifold case, it's going to go down the... sorry. It's going to go into pending.'

'Which means no further action,' Phryne translated.

'Yair,' said Jack, and drank more beer. 'I've searched and I've asked and I've been all round the traps, but nothing's come to my notice.'

'Get up and tiptoe to the smaller parlour door,' said Phryne. 'If he's still asleep, don't wake him.'

Robinson did as she asked. Then he tiptoed back.

'Strewth! That's one of them!'

'That's James Barton, who ran to me for protection against the others, whom he swears are trying to kill him,' she informed him. 'Later, when he wakes, I shall have information out of him if I have to draw it like teeth.'

She snapped her own pearly white teeth and Jack Robinson drank more beer. He was fairly sure that, given the right circumstances, Miss Fisher would definitely bite.

'All right,' he conceded. 'I'll keep it alive a couple more days. Still got some avenues to pursue. We ain't going to solve that wharf case, anyway. No one saw nothing. You just have to ask them. But you'll let me know?'

'As soon as I know anything,' Phryne promised. 'I have to do something about the Bonnetti baby first. I have agreed—as a favour to the Church, no less—to find out about this wretched infant, and if I can just tell you about it...' She summarised the Bonnetti baby case, and added, 'If you would just be a dear, Jack, and send out a notice to all pawnbrokers and dealers for anything which might have come from that house.'

'That's a tall order, Miss Fisher!'

'Not really. I believe that a collection of Dresden figures has been stolen and sold. There will be more.'

'How do you know?'

'I saw their imprints left in the dust on a mantelpiece. They all should be marked "Bonnetti" on the base. It's a standard precaution. All my ornaments and paintings have "Fisher" on them. I'm serious, Jack, I think that someone is looting the estate. But I'll have the whole solution soon. Dot has to go and see a priest.'

'Sometimes,' said Jack Robinson, with the clarity induced by alcohol on top of a night's lost sleep, 'you frighten me.'

'And I frighten myself,' Phryne assured him.

Jack Robinson left. As he had drunk his beer out of the bottle he did not add to the washing up. Dot, released from scullion's duties, put on her hat and told Phryne that she was going to see the priest at St. Mary's, young Father Kelly, who had lately come from Donegal and was homesick for the soft green fields and limestone outcrops of the Gaeltacht. She had the O'Rourke inscription in the palm of her white cotton glove. The incomprehensible Irish inscription, written by the dying Patrick O'Rourke on the wrapping around the coin: *Tá sí milse ná seo rud eile*. Dot did not mean to lose it.

Thus it was only Phryne who was attending when James Barton awoke from a sweet sleep and felt the need to confess. Lin Chung, who had supervised his nap, had excused himself to attend to some business and was talking on the telephone in the hall. The young man was awake, his eyes were relatively clear, but his hand was shaking as he laid it on Phryne's wrist.

'I can stay here?'

'For the moment,' said Phryne. 'Until the danger has passed. Providing that there is a danger, of course. Drink some water, James, and tell me what's on your mind.'

'Murder,' he said. 'I just got out of there with a whole skin.'

'I know the feeling,' responded Phryne.

'It's those damn hidden masters. Pris is entirely under the influence of Blanche and she is under the influence of Steph and they are all under the influence of Gerald and it's all gone to hell.'

'Would you care to particularise?'

'They've been getting muddled messages from the spirits,' he said. 'About who to trust and what to do, and where the bloody treasure is. There are two spirits, Selima, who was a slave girl in

Ancient Rome at the court of Heliogabalus and was smothered in roses, and Zacarias, who is some sort of Jewish high priest or prophet and was stoned to death. Both of them come through the medium of this utterly bogus Indian called Charging Elk. I mean, Indians don't really say things like, "How! White man speak with forked tongue," do they? I mean, outside the movies?'

'I have never met an American Indian so I cannot tell, but I think it very unlikely,' Phryne assured him. 'Got it so far; two spirits brought through the veil by Charging Elk, the Synthetic Indian.'

James managed a smile. It wasn't a very good smile, but it was better than his expression of unsettled panic.

'Well, it all went along merrily at the beginning, when we got a lot of information, I mean they got a lot of information, and the spirits appeared to make sense, or at least sentences. But since…'

'Augustine died?'

'He was a good…' James began, but Phryne held up a monitory hand.

'Don't. Is it since Augustine died that the spirits have lost their coherence?'

'Yes,' said James, faintly astonished. 'But he wasn't at the seances.'

'No matter. Go on.'

'Well, Selima appears to be sulking and all they can get is Zacarias, and he said…he said…' He broke down, sobbing.

'Buck up, James, do!' urged Phryne. 'I can't protect you unless I know what the danger is! Spit it out!'

'He said they needed a scapegoat, a sacrifice for the endeavour, and I would do because I was an unbeliever anyway. And Gerald just nodded and got out one of his sacrificial knives and Val and Luke had ropes in their hands and the girls were nodding. I just leapt through the window and ran to my car and came here because they're afraid of you, Miss Fisher.'

'And you really think they meant to kill you?'

'Yes, I do,' he said.

Phryne was convinced, at least, that James did believe it. She patted the shaking hand.

'Right, my dear, you're here for the duration. Would you like Lin to take you home to pack a bag?'

'No! What if they're waiting for me?'

'Then we shall send Li Pen as well and they will be very sorry.'

'Who's Li Pen?'

'Lin's bodyguard. I would back him against twenty men. Against Valentine and Luke he wouldn't even break into a light perspiration and they would be tied into knots. Turk's heads, for preference.'

'No!' James shuddered.

'Can you forgive me if I lend this shivering wreck one of your suits of pyjamas, Lin dear? Then he can have a nice bath, take his next dose of Dr. Shang's medicine and we'll tuck him into bed. I'll bribe Dot to wash his shirt and underwear, they ought to take, oh, minutes to dry in this weather.'

'Certainly I can forgive you,' said Lin. 'I will supervise the bath and change. Where are you putting him to bed?'

'Spare room, next to the girls. You can use their bathroom. I'll get the jammies.'

'Might I suggest the pale blue ones which you do not much like?' asked Lin as she went out. 'Come along, Mr. Barton,' he said kindly. 'Take your next dose and a bath will make you feel better.'

'What about a drink?' asked James hoarsely, having swallowed the evil brew.

'I think we could manage a brandy and soda,' said Lin, observing him closely. He was aware of what Phryne was doing. Anyone who had helped or even observed the drowning of Augustine Manifold would show some reaction to baths.

But James exhibited no emotion except his prevailing one of muted terror. Lin ran a bath, helped him strip, handed the discarded garments to Phryne, and ushered the young man into the pale blue gentlemen's nightwear, and then into the spare room's comfortable bed, without noticing anything amiss except his habitual failure of nerve.

James Barton drank his weak brandy and soda, sighed, and closed his eyes.

'Augustine,' insinuated Lin. 'What happened to him?'

'I dunno,' blurred James. 'I was asleep.'

Lin suppressed a curse and went out, closing the door against the hot light. He told Phryne what Barton had said.

She tsked. 'I knew we'd have to do something outrageous to solve this one,' she said. 'Never mind, it should be fun. You told me once you could make me a spirit. We were in the ghost train at Luna Park and you said you could make it a journey into terror and nightmare. Was it true?'

'Given the right conditions, yes,' he said. Phryne never ceased to surprise him.

'Name your conditions,' she said.

Bert looked at his passengers in the rear-view mirror. Phryne had hired his vehicle for the duration of the Manifold campaign, and after a rousing argument about socialism he had decided that he liked the two communist chooks who were presently balancing their charity accounts in the back seat of the bonzer new taxi. He and Cec had done a lot of watching in their time as soldiers, on hot cliffs at Gallipoli and in deep Flanders mud.

He wasn't going to miss a bloke on a great big motorbike. And he wasn't going to lose him, either. Round the corner Cec was waiting in the battered van which was still going, more or less, though held together with baling twine and spit. If all else failed he knew several ways of bringing a motorbike down, sometimes without killing the rider. He hoped this would not be necessary. The cops always went crook about any little disturbance. They were funny like that.

The Manifold shop had opened again. So far business was brisk. Naturally all the silvertails wanted to gig at a place where the proprietor was murdered—nothing better to do after they had trodden on the faces of the starving poor for the day. Cec had been in to have a bit of a yarn with his cousin Cedric, and he had reported that this Simon bloke always turned up just after dusk, as though he had something to hide. Well, that could be said of many blokes. If the bloke was just dealing in a little merchandise which had fallen off the back of a truck, Bert wasn't going to go all righteous on him. But Miss Fisher said that something very unpleasant was going on, and Bert's not to reason why.

Besides, he liked listening to the flow of socialist patter from the back seat. Made a nice change from his fares complaining about the Test cricket.

'If we transfer four pounds from the Girls' Friendly to the Orphans' Picnic Fund we can borrow six pounds ten from the Provision of the Works of Marx and Engels and still hire the hall for the Mothers' and Babies' Hygiene and pay the cook for the Factory Girls' Cookery and Household Management,' said Lady Alice, biting the end of her indelible pencil and spreading a purple stain across her lower lip.

'Yes, dear, but if we take six pounds ten out of the Provision of Works Fund, we won't be able to pay for the new books that are coming in from Russia this Thursday,' worried Miss Eliza.

'Drat, I'd forgotten that. Well, what about pinching five pounds out of the Working Girls' Retraining…no, that won't do…'

Bert was about to suggest stinging Miss Fisher for the whole of the Provision of Works Fund, but refrained. They were enjoying themselves too much. Good works, Bert thought with a touch of sentiment. Who would have thought that two nice comfy pussies would have spent so much of their time and energy on caring for the downtrodden masses and the lumpen proletariat (some more proletarian than others)? It made world revolution seem slightly more possible.

Not much traffic on the road. Twilight was fading and pretty soon it would be dark. No sign of a big motorbike.

Bert was about to suggest that they turn it up for the nonce when he heard the sound of a hungry engine, roaring.

'Comrades!' he said to the pair of accountants. 'I reckon that might be our bloke now.'

'Yes, indeed,' agreed Miss Eliza. 'And there's Sophie meeting him. No embrace, kiss on the cheek. Probably hasn't gone too far to be easily reversed, Alice.'

'She's very plain,' said Lady Alice dubiously. 'She'd be grateful to him. It's going to be a blow to the poor girl if he's up to what Phryne thinks he's up to.'

'There are always blows,' said Eliza. 'And she's got a profession, and a respectable one. Oh, he's leaving. Can we follow, Comrade Bert?'

Bert had never met a woman who could say 'comrade' as though it was 'mister'. He started the engine and let the taxi slide out into the street.

'But what if he sees us?' asked Lady Alice.

'You can leave that to me and Cec, Comrade,' Bert assured her, relighting his stub of cigarette. 'That big bike sounds like a smithy and goes like a bat out of hell, but me and Cec know this city like the back of our hand.'

'Carry on, then,' said Eliza.

The bike sped up, flying around the Esplanade on the way to the city, and the taxi kept pace, sometimes falling back, sometimes drawing almost level. Behind, the unmarked van trundled on its way, unnoticed amongst the remains of the commercial traffic as the city dismissed its workers, closed its shops, and settled down into a respectable slumber.

Down Swanston Street like Bert's bat out of hell roared the big bike. Expertly driven, the taxi and the van dogged its heels. Past the brewery, up the hill to Parkville, past the university and onto Johnson Street.

'I reckon we're going to Kew,' said Bert. 'Anyone we know in Kew, Comrade Eliza?'

'Gerald Atkinson,' replied Eliza. 'Oh, dear, I'm afraid this looks very disappointing for Sophie.'

'Kew it is,' said Bert some time later. 'That's Studley Park. You know, he hasn't looked around once, that bloke.'

'So he's innocent?' asked Lady Alice.

'Or very confident,' replied Eliza Fisher.

'Bingo,' said Bert with deep satisfaction, as the big bike halted outside a large mansion.

'Yes, that's the Atkinson address,' Eliza confirmed. 'Oh, dear!'

The figure of a young woman had run out from the side gate and embraced Simon in the full glare of the streetlight. He kissed her on the mouth, laughing. Then he swung her around, tripped over the kerb, staggered, laughed again and kissed her again.

'Well,' said Lady Alice. 'Keep following, Comrade Bert,' ordered Miss Eliza.

'Well, there might be water up in them caves,' insisted Curly. 'I seen them limestone caves before.'

'If we don't find water, we're dead,' said Jim. 'And the neddies too. Up we go, then.'

They scrambled and clawed their way up the baking cliffs. Vern found a long crack in the stone and slipped inside.

'You beaut, Curly, there's water all right. A soak. Tastes a bit chalky. Bring 'em in, there's room for all, it widens out here. Do a recce of that little cave, Jim, we might be able to light a fire.'

'Yair, we can light a fire. There's a triangle on this rock and some carving. *Adelphos*, whatever that means. There's a hollow behind. I'll just pull out this stone…Come and look,' Jim requested.

They came. They stared.

'Do we call an officer?' quavered Jim. The others looked at him. Vern knelt and counted them out of the lid of the broken stone box.

'Gold coins. Forty. That's ten each. Nip out and get some of that pitch, Jim. We can solder 'em into a bandolier. And we say nothing, right? We keep shtum. This is our ticket into civvie street.'

'Right,' said the four.

Chapter Sixteen

All that glisters is not gold Often have you heard
that told…Gilded tombs do worms enfold.

William Shakespeare
The Merchant of Venice

Phryne was about to suggest to Lin Chung that a pre-dinner nap would be a pleasant thing when the doorbell, which fairly soon she was going to disable with a handy hammer, pealed again. It was six pm and getting dark and Phryne wanted to wash and change for a civilised dinner, assuming her staff had not given notice by then.

'Well, Mr. Butler? We are having a day, aren't we?'

'A lady to see you, Miss Fisher,' he replied, offering her the silver salver. Phryne took the card. Then she looked at Lin and abandoned her lascivious ideas for the present.

'Sorry, Lin dear, I really do have to see this lady.'

'I'll start designing my journey into horror,' he offered, and went into the smaller parlour in search of pencil, paper and freedom from interruptions.

Phryne shook herself into order, adjusted her expression to 'bland', and went to greet Mrs. Joseph Bonnetti.

As Phryne remembered from the Lord Mayor's Show, she was a large, florid woman in a flowered hat. She still was. But the hand in Phryne's was the second trembling one of the day. Phryne sat her down and offered a drink, which Mrs. Bonnetti accepted. She gulped down her glass of the ordinary sherry and accepted another.

By this time Phryne felt she had deserved a cocktail and Mr. Butler did not fail her. It was a strong concoction of Campari, cherry brandy and gin, rather stressing the gin. Miss Phryne had behaved generously and Mr. Butler was not one to stint a lady in distress. Especially when it was her liquor.

'What can I do for you, Mrs. Bonnetti?' asked Phryne.

'I was not at the conference in the old lady's house,' said Mrs. Bonnetti. 'You might have noticed that.'

'I did,' said Phryne, sipping. One could not gulp a Negroni of this strength and keep breathing.

'You might also have wondered where I was?'

'Well, yes, I did rather…since it was a family gathering, I thought that you might have been there.'

'I was excluded,' said Mrs. Bonnetti, with strong disapproval. 'My husband said that it was a Bonnetti matter. He is terrified, Miss Fisher, he always gets more autocratic when he's scared. Something frightful is happening.'

'Your brother-in-law was just here, flourishing money and telling me to stop investigating,' Phryne told her.

'That fool!' Mrs. Bonnetti snorted. 'I have never been able to understand what Sheila sees in him. If I was her I would have shown him the door—and made sure he went through it— years ago. Then again, she is not altogether…but I am digressing.'

Mrs. Bonnetti settled her hat, gulped her second glass of sherry, and laid a hand on Phryne's sleeve. 'I want you to keep on,' she said.

'Why?' asked Phryne, which was not part of her brief.

'Because if it is some fearful disaster, if it is an hereditary disease or weakness or madness, I need to know. I have three children. They have children.'

'I don't think it's a disease,' Phryne said, assessing how much courage her interlocutor possessed. Considerable, she judged.

Mr. Bonnetti was a pater familias of the old school and would be outraged if he found out that his wife was here. 'I think it's a scandal.'

Mrs. Bonnetti waved a dismissive hand. The artificial orange roses on her hat shook as in a strong breeze.

'If so, it's an old scandal. No one is going to care, in this year of grace 1929, that Kathleen Bonnetti had a lover before she married the old man so long ago. There is something alive and present day about this, and I need to know. The situation at the old lady's house is strange. That butler, Johns, is insolent. Yet he goes unreproved and he keeps his place. If he was my servant he'd be out on the street in his nightshirt.'

'Yes,' said Phryne consideringly, believing her without difficulty. 'I have Mr. Johns in mind. I believe that he is selling things from the old lady's house. Ornaments and so on.'

'Is he? So he is a thief, as well? We should call the police!'

'No, not yet, remember that this scandal is so important to your husband that he keeps Johns in his employment. And that possibly one of the reasons why you were not asked to that meeting is that you would, as I did, notice the gaps in the dust on the mantelpiece.'

'The Dresden shepherdesses!' gasped Mrs. Bonnetti.

'Probably. I've asked my policeman to put out a notice to all pawnbrokers so we might get him that way. In any case, we will continue until we know the truth. But it might be a very unpleasant truth,' Phryne warned.

'If it's unpleasant, we will deal with it,' replied Mrs. Bonnetti, getting to her feet with some difficulty. 'The Bonnettis have been a prosperous but rather unlucky family. Their mother and father were happy enough, but Sheila married a waster, Maria is a nun, Bernadette lost her wits, and only my husband appears to have retained his grip. And I am not going to allow some dreadful secret to poison the rest of our lives. Out into the sun with it, I say, and then we can deal with it. Whatever it is!'

'Commendable,' said Phryne, recognising real resolution when she heard it. She said goodbye, and Mr. Butler saw Mrs. Bonnetti out, her orange roses still agitated as by a tornado.

Phryne drank the rest of her cocktail. It was now six thirty. She was expecting Eliza back for dinner, with Bert and Cec, reporting on Sophie's boyfriend, the mysterious Simon of the large Harley-Davidson. She was not expecting anyone else. She was just about to join Lin in the smaller parlour when the bell rang again. Phryne swore most indelicately.

This time she had no need to offer tea from a kitchen that was probably getting pretty cross by now, as Mr. Rosenberg would not have been able to accept it in a non-kosher home. So she offered him some port and sat him down in the best armchair.

He was a small man, hunched by years of close work, and short-sighted to a degree. He wore a good but very old dark grey suit and a yarmulke. His hands, Phryne noticed as he reached out to take his glass of port, were very beautiful: spotless, white, smooth, long fingered and deft. Watchmaker's hands.

'Miss Fisher, my daughter says that I can trust you,' he began. 'This is very nice port,' he added. 'A good year. Well. I am concerned. I am worried, even. You know that I run a little shop in the Centreway, just a few things, small things? Coins, stamps, maybe a few precious stones, artifacts?'

Phryne nodded. The old man sipped more port and paused. His breath was short. His lips had a bluish tinge which made Phryne fear for his heart.

'Take your time,' she said soothingly.

'No, I'm all right, nice lady,' he answered. 'Not sick. Just old. See, look, a pretty thing,' he said, and showed her a small velvet packet which he produced from his inner suit pocket. Inside an object was encased in oiled silk. Phryne opened this envelope and looked at a golden coin, almost as big as a penny.

'Byzantine,' said Mr. Rosenberg. 'Now I know a little about coins, yes? I know there are only seven of these Antiochus the Seconds. One only in Australia. In the collection of an old Italian gentleman, which was inherited by his wife, who died—'

'Recently. Mrs. Bonnetti?' asked Phryne.

'Mrs. Bonnetti. I tried to buy this coin from her husband, he often dealt with me, he said I was the only honest dealer in Melbourne. He was a nice man—I used to go there sometimes with a coin I had found and drink port with him. I liked him. But he wouldn't sell me the Antiochus. "It's for my son," he said. Then this coin comes into my shop. You can imagine how I felt.'

'Who brought it?'

'A man, that's what my assistant says. He came in this morning when I was at the doctor's. She is a good girl, Helen, my sister Miriam's daughter's child, but she is an artist—you know? She works for me to get money to buy more paints. Knows nothing about coins. But a good girl, she sees this is old, she tells the man, you can leave it, come back tomorrow, I have to ask my great uncle. Me, I don't know what it's worth. He doesn't want to leave it, but she says, fine, take it away, you won't find another man who knows as much as my great uncle, God love her, and he finally grumbles but he leaves it and goes out kvetching. Rachel comes back from the shopping and finds her about to clean it, and she shrieks and snatches it away and tells her it's worth ten thousand pounds. Then Helen has to sit down and drink brandy. When I come back the shop is closed, both of them are in the back room, laughing like fools, and the Antiochus the Second sitting there on a tea towel like a big gold sequin.'

'What did the man look like?' asked Phryne, as Mr. Butler refilled his glass.

He shrugged fluidly. 'Helen, she says swarthy, tall and broad shouldered, wearing a good coat, hat pulled down so she couldn't really see his face. But rude, she says, curt, as though she was a scullery maid. Soft hands, not a labourer. She didn't like him a lot. Said she wouldn't paint him if he paid for it.'

'She's a good observer!' said Phryne.

'Artists, they see things. But on coins, she is a little ignoramus. Now, nice lady Miss Fisher, what would you have me do?'

'I would have you finish your port. How did you get here, by the way? Is there someone waiting in a car?'

'I took the tram,' he said. 'My doctor he says rest but I will get enough rest when I am called to heaven by the Master of the Universe, no? I felt that this was important.'

'Oh, it is,' said Phryne. 'I will call my policeman friend Jack Robinson and he will arrange to have someone pick up the man when he comes tomorrow. No trouble,' she assured him. 'No noise. Nice and quiet. Assuming, of course, that he comes back.'

'For this,' said Mr. Rosenberg, stowing the coin and getting carefully to his feet, 'for this I think he will come back. You choose me a nice quiet policeman, no? Otherwise the man will fight and I have Rachel and Helen to think of, God help me. And the stock, some of which is breakable.'

'I know just the person,' Phryne replied. 'Are you sure I can't call you a taxi?'

'Taxi? No, I take the tram again, it is nice to get out for some sea air. Rachel is right,' he told Phryne, taking her hand. 'You are nice lady.'

'There is something you can do for me,' Phryne told him. 'Wait just one moment.'

She opened the drawer in her small desk and took out the coin which had been found on Augustine Manifold when he was dragged from the sea. Mr. Rosenberg grunted, came over to the desk and switched on the light, took a loupe out of his pocket and screwed it into his eye. Then he turned the coin around under the strong illumination. It shone as gold as...well, gold.

'And you got this where?' he asked.

'It was in Augustine Manifold's pocket,' Phryne told him.

'Poor Augustine, he was a good fellow,' said Mr. Rosenberg, turning the coin over again. It glowed.

'Do you know what it is?'

'Oh, yes, it is a shekel, a pre-Roman shekel. After the Romans conquered Israel they called in the coinage, melted it down with the temple treasure, and issued new coins with Judea Captiva on them. This has no mourning figure, no head of Vespasian or Titus.'

'Where could it have come from?'

'From Palestine, maybe. I have seen some of these. They were popular in the Ancient World, nice lady, the gold content is very high. They were alloyed just enough to make them coinage. Some were still in circulation in the eighteenth century. Interesting. If you find that Augustine had more of them, I would like to make an offer. Now I must go,' he said. 'Rachel will be worrying. Ever since her husband got run down by that van, she worries. Good night,' he added.

Mr. Butler saw him out. Phryne was on the phone as he came back from shutting the door yet again.

'Who was that nice young officer who helped out with the Pompeii loot last year, Jack dear? Thin, youngish, had a beard? Oh, you made him shave it, what a shame. Had a German name… Pinkus, was it? Yes, that one. Well, if you send him along to Mr. Rosenberg's coin shop tomorrow I think you will be able to pinch the person who has been looting the Bonnetti estate. Better be armed, I think. We don't want this to turn ugly, do we, in such a confined space full of treasures? I've just sent Mr. Rosenberg home. It might be an idea to keep a bit of an eye on him, too, he's walking around with ten thousand pounds worth of coin in his breast pocket. I know, but I couldn't shanghai the old gentleman and fling him into a cab, could I? Well, then. Let me know how it goes. I suspect things are about to break, Jack dear. In both cases. Good night to you too, my dear old chap.' She broke the connection, thought a moment, then scrabbled through her notebook. 'Mr. Butler, could you get this number for me? Inform Mrs. Phillips that her father has been to see me and is on his way home. If he isn't there in an hour, perhaps she could call? I worry, too,' she added with a grin. She was feeling breathless with excitement. Facts were coming in and the whole scenario was beginning to make sense, which was an immense relief. One reason why Phryne solved puzzles is that she hated mysteries.

'Certainly, Miss Fisher.'

Mr. Butler took the phone from her hand. Not wanting to disturb Lin while he was making magical designs, she flung herself down on the couch and lit a gasper. She looked at her watch. Getting on for seven. Time to bathe and change for dinner.

First, however, she needed to find out if there was going to be any dinner.

Phryne approached the kitchen door with some care. Mrs. Butler, when moved, had been known to throw things. But when she opened the door the scene was of genteel cordiality. Mrs. Butler was sitting in her cook's chair with her feet up, Dot was pouring orange crush for all, and Ruth was describing her Home Management teacher's false teeth, which slid and clicked whenever she said 'shervant shituation'.

Phryne entered on a gale of giggles, which stopped as soon as she came in.

'No, no, no one move, I was just about to go up to get ready for dinner and I thought I'd find out how the shervant shituation was.'

This set the girls and Dot off again and made Phryne feel less like the spectre at the feast.

'Dinner's all ready, Miss, all cold, even the strawberry shape has set,' Mrs. Butler informed her.

'Wonderful. I hope we have only four more people to come, just Eliza and Lady Alice and Bert and Cec. Then we bar the doors and loose the dogs and inform the sentries that they are to shoot on sight. I want a nice quiet evening, and I expect that you do, too.'

'It's been fun,' Ruth told her.

Jane nodded. She had been allowed to dissect the cooked roast duck with cherry jelly which was the centrepiece of Mrs. Butler's cold collation. She found it strange that while Mrs. Butler had no anatomical knowledge per se, she knew how a duck fitted together and how to take it apart. And Jane had smuggled a lot of scraps to Ember, who was now sitting in the middle of the sacred kitchen table, on a tea towel, washing himself with greasy, overfed languor.

'Time we all got ready,' said Dot, finishing her drink and putting the glass in the sink. 'Come along, girls, you can have first wash. Is that young man all right?' she asked Phryne.

'Perfectly so, and in any case I've locked him in,' Phryne replied. She did not know anything about James' preferences, but they were not going to include Jane or Ruth.

'Then we thank Mrs. Butler for a nice afternoon and off we go,' Dot instructed. 'And we take the cat,' she added.

Jane gathered Ember to her unformed bosom and carried him, purring, out of the room and the others followed.

'All right, Mrs. Butler?' asked Phryne.

'Oh, yes, Miss,' said the cook, wriggling her toes in her lisle stockings. 'Nothing to what Mr. B and I did in the old days— there were always a string of visitors hanging on the bell. The afternoon goes fast. It's all right being flat out like a lizard drinking, once in a way.'

'But only once in a way,' said Phryne, who had got the message. 'Right, I'm off. Thank you so much, Mrs. Butler. Pink flowers on the hat, am I right? And perhaps white feathers?'

'Right you are, Miss,' said Mrs. Butler.

Phryne, bathed and scented, dressed in her favourite at-home dinner dress. It was ankle length, modest in cut, with a sweetheart neckline and thin straps. She smoothed down the material, a fine claret coloured silk which draped like velvet. It had been an interesting day, and further revelations were to come. She heard the bell ring for what she hoped would be the last time today, and Eliza's voice in the hall. Good.

She sat down at her window to watch the sun set, smoke a meditative cigarette, and get her thoughts into order. She scribbled for some time in her notebook.

A little later she rose and descended to find her parlour augmented with Eliza and Lady Alice, accepting cocktails, and Bert and Cec, accepting beer.

'There she is!' Bert raised his glass. 'You look bonzer, Comrade!'

'Thank you, Comrade Bert,' said Phryne, wondering if he had been imbibing already.

'You always look lovely in that dress, Phryne,' her sister told her. 'We are celebrating our first successful mission as spies.'

'Oh?' asked Phryne. 'Did you enjoy it?'

'Rather,' said Eliza, seconded by Lady Alice. 'I've always loved driving fast, but father would never let me drive the Rolls, you know, and the gardener's car would go about twenty miles an hour, even down Dewberry Hill.'

'You drove down Dewberry Hill in that old rattletrap?' Phryne was amazed. 'You're braver than I! How very enterprising of you, Eliza!'

'It wasn't so much going down,' replied Eliza thoughtfully, 'as stopping at the bottom without brakes. I ended up in the hedge about three times out of five. But it was a stout hedge.'

'She is very enterprising,' agreed Lady Alice. 'We even managed to make the accounts balance—well, almost—while we were lurking.'

'Miss Fisher, Mrs. Phillips reports that her father has returned safely. And dinner is served,' announced Mr. Butler.

The table was laid buffet style, an invention which Phryne approved of, because you could see the whole choice of food at once and collar your favourites. Mr. Butler approved of it, because it meant that he did not need to wait on the diners, and his feet hurt. Dot and the girls liked it because it seemed so luxurious to have all that food in view. Mrs. Butler was not sure. Bert had never seen such a thing before, but his opinion was formed in a moment.

'You beaut!' he enthused. 'What a spread! Come on, Cec mate, pass me the cold steak and kidney pie.'

Lady Alice and Eliza were so hungry that they didn't even murmur a protest about how many poor families this feast could feed. Everyone found a plate and began to help themselves. Cold chicken, cold duck with cherry jelly, five kinds of salads, three kinds of bread. A French cheese and egg pie. A steak and kidney pie. A pork pie filled with delicious seasoned jelly. Small cups of chilled bouillon.

There was a general sigh of delight as the company found their particular tastes and indulged. Jane found that dissecting the dinner didn't change the taste at all.

'I like this eggy pie,' observed Bert.

'And this is wonderful chicken,' said Dot. 'So tender! I didn't think we'd be hungry after all the scraps the girls and I have eaten today.'

'Whereas Cec and me have been doing Boy Racer all through the city,' Bert replied, reaching for another slice of—pork pie, this time? 'And he had the hardest yakka, 'cos that old van ain't up to much these days.'

'It's all right,' said Cec, replenishing his plate with *salade russe*, for which he had acquired a taste on the very first occasion that Phryne Fisher had irrupted into their lives. 'Just a bit old and a man can't get the parts for it, so we had to make a few of them. The door stays on all right if you remember to tie it up. But I almost lost you, Bert. That Harley was breaking all the speed limits.'

'Yair, where's a copper when you need one?' grinned Bert.

'All right, Eliza, what happened?' asked Phryne, who had ordered a plate of delicacies conveyed to Lin Chung, who was still designing and did not want to be disturbed. James Barton was still asleep. Phryne had taken the plate of alligator pear vinaigrette to herself. No one else had had the nerve to try it yet. It was buttery and perfect. 'We are agog to hear your adventures!'

'Oh, Phryne dear, it was fun,' confessed Eliza. 'And Comrade Bert is a most expert driver. The big motorbike ridden by the man we are calling Simon came first to the Manifold shop. Comrade Cec went in to talk to his cousin Cedric first,' she said, trying to keep her facts in order.

'Ceddie,' said Cec, 'told me that this Simon was always hanging around Sophie, and Ceddie didn't like his looks. Had seen him off a couple of times, but what can a man do when the sheila lets the mongrel in? Says he told Soph the bloke was a wrong 'un but she didn't listen.'

'They're good at that,' observed Bert. 'Women. Not listening. My landlady—' He was suddenly aware of a silence and looked around a table entirely populated by women. The silence lengthened. Dot, Phryne, Eliza, Lady Alice and both girls stared at him. 'Can someone pass me some of that thin soup?' he asked desperately.

'He kissed Sophie goodbye, the hound. Then we started off,' said Eliza. 'The bike roared through the night and we followed. If we talk of breaking speed limits, Comrade, I don't like to think how fast we were going.'

'Ah, well,' said Bert, burying his blushes in bouillon. 'Not that fast. We had to keep Cec in view, and the bloke on the Harley as well. Luckily he never thought to hare off down some of them lanes, or we would have lost him.'

'Then we raced through to Kew, where he stopped outside the Atkinson mansion. There he loitered with intent until a maid came out and threw herself into his arms.'

'Gertrude,' said Phryne. Her heart sank. Gertrude had tended her kindly when she had arrived at the Atkinson home soaking wet. She had even sold Phryne her new pink slippers. Somehow the thought of the slippers made Phryne feel sad. And hadn't she said that her young man was a baker and they were saving up to get married? That must have been what Simon told her. The hound.

'They were clearly well acquainted,' continued Miss Eliza delicately. 'He spoke to her and then he kissed her goodbye— and then we were off again. This time to Richmond, it transpired. He really let the bike out on those curves.'

'Going like a bat out of hell,' agreed Bert, who had recovered his spirits.

'That's where I nearly lost you,' Cec informed him.

'But luckily there was a traffic lock on Studley Park Road,' continued Eliza. 'And he had to slow down. He actually got off the bike and rolled a cigarette and waited for the cars to go past. A truck, I believe, had shed its load and there were peaches all over the road.'

'Not a lot of traction in stone fruit,' said Bert.

Jane immediately began calculating. If a standard peach was crushed under a weight of, say, one ton, how slippery would it be under motorcycle wheels?

'So that when he went on we could easily follow,' said Eliza. 'And then—he went home. You'll never guess where he lives, Phryne, not in a million years.'

Phryne had an idea but she wasn't going to spoil her sister's triumph.

'Can't imagine,' she said, putting down a forkful of tomato salad with basil and olive oil. 'Where?'

'With Miss Collins,' said Eliza. 'Veronica Collins. She is one of them. I saw her at the funeral.'

'Oh, yes, I heard her mother kept a boarding house. Gosh,' said Phryne. 'That young man does spread himself around, doesn't he?'

'By the way he was embracing Miss Collins,' said Eliza primly, 'I'd agree with you.'

'Fervently?' asked Ruth, who loved romances.

'Most amorous,' said Lady Alice, to whom they were a secret vice.

'Gosh,' said Ruth. 'That's three!'

'Indeed it is,' agreed Phryne. 'Well, Simon is a bounder. How very useful you have been, Eliza dear. Can I make a small contribution to the charities to express my gratitude?'

'This dinner is enough,' protested Eliza. 'And it was very exciting!'

'You want to put six quid into the Provision of the Works of Marx and Engels Fund,' said Bert, who had been listening to the accounts in his back seat. 'Then everything will balance proper.'

'That would be very generous,' agreed Lady Alice. 'And they would balance.'

'Six quid it is,' said Phryne. 'And cheap at the price.'

Dessert was Ruth's chocolate ice cream, fruit, cheese and coffee. The girls helped Mr. Butler clear the table. Dot was under the influence of some strong emotion but did not respond to Phryne's inviting glance. Therefore, the dessert was consumed— with many compliments on the ice cream—and the visitors were farewelled with money and thanks. The girls took their hot milk and put themselves to bed, to play a game of ludo until they were drowsy. Phryne and Dot sat at the denuded table over their last drinks, Dot with her hot chocolate and Phryne with her liqueur, her coffee and her cigarette.

'A long day, Dot dear, and I forgot to ask you about Father Kelly.'

'Poor man, he is so homesick. I had to listen to him talking about his Donegal for an hour. Such a long way from home. I did tell him that there is a Gaelic speaker at the Caledonian Inn. The publican. My dad knows him. He's homesick too. At least he can listen to his own language there, and get a drink of Irish whiskey. That must be so hard,' said Dot. 'I'd hate it if I never heard Australian again.'

'Indeed,' coaxed Phryne.

'Anyway, I asked him what the inscription meant and he said it was Irish all right and he told me what it meant. And I lit a candle for the boy Patrick and for the poor girl Kathleen as well, and paid for a few masses. It didn't cost much, Miss.'

'Dot dear! You may pay for as many masses as you please,' said Phryne. 'What did the message say?'

Dot told her.

Phryne took a long gulp of coffee. 'Well,' she said at last. 'We'd better set up a meeting with the Bonnettis, Dot dear, as soon as possible, don't you think?'

'But who is the child, Miss Phryne?' asked Dot.

'Oh, I think I know that,' replied her eccentric employer. 'We'll do it tomorrow if we can. Pack up all the things we have of both parties, Dot dear. And we can, at least, as Mrs. Bonnetti says, drag it all out into the sun and deal with it.'

'If you say so, Miss Phryne. I'm going to bed—unless you need me?'

'No, you've had a long day, sleep in tomorrow. Nothing— God willing—will happen until the afternoon. I'll just see how James Barton is, and Lin Chung. Good night, Dot, sleep tight.'

Dot trailed away up the stairs. Having given Miss Phryne the translation, she felt relieved of a burden. And she was so tired.

She washed briefly, donned her softest cotton nightdress, and fell asleep as she was saying her prayers.

Phryne prowled to James Barton's room, but he was sleeping like a baby. She saw that he had a chamber pot and a supply of snacks and a carafe of water. The cigarette box was full and there were matches in the box. He would do for the night and she locked him in again.

Then she joined Lin in the smaller parlour. He was surrounded by sheets of screwed up paper and he had clearly eaten his dinner while writing. But he turned to her a face alight with accomplishment and showed her a page of specifications and sight lines and wiring.

'I shall make for you, Jade Lady,' he said, 'a journey of nightmare and terror.'

She kissed him rather thoroughly.

◇◇◇

'We're a four,' Vern instructed Bill, the youngest. 'We live together and ride together. We're mates. And these are our horses. They get twenty-two litres of water a day where we get one. They get fed three times a day and rested ten minutes an hour. Though with this new bloke I dunno how much rest we're gonna get.'

'Saw Banjo,' said Bill. 'Back at camp with the Methusaliers.'

'Did yer? What's he like?'

'Old bloke,' said Bill. 'Gives the best horses to the troopers, says the HQ officers can ride screws. Said this new general's a cavalryman. Says Allenby's been trying on generals like a man in a hatshop tries on hats. He's sent half of HQ home and moved out into the desert. I reckon we'll see Damascus soon.'

'And then home,' sighed Curly.

Chapter Seventeen

Come on, poor babe:
Some powerful spirit instructs the kites and ravens
To be thy nurses!…
Poor thing, condemn'd to loss!

William Shakespeare
The Winter's Tale

Phryne woke and blinked sleepily. It was evidently late. The sun had moved over her coverlet. Ember had already departed, perhaps to breakfast, perhaps to lunch. Lin Chung was lying asleep beside her. Yesterday had been strenuous and Phryne was not minded to sleep again or even to make love, as it would be cruel to wake her lover. She lay back in her silk nightdress and enjoyed the soft sunlight and the down pillow and the feeling of utter repose.

A soft tap announced Dot. Phryne slipped out of her bed and went into her sitting room.

'I slept in until nine,' said Dot, who had never done such a thing while she had her health. 'So did Mr. Butler and that James Barton just ate his breakfast and went back to byes like a baby. The girls just got up and Mrs. Butler didn't rise until eight, she said it was like a holiday. She says she doesn't mind serving breakfast instead of lunch, but would you like some of either, and Mr. Lin?'

'A nice question. He was up until all hours designing the surprise for the Atkinsons. Send up a cooked breakfast for him and the usual for me, Dot dear, and just turn the hot tap as you pass? I am going to have a bath. Then we shall come down and plot.'

Dot did as requested and Phryne bathed in a new bath scent, Ocean, which smelt of salt water and frangipani, a strange but interesting combination. When she heard the rattle of the dumb waiter she wheeled the trolley out.

Lin woke to the scent of bacon. This made him remember Cambridge, which had been cold. But he was warm and dressed in silk pyjamas. Half of them, at least. He was rummaging for the bottoms when Phryne came in.

'Early lunch,' she said. 'Or maybe very late breakfast. Will you partake?'

'I will,' he said.

'And would you like my bath?'

'That, too,' said Lin Chung, and abandoned the search for his trousers. There was not a square inch of him which Phryne had not seen. He stripped off the top instead and went to bathe in Ocean-scented water.

Phryne had already eaten her croissant and was drinking coffee when he reappeared and loaded a plate with bacon, scrambled egg, sausages and grilled tomato. Phryne averted her eyes and began to dress.

'I need to tell a respectable family a terrible secret,' she said, looking at her array of clothes. 'What do you suggest? Black?'

'Dark blue,' said Lin, with his mouth full. 'A suit.'

'Good notion,' approved Phryne. She had assumed the dark blue suit and was selecting a hat by the time Lin Chung laid down his fork and filled his teacup.

'I need to find a place in which to produce your performance,' he said. 'So I shall be away perhaps all day. Dinner tonight?' he asked.

'Indeed,' said Phryne. She sprayed herself with Floris Stephanotis, kissed him warmly, and was gone with a tapping of her Louis heels.

Lin shrugged and drank more tea. What a woman. She was a force of nature.

Phryne advised Mr. Bonnetti that she and her assistant would be pleased if a family council could be reconvened at two in the afternoon. He had agreed. She had requested that his wife should be present. To this he had also agreed, a trifle hesitantly. Phryne thought that of all the Bonnettis, the woman with the orange roses was the one who might be able to hold the family together under the revelation Phryne was about to make. She checked her little bag, which contained her little gun. No way of knowing how this might go. Then she rang Jack Robinson, heard his news, and made her request. This, after the usual objections, he granted, as he usually did.

Then she collected Dot, who carried the box containing amongst other things, Patrick O'Rourke's pitiful remnants, the letters and the shawl of the girl Kathleen. She intimated her destination to Mr. Butler, and had herself driven to the Bonnetti house. She only made one stop on the way.

Her two guests were silent. It was, one observed to himself, like watching a rather good performance of *St. Joan*. The GBS *St. Joan* of course. The profile was set, the lips firm, the whole being radiated divine purpose. Better to do as the nice lady says, and then no one would get hurt.

In all probability.

The Bonnetti mansion was as tall and imposing as before, but Phryne allowed no flinching. She swept her supporting cast up the endless stairs, observing tartly that filial piety would, one thought, require a son to water his mother's geraniums. To which Dot agreed. 'Pity to let them all die like that,' she said. 'Those red ones are rare.'

'We shall speak to the butler about it,' Phryne responded.

The door was opening in anticipation of their arrival and the looming Mr. Johns allowed them to pass him and enter the hall. This had been vigorously cleaned. The gold picture frames glowed. The carpet smelt of orange vinegar, tea leaves and elbow grease. Mr. Johns conducted them into the Bonnetti dining room, now fresh, dustless, and populated with Bonnettis. Phryne raked the room with an assessing stare. Mr. Adami, looking nervous. Mr. Bonnetti, looking anxious. Ditto Mrs. Bonnetti, Mrs. Bernadette, her attendants Dr. James and Tata, Mrs. Johnson and Mr. Johnson, who looked hysterical. The Bishop, looking down at his folded hands. All present and correct.

'Mr. Johns will stay, if you please,' she said icily.

At a gesture from Mr. Bonnetti, Mr. Johns took up a station near the door.

The big windows had all been opened and a sweet scent was being blown in from a mass of creamy roses.

'Miss Fisher,' said Mrs. Bonnetti, trying for and almost achieving a social manner. 'Will you sit down? Perhaps some tea?'

'Tea might be a good idea,' said Phryne. Her inflexible manner was inflicting the willies on her employers, which was just what she had in mind. These foolish people had put her to a great deal of trouble. Their lack of trust in each other had caused a good deal of damage—to each other. Another object lesson of why humans should have stayed in trees, where they could not behave in such an idiotic way. Or possibly we should never have emerged from the sea. Evolution, Phryne sometimes thought, had a long way to go before the Homo became even close to Sapiens.

Tea arrived, wheeled in on a series of trolleys by three Italian servants. The general shake-up of the housekeeping meant that someone had spent the intervening time with the Silvo, polishing the huge silver teapot, the Modern Dutch cow creamer, water jug, sugar basin, slop basin, strainer and silver spoons. And someone else had carefully washed and dried a precious Meissen tea set, cups, plates and saucers. It was all very decorative—and had not been looted—and the servants distributed the crockery and cutlery nervously, as though they had been told very firmly how valuable it was.

Dot thought that it was very pretty, but there was no point in having a tea service which would be ruined if someone dropped a cup.

Phryne waited until everyone had gone through the tea ritual—strong or weak? A little more water? Sugar? How many lumps? And milk? She sipped to clear her voice.

'Well, Miss Fisher, here we all are,' said Mr. Bonnetti.

'Yes, indeed. You will recall that I was asked to find out if there was a child of Kathleen O'Brien and Patrick O'Rourke. There was.'

'We knew this already.' Mr. Johnson's voice was ragged with strain.

'If you would be so good, Mr. Johnson, as to allow me to continue?' Phryne asked.

Mr. Johnson, at a signal from his brother-in-law, subsided.

'I now know that the child lived, against the odds. And I know who the child is.'

'No!' screamed Mr. Johnson.

'Sit down, now,' said the Bishop firmly. 'Mrs. Bonnetti is right. We must have this secret out of its lair, and defy the foul fiend.'

'Ordinarily, the existence of the child would not matter,' Phryne continued. 'But strange things have been happening in your family, Mr. Bonnetti, and because all of you were spitting on your hands and bending your best endeavours to make sure that no one else found out anything, you have got yourselves into a pickle. And you made yourselves into perfect victims for a man with no scruples. You received a message saying "the child is among you" and each and every one of you lost his or her wits.'

'Don't say it!' cried Mr. Johnson.

'Will you put a sock in it?' demanded Phryne. 'Shall I have you removed from the room?'

'No, no, I'll stay,' he said biddably. Then without warning he threw himself across the table, to the detriment of the Meissen, both hands grasping for Phryne's throat.

'Meddling bitch!' he yelled.

Phryne drew away disdainfully, out of reach of those murderous hands, and drew her little gun. The room went quite still.

'Pick Mr. Johnson up and put him back in his chair,' she told the Italian servants. They looked at Mr. Bonnetti, who nodded. They did as they were told.

'Sheila, block your ears, don't listen!' he shrieked.

'Tom, what's wrong with you?' she exclaimed.

Phryne went on, keeping hold of the Beretta in case of further assaults.

'What Mr. Johnson doesn't want you to hear is that he was being blackmailed. By, as I said, a subtle and ruthless man. What he didn't tell you when he married you was that although he came from a nice respectable family, he was not their son by blood. He was adopted. By the coincidence of his birth, which was in January 1865, the blackmailer made him believe that he was the child of Kathleen O'Brien, and that—'

'Oh, dear Lord Jesus,' said Bishop Quinlan.

Mr. Bonnetti jumped to his feet to embrace his sister, who was sagging. He looked shocked but also puzzled.

Phryne held up a hand and the buzz of talk stilled. She realised that she was still holding her pistol in it and put it down.

'He handed over all the money he could steal, extort or borrow to this man. The police have traced the postbox. It was a perfect plot and as long as he didn't actually trust anyone with the secret, like his brother-in-law and head of the family, he would have been bled white. I doubt he was actuated by love of his wife,' she said with some distaste. 'But he knew that his nice cosy billet and his unending stream of cash for his businesses would dry up if this was found to be true.'

The Bishop was now sitting next to Mrs. Johnson, holding her hand. He was praying under his breath. Sheila Johnson was echoing the words.

'But, of course, it's not true—is it, Mr. Bonnetti?'

'No,' said Mr. Bonnetti heavily. 'It is not true.'

'Because that same subtle man was levying the blackmail on you, too,' said Phryne. 'He sent the "child is among you" notes. He said he was, in fact, the child. Because you wanted to be relieved of his attentions, you employed me. But you also kept paying.'

'What else could I do? It might have been true. In the beginning, he didn't want much. Then...'

'The demands escalated,' said Phryne. 'They became intolerable. And he seemed to know things. Secret family things.'

'Yes,' said Mr. Bonnetti.

'Gentlemen,' Phryne said, now addressing her fascinated guests. 'Do you know anyone in this room?'

'Oh yes, dear,' said Mr. Wright. 'I'd be sure if he turned his back…yes. What do you think, Archie?'

'I never forget a back,' said Mr. Lawrence. 'Not after I chased it all the way through the cemetery looking for a contribution to a funeral. Besides, we know him, Albie.'

'We do?'

'Walking gentleman in all those Shakespeares. Spear carrier—nice legs he had—in that scandalous production of *Caesar and Cleopatra* where Maggie Arnold wore that muslin gown that you could see straight through. It revealed that she was not wearing any undergarments. That's our Toby.'

'So he is,' marvelled Mr. Wright. 'Been getting any work lately, Toby? This is Toby Johns,' he told the company. 'Used to be an actor. Not a very good actor. Last time we saw him was at Patrick O'Rourke's funeral. Then he left the stage, it seems.'

'Which is where he got his secret family knowledge,' said Phryne. 'From Patrick O'Rourke.'

'So he is not the child,' said Mr. Bonnetti, astounded. His wife was glaring at him from under her tea-time fascinator of mauve feathers.

'No,' Phryne told him. 'He is a thief. You have been allowing him to loot the estate and practise *droit de seigneur* among the maids, not to mention oppressing your Italian staff.'

This brought heartfelt agreement from the Italians. '*E vero, bella signorina!*' said one.

'He was fortunately caught trying to sell the Antiochus the Second to Mr. Rosenberg and he is presently under arrest. Would you like to come in, Constable Pinkus?'

'Yes, ma'am,' said a tall young man, resplendent in full uniform, from the door behind Mr. Johns.

'You don't dare,' sneered Mr. Johns. 'I know your secret.'

'No, actually, we do dare,' said Phryne. 'Because you don't. Now are you going quietly or do I have to shoot you? I would be delighted to oblige. A few holes in your anatomy is the least you deserve for your settled cruelty over so many years. You contemptible man,' she added, picking up and levelling the pistol. 'Try to run, would you? Please?' she coaxed. 'Left leg or right?'

'You bitch!' cried Mr. Johns.

'Music to my ears,' said Phryne, unfazed.

Under the threat of the little gun, Mr. Johns allowed himself to be handcuffed. 'It was easy,' he yelled into their faces. 'You made it so simple! You wouldn't talk to each other, you never trusted each other, you made it too, too easy! Hypocrites! I hated you, I hated you all. You, Bonnetti, and your affectation of father of the family, wouldn't even confide in your own wife! She would never have let me get away with it. You, Johnson, terrified that your meal ticket was going to throw you out. For incest! And you,' he snarled at Mr. Wright and Mr. Lawrence. 'I was a good actor! They were just envious! I never got a chance! But I played butler to perfection, to perfection! Difficult. I couldn't let up for a moment. But I did it and no one suspected me! You're all fools!'

His voice was rising into hysteria. He was promptly escorted out, to the massed but smothered parting curses of the Italians.

'It seems that our late butler might be right,' said Mr. Bonnetti heavily, refusing to look at Mrs. Bonnetti. 'We are all fools.'

'Of course,' said Bernadette, coming out of her habitual trance, 'I never liked that Johns and I tried to tell you, but no one listens to me.'

'Tom, how could you?' demanded Sheila Johnson. 'You wasted all that money on a blackmailer, you never said a word to me, and they were my children, they might have been tainted, children of incest, how could you?'

'You would have sent me away,' he pleaded, rubbing his patchy red face with both hands.

'And I shall,' she said firmly. 'Oh, I shall. Mr. Adami?'

'Ma'am?' Mr. Adami was glad of a distraction.

'Draw up a Separation,' said Mrs. Johnson. 'From this hour. I want him out of my house. I'll give you an allowance,' she said. 'But you'll never lay a hand on me again, never come roaring into the house with your whores, never kick my dog or pawn my jewels or waste my substance. If you come near me again I shall call the police. Clear?'

Tears rolled down his face. This had always worked before but now there was an unfamiliar light of resolution in his wife's eyes.

'Sheila, you can't mean it! I only wanted to protect you!'

'No, you wanted to protect yourself,' she said. 'And it's been a very expensive exercise.'

'Bonnetti, can't you do anything?' He appealed to his brother-in-law.

'Perhaps I could, but I'm not going to,' said Mr. Bonnetti. 'It occurs to me that I have been very remiss in my duty to protect my sister, and perhaps it is not too late to begin. You may leave,' he said.

'Oh, no, don't let him go,' cried Mrs. Johnson. 'He'll go home and kill Antoinette, my poodle. He's always threatened to do that. He hates her because she loves me.'

'Then you shall sit down in the smaller drawing room, Mr. Johnson, and Mario will stay with you. And there you shall sit until we have completed this meeting. Then we will go to my sister's house, remove your belongings, bestow them somewhere else, and arrange for her to have a little company, in case you feel like making trouble.'

Mario, who was strong and swarthy and already delighted by the fall of Mr. Johns, grinned an unnerving grin. He had a mouthful of gold teeth and the self-assured air of one with a knife in his sleeve. And another in his sock. He took Mr. Johnson by the shoulder and he, after all, went quietly.

Mr. Lawrence and Mr. Wright had been whispering to Miss Fisher while the family discussion had been going on. She nodded and smiled at them. Dot was feeling stunned. So much noise! Ladies and gentlemen acting like that! She was shocked and fascinated in roughly equal proportions.

'So, Miss Fisher, what about the child?' asked Mrs. Bonnetti. 'Did you find him?'

'I found the child,' said Phryne. 'Dot, would you read the translation of the Irish writing for me? This was found amongst the pitiful belongings of Patrick O'Rourke, who died in extreme poverty. It was wrapped around a golden guinea. What did Father Kelly say about it, Dot?'

'It says "*Tá sí milse ná seo rud eile*", which means "this is for my sweet daughter",' said Dot.

'And I think it's time we gave it to her,' said Phryne, and laid the coin in Tata's hand. Silence fell with a thud. The company stared. Tata looked at the golden guinea.

'And you knew Tata,' said Phryne. 'Mr. Wright, Mr. Lawrence?'

'She was at the funeral,' said Mr. Lawrence. 'Wearing an old black cloth coat with a rained-on fur collar.'

'That was Mother's,' said Mr. Bonnetti. 'I was there when she gave it to Tata.'

'I got the idea,' said Phryne chattily, to give everyone time to recover a little, 'when an eminent doctor mistook the daughter of my house for a servant. I thought, am I doing the same thing? Who notices Tata? Mr. Bonnetti talks to her as though she was deaf or simple, but she isn't simple or deaf. She's just always been there. Part of the furniture. I bet you don't even know her name. She isn't a person. She's a title.'

'You're right,' he said numbly. 'I don't know her name. What…what is your name, Tata?'

'Julia Flaherty,' said the elderly woman in a firm voice. 'You know, I always wondered if this day would come. I never knew how I would feel.'

'Tell us,' encouraged Phryne.

'I was adopted by a good Catholic family and given the name of Mary Flaherty, though the nuns said my mother named me Julia, so I went back to Julia as soon as I could. We lived near the Sisters of Mercy's home. Soon after I was adopted my mother and father had their own children. They tried to be fair but there was always a difference and I was unhappy. I started asking questions and found out the name of my real mother. The Flahertys said that she didn't want me and had given me away. I was very young. So I ran away in the night and came to Melbourne and got a place in the household of this woman who had abandoned me. I was prepared to hate her. But she was kind and sad, and I thought that might be because of me, so I cared for her children as best I could. I found my father—I even saw him act—but I knew that he had abandoned my mother, and me, and I never tried to speak to him. Then it was too late.'

'Tata—I mean, Miss Flaherty—I mean, Julia, that was Mother's middle name, that's why she called you Julia. You knew we were looking for you, why didn't you say anything?' asked Mr. Bonnetti.

'I didn't know what to do,' she said simply. 'You might not have believed me, and then I would be dismissed, and I am old now, where would I go?'

'She loved you,' Dot said suddenly. 'She wrote about it. She made this for you,' and Dot unbundled the cobweb fine shawl and threw it over Tata's shoulders, where it settled like a benediction over her black dress and white apron. 'They both loved you. But they were ill-fated. She never would have abandoned you if she had had her own will.'

'I nursed her,' said Tata, stroking the shawl. 'I held her in my arms when she was dying. I knew she was my mother and I think, at the end, she almost knew about me, too.'

'That would explain the will,' said Mr. Adami, pleased that something was making sense at last.

'But what are we going to do with you?' asked Mr. Bonnetti helplessly. 'I mean, we have treated you very badly, Julia, what would you have us do?'

'If you want to do something for me, then dismiss this charlatan and get Bernadette off those sedatives,' said Julia. 'She was despondent when the last baby came, a lot of women are. And she needed medicine for a few years, a lot of women do, such a hard time, the climacteric. But she doesn't need it now and hasn't for some years. It suited you that she was not interfering in your family affairs,' she told Mr. Bonnetti calmly. 'She is capable of being quite tiresome, but she should not be drugged like this.'

'Quite so, off you go, Dr. James, there's a good fellow,' said Mr. Bonnetti promptly. 'We shall give you a generous severance, but no more valerian.'

'She can't just stop taking it like that!' exclaimed the doctor, who did not offer any other words in his own defence. It had been a nice, comfortable position with an undemanding patient, but someone was bound to notice eventually.

'No, we shall wean her off it slowly,' Julia told him. 'Now, do as the master tells you.'

Dr. James left. Tata took off her cap and apron and became Julia. The room was emptying. Last act. At least it was not like the last act of *Hamlet*, thought Mr. Wright, and repressed a giggle. This high-octane emotion was all right for the stage, but he preferred a quiet life these days. Mr. Lawrence nudged him. He hadn't had so much fun in decades.

'I have a suggestion,' said Phryne. 'A voyage. Julia and Bernadette. A cruise ship—why not the *Hinemoa*?—to Europe. Sleepy days, good food, a little promenade on the sun deck. A reduced dose of valerian. And then a few trips to nice, bracing places—Skegness, perhaps? Switzerland? And when they come lazing home, Julia will have become a sister rather than a nurse, and Bernadette will be off the stuff.'

'Wonderful,' said Mr. Bonnetti. 'Agreed?' He looked around the table. Everyone nodded. Incandescent Mrs. Bonnetti, who had things to say to her husband. Sheila Bonnetti, freed of an appalling husband. Bernadette, shortly to be restored to whatever sanity she had been born with. Julia, restored to her proper place. The loathsome Mr. Johns was in custody. The unuxorious Mr. Johnson was in the care of a grinning Sicilian with a blade. Just what she would have wished for all of them.

Phryne felt that the day's work was done and stood up.

'Must go,' she said. 'My account will be in the mail. Goodbye,' she said, collected her followers, and left. The front door stood open. A warm scented wind blew in. It smelt wet. Someone was watering the geraniums.

Phryne laughed suddenly and ran down the stairs. As her panting followers came up, she loaded them into the big car and gave her orders.

'Mr. Butler, to the pub! We all need a drink.' 'Thank goodness for that,' whispered Mr. Wright. 'I thought she'd never ask,' agreed Mr. Lawrence.

'When the next war comes along, I'm gonna go down to the docks with the troops and sing "Boys of the Old Brigade" and then I'm gonna turn around and march right back home,' said Vern.

'Too right. Halt! Who goes there?'

'Oh, it's just Zeke, the poor old coot. He's got religion again.'

The voice came closer, wailing, 'The indignation of the Lord is upon all nations: he hath utterly destroyed them: he hath delivered them to the slaughter. The streams thereof shall be turned into pitch and the dust thereof into brimstone, and it shall not be quenched by day or by night forever!'

'Put a sock in it,' suggested Curly easily.

'They have stretched out upon Ashkelon the line of confusion and the stone of emptiness: they have swept it with the besom of destruction: it shall be an habitation for owls and a court for dragons.'

'Not that he's wrong, mind you,' said Vern.

'Too right,' said Curly.

Chapter Eighteen

Glendower: *I can call spirits from the vasty deep. Hotspur: Why, so can I, or so can any man; But will they come when you do call for them?*

William Shakespeare
Henry IV, Part I

Phryne felt she had had enough of the wild extravagances and small meannesses of human nature for the time being. She extracted Dot from her plunge into theatre gossip with the two elderly Thespians and went home quietly, which was the only way Mr. Butler knew how to drive.

Then she left Dot to convey the solution of the Bonnetti puzzle to the enthralled staff, walked up to her own cool airy room and fell onto her bed, barely having the energy to take off her shoes and stockings and shuck the neat dark blue suit.

It had been an interesting afternoon. A period of reflection and repose was indicated. One mystery down, and one to go. A bee buzzed drowsily in the wisteria. Seconds only intervened before reflection gave way to repose and Phryne was asleep.

When she woke she bathed lazily and had another nap, knowing that she was going to dine at the Cafe Saporo. Mrs. Butler, she considered, had served up enough large dinners lately. The whole party could walk to the cafe and back again, which also gave Mr. Butler the night off. She dwelt affectionately on the memory of two aged actors, arms around each other, drinking Patrick O'Rourke's health in pub whiskey, and Dot—Dot!—joining in a chorus of 'She Was Poor But She Was Honest'. They had left seconds before they were thrown out of the pub, which in any case closed at six. And she thought how pleased the Sisters of Mercy and the Actors' Benevolent Society would be with Phryne's fee, which she was dividing amongst them, with a few deductions for new hats, vintage port and theatre treats incurred in the Bonnetti cause.

And it was probably time she got up and dressed and went down to see how James Barton was, and whether Lin Chung had returned.

So she selected a cool cotton dress and a shady hat and sauntered down the stairs to her quiet house, carrying her sandals in her hand. Mr. Butler emerged from the kitchen to enquire as to her wishes.

'The young ladies are in the larger parlour, Miss Fisher, reading their library books, which have to go back tomorrow. Mr. Lin is in the smaller parlour, and Mr. Barton has arisen and is with him. They are drinking tea.'

'I would like a glass of orange crush, if you please,' said Phryne. 'You know that we are going out for dinner?'

'Yes, Miss, the Cafe Saporo has confirmed your booking. Very obliging of you, Miss. Mrs. Butler is looking forward, she says, to a boiled egg and a good sit down. And I am, too.'

'I bet you are. Very good, Mr. Butler. Where's Dot?'

'In the garden, Miss. Sewing. She says that the light is better.'

'Good, thank you, Mr. Butler. Enjoy your egg.'

The butler bowed a little and Phryne went into the smaller parlour. She found Lin Chung attempting to make conversation with James Barton, who was more than a trifle dazed.

'I say, you are a Chinaman, aren't you?' he was asking. 'Or is there something wrong with my eyes?'

'Nothing wrong with your eyes,' said Lin patiently. 'I am, as you see, Chinese.'

'Hello, sweet man.' Phryne strolled in. 'Can I get you anything? Muslin, paraffin wax, flying trumpets, the complete works of Harry Price?'

'No, thank you,' said Lin, smiling at the enumeration of the elements of faked seances and the man who proved them spurious. 'My effects are nothing like as crude.'

'I am really looking forward to this. Hello, James. How are you feeling?'

'Still sleepy,' confessed James Barton. 'Bit woozy. Must have been that ghastly medicine.' He sat up suddenly. 'They haven't come for me, have they?'

'No, and if they did, they wouldn't get you. Now, James dear, I am going to ask you to describe a seance at Mr. Atkinson's house, and I want you to remember everything. I am going to make notes. Then you can have a nice boiled egg for dinner and get some more sleep.'

Lin waited for James Barton to thank Phryne for her kindness and care. But he didn't. This young man had no manners, Lin thought: no manners, no breeding, and no backbone. Altogether just the sort of young man that, according to Grandmamma, characterised the modern generation. Lin drank more tea and listened as James, slowly and then with more fluency, described the appearances of the spirits as seen by the medium Stephanie Reynolds in her red sari. Selima in her short white tunic crowned with roses. Zacarias in his long white robes with a tall conical hat. Charging Elk in buckskin, with a feathered headdress, and a bare chest strung with bears' teeth and wampum. He imitated their voices for Phryne. Then he excused himself to go and lie down again. The effort had quite exhausted him. As breakdowns go, James Barton's was not a nervous one. Phryne wondered if he had traumatic symplegia, like that Wodehouse cat, Augustus.

'Is that enough information?' Phryne asked Lin Chung.

'Oh, yes, more than enough. I have located and rented a little house, which I have altered and wired for my effects. Which do not, by the way, involve cheesecloth ectoplasm. I have spent more than eight pounds,' he confessed.

'Which shall be repaid. This is very kind of you, Lin dear.'

'No, not at all. I have not had a chance to play magician since I left the troupe in China. But I have to tell you, Phryne, some of my effects are…I do not know the term…perhaps, biological? They will scare all of us, you, me, them, the dog if there is a dog.'

'Interesting. That's all right, Lin. We're brave.'

'I just wanted to warn you,' he said affectionately. He was feeling very well. Grandmamma had finally approved of the ice and fan arrangement, and she had slept all through the night. For three nights running, now. So, therefore, had her maids, her servants, the cooks and servers, and the Lin family daughters and granddaughters. And Lin himself. The relief was profound. He took Phryne's hand and kissed it.

She returned the kiss and retrieved her hand. 'Now, pass me a sheet of paper. I need to write an anonymous letter.'

'To whom?' asked Lin.

'To Gerald Atkinson,' she said. 'Give me the address of your little house. And when would it be please you to commence your performance?'

'Oh, after midnight,' he said. 'All the best ghosts arise at midnight.'

'And do you want Miss Reynolds as your medium?'

'She should prove admirable,' he said. 'If she is a fake, I will scare her into honesty. And if she is real—then Augustine Manifold must be fairly annoyed by now.'

'Sometimes, Lin dear,' said Phryne, blotting her letter, which was written in ragged black capitals, 'you make my spine tingle. And other parts of me, of course. Now, let's get James his supper and gather our family for a nice walk down to the cafe. I can post this on the way.'

'Jade Lady,' said Lin.

Phryne saw James Barton locked in for the night and led her family into the street for a soothing walk to Cafe Saporo, a

Fitzroy Street restaurant run by the Patti family, Italian immigrants, which catered for simple people and large appetites. It was no use taking the girls to her favourite French bistro, Cafe Anatole, because they did not like French food. But Saporo would provide basic well-cooked English food for them and Dot, and pasta primavera and garlic prawns for Phryne and Lin.

In spite of her late breakfast or early lunch, Miss Fisher felt that she had missed out on one meal today, and did not mean to miss out on another.

The Saporo was pleased to see Phryne and her family. Signor Patti welcomed them in, sat them down at a table with a red-checked gingham cloth, and brought bread and glasses of grenadine without asking. Pasta primavera was produced, with steak, eggs and chips for the others. Dot was still expounding the mystery of the missing child as they ate and the girls hung on her every word. Phryne was content to let someone else tell the story.

Phryne finished her garlic prawns, wiped her mouth on the napkin, and suggested mixed gelati for dessert. With it came a beaming Signora Patti and a bottle of grappa.

'Signorina Prudenzia,' announced Signor Patti. 'Drink with us!'

'Certainly,' said Phryne. 'But what's the occasion?'

'We heard that you found out that dreadful man who was butler to the Bonnetti. He beat my son, once, and he…attempted the virtue of my daughter who worked in the kitchen. But now he is in jail, and we do not have to kill him, so we rejoice.'

'A good reason,' approved Lin Chung, holding out his glass. 'We have a saying. "If you seek revenge, remember to dig two graves."'

It was, of course, illegal for such cafes to sell wine. God forbid that anyone in Victoria should enjoy themselves after six o'clock, except in the Melbourne Club. But there was nothing to stop the delighted Signor from giving it away. This was special grappa which his cousin made and, although to Phryne it reeked of floor varnish, to the Signor and the Signora it was a precious taste of home. So Phryne drank and smiled.

Then they tottered home, the girls and Dot to finish the last pages of their library books, Lin Chung to depart for his own house, and Phryne to beguile a sleepy hour or so with the latest Dorothy Sayers.

In the middle of the night she woke, switched on her light, scrabbled for her notebook and feverishly flicked through the pages. Then she wrote a memo to herself in large letters and lay down again, not altogether sure what had triggered off that strange chain of thought.

Pondering it, she drifted off again.

Morning brought a series of florists' vans. A large bunch of roses from Mrs. Bonnetti. Orange ones. A larger bunch of roses from Mr. Bonnetti. White. A sheaf of paradise lilies from 'Bernadette and Julia'. And an orchid from a grateful policeman, who brought it himself.

'A lovely thing, Jack,' said Phryne, turning it around. It was royal purple, shading to pink, with striations of a darker magenta.

'Yes, but I reckon you've got enough flowers for today,' he said, looking at the array which Mr. Butler was carrying into the kitchen to be put in buckets until Miss Fisher could arrange them.

'No, no, this is lovely. Come in. How clever of you to get them to flower.'

'Taken me years to get that shade of blush in the middle,' he confessed. 'Just thought I'd see how you were going, and tell you about the Johns case.'

'Oh, yes, please.' Phryne popped the orchid into a cocktail glass of cool water and put it on the desk to admire it.

'Well, he came back, as you know, and Constable Pinkus nabbed him real neat. Not so much as a stamp stirred in Mr. Rosenberg's shop. Then we took him to the Bonnetti house and Pinkus heard every word he said. Then on the way back to the station after he was cautioned, he said it all again. He's proud of it!'

'What an unpleasant man,' said Phryne.

'Chatty, too. I was afraid that the family would want to keep it all hushed up, but now they've got their Julia back they seem to have cheered up a lot. All of them happy to make complaints, even that Johnson coot. I reckon Johns is looking at twenty years for blackmail. And we've got most of the money back. He never spent it. He just liked extorting it. No accounting for tastes. Now, how about the Manifold case?'

'By early tomorrow morning, Jack dear, I expect to have it solved. Or perhaps I should say, if I can't solve it with this trick, I will not be able to solve it. And that would be a pity, because mysteries make my teeth itch. This is the address.' She scribbled it on a leaf of paper. 'Perhaps you might like to send someone to lurk outside at about two am or so? Just tell them to arrest anyone who leaves the house.'

'For you,' said Jack Robinson gallantly, 'I shall come myself. See you tonight, then. When's your kick-off?'

'One in the morning,' said Phryne. 'When all the best ghosts, I am told, arise.'

'Good-o,' he said peaceably, and left.

Phryne caught Dot as she and the girls were about to set out for the library.

'Dot, I need you to run an errand for me. To the Atkinson house. You've got some leaflets about girls' societies and parish meetings and things, haven't you?'

'Yes, Miss Phryne,' said Dot, putting down her bag of books.

'Then I want you to take some to the Atkinson house—take the car on after you've been to the library—and talk to Gertrude. I want you to find out something for me.' Phryne told Dot what she wanted to know.

'Might be a bit difficult to slip it into the conversation,' she said. 'But I'll do it, Miss.'

'I know you will,' Phryne responded, and watched Jane and Ruth haul large shopping bags out to the car while Dot ran up to her room to collect some Improving Literature. 'After this, ladies,' she said to them, 'we shall go on holiday. To the sea. We shall shut up this house and find a nice place to stay and you can send Mrs. Butler a postcard. Queenscliff, perhaps. I hear that it is very charming.'

'Do you mean it?' asked Ruth, eyes shining.

'I do,' said Phryne. 'I am getting very tired of my fellow humans,' she added. 'I think I'd better get away from them for a while.'

Ruth made no comment, as Miss Phryne looked a bit strained. Jane pressed Phryne's hand. She had never been on a holiday. Then she frowned. She was calculating how many clothes she would have to leave behind so that she could take all her books. Cubic capacity of one suitcase…*Gray's Anatomy* versus how many cotton dresses?

Phryne, at a loose end, donned her own bathing costume and went for a vigorous swim, returned to a bracing cold shower, put on a housedress and spent the afternoon peacefully arranging flowers, which was so engrossing a task that she almost forgot about the Atkinsons. She was not looking forward to seeing them again.

By the time the girls had returned and gone for their own swim, the house was filled with the scent. White roses and trailers of white jasmine lolling from a Fantin-Latour style silver epergne in the sea-green parlour. Orange roses and paradise lilies in a tall arrangement in the hall, surrounded with bamboo stalks. The orchid in a rotund brandy glass on Phryne's little table. Phryne belonged to the Beverley Nichols school of flower arranging. Let them arrange themselves, no spikes, no torture. Just allow the beauty of the flowers to shine in the right vase and the right place. Beautiful.

Dot admired them. She had also done as Phryne wished and had an answer to her question from Gertrude, the maid at the Atkinson house.

'Puts them in to soak on Sunday night,' she said. 'Aren't the white ones lovely?'

'I made a little posy for your room,' said Phryne, producing it. It was a few orange roses, with sprays of jasmine around them, in a squat terracotta pot. Dot turned the arrangement in her hands.

'It's lovely,' she said. 'You are clever, Miss Phryne! My favourite colours.'

'The afternoon letters, Miss Fisher.'

Phryne took the envelope from the silver salver and thanked Mr. Butler. She tore the envelope open and read the single sheet inside.

'Telegram from Jack Robinson's watcher. I'm told that the Atkinsons are going to a certain address in Maidstone tonight,' she said, pleased. 'Good! It worked. This is the effect of my anonymous letter, which said that if they held a seance in this place, they would find Blackbeard's treasure. I'd better go up for a nap. This might be a testing evening.'

'You will be careful, Miss?' asked Dot.

'Of course. I shall have Lin and Li Pen, and also the full backing of the Victoria Police. And this is my last throw, Dot, so if you feel like doing a little praying, I would appreciate it. In this production, I will need all the help I can get.'

Dot bore her flowers away. There was just time to start a rosary of intention.

Phryne lay down but could not sleep. So she got up.

She passed the rest of the evening by eating an abstemious dinner with only one glass of wine and by playing a noisy set of games with the girls; ludo, snakes and ladders, Chinese chess. She ended the session by losing seventeen pennies to Jane at Red Ace. Then she sent them to bed, ascertained that James Barton was sleepily reading Agatha Christie, and climbed the stairs. She put on trousers and a top of unrelieved black. Over that she had a petticoat pocket containing her gun and other necessities. Over that she had a loose Erté-inspired gown in violet and silver and a turban to match.

Lin came to the door at midnight. He had borrowed a smaller car than his usual Rolls. He too was wearing unrelieved black and looked so attractive that Phryne had to clasp her wandering hands firmly in her purple and silver lap.

Maidstone was sparsely inhabited. 'We have a lot of market gardens down on the river,' Lin told her. 'I have borrowed a house which is at present empty. Did you speak to Detective Inspector Robinson?'

'Yes, and he will be here, so tell Li Pen not to throttle him by mistake.'

'As you wish, Miss,' said someone in the back seat. Li Pen had made something of a specialty of not being seen and Phryne had not known he was there. She jumped.

'And the same goes for anyone wanting to get into the house. Let them in. Just don't let them leave.'

'As the lady says,' agreed Li Pen. Though he was a monk and had nothing to do with women, he approved of Phryne. They had once rescued Lin together and he admired her courage and resource. Besides, she had introduced him to his favourite food, Vegemite.

Lin stopped the little Austin near a weatherboard house, seemingly in the middle of nowhere. It had a street number but appeared to be the only house in that street. Which ought to mean that the Atkinsons would find it no matter what they had been smoking. Lin gave Phryne the basket which Mrs. Butler had put up for her.

'There is a table and sufficient chairs in the main room,' he told her. 'We're early. Will you be all right on your own?'

'I will,' she said, and walked up two steps to a front door. A single electric bulb was burning inside. Lin ushered her inside, kissed her, and melted into the darkness.

Phryne walked through the bare dusty hall, past an unoccupied bedroom, and found the main room, where there was, indeed, a large battered table and a lot of chairs. She sat herself down with her face to the door and put the basket on the floor beside her. Good old Mrs. Butler! The basket contained a flask of coffee and Phryne drank a cup.

There was almost no sound either inside or outside. The Maribyrnong River must be near, if this was a market garden, but it was modest and did not make itself obvious. The house smelt disused, of dust and creeping mould, and Phryne found that she was shivering. And afraid, though there was no one in the room, and the bare electric bulb was the essence of practicality. This must be Lin's 'biological' effect. Either that, or she had entirely lost her nerve.

There was a low humming noise, which lay just on the edge of hearing. A motor? Someone coming? She wished they would get on with it. Then she heard a short snatch of music, a flute or whistle, which was abruptly cut off.

Moments before she felt that she had to get up and move, she heard the front door open, and a chatter of voices. Stephanie Reynolds talking about the masters. Blanche White murmuring some response. Veronica Collins complaining about a torn stocking. Gerald Atkinson bidding them all to be silent.

They came in and looked at Phryne as she sat in her purple and silver and stopped in a clump. Then they smiled. Luke and Valentine took up their posts at the door. The others came forward and sat down in the chairs.

'My dear Phryne, how lovely!' said Gerald. 'Why are you here?'

'Anonymous letter,' said Phryne. 'And I don't know anything more about it. I was just about to leave. This place is giving me the willies.'

'You are not used to spiritist phenomena,' explained Stephanie condescendingly. 'I'll take that chair, Blanche. You and Pris beside me on this side, Ronnie, Gerald and Phryne on the other. Luke, Val, you'll have to join, the table's too big to hold hands without you.'

They did as they were told. Stephanie opened a hamper in which were candles in holders and various glasses and bottles. The company sat down, poured themselves a drink, and watched as the candles were lit. They were red shaded and gave a soft light in which it might be possible to develop photographs.

But they weren't comfortable. Luke kept watching the door. Priscilla was huddling close to Blanche White, whose dark eyes had dilated with fear. Gerald was tapping the table and seemed unable to stop. Veronica was twitching as though she was sitting on an ant hill. The biological method was working on them. Phryne still shivered. She drank more coffee, declining the various liqueurs circulating the table.

Then Valentine put out the light. They all joined hands and sang 'Worship the King'. The voices were off-key and Phryne thought this a bad choice of hymn. 'His chariots of wrath the dark thunderclouds form, and dark is his path on the wings of the storm.' Not comforting, though she had always associated 'pavilions of splendour' with cricket…

Her mind was wandering. Her hands were being held by Gerald on her right and Luke on her left. Luke's hand were shaking, Gerald's were sweating. Phryne's, she was sure, were as cold as ice.

'Is there anyone there?' asked Stephanie Reynolds. 'Charging Elk, are you with us?'

There was a long silence, then out of the mouth of the medium Phryne heard someone say, 'How! Charging Elk comes back from the happy hunting ground.'

'We want to find the spirit of Augustine Manifold,' said Gerald. 'To tell us where Blackbeard's treasure is.'

'Passed on,' said the voice of Charging Elk. 'Will ask.'

Then he cut out and the people relaxed a little. It always took Charging Elk a few minutes to find the deceased in the afterlife. Phryne was aware of a smell. It was the house's own scent of mould and dust, with something else…was it roses? decayed roses…something very decayed. Rotten meat and wet earth and decayed roses. The scent of a fresh grave. She shuddered. The women picked it up first. Priscilla buried her nose in Blanche's shoulder. Blanche sneezed. Veronica coughed. Then Gerald and Valentine smelt it. Noses wrinkled, but they could not loose their hands. The smell grew stronger until it was a stench. Priscilla retched.

A light was growing so slowly that Phryne had not noticed it. It grew from a spot to a circle. It got brighter. It got bigger. Charging Elk appeared in it.

He was beautiful. He had the feathered headdress and across his bare chest were strings of teeth. Stephanie Reynolds cried out in love and longing. Then his voice came, louder and closer.

'White man here,' he said, and blinked out. Again the circle glowed. Gradually a picture formed. Phryne knew the face. A plain man, with a weak mouth. She had not remembered that he had brown eyes and shiny brown hair.

'Augustine,' called Gerald. 'Oh, my dear fellow!'

'Augustine,' said Stephanie. 'It is you!'

The graveyard stench was distracting Phryne. She was not going to vomit if she could help it, but fairly soon she was not going to be able to prevent it. Then a voice manifested itself.

'You killed me,' said Augustine.

'No, no, my dear, don't say that!' cried Gerald, tears streaming down his face.

'You killed me,' repeated Augustine. 'I never harmed you.'

'We did just push you about a little,' said Gerald. 'Luke and Valentine did. I agreed. But killed, no, my dear, don't say that. It wasn't us! You went out, you know, and then something happened to you! What was it?'

'Water,' said Augustine. A splash and a struggle were heard, loud and horrible. The stamp and crash of a struggle, the panting of two fighters. Then the gurgling of a drowning man, shockingly vivid.

'What about the map?' asked Luke, chokingly.

'I know of no map,' said Augustine.

The house door crashed open. Someone came in. He shoved his way into the room and yelled, 'It's all a trick!'

Damn, thought Phryne, and we were going so well. She could loose her hand from Gerald's feeble clasp and get to her gun fairly fast. Who was this intruder?

'Simon?' asked Gerald. 'What do you mean?'

'I mean, it's all electricity and gramophone records!' cried Simon in triumph. 'I'm pushing this screwdriver into this light switch. It'll fuse the lights. Then see where your apparitions come from!'

He laughed aloud. They saw him drive the implement into the switch, saw a flash as the household electricity was disconnected, and heard the crack as the fuse exploded. Simon stood as if rooted to the spot. He stared in utter disbelief.

Augustine Manifold had not gone. Phryne saw Valentine and Veronica reach out and drag Simon into the circle.

'It was you,' said the apparition slowly. 'You killed me.'

'No!' breathed Simon. So this was Rachel Phillips' rotten younger brother, the disinherited waster with the greyish import of dubious goods. The trader with the motorbike who was simultaneously romancing Sophie Westwood from the Manifold shop, Gertrude the Atkinson maid and Veronica Collins.

The extent of the fraud which had been practised on Gerald Atkinson became apparent and was so ingenious that Phryne forgot about being sick. Simon had manufactured the Blackbeard plot, had used Augustine as a front without his knowledge, and was able to get into the shop because of Sophie. He knew what was happening in the Atkinson menage because of both Veronica and Gertrude. But why had he killed Augustine?

'You murdered me,' said Augustine, but this time it was the medium who spoke. The picture was still on the wall, but Stephanie Reynolds' mouth was moving.

'You wouldn't tell me,' moaned Simon. 'You wouldn't tell me where it was! I needed it! The Blackbeard story was just to get the money to go to Palestine.'

'The Temple treasure,' said Phryne, very quietly. Simon twitched at the new voice but went on whimpering.

'I didn't know,' said Augustine. 'You killed me for nothing. You filled me with whisky under the threat of your gun, then when I still didn't talk, you drowned me in a washing tub, you bound my body to your own back and got onto your bike, you took me to the pier and threw me into the black water.'

The room filled with the thunder of waves.

'But I needed it to show my father he was wrong about me,' pleaded Simon. 'I was clever! I seduced three tarts and knew everything that went on, I even had your stationery and your seal and these idiots believed everything when I said I came from you! Tell me where it is, Augustine! My father disinherited me! He showed me no respect! I wanted the Temple treasure to show him, he believes in all that Jewish stuff, he would have been—'

'You are damned,' said Augustine Manifold flatly. 'Goodbye, Gerald, I'm going on. My dear…'

'Oh, my dear,' wept Gerald.

Gradually, the smell faded, the light faded, and Stephanie Reynolds shifted in her chair. Simon gave a sob, shook his hand free, and ran out of the house. Phryne heard a shout and then the sound of a car starting up. Not a motorbike. With any luck, Jack had caught his man. The feeling of imminent horror which had been so strong had also ceased. Phryne stood up.

'I'm so sorry, Gerald,' she said to him.

'He called me "my dear",' wept Gerald. 'He forgave me. Well, my darlings,' he said to his disciples. 'We know now. What's the matter, Ronnie?'

Veronica was crying.

'I thought he loved me,' she said.

'He was a greedy little swine of a pi-dog,' said Blanche. 'Come along, Ronnie. You can do better than him. It's late and we need a drink. Are you coming, Miss Fisher?'

'I need to sit and think for a while,' said Phryne. 'Leave me a candle, would you?'

The Atkinsons, expostulating, silent or weeping, saw themselves out.

Phryne got out the basket and found the flask of brandy, from which she poured a rather large drink. Lin joined her when the big cars had gone.

'They got Simon. Li Pen caught him and Jack Robinson took him away, confessing freely.'

'Good. Why did the manifestations continue when Simon killed the lights?'

'That would be because of my generator,' said Lin. 'And the voice from Stephanie's mouth?' 'That would be the spirits,' said Lin. 'Is that brandy?'

◇◇◇

'Can you see him, Vern?'

'Yair, I can see him, Curly. Clear as day. And I can see the moonlight through him, too.'

'D'you reckon he's a crusader?'

'Nah, they had them big pots on their heads and all that metal. He's only got a tin helmet like ours and that sort of string vest knitted out of wire. Horse's a bit hairy round the hocks, too.'

'What's he doing here, then?'

'I reckon,' said Vern, lighting his stub of a cigarette, 'I reckon he's saying, the poor bugger, "About time you blew in, you blokes. It's been seven hundred bloody years."'

'Well, we got here in the end,' said Curly.

'Yair. And we took the Holy Land back.'

Solemnly, with strict, formal movements, the soldiers saluted the ghost.

Chapter Nineteen

O Lord! methought what pain it was to drown!
What dreadful noise of water in mine ears! What
sights of ugly death within mine eyes! Methought I
saw a thousand fearful wrecks; A thousand men that
fishes gnaw'd upon; Wedges of gold, great anchors,
heaps of pearl, Inestimable stones, unvalu'd jewels,
All scattered in the bottom of the sea

William Shakespeare
King Richard III

Phryne woke feeling as though she had been dragged through several hedges backwards. Her recollections of the night before were clear but confusing. Which part of those fascinating manifestations had been Lin's magic? Which had been your actual Augustine?

She bathed at length—not in Ocean, she was going to have to get over that drowning first—dressed and ate her croissant and puzzled while Dot kept the girls occupied by planning what they would take on holiday. A very pleased Jack Robinson came with another orchid and a report on events. Gertrude was distraught. She had thought that Simon was a baker and that they would marry. Veronica Collins, however, was bearing up. Simon was perfectly unrepentant and had cursed his own father when the old man came to visit him.

'He's a piece of work all right,' he said, accepting a glass of beer. 'He's been mad about this Temple treasure—thought the prof was searching for it, as he might have been, of course. There was a rumour that some of it was found during the war. Soldiers' tales! Simon believed it. Burgled your house on the off chance there was a code in your Greek plays. Walked a tightrope telling that Atkinson mob about pirates. Ran all those women against each other to find out all he could and then finally killed poor old Augustine for knowledge he didn't have. He'll hang,' said Jack Robinson, finishing the beer. 'And good riddance.'

When Lin arrived at eleven Phryne sat him down with a brandy and soda and demanded, 'All right, explain.'

'If you explain how you knew it was Simon,' he bargained.

'Deal. I didn't precisely know it was him,' she added. 'I just thought it might be, if it wasn't the Atkinsons. It was being drowned in soapy water, you see.'

Lin did not see.

'Two places you find standing water with soap in it. One, in a bathroom. I thought they might have tortured Augustine by plunging his head under the water, then pulling him out again, and left him under once too long. Schoolgirls do it to unpopular girls.'

'And unpopular boys,' said Lin, taking a gulp of his drink.

'But then I thought, if it wasn't them, where else would you find soapy water? In the copper on a Sunday, where the maids leave their smalls to soak until Monday, which is wash day. I knew that Gerald would have his linen sent out, so I asked Dot to ask Gertrude about it, and she agreed that the washtub would have been full of soapy water on Sunday night—which is when Augustine disappeared. Simon collared him on his way out, and dragged him into the backyard. The questions which the Atkinsons asked him must have made Augustine suspicious so Simon knew he was about to be exposed. Simon filled Augustine with whisky to make him drunk and confess. He got drunk, but he didn't confess because he didn't know. Then Simon tortured him for the location of the Temple treasure, and held him under too long. When he realised that Augustine was dead, he strapped the body to his own back, zoomed off to the sea, and threw him in. Just as the spirits said, if it was the spirits. Now you.'

'A certain level of sound makes animals nervous,' explained Lin Chung. 'We have known this for many years. There are places where the earth makes this sound, too low to hear, where men cannot live and cattle cannot graze. I rigged up a generator for my electricity for my lantern slides, and also to send out this sound, which gives everyone the…what was the word?'

'Willies. It worked. I was afraid, all right. And the dreadful smell?'

'Just an incense I made from wet earth, carefully aged ox liver and essence of roses. Blown into the house by a fan. The sounds were records on a wind-up gramophone. They are used for radio plays. I borrowed them from my cousin. The images were cast onto a screen, which was canvas but painted to look like plaster with which I replaced a section of parlour wall. The initial voices were me. The later ones—well, they weren't me. That's all I can say.'

'Brilliant,' said Phryne, and kissed him. 'I am going on holiday,' she said. 'After my birthday. Any chance that you might take a trip to Queenscliff?'

'Every chance,' he said fondly.

Mrs. Manifold received Phryne in her decorated parlour. There was Morris paper on the walls and Morris tapestries on the chairs and an array of Pre-Raphaelite paintings on the walls. The tea, however, was herbal and thin, though hot. Mrs. Manifold sat as straight as a poker in her hand-woven daisy smock and her bare head.

'You have found the murderer?' she asked in her harsh voice.

'I have,' said Phryne.

'Who is he?'

'Simon Rosenberg, who used to deal with your son. He made him drunk then drowned him in a washtub and threw the body into the sea.'

Phryne did not mince her words. Mrs. Manifold was owed the truth and would not have welcomed any polite evasions.

'The police have been here to speak to Sophie. They say that she helped this murderer.'

'No, you misunderstood. He is a very pleasing young man. Two other women were fooled by him, and one of them is distraught. He seduced Sophie to let him into the shop. That is all she did. And I have no doubt that she is very sorry.'

'She is very sorry,' conceded Mrs. Manifold.

'Will you dismiss her?'

'No,' said the old woman. 'She knows the business. And she has backbone. She will not be fooled again.'

'Indeed,' said Phryne, a little chilled despite the tea.

'Will he hang?' asked Mrs. Manifold.

'Oh, yes, he will hang,' responded Phryne.

'Go down into the shop,' Mrs. Manifold said slowly. 'Take anything you want. Thank you. Goodbye,' she said.

Phryne went into the shop, where Cedric Yates was awkwardly patting a sobbing Sophie on the shoulder.

'You have a go, Miss, she won't listen to me,' he said.

'Wouldn't matter who was patting her,' Phryne replied. 'Her heart is broken. Sophie? You go up to your room, now, and lie down for a while. You'll have to mind the shop, Mr. Yates. I'm to choose my reward for finding Augustine's murderer.'

'You did a bonzer job, Miss. Cec said you was clever. What do you fancy, then? A painting? An ornament? Some of that jewellery?'

'Yes,' said Phryne, wanting to get out of this place. 'There's a Fabergé necklace with mistletoe and pearls. Ask Mrs. Manifold to box it up and send it to me.'

'If you can wait, I'll do it now,' he told her. 'Just a tick. I got Sophie's keys.'

Phryne identified the necklace and trailed around the room, noting the Dulac lady with the bears and the dynamic Fauve sketches. So much beauty. So much waste. And poor Augustine murdered, not knowing anything about the Temple treasure. She hoped that it had been him speaking through the medium and that he had forgiven the Atkinsons, who were guilty of nothing more than greed and drug abuse...

'Here you are,' said Cedric Yates, handing her a parcel. 'All done up nice. You did good, Miss,' he said, as he opened the door for her. 'You did real good.'

Phryne went home for a nap. When she came in she heard Priscilla's voice in the parlour.

'You can come back,' she was telling her brother. 'It's all right now. And Stephanie is leaving us to join a guru in India. It's all been a shock for us. And Luke was only joking, you know, with the knife.'

'I'm not going back,' said James firmly. 'Nor are you, if you have any sense. But I'm glad it's all settled, Pris. I'll be waiting at the old house, if you want to come home.'

'I'll give you a lift,' said Priscilla. James passed Phryne at the door, said, 'Er, thanks, Miss Fisher, goodbye,' and left. Mannerless, but at least he had gone.

'Hello, Mr. Butler, I'll just settle down here at the phone for a while,' said Phryne. 'I need to ring the Queenscliff Hotel, and then the Windsor. It'll be my birthday soon.'

'I'm sure it will be very happy, Miss,' observed Mr. Butler.

As he would, with a month on board wages and no drinks to serve, he went to direct the Thursday housemaid to change the sheets in the spare bedroom and clean thoroughly. The chief virtue of that somnolent young man, Mr. Butler considered, was that he had gone.

Dear Professor

I am afraid that you will be thinking me such a fraud so I will explain what has been going on with Mr. Atkinson's people. Mr. Atkinson, who is a dear friend, has enthusiasms and it does me no harm to indulge them. I have allowed them to believe that I have some line on this treasure, assisted by Simon, who is otherwise not in my confidence. But just lately I have begun to think that he is playing some sort of double-game, I no longer trust him, not that I ever really did. So I am telling you all about it. If you will allow me to trespass on your time.

When I was looking around the ruins of an old hotel in Bendigo, looking for any little bits and pieces I could repair and sell, I came across a big iron pot, still sealed. I bought it along with a lot of other old wares, and it was some time before I got around to opening it. The lid had been welded on. Inside was a bushranger's hoard of gold dust, already beginning to melt around the edges. It was enough to keep Mother in comfort and allow me a house of my own, which as you know was what I have always wanted. There was no way of finding the owner, anyway. I reckon the pot was hidden in about 1853.

So I got a pal of mine—no names, no pack drill—to melt the gold into ingots, and they are beneath the floor in my work room under the board that creaks. If something happens to me, can you make sure that Mother gets the gold, and that my workman and the girl are looked after?

I'm probably worrying you for nothing. But still.

Yours faithfully, Augustine Manifold

PS I got a clue to your Temple treasure, too. I got the vendors to trace out the carvings. I'll give it to you when we next meet. AM

It was a very merry party. The Windsor had been Phryne's home before she had found her little house, and she doted on every curlicue in the Grinling Gibbons-like carving on every little chequer of coloured glass in the windows, and every black and white tile on the floor.

She had chosen the Grand Ballroom for her tiny party, as her guest list had become alarmingly long. The company would not have fitted into the Esplanade house, even if Mrs. Butler could have cooked for so many.

The dinner had been good, with all her favourite dishes. Lobster mayonnaise. *Goujons de poulet Princesse.* Her birthday cake had towered like a wedding cake. Now her guests were dancing, and Phryne, leaning on Lin Chung and sipping champagne, watched them.

Jane and Ruth had been taught dancing at their select academy, but they had never thought that it could be fun. Now Ruth was in the arms of Mr. Archibald Lawrence, who was telling her about great romances of the theatre, which so enthralled her that she forgot about her feet. Jane was dancing with Mr. Palisi the undertaker, doubtless swapping reminiscences of dead people they had met. Dot swept along, dancing with Hugh, her intended, who danced very well for a policeman. Cedric Yates danced with Sophie, who seemed to have recovered a little. He was awkward with his one leg but Sophie did not seem to mind. Mr. Wright danced with Mrs. Manifold. He had always been a brave man.

Her friends from the circus were present, as the illness of the premier elephant had stalled their circuit and they were all in town. Strong man Samson, gypsy Alan Lee, Farrell himself, Doreen without her snake. Mr. Burton, an eminent and elderly dwarf, was dancing with Dr. MacMillan and conversing about Border ballads.

'Lovely party,' said a hurried voice. 'But we've got to go. We've heard of the most astounding physical medium, my dear, and she ought to lead us to the Temple treasure!' Gerald Atkinson, breathless, kissed Phryne's hand and led his entourage out of the room.

Phryne began to giggle, leaning on Lin Chung's beautifully tailored middle. Two women conversing over the shoulders of the men they were dancing with paused near them.

'Oh, yes, dear, you have to persuade her to sell things to you,' said one. 'It's frightfully exciting, just like Paris!'

'They say she was an artist's model,' said the other. 'Perhaps I'll look in at Manifold's tomorrow. I want to match that Royal Doulton cup, they don't make that design anymore. And they say she has a little man who can glue anything together, no matter how frightfully shattered…'

The Bonnetti family were dancing, mostly with each other. Julia, resplendant in a teal-blue gown, sat decorously by the wall, sipping champagne cup. Bernadette sat with her, already seeming to be more awake.

There was a good showing of Melbourne's best and brightest, though Miss Fisher's parties were always thought to be a bit— well, mixed. One could find oneself dancing with a well set-up young policeman, perhaps, or a Chinese, or an artist. Which was, of course, what one liked about them.

Professor Rowlands, escorting a beautiful, plump woman with long red hair, had already found a University Fellow who would love to lease his Queenscliff house and staff to Miss Fisher for as long as she wanted. He was going to Arnhem Land to investigate song cycles and was expecting to be away for three months.

Phryne surveyed the dancing throng. 'They're very decorative,' she said idly.

'The thing I want to know,' said Lin, not attending, 'is, where did Augustine get those forty pre-Roman shekels that Mr. Rosenberg just bought?'

'Some things we are not meant to know,' said Phryne solemnly. 'You could go and ask Gerald's new physical medium, of course,' she added.

'No,' said Lin. 'I am giving up magic for the present. What were you saying about the crowd?'

'They're very decorative,' Phryne repeated. She wreathed her arms around his neck.

'I am a very lucky woman,' she said.

'You sure about this bloke, Curly?'

'Sure. He's ryebuck on a straight wire. And we got to sell 'em to someone straight. You need to buy a van, Vern needs to buy a house, I got to have something to live on and Jim's wife's sick. I melted the pitch off all of 'em and I reckon the boss'll give us a good price. Are we on?'

'We're on,' the others agreed.

Cedric Yates, called Curly because of his straight hair, left his mates and went into the shop to show Augustine Manifold the coins, which had been glued into bandoliers and carried out of the Holy Land into Australia, to wait for a time when they needed the money.

Because Augustine was a good bloke, they told him where the coins came from.

Afterword

This book has left me feeling a bit like a Dr. Who casualty; time-sick. Fortunately I can vouch for all of my facts. The crinoline was more comfortable than five petticoats: contemporary women said so. The Light Horsemen did see a ghost (and didn't know it for a crusader because they thought crusaders wore plate armour, which in fact didn't come in for another four hundred years). And antique shops continue to weave magic for people who like the past. This book is in loving memory of my Great Uncle Donald ('Doody') McKenzie, who was in the charge to Beersheba with his brothers. His bandolier was sitting on my desk as I wrote.

Please feel free to email me on kgreenwood@netspace.net.au if you would like to talk to me.

Bibliography

Cemeteries

Morgan, Marjorie, *The Old Melbourne Cemetery 1837–1922*, Australian Institute of Genealogical Studies, Oakleigh, 1982.

Sagazio, Celestina (ed.), *Cemeteries: Our Heritage*, National Trust of Australia, Melbourne, 1992.

1864

Burt, Alison, *Colonial Cook Book*, Summit Books, Sydney, 1970.

Various websites on costume. *The Girls Own Paper* collected volume, London, c. 1890.

Archaeology

Albright, WF, *The Archaeology of Palestine and the Bible*, Pelican, London, 1949.

Baiget, M and Leigh, R, *The Dead Sea Scrolls Deception*, Corgi, London, 1991.

Hallam, E (ed.) *Chronicles of the Age of Chivalry*, Greenwich, London, 2002.

Rowley, HH, *From Moses to Qumran*, Lutterworth Press, London, 1963.

Shanks, Hershel, *The Mystery and Meaning of the Dead Sea Scrolls*, Random House, New York, 1998.

Vermes, G, *The Dead Sea Scrolls in English*, Penguin, London, 1962.

White, Anne Terry, *Lost Worlds,* Harrap and Co, London, 1943.

Woolley, Sir L, *Digging Up the Past*, Penguin Books, London, 1930.

The King James version of the Holy Bible.

Arts

Greenhalgh, Paul, *The Essential Art Nouveau*, V&A Publications, London, 2000.

Morris, William, *The Wood Beyond the World*, Oxford University Press, Oxford, 1980.

Robinson, Julian, *Golden Age of Style*, Orbis Publishing, London, 1976.

Various websites on the Pre-Raphaelites, especially Holman Hunt.

War

Baker, Sidney J, *Dictionary of Australian Slang*, Roberston and Mullens Ltd, Melbourne, 1944.

Bostock, Henry P, *The Great Ride*, Artlook Books, Perth, 1982.

Gardner, Brian, *Allenby*, Cassell and Co, London, 1965.

Hughes, Matthew, Allenby and British Strategy in the Middle East 1917–1919, Frank Cass, London, 1999.

Idriess, Ion L, *The Desert Column*, Pacific Books, Sydney, 1932.

Jones, Ian, *The Australian Light Horse*, Time-Life Books, Sydney, 1987.

Kent, David (ed.), *The Kia Ora Coo-Ee*, Cornstalk, Sydney, 1981.

Paterson, Andrew Barton (Banjo), 'Happy Dispatches', Australian War Memorial website.

Shermer, David, *World War One*, Octopus Books, London, 1975.

The Times History of the Great War, *Times* newspaper (collected), 1918.

Classics

Josephus, *The Jewish War*, trans. GA Williamson, Penguin Books, London, 1959.

Plautus, *The Rope and Other Plays*, trans. EF Watling, Penguin Classics, London, 1964.

Places

Evans, Wilson P, *Port of Many Prows*, Victoria Press, Melbourne, 1993.

To receive a free catalog of Poisoned Pen Press titles, please contact us in one of the following ways:

Phone: 1-800-421-3976
Facsimile: 1-480-949-1707
Email: info@poisonedpenpress.com
Website: www.poisonedpenpress.com

Poisoned Pen Press
6962 E. First Ave. Ste. 103
Scottsdale, AZ 85251

THE AGENT
RUNNER